BY SILVIA MORENO-GARCIA

*Signal to Noise*

*Certain Dark Things*

*The Beautiful Ones*

*Gods of Jade and Shadow*

*Untamed Shore*

*Mexican Gothic*

*Velvet Was the Night*

*The Daughter of Doctor Moreau*

*Silver Nitrate*

*The Seventh Veil of Salome*

*The Bewitching*

# THE
# BEWITCHING

# THE
# BEWITCHING

# SILVIA
# MORENO-
# GARCIA

NEW YORK

Del Rey
An imprint of Random House
A division of Penguin Random House LLC
1745 Broadway, New York, NY 10019
randomhousebooks.com
penguinrandomhouse.com

Library of Congress Cataloging-in-Publication Data
Names: Moreno-Garcia, Silvia, author.
Title: The bewitching / Silvia Moreno-Garcia.
Description: New York : Del Rey, 2025
Identifiers: LCCN 2025014950 (print) I LCCN 2025014951 (ebook) I
ISBN 9780593874325 (hardcover ; acid-free paper) I ISBN 9798217091232
(International edition) I ISBN 9780593874332 (ebook)
Subjects: LCGFT: Horror fiction. I Witch fiction. I Novels.
Classification: LCC PR9199.4.M656174 B49 2025  (print) I
LCC PR9199.4.M656174 (ebook) I DDC 813/.6—dc23/eng/20250404
LC record available at https://lccn.loc.gov/2025014950
LC ebook record available at https://lccn.loc.gov/2025014951

Printed in the United States of America on acid-free paper

2  4  6  8  9  7  5  3  1
First Edition

BOOK TEAM: Production editor: Loren Noveck •
Managing editor: Paul Gilbert • Production manager: Sarah Feightner •
Copy editor: Hasan Altaf • Proofreaders: Laura Dragonette,
Susan Gutentag, and Monica White

*Book design by Fritz Metsch*

The authorized representative in the EU for product
safety and compliance is Penguin Random House Ireland,
Morrison Chambers, 32 Nassau Street, Dublin D02 YH68, Ireland,
https://eu-contact.penguin.ie.

*For Bobby Derie*

# THE
# BEWITCHING

# 1998: 1

BACK THEN, WHEN I *was a young woman, there were still witches.*
That was what Nana Alba used to say when she told Minerva
bedtime stories; it was the preamble that led into a realm of shadows and mysteries.

Shortly after Minerva first arrived at Stoneridge, she'd looked
toward the thick mass of trees that constituted Briar's Commons
and heard a shrill cry that sounded like an infant's wail. For a moment she'd shivered in fear, thinking of her great-grandmother's
tales of witches who drank the blood of the innocent on moonless
nights. But it had been only a peacock.

She was used to the birds now, the gray peahens and the beautiful males with their dazzling displays of iridescent feathers. They'd
sun themselves on the lawn in front of Ledge House and sometimes they'd even sit on the porch of the old mansion. The story
went that when the college acquired the building and turned it
into a dorm, the peacocks had been part of the deal. A superstitious old dean reckoned they were lucky. Thus it had become tradition to keep a few of them by the dean's house, though the birds
liked to drift toward other buildings and roamed the campus with
impunity.

Now as she stood near the window, she heard the same cry.

She couldn't see where the peacock was stationed. It was likely somewhere by the entrance, watching the last of the students make their exodus from Ledge House.

Her friends had told her she'd never get used to the cold and the snow of New England, hailing as she did from the temperate climate of Mexico City, but she'd handled the winter without misfortune. It was the summer that made her anxious.

The campus was closing for the season. Within twenty-four hours all the dorms and facilities would stand silent and still, with a few resident directors like herself left to oversee the buildings. The library would be open, albeit with reduced hours, serving the students—mostly grad students—who would not fly or drive home for the summer.

The campus by the sea, with its greenery and its beautiful Victorian houses, with the sun shining and the ducks swimming placidly in the lovely ponds, ought to have inspired joy and relaxation. But everything irritated her. The quiet of the summer was the perfect chance to work on her thesis, if she'd had anything to write about.

Her progress had stalled. She'd done little in the winter and even less in the spring. Her adviser would expect a certain number of pages come fall. Minerva doubted she'd be able to produce much; her outline was a jumble of nonsense.

She couldn't afford to be anything except excellent. Her tuition at Stoneridge College was covered courtesy of a scholarship for academic high achievers. Her room and board were paid through her work in the language lab, helping Mr. Marshall with the flock of bored undergrads who needed a second-language course to graduate, and supplemented with her job as a resident director.

She'd always been able to juggle dozens of responsibilities without a hitch. Back in Mexico City, when she was in secondary school, she helped take care of Nana Alba. She'd come home, peel off her school uniform and change into comfy clothes, make dinner, give the old lady her medications, then complete her homework while keeping an eye on her. Great-Grandmother Alba died at the ripe old age of a hundred and one, and everyone said a nurse couldn't have done a better job taking care of her.

Could someone plateau at twenty-four? Could your brain shrink? She felt tired and listless all the time. Often, she was sad for no reason. She was in grad school, obtaining an English literature degree from the same college Beatrice Tremblay had attended. It was her childhood dream come true.

They'd said she'd be shocked by the cold of a Massachusetts winter, but the truth was Minerva knew all about New England. She'd lived in it, through the stories of a multitude of writers. She'd ambled through Peter Straub's Hampstead, H. P. Lovecraft's Arkham, Stephen King's Derry. Imaginary towns, but towns based on real locations, real places. She'd preferred to slip into the tales of Shirley Jackson rather than go out dancing with her friends, and instead of asking for a quinceañera party she'd managed to persuade her mother to buy her a first edition of Tremblay's *The Vanishing* and a cache of other horror novels, which she'd spotted in a dusty used bookshop on Donceles among a slew of old, forgotten titles.

Minerva had studied and saved, researched her options and budgeted, spent countless days paging through the college guides and data sheets at the Benjamin Franklin Library—which contained information on American scholarships available to international students—until she'd found a way to make her grad school fantasies a reality.

Now she was slipping up.

The peacock cried again, as if urging her out. She grabbed her clipboard and headed to the front of the house. She waved at one of the undergrads, who was loading her car, and set off toward Briar Hall, cutting through Briar's Commons, which the students called the Witch's Thicket because a witch had supposedly lived there in the time of the Salem trials. Or else the Devil dwelled under a tree. The stories contradicted one another as all good oral narratives must.

Salem was a few train stops away from the college, but there didn't seem to be a real basis for the story about the witch. As for the Devil, he seemed to live everywhere in New England. There was a Devil's Rock and a Devil's Footprint and a Devil's Pulpit.

Devil or not, Briar's Commons had served as the inspiration for *The Vanishing*, so it had some artistic merit. She'd felt giddy the first time she looked out the window and saw it, recognizing it from Tremblay's novel.

A single narrow dirt path cut through Briar's Commons and connected the eastern dorms with the rest of the campus, or one could take a wider, better-kept road that snaked around the patch of trees and had actual lighting at night. Stoneridge College at one point had tinkered with the idea of leveling the whole area and making a parking lot or a new dorm or something or other. But it caused a panic among local nature enthusiasts and the more ecologically minded students. Instead, the college had expanded west and north. South lay the sea and a couple of stretches of sand that passed for beaches.

Minerva walked briskly along the oak-dimmed path, clipboard in one hand. She thought about Nana Alba's tales of witches and the particular tale that had haunted Minerva since childhood. The peacock's cry, the silence of the path, further increased her melancholy. She missed her great-grandmother, had never stopped missing her even though Minerva's mother said she would. Just like she'd said Minerva would grow out of her teenage blues.

She'd written to her mother that day. She tried to limit phone calls back home with the excuse that long distance was expensive, but in reality it was easier to pretend she was fine and happy when she was typing on the computer or mailing letters. She'd mailed a bunch of photos from around campus to her mother the previous week. That, plus the short email that discussed nothing of importance, should keep her happy. Minerva had no desire to discuss her problems with her mother, who believed herself a psychoanalyst after reading too many self-help books.

Minerva emerged in front of Joyce House, which had the honor of being the oldest structure on campus, built in 1750. It was shuttered, with renovations to begin next year. It dearly needed this renovation; the once picturesque structure was now dull and battered, but she found it entrancing. Often, when doing her rounds, she looked at its upstairs windows and felt an almost electric tug.

It was the lure of history; she adored older buildings and was re-pelled by the new.

They said the building was haunted, but then people said the same of all the old dorms. It did not frighten her. A few months before, close to Halloween, she'd noticed a glow coming from one of the upstairs windows and had ventured inside in the company of a campus security officer. Someone had broken into the dorm and attempted a séance, but they'd run off, probably spotting Mi-nerva when she was waiting for an officer to arrive and escort her inside. They'd left behind a Ouija board and a few candles. It was a fire hazard, and as a result security had boarded up the down-stairs windows, since it was terribly easy to lift one open from out-side. Minerva had never discovered the identity of the culprits.

The wooden boards on the ground floor marred the looks of the building even more than its age, giving it an air of terrible neglect.

A ways away from Joyce House there was a smaller dorm, this one built in the 1950s when the college was still an all-girls' institu-tion. That was Briar Hall, with its front door painted green and a cheerful garden gnome standing guard next to a clump of daisies.

The front door was propped open. Hideo Ogawa was helping a student carry a TV out of the dorm. Hideo was also a resident di-rector. He managed three buildings on the northern side of the campus. Minerva technically also managed three, but with Joyce House closed, in practice she was down to two. The resident direc-tors were responsible for two or three buildings, depending on their size, and the corresponding undergraduate resident assis-tants. But in the summer, with so few of them on campus, they might be watching over twice as many buildings.

"Taking it to storage?" Minerva asked.

"Yeah," Hideo said. "That and a couple of boxes."

International and out-of-state students could ask to leave their belongings behind for the summer in one of the storage spaces on campus, although these could be quite contested. There was no storage space at Briar, and Ledge House's basement storage was crammed full already, so they must be heading to August Hall, which was Hideo's dorm. That was a much more modern facility;

it even had an elevator to take you up its three floors, although Minerva preferred the old houses and mansions that had been converted into student housing. Amazing what the Great Depression had done to real estate. The college had acquired a bunch of properties and land shortly after that time, doubling its size, back when properties were somewhat affordable on the North Shore.

Hideo and the student maneuvered the TV into a car, then Hideo turned toward her.

"You've checked out everyone at Ledge House?" he asked.

"I have a couple of stragglers," she said, looking down at the pink forms resting on her clipboard. "A couple more students here, too."

"I've got to drive this over to August Hall and then I'll check out a bunch of folks at Plymouth Hall. Will you be home around five?"

"Where else?" Minerva said. She didn't own a car. The walk to Temperance Landing was a good forty minutes. When classes were in session, she could ask another resident director for a ride or wait for the minuscule van that passed as a shuttle, ferrying students to the train depot at Temperance Landing, from where they could catch the train to Boston. Or it would drop them at the Stop & Shop, the multiplex, and a host of other spots. In the summer, however, the shuttle did not operate.

"Good, I need to show you something."

"Sure. Drop by."

Minerva went inside the house and up the stairs. Even as she knocked on the door, she hoped Conrad Carter would tell her he hadn't obtained the proper paperwork. He had filed it late and the housing office said students who wished to remain on campus could do so only under extenuating circumstances. Conrad Carter had family in Dover and Minerva suspected he wanted to stay at the dorm because he was too lazy to haul his things into a storage unit.

Conrad opened the door and squinted at her. He was wearing a sweatshirt and pants and looked like he had rolled out of bed a few minutes ago.

"I'm coming to inspect your suite and check your paperwork for the summer stay," she said.

"Ah, yeah." He rubbed the back of his head. "Give me ten minutes."

"Our appointment is for two-thirty," she reminded him.

"Wait, okay?" he said. It was an order, not a request.

Minerva guessed he was going to hide his bong. Late in the autumn, Conrad Carter had been the usual trouble, which meant he'd argued with his roommate. Most of the student quarters in this dorm were doubles, with two beds in each room. There were, however, a few precious suite-style rooms, which looked like mini apartments. Two single rooms divided by a small living room area, plus a private bathroom. These suites were reserved for seniors or grad students.

Conrad Carter had been assigned to a suite; he had one room and Thomas Murphy had the other one. They were a bad fit from the beginning. Conrad played his music too loudly and dirtied the bathroom. Thomas had lodged a complaint, but when a student washed their bowl of noodles in a bathroom sink and clogged it, the usual procedure was to simply have a chat with them. Which Minerva did. Conrad Carter kept playing his music and annoying his roommate. She caught him smoking pot and wrote him up, which meant nothing, because you needed far worse infractions to merit anything close to a punishment and Conrad knew it.

Thomas did not return after winter break, and Conrad seemed to have considered this a chance to increase his annoying behavior. Even though he lived in a dry dorm—there were underclassmen on the first and second floors—Minerva wrote him up for throwing three parties with plenty of beer. What was worse, he had freshmen and sophomores with him. Drinking with eighteen- and nineteen-year-old students was definitely an infraction.

Conrad, however, had skated through without any issues—his dad was friendly with a couple of school trustees. In March, Conrad had elbowed away one of Minerva's resident assistants who had been doing the rounds of the building and suspected he was carrying liquor in a shopping bag. Minerva tried opening a disciplinary inquiry, which did not proceed because Conrad said he hadn't elbowed anyone, it had been an accident, and the resident assistant had been too scared to ask him to open the bag, so no actual alcohol had been confiscated.

But Minerva didn't think it was an accident. Conrad was an asshole, plain and simple, and after she lodged her inquiry, he seemed especially eager to annoy her. He hadn't always been like that; she'd liked him in the beginning, and before Halloween, when they'd walked back to campus . . . but no matter, they were hardly on friendly terms now, and she had a job to do.

Minerva began looking around the living room and going through the pink checkout sheet. Although technically Conrad wasn't leaving, she had to make sure the suite was in decent shape, have him sign off on any damage, then also have him sign a new sheet for the upcoming year. The living room and bathroom were messy, but she saw nothing out of the ordinary.

Minerva poked her head into the room that had belonged to Thomas Murphy. There were two boxes next to the window. She'd seen them months before. Instead of coming back to campus, Thomas had emailed the registrar's office and told them he was dropping out, which meant Minerva had been alone when she'd inspected the room. There was no damage, so she'd simply informed her boss that Tom had left two boxes, assuming he'd pick them up later.

Minerva opened the flaps of one box and peered down at its contents. Books.

"You can go into my room now," Conrad said as he stood in the living room and sipped a can of Red Bull.

She quickly closed the flaps of the box and turned around to look at him.

"Tom didn't return for his stuff. You hadn't mentioned that," she told him.

"I didn't know I had to. I figured he'd come and get it if he needed it."

"In the fall you'll get a new roommate, and the room must be empty."

"You want me to chuck it out?"

"No. It's fine. I'll talk to housing services, they'll send someone. You have the R5 form?"

"You know I do."

"I still need to see it."

"You're always by the book, aren't you, Minnie? Dot your i's and cross your t's."

She detested nicknames. She was Minerva, not Minnie or Min or Nini or any other variation. He was smiling, probably thinking it was cute to butcher her name, but she returned his smile with a serious stare. She didn't need Conrad thinking summer break would soften her.

She held out her hand. He spoke under his breath and went back into the bedroom. He came back and finally gave her the permission slip for summer residency.

"You can't have overnight guests during the summer," she reminded him. "And please don't park at the front, the parking lot is—"

"I know where the parking lot is, Minnie."

"Minerva," she said coolly, the chill of autumn in her voice even with the heat of the summer gently baking the dorm. "Can I look at your room?"

"Be my guest," he said, bowing and pointing in that direction.

Conrad's room was a jumble of clothes, tangled bedsheets, and assorted soda cans piled by the window, but there was no damage to the walls or floor and all the furniture was accounted for.

He signed on the appropriate lines and Minerva continued her inspections. By the time she was done signing everyone out of the dorms, it was four. Minerva closed the front door of the dorm and headed to her apartment.

Ledge House was three stories high, with dorm rooms on the second and third floors. The kitchen had been modernized, with a refrigerator, a microwave, and a double sink. But the rest of the ground floor remained much as it had been when the building had functioned as the summer home of nineteenth-century Boston socialites.

The large parlor with its plush couches, floral wallpaper, velvet curtains, and seascapes evoked the Victorian era, even with the large TV above the nonfunctioning fireplace, which the girls in the dorm mostly used to watch *The Real World.* The dining room still had the long mahogany table where fine suppers had been orga-nized, although nowadays it was more likely to serve as the spot for a pizza night. The billiards room had been converted into a study lounge, but the dusty, ornate chandelier remained above the grand staircase.

The resident director's "apartment" was made up of several interconnecting rooms, the first of which had once been Ledge House's library. There were bookcases crammed with forgotten leather-bound volumes, as well as a multitude of stuffed birds— two ducks, two doves, several startled canaries—perched on the walls. A walnut birdcage housed a taxidermied owl. The fireplace in this room was still functional, and although the rugs were not original to the house, they had an old-fashioned look that matched the rest of the room. The library had two couches and a large leather chair. This was where Minerva held her meetings with her resident assistants, and the cabinets she used to file her paperwork were discreetly tucked in a corner.

Hideo thought the dead birds were creepy, like something out of *Psycho,* but Minerva liked them. She had names for each of them— Poe, Stoker, Shelley. Nana Alba loved birds. She'd kept canaries and doves. A parrot had often perched on her shoulder, talking merrily. In her old age Nana Alba would forget that the bird had died and speak to it, offering it a peanut and smiling placidly.

The library with its collection of stuffed birds connected to a hallway with built-in shelves, which Minerva used to store linens and supplies. Then came her bedroom. This was a very large room, not quite as big as the library, but still substantial. There was no closet; instead she had a wardrobe and a dresser, neither original to the house. By the look of them, this was furniture from the seventies, from around the time the college had gone coed, though several dorms, including Ledge House, remained single-sex. The bed was even more recent, large and comfortable, and her desk and chair were duplicates of the ones that the undergrads had in their rooms.

Minerva had been told she could hang new paintings in her bedroom, and she'd purchased a beautiful map of Cape Cod at an antique shop in Newburyport. Yet she'd never hung it. It remained resting against a wall in its frame, half hidden behind her laundry basket. Atop the dresser sat pictures of her family: Nana Alba rendered in sepia tones in her youth, then her mother, then Minerva with her hair in braids next to Nana Alba, and then the three of them together. Plus snapshots of a few friends from back home, whom she hadn't spoken to in ages, and of her more recent acquaintances.

The bedroom had two doors, one of which led to a small bathroom, the other to a room, more a nook than anything else, with a table and a couple of chairs. There was a sink, a microwave, and an electric kettle, but no stove. Hideo had gifted her a rice cooker, but if she wanted a real meal, she needed to use the dorm's kitchen. This mini kitchen had a door to the back porch and then there were steps that led to a beach, which was not like the beaches she'd visited in Mexico—all warm, soft sand. Barberry bushes delimited this beach, and it was more rocky than sandy.

Minerva grabbed her computer, made herself a cup of coffee, and sat in the kitchen, eyeing her laptop and her copy of *The Vanishing* yet not touching them. She did not know where this listlessness came from. It attacked her in waves, drowning her. She'd once asked Nana Alba how she'd survived a war, suffered through the years of meager crops and too many hungry mouths.

*You simply live through it,* she'd said. Minerva was not sure she could ever imitate the stubborn certainty in Nana Alba's voice. Perhaps Minerva was made of a softer substance.

By the time Hideo showed up, Minerva had not even turned on her laptop. He unzipped his backpack and took out a comic book tucked in a clear plastic sleeve. It had a scared-looking man on the cover.

"It's Shigeru Mizuki's adaptation of *The Dunwich Horror,*" he said. "I have a collector in Peabody that wants it. I thought I'd let you take a peek before I drop it off."

"Will you look at that," Minerva said.

Hideo was also an English student. They'd met during resident director orientation when he'd pointed at her beige trench coat and said she looked like a private investigator from an old movie, and she in turn said he looked like Freddy Krueger with the striped sweater he was wearing.

They'd bonded because of Minerva's interest in Weird fiction and horror authors, though Hideo was a Henry James aficionado writing a thesis on his ghost stories, not really a Lovecraft groupie. Aside from working as a resident director, he sold an eclectic mix of manga, movies, and Japanese pop culture artifacts, which his cousin shipped him from Osaka.

"You working?" he asked, and grabbed the beat-up paperback that sat on the table. It was a reprint copy with bad artwork and had no collector's value. Her first edition of *The Vanishing* was in the bedroom. She also had two copies of Tremblay's *Wicked Ways and Other Stories,* one of which she'd thoroughly marked with annotations and Post-its.

"Trying to. But there's no getting around it, I need to look at Beatrice Tremblay's diary and her private letters. Right now, what I have is what's in the college's archive, and that's just roughs of manuscripts, correspondence with her agent, business stuff."

"I thought you'd located some letters to Lovecraft at Brown?"

"Yeah. Two letters. One of them excitedly discusses ice cream flavors. Lovecraft rarely kept the letters of those who wrote to him, so I guess I'm lucky there are two, even if one of them waxes poetic on coffee-flavored ice cream."

It was actually Lovecraft who had first guided Minerva toward Beatrice Tremblay, though she'd long since grown more interested in her than in the man from Providence. Lovecraft had been an avid letter writer, which was a boon to history. He corresponded with all the Weird writers of the era: Clark Ashton Smith, Robert E. Howard, even a young Robert Bloch.

Despite rumors that Lovecraft was deathly afraid of women, the man was xenophobic but not gynophobic. Therefore, he also maintained a healthy correspondence with professional and amateur women writers of all types. Gossip indicated he had once been infatuated with the poet Winifred Virginia Jackson, who dated the African American poet William Stanley Braithwaite—she could imagine the shock on Lovecraft's face upon hearing about such a rival. Well, if he had been a rival. A lot of Lovecraft lore was mutated hearsay.

Among Lovecraft's correspondents, who included obscure revision clients such as Hazel Heald—with these "revisions" sometimes amounting to full-fledged ghostwriting for a few dollars—and authors of a certain renown, such as C. L. Moore, who penned the Jirel of Joiry stories, there was a young aspiring writer named Beatrice Tremblay, though back then she had signed her letters "Betty."

Beatrice would go on to correspond with other writers and publish a robust number of short stories, a couple of novellas, and one novel. Her name, first glimpsed as a footnote in a paper about Lovecraft, had incited Minerva's curiosity because Lovecraft and Tremblay had apparently corresponded on the subject of witchcraft, and also because she was a woman and a writer of "weird tales," a combination that, although not unique by itself—Greye La Spina, Everil Worrell, and Mary Elizabeth Counselman were women who wrote such stories—was noteworthy because history seemed to have forgotten most female horror authors.

Minerva had tracked down one of Tremblay's stories, translated into Spanish and reprinted in a horror anthology that had been put out by Minotauro in the eighties, and had fallen hopelessly in love with her prose.

New England and witchcraft featured prominently in Tremblay's work. Minerva's original plan had been to dig into the autobiographical elements in *The Vanishing* and tie it all together in an essay with the context of New England's history and folklore.

The first edition of *The Vanishing* contained a cryptic note at the back that declared, "This is based on a true story." And at

Brown, in one of those two letters kept at the John Hay Library, there was a paragraph that read:

I have been toying with writing a novel based on certain experiences of mine, which, as I indicated when we met in Providence last summer, were of a most eerie and disturbing nature. The working title is *The Vanishing,* and it concerns the disappearance of a young woman whom I briefly befriended. I know you've asked me for more details on this tale, which is a true account as baffling as the Lost Colony of Roanoke. Perhaps I might be able to show you my notes when I go down to Providence, which looks plausible in the fall.

The letter had been dated January 1937. Lovecraft passed away in March. Beatrice and Lovecraft had never discussed *The Vanishing*—she wouldn't write it until decades later; it had a long gestation. Of their first meeting, there were no great details and no information on what they had conversed about. Minerva knew Beatrice had almost concluded her studies at Stoneridge by the time she went to Providence to meet "Grandpa Theobald"— Lovecraft liked to call himself that. She also knew that she'd stayed for three days in Providence and that Lovecraft had given her something of a tour of the area.

He'd done the same thing for Helen V. Sully in 1933 when she'd visited Providence, and spooked her by taking her to a graveyard at night, and in 1934 Lovecraft had headed to Florida to meet with a teenage fan, R. H. Barlow—Lovecraft did not actually know his pen pal was sixteen until he arrived—who had invited him for a visit at his family's house. Which is to say, rather than being an old, scared man hiding inside a dilapidated mansion, Lovecraft did have a social life.

Lovecraft's impressions of Beatrice had been preserved in a letter to Jonquil Leiber in 1936, in which he detailed his meeting with an "interesting" young woman named Beatrice "Betty" Tremblay who was fascinated by matters of the occult and witchcraft, thus birthing the footnote that had entranced Minerva.

Minerva's mission to rescue Beatrice Tremblay from the jaws of oblivion had seemed to her achievable in the beginning, but the material in the archives of Stoneridge was dry and impersonal, unless you were eager to know that the price of *Weird Tales* in 1932 was twenty-five cents.

"What about her journal? Didn't you find out someone in the area had Tremblay's personal papers?"

"Yeah. Carolyn Yates."

"You know the remodel job at Joyce House? It's being financed by the Yates Foundation. It's not *that* Yates, is it?"

"Yep. They went to school together. Beatrice left her business correspondence and a bunch of roughs, outlines, and notes to the college; her journal and personal letters went to Carolyn. The problem is I can't get hold of them."

"She's given you the brush-off?"

"I wish. I can't even get the woman on the phone. Because she's a valuable donor, I must go through the alumni office, and they said her secretary turned me down. I got so upset that a few weeks ago I cornered her grandson in the library and asked him about it."

"He goes here?" Hideo asked. "What's his name?"

"Noah."

"What's he studying?"

"I think economics, but he might be switching to something else. Rose at the registrar's office said he's cycled through several universities. You want a cup of coffee? I'll brew a fresh pot."

"No, thanks."

Minerva stood up, fiddling with the coffee maker. Like the other appliances in the kitchen, it was an ancient, temperamental machine from the seventies. The wiring didn't help. An old building like Ledge House couldn't have two things hooked up to one electrical outlet or the power might fail.

"He's not that balding guy with the ponytail, is he? The one who has one of the singles in Catherine House?"

"No. He's our age."

"Well, okay, so what did he say?"

"He told me to contact his grandmother's secretary. This is

going to be the dullest thesis in the world. I'll never secure doc-toral funding."

"Why don't you switch it up? Focus on Lovecraft."

"Lovecraft's played out," she said, pushing the brew button. "De Camp wrote a bio about him in the seventies and then Joshi came out with an even better bio. Tremblay is fresh. Anyway, how's your work going? You keep changing your topic."

"I think I'm going to compare the ghost stories of Henry James with *Kwaidan*."

"The movie or the book?"

"I don't know," Hideo said with an effortless shrug.

"I love those types of ghost stories."

A scratching noise by the door made Hideo frown. Minerva opened the door and let in an orange tabby, which stared at Hideo while she looked for the can opener.

"You have a cat?"

"It's a stray. It started coming around for no reason."

"If you're feeding it, it has a reason. Did you name it?"

"Karnstein."

"It's definitely yours if you named it."

Minerva opened a can of cat food and poured it into a shallow ceramic dish, which she set down on the floor. The cat began munching on it.

"I should get going. I need to get this to my client," Hideo said, and slid the manga back into his backpack. "Are you going to Pa-tricia's party tomorrow?"

Now that the campus had been vacated, Minerva had intended to focus on her thesis. Realistically, she was probably going to spend twelve hours a day in bed, but she at least wanted to imag-ine she could achieve a modicum of efficiency if she was not bound to the needs of students.

"I'm not sure," she said.

"I can drive you to Patricia's and back. I want to see if there are good-looking guys there, I haven't hooked up with anyone in three months. Who was the last guy you went out with?"

She preferred to keep her thoughts veiled, to not overshare, and there wasn't anyone to talk about, not really. In the winter, she'd watched a movie with a guy from Brookline whom she'd met through a message board. But although she'd gone out with him a few times, by the spring she'd stopped responding to his emails and calls. It wasn't that she meant to cut him off—she simply figured she'd reply another time, and it was hard to go on dates when she didn't even want to change out of her pajamas. Her energy was exhausted simply by following her everyday routine and maintaining a semblance of normalcy. Perhaps she'd be able to cocoon herself during the summer, to emerge revitalized.

She'd never been much for romance, anyway. There'd been Jonás in university, although that had felt like an obligation, like she should at least try to have an adult relationship. But she'd suspected it would never lead anywhere and had been unwilling to consider going long-distance or, even worse, to reject the scholarship offer. At Stoneridge she had tiptoed around . . . well, there had been that thing with Conrad Carter, which was not even a thing.

"Isolation is not going to allow you to craft a more brilliant thesis, you know," Hideo said, as if guessing her thoughts.

"I'm not isolated," she said, and picked up her cup of coffee, taking a sip. Then she pretended to look for sugar, avoiding Hideo's gaze.

"Jessica said you want to do your night rounds alone during the summer."

"It's more convenient."

"We're supposed to walk in pairs."

"Everyone says it'll be quiet."

"Sure, but don't you want to talk to some of the few people around? I've barely seen you in the last month and a half. You keep making excuses."

"I'll go with you to the party," she said, which was the best evasive maneuver she could come up with. She didn't want to discuss her research roadblocks or her problems with anyone, even if he was a friend.

After Hideo left, Minerva looked at the cover of *The Vanishing,* which showed an open door and an empty room. It was interesting how Nana Alba had also told her a story of a disappearance that was tied to witchcraft, just as Beatrice Tremblay's novel had connections with the occult. Perhaps that was why she'd loved the book so much, why she'd devoted years of her life to pursuing this tale. This was what got her pulse racing, not lovers or romance—it was the thrill of research, of odd questions and murky answers.

"Back then, when I was a young woman, there were still witches," she said, and tapped her fingers against the book.

# 1908: 1

ALBA WANTED TO MAKE sure that the set of porcelain mancerinas was ready. She knew her mother would ask that chocolate be
served and had done her very best to time it correctly, calculating
how long it would take for a cart to roll down the roads and toward
the farm after the five o'clock train made its stop. But the mancerinas with their painted birds and insects, old and fine artifacts from
another era, were kept in a locked cabinet. Alba hurried around
the house, trying to find the key.

"Can't we pour the chocolate into a cup?" Fernanda asked.
"Why do we need that funny little plate to hold the cup up?"

"It's the way chocolate is supposed to be served," Alba said.
"When noble people held their parties, they always drank their
chocolate in a mancerina."

"We're not nobility and those dusty antiques are best kept
locked away," Tadeo said.

Alba ignored her brother and turned to the young maid. "Look
in that drawer, Fernanda, for God's sake. My uncle Arturo is
bound to be here any minute now. Oh, and cut one of the carnations that are growing in the white flowerpots, the red carnations
by the kitchen windows, not the pink ones in the back. Put the
flower on the tray when you bring it in."

"You'd think the Pope is visiting," Tadeo said.

Tadeo did not care much for their uncle, calling him a snob and even "Uncle Catrín" when he was in a bad mood, but Alba disagreed ardently. Although Arturo Velarde was twenty-four, merely five years older than Alba, she considered him the most mature, sophisticated, and intelligent man in the entire nation. He spoke French fluently, had memorized verses by Verlaine, Manuel José Othón, Juan de Dios Peza, and many others, and had even published a few poems of his own.

For his sake she'd worn the green dress with the high waistline, because green was Arturo's favorite color and she thought that the dress had a Parisian touch to it that he'd be sure to admire. On her finger she wore a delicate ring with a jade stone that her father had given her for her fifteenth birthday, and matching earrings framed her face. She wanted to look like the women who appeared in magazines, sleek and sophisticated.

"Mr. Quiroga, your uncle is here. I need help carrying his things," Jacobo said. "Have you seen Belisario?"

Alba still winced when people called her brother "Mr. Quiroga," though it was accurate. Now that their father had passed away, he was the only "mister" around, and yet he was less than a year younger than Alba, just eighteen years old.

"Belisario is on an errand," Tadeo said.

"That's a bad thing, then," Jacobo replied, and scratched the collar of his shirt. "I don't know how I'll manage."

"You can't carry a valise by yourself?"

"He has two trunks, Mr. Quiroga, and two valises."

"Of course he does. I'll help you."

Fernanda found the key to the cabinet and Alba told her to pour the chocolate while she hurried to the parlor. This was the best room in the house. On sturdy bookshelves rested the Quirogas' books, everything from a fine encyclopedia to volumes on ancient mythology. Her father had not been much of a reader, but he'd had a younger sister—dead of a fever many years now—who'd had a fondness for novels. Alba's mother had added to this collection, and now Alba carefully dusted each book and catalogued it with care. When her uncle mailed her a new volume of poetry, she reverently placed it next to the others on a shelf designated for her most treasured reads.

The sofa in the parlor was upholstered in pink damask and the two armchairs facing it were of the finest leather. In front of a window there was a table with gilded legs and upon it a vase of fine china gifted to her mother on the occasion of her wedding. A few chairs were arranged by this window, and when they had company they moved them next to the couch so that everyone could listen while Alba or her mother played the piano. But they had not had many visitors since her father's death four months earlier, and the parlor had become sad and dreary to her.

Now, as she walked in, Alba thought the room had been entirely changed: the sun shone bright through the open windows and the parlor seemed light and airy. Standing there, glancing out one of those windows, was her uncle Arturo. He wore a three-piece suit that served to emphasize his slimness. His jacket and his trousers were a dark gray color, and his vest, with its daring bright blue hue, was in sharp contrast to the subdued gray of the rest of his clothes.

His hair, of a rich brown that was almost burnished, flecked with gold, was slicked back with macassar. His eyes were a light, liquid brown, the eyebrows elegantly sketched, and his full lips granted him a languorous expression, which he often enhanced with a decadent half smile. He had an easy, relaxed air about him that seemed to match his handsome face.

She had thought so much about him in the last few months, wishing dearly he'd visit Piedras Quebradas. She had even cast a little spell she'd learned, summoning him. She did not often indulge in such practices, for fear of what others would think if she admitted she believed in folk magic. Her mother abhorred superstition and even though her father had believed in enchantments, in monsters and witches, she tried to be like her instead of him. Besides, Alba understood these games children played must be sloughed off as she became a worldly woman.

Arturo turned his head. "Alba," he said, delight clear in his voice, and opened his arms to her.

Alba rushed forward and hugged him, closing her eyes. "Arturo! You've come! I so hoped you would come! Tadeo is terribly bossy, and Mother . . . it's dreary."

He was there! How she'd missed him. It had been well over a year, almost two, since he'd last visited Piedras Quebradas. But he was finally there, and she clutched him tight. For a minute they embraced and stood so close she was able to hear his heart beating in his chest, then he stepped back.

"I can imagine," Arturo said, and began drawing her toward the sofa so that they might sit together.

"Mother is cross with me every day. I do my best, but I've never been good with the little ones, and now that Father isn't around, Magdalena complains all the time and the twins are even more of a handful."

As the eldest child, Alba kept an eye on the younger children, played with them or watched them when her mother was busy. But Mother was eternally irritated now, and Tadeo could hardly help her, busy as he was in the fields or with the animals. She sometimes believed Tadeo liked horses more than he liked people.

Alba found herself juggling household responsibilities and tending to her siblings. Lola was six, docile, and took her little brother, Moisés, by the hand, which at least meant she watched over him. But the twins! They were seven and didn't want to learn their letters, wash their hands, or comb their hair. Alba was in a constant battle with them.

Magdalena was terrible in her own special way, always mumbling under her breath and pointing out Alba's mistakes. Even though she was only eleven, she attempted to bully Fernanda and undermine her big sister. Alba would have had Magdalena chopping wood all day long, and the twins too, but their mother wanted them to practice their penmanship, read books, learn the names of faraway countries. Alba was no schoolmistress to teach all this, and yet her mother said this was a woman's obligation: to handle the household and the children.

"Now, now, don't look so sad. I've brought new sheet music and a trinket you might like," Arturo said. "We'll scrub this house free of any gloom, won't we?"

Her eyes widened with delight. "Sheet music! And books? Have you brought any books?"

"Yes. Baudelaire, Rubén Darío, and Amado Nervo. *That evening in the poplar grove, mad with love, the sweet one I idolized offered me the wild rose of her mouth*," he recited smoothly.

"You must read to me, and you must play the piano, and you must make me terribly happy."

"I will," he said, his voice soft as silk. She wished to throw her arms around his neck and hug him again, but then her mother walked in and Arturo smiled one of his dazzling smiles.

He stood up and took her hands between his. "Luisa, my deepest condolences. I'm terribly sorry that I couldn't be here for the funeral."

"Thank you. I'm glad you'll be here for tomorrow's remembrance mass, it is a great comfort to me," she said, and pressed a hand against his cheek. "My darling brother, how have you been?"

"Very well."

"You are not missing any meals? Julia complains that you never have your breakfast and you stay out late. Let me see. Yes, you have dark circles under your eyes. Silly boy, are you behaving yourself?"

"I behave most properly. You can rap my knuckles if you think I'm lying," he said. Luisa slapped his hand in mock admonishment. She smiled.

When Luisa Velarde was sixteen, her mother died, leaving her with the responsibility of caring for her siblings and running their house. Her younger sister, Julia, had already been thirteen and capable of fending for herself, but her little brother, Arturo, had been two years old. Luisa had endeavored to fill the role of mother for him, to ensure that he would never lack for anything.

When Luisa married a farmer from Hidalgo, she had wept bitter tears and Arturo had cried with equal abandon. Then, when he was nine, the family sent him to live with Luisa. The boy had missed his eldest sister. Besides, Julia had never been the mothering type. She was relieved to have the child in someone else's hands, and Arturo's father was a busy man who had no time nor patience for fussy children.

Arturo lived at the farm for a few years. The mountains, the gorges, the rivers and trees, did not suit him. When he turned fourteen, Luisa determined that he ought to attend a boarding school, for he was an intellectual, taciturn child. Alba's father had tried to show him the ways of the farm, but he had not taken to it. He'd gone away, attended the boarding school, polished his French and his piano playing, enrolled in university.

By the time he returned to visit the farm, Arturo was a youth of nineteen with dreams and prospects. Alba was delighted by the sight of him, and even when he dropped out of university and their family chided him for it, she thought him a most brilliant man.

Each of his visits was delightful. No matter whether it had been more than a year or just six months since she'd last seen him, he seemed to have grown more sophisticated, his clothing more fashionable, his manners more attractive. He lived in the city with his father and Julia and attended all manner of dances, exhibitions, and gatherings. When he spoke, it was like sweeping into the pages of *El Mundo Ilustrado.*

Fernanda walked in carrying a tray with the mancerinas and the pretty carnation in a flower vase. Dolores walked behind her. In her hands she held a dish with a silver dome that concealed what lay under it. The staff at Piedras Quebradas was modest. Dolores and Belisario had worked there for ages, she as the cook and maid, he as the right-hand man to Alba's father since long before he'd married. Jacobo had been there for a couple of years and Fernanda for almost ten months. During the planting weeks and the busy harvesttime, they hired a few extra hands.

They grew barley, corn, and beans in the fields. They kept chickens, pigs, rabbits, and goats. Her father's most precious investment had been his horses. They had a beautiful white stallion that they put out to stud for a fee.

Her father had done well enough and yet there was no denying

that theirs was a provincial life and a provincial existence. Alba
worried that Arturo would find something lacking in his lodging
or in the food. She had managed, through clever bribery and the
use of sweets, to persuade the children to play in the nursery, at
least for a little while. She did not want them stumbling into the
parlor and running wild, playing at pirates, while Arturo drank
his chocolate.

"But what is this? *Une tasse trembleuse, pour moi?*" he asked,
and smiled as Fernanda handed him a cup. "And this warm chocolate. You needn't have bothered, really."

"I baked an almond cake, too," Alba said, lifting the silver dome
from the dish and motioning to the maids that they might step out
and check on the younger ones.

"How lovely. You're an excellent cook."

"Not when it comes to making tortillas," Tadeo said as he
walked in and wiped the sweat from his brow. "She acts as if there
are ants in the dough, she won't palm them into shape."

"I do make tortillas. I make everything," Alba said angrily.

In truth, she was impractical, and liked to cook elaborate dishes
or sweet treats. The thought of plucking a chicken or skinning a
rabbit was abhorrent, and she submitted to such mundane tasks
only when her watchful mother demanded it. But she didn't want
Tadeo speaking so bluntly about her, even if it was true.

"Well, your luggage is up in your usual room, Uncle Arturo,"
Tadeo said. He plopped himself down in one of the armchairs
while Arturo settled into the other one. "It looks like you're coming for a year and not merely for the mass."

"I thought I'd stay for a little while and help around the farm,"
Arturo said, lifting the porcelain cup and sipping his chocolate.

"Help how?"

"Your father's death is a great burden to your mother."

"A burden we're shouldering, yes."

"You needn't shoulder it alone."

"Exactly what could you do for us?" Tadeo asked, raising a
skeptical eyebrow.

"I'm not as useless as you think, dear nephew," Arturo said. His poise was admirable. Alba watched him with zeal, observing how he tilted his head and held his cup.

"I've never known you to be interested in tilling fields or butchering a pig."

"It's a balm simply to have you with me, dear brother," Luisa said, and then she looked at Tadeo. "You must watch your tone, Tadeo, or your uncle will think you rude."

"I'm sorry, Uncle," Tadeo said, but he stretched out his legs and shrugged with insolence.

Alba's brother took after their father; he was broad of shoulder, tall, and strong, and although still young he had that shell of toughness of the Quirogas. Alba, on the other hand, was like her mother, like the Velardes. Delicately sculpted, elegant, with brown curls cascading down her back and long fingers that slid upon the piano keys with ease.

Why had her father, rougher, with little interest in fashions and soirées, picked a lady from the city for a wife? And why in turn had a girl who liked the scent of perfumes more than the fresh country air accepted the proposal of a young farmer? Alba liked to think it had been love at first sight, and yet the thought of two people who were so wildly different made her frown. She wished to marry someone who shared her interests, who was sensitive and idealistic, not her complete opposite. This was why she was hesitant with Valentín. He was nice, but he was like all the men in Paraje de Abedules, one more farmer who wanted to discuss animal husbandry, not couplets.

Arturo carefully wiped his mouth with a napkin and set aside the mancerina. "No need to apologize, Tadeo. However, I'm afraid I'm exhausted. Riding on that rickety wagon is torture. I've said it before: it's a shame you don't have a proper carriage."

"Why should we have a carriage?" Tadeo asked. "It would go to waste. Besides, if the wagon bothers you, you could have availed yourself of a horse at the station. One of the townspeople would have lent it to you and you'd have arrived sooner."

"I hate horses more than I hate wagons. And they hate me in

turn. Anyway, I should nap. It's no small feat to make it to this little farm in one piece."

"My boy, we are so careless to keep you here when you must be falling asleep," Luisa said, rising with Arturo. "Come, I'll walk you to your room, and if anything is amiss, you can tell me and I'll have it fixed."

Luisa and Arturo walked out of the room. Tadeo immediately cut himself a large slice of almond cake and grabbed one of the porcelain cups.

"Will you put that down? I didn't bake it for you."

Her brother twirled a fork in the air. "What? You want it to go stale? The man is sleeping, I might as well eat your silly cake."

"He's retreated upstairs because you're rude."

"I don't think it's rude to speak the truth. He looks like he's packed to go on a trip around the entire state of Hidalgo. Aunt Julia says he's a spendthrift and she doesn't want him living with her anymore. Now he suddenly shows up with all his shirts and neckties when he couldn't bother to come for Father's funeral? He's come to live here. But I don't give free room and board."

"You're shameless, Tadeo Quiroga," she said, and crossed her arms. "This is our uncle we're talking about."

"Our uncle who spends his days at the Jockey Club and has a lover."

"How do you know that?" Alba asked, incensed, clasping her hands together.

"The Jockey Club? Why, it's where all the rich young men go, and Uncle Arturo may not be rich, but he likes to live richly."

"I meant the other part."

"That's what Aunt Julia wrote to Mother. That he is either spending all his money at the racetrack or keeping a lover. Otherwise, she can't figure out what he's done with his bank account. I'm telling you, he's not coming here to live off us. I have a hard enough time handling Piedras Quebradas right now to have to handle *him,* too."

"When did Aunt Julia write such a thing? I didn't see the letter."

"She wrote to us, and Mother wouldn't let me show you the letter because of those things she said about Uncle Arturo. She doesn't think a young lady should hear such tales."

"She's correct. They're filthy lies," Alba said primly, though she felt furious at this gossip, and if she'd had her darning needle handy she would have poked her brother with it.

"Well, I'm telling you because right after she wrote, Uncle Arturo also wrote to say maybe Mother should accept Mr. Molina's offer. I think that's why he's here, because he wants her to sell the farm."

Alba understood her brother's animosity; he loved the land. But she didn't feel the same love for Piedras Quebradas. She didn't mind helping her mother with the garden where they grew vegetables and herbs. But she hated when they castrated the pigs or cut off a chicken's neck with a sharp axe. She felt like screaming every time her mother killed a chicken and the corpse twisted and shook, seeming almost to dance.

"When you're married and keep your own house, you'll have to do as much, even if you have the help of your maids," her mother had told her on one occasion, when she practically fainted at the sight of the bird's carcass.

"I can't. I'm no good at it," Alba said, and stared at the blood spatters left by the poor chicken. She wanted to paint pretty watercolors, like the one she had gifted Tadeo for his fifteenth birthday, or raise gentle doves, not chop the necks of birds.

"I didn't know how to kill a chicken when I came to Piedras Quebradas, but I learned."

But Alba had never wanted to learn. She wanted to be a lady, soft and poised, like her mother had been in the city before she married, like the women in the society pages.

"I'm headed upstairs, too," Alba told her brother. "You must be nicer tomorrow."

Once Alba reached her room, she locked the door and closed her eyes. She knew that in a few minutes she'd be needed, either to tend to the children or to help with a chore.

She opened her eyes and sighed. She could understand why Uncle Arturo wanted to visit the Jockey Club and spend his days in merriment. Who'd prefer to clean out the hogpen? Perhaps Tadeo, but he was a silly boy, even if the servants called him "Mr. Quiroga."

Alba walked around the room, her hands gliding along the white curtains that encircled her bed then resting on a book she'd abandoned upon her pillow, a slim volume of Greek myths, stories of Cupid and Psyche, Hades and Persephone, Helen's love affair with Paris. She wondered whether her uncle had a lover, as they said. If he did, she'd be a seductive woman with a sharp tongue. She'd be lovely and would dress in beautiful gowns.

No doubt the lover rubbed nice creams, like the one Adelina Patti advertised in magazines, against her skin and pressed rice powder on her cheeks. She wore lace of Alençon and owned a hat with an ostrich feather.

How annoying, Alba thought, that on their farm she must wear simple muslin dresses, white, or perhaps with a pattern of flowers, while in Mexico City women were outfitted in silks. Her mother would never allow her rice powder, let alone rouge, and Arturo's lover must have access to both.

Alba leaned forward, looking into her mirror, and pictured her cheeks dabbed with color, her lips streaked with carmine.

There was a knock on the door. She stood up straight and placed the book in a drawer, fearing it might be Tadeo. He mocked her reading tastes, but then all the reading he wanted to do was about horses and pigs. "I'm resting for a minute," she said.

"It's Arturo."

She looked at her reflection, quickly pressing her hands against her hair, smoothing it back, making sure an errant curl was tucked behind her ear.

"Is there something amiss with your room?" she asked as she opened the door and gazed into his smiling face.

"No. It's cozy enough. I wanted to give you that trinket I spoke about."

"How sweet of you to remember me."

"Here," he said, and from his pocket he pulled out a chain with a single pearl dangling from it.

Alba rushed to her mirror excitedly, holding the necklace up. She angled her head left and right.

"I saw it and thought of you. How do you like it?"

"It's darling!" she exclaimed. "Come inside. Help me put it on."

He swept her thick, long hair away from her nape and with careful fingers manipulated the clasp. She watched his reflection in the mirror, his eyes fixed on his task, and wondered if he'd bought something just as pretty for his lover. He looked up at her, their eyes meeting in the mirror, and she blushed.

"But it's not a trinket, you shouldn't have," she said, looking down.

"I'm aiming to cheer you up. Will you wear it tomorrow?"

"Of course! Although tomorrow is the mass and I ought to wear my crucifix and that scratchy gray dress Mother picked for me," she said, frowning.

"You can't wear both?"

"I could. As long as Mother doesn't see it, or she'll say it's vulgar to pair the cross with anything else. But the chain is long. . . ." She trailed her fingers down her throat, to the spot where the pearl rested, almost between her breasts. "I'll wear it close to my heart, always," she said, and looked up at him.

A smile stole over his face and her heart was near to bursting with joy at the sight. He stepped away from her. Hands in his pockets, he walked to the door.

"Will the Molinas be at the mass tomorrow?" he asked when he reached the doorway.

"Yes, they will," she said, following two steps behind him. "The Molina girls will be pleased to see you. They think you're dashing."

"Am I, then?" he replied, and laughed.

He lingered by her side until there came the sound of a wail from down the hallway and Alba sighed, guessing that one of the twins was being naughty with the other. She had perhaps five minutes to herself before her presence in the nursery became imperative.

"I'll try to take my nap now, or your mother will box my ears," Arturo said.

"Thank you once more."

Alba closed the door and hurried back in front of the mirror, admiring the new piece of jewelry. She bit her lips, hoping to add a pinch of color to them, and traced a line with her index finger down her neck.

# 1998: 2

MINERVA DIDN'T KNOW MOST of the people at the party, and the ones who attended Stoneridge were at best faces without names. Many guests, many strangers. A couple of people approached her, yelling their names, indicating via gestures or expressions that they'd been introduced at one point, perhaps at another party, perhaps they'd seen each other in the cafeteria, but Minerva couldn't hear what they said and couldn't make herself understood with all the noise.

She found refuge on a couch and sat clutching a bottle of beer but did not drink. The TV was on, showing *Pinky and the Brain*. They'd turned the volume off, so she couldn't hear what was happening on the show, not that it mattered. She wasn't watching it. She had merely picked that spot to hide. It was located away from the table where Patricia and her roommates were playing beer pong. She was afraid Patricia would ask how she was doing. If Minerva said she was feeling like shit, Patricia would offer her a Jell-O shot, suggest that she join the beer pong game, or any number of inanities.

Minerva liked Patricia. She was fun, energetic, and kept finding interesting holes-in-the-wall to visit. She liked Hideo, too. Lots. At night the three of them talked on ICQ about meaningless and profound topics, then they gathered in the morning in the cafeteria. It had been Patricia who showed Minerva how to make a snowman—she'd completed her bachelor's degree in the States, so she already knew the minutiae of winters—and Hideo frequently popped by Minerva's dorm with lychee candy, which she'd never tasted before.

They were her friends, or they had been until the last month, when she'd avoided them, too wrapped up in academic pursuits and thesis burnout to seek their company. Same as she was avoiding her mother—she didn't want to talk to anyone. Inevitably, they'd ask about papers, research, everything she didn't wish to discuss.

She shouldn't have come. Not in her current mood, not with the anxiety that kept simmering in her belly. The reason she'd shown up was because she had a feeling she ought to, the thought embedded in her mind almost like a thorn. Nana Alba used to call these feelings portents and said they should be heeded.

Minerva rubbed her temples. Hideo was having an animated conversation with a tall blond man and she knew he'd never agree to drive back to campus before two A.M. He'd said so when they left: *Party night! End of term!* He'd said it with such enthusiasm, too. As if it meant anything, as if it were a national holiday.

Minerva supposed she could walk back. Patricia shared a house with three other students in Temperance Landing and it might not be that convenient to walk home at night, but at least she was wearing comfortable shoes.

The girl sitting next to her laughed, and in her excitement she elbowed Minerva. Minerva spilled beer on her own shirt. The girl didn't notice. Minerva hurried to the bathroom, locking the door.

She dabbed at her shirt with a towel, trying to blot out the stain. Hideo had said she should "doll herself up" when he phoned her earlier in the day, but Minerva had merely put on a flannel button-down over a T-shirt. She gave up on trying to clean the stain and tied the flannel around her waist so the mess at least wouldn't show.

She unzipped her oversize leather purse, took out a bottle of aspirin, and swallowed two pills. She wished she had brought her

Discman, although she realized how antisocial she'd look if she walked around a party with headphones on.

Someone knocked on the door. Minerva ignored them. After a few minutes they went away, probably to the upstairs bathroom.

Minerva remained sequestered in the bathroom for ten minutes. She timed it. Then she left her beer by the sink, stepped out, slipped through the laughing young people, and walked down the front steps of the house.

The sky above her head was a cloak of indigo and the noises of the party turned into a distant hum as soon as she closed the door behind her. A moth fluttered by, attracted by the glow of a lamppost. She took a deep breath. The night felt velvet soft, almost alive, thrumming with secrets.

"Damn it," a guy said. He was a few paces from where she stood, looking at the ground, clutching his bottle of beer and muttering to himself as he walked around a tree.

She was going to leave him there, circling the tree and slurring his words, but she wondered if he'd be safe by himself. Maybe she could coax him back inside, call him a taxi. Although at this hour of the night there would be no taxis. In such a small town, rides were scarce at the best of times. Well, she could at least get him seated on a couch where others might watch over him.

"You okay?" she asked.

"Kind of. Can't see where I dropped my cellphone without my contacts," he replied.

She looked down, searching in the tall grass. Her hands brushed against a lump of plastic and she picked up the phone.

"Here. You sure you're okay?"

He nodded and tucked the cellphone in his back pocket. When he swept his hair back from his face, she realized she was standing in front of Noah Yates. He was dressed in what was essentially the preppy uniform of men at Stoneridge, with beige slacks and leather boat shoes. Instead of a sweater or a bomber jacket—which was practically mandatory for guys his age—he wore a suede jacket. In short, he seemed like he was emulating the men in the J.Crew catalogues. All-American Norman Rockwell. Rather bland, despite his expensive ensemble.

He took a swig of beer.

"Shitty techno. Makes my eardrums bleed," he said while he swayed a little and stepped back. "I got a splitting headache from it."

"You want an aspirin?" she asked, not knowing what else to say.

"Sure."

She placed one on his palm and he popped it into his mouth, taking another drink. But the bottle was empty and he tossed it away. He pulled out a silver flask from a jacket pocket and took a sip, then tipped the flask in her direction.

"No thanks."

"Orange juice," he said loudly.

"Sorry?"

"What I need is orange juice. Eggs, coffee. A damn waffle. What time is it? Fuck. I want brunch. This shithole town doesn't have a twenty-four-hour diner, do you realize that? How fucked up is it that we can't even get a twenty-four-hour Denny's?" He took another sip, then he squinted. "Don't I know you?"

She almost jumped with relief at his words. This was the opening she needed. "Yes. We met at the library. I asked if you could get me in touch with your grandmother."

"Carolyn?"

"It was about Beatrice Tremblay's papers. I'm Minerva Contreras." She extended her hand.

He looked puzzled, then his eyes finally seemed to focus on her—he was quite drunk, and his nearsightedness must not have been helping the situation—and something seemed to click inside his head. He shook her hand, hesitating for a moment, then clasping it with vigor.

"Yeah, yeah. I remember now. The ghost-story girl. What happened?"

"You told me to contact her secretary. I'm still waiting to hear back."

She ought to say he'd been incredibly rude to her. The man had practically barked the moment she started speaking. But it would do her no good to point it out. At least the booze mellowed him.

"You're with the English lit department, right?"

"Yes. Nell Quinn is my adviser."

"I'm economics. Presently," he said. He ran a hand through his hair. "Ghost stories. What you like . . . you like ghost stories, right?"

"Witches' stories," she corrected him. "I said I was studying Tremblay's work and wanted to explore its connection to New England's witchcraft folklore."

"It's the witching hour. Midnight, no?"

"Five to it," she said, consulting her wristwatch.

"Miner—Minerva, ah . . . international student, no? From . . . fuck, don't tell me . . ."

"Mexico," she said.

"I was in Cancún for spring break three years ago," he said. "I'm Noah."

She hitched her purse up her shoulder. "I know."

"Oh, yeah, you do," he muttered. "They tell ghost stories in England for Christmas, bet you didn't know *that,*" he said excitedly. "Every year—"

"My friend studies Henry James, so yeah, I know."

"You're not much for making conversation, are you?" he replied, irritated. Then he paused. "Fuck, I'm going to vomit."

He leaned against the trunk of a tree and bent down. He puked, and then coughed so much she thought he'd dislodged a lung. "Are you okay?" she asked. It seemed it was the one question she could ask him.

He wiped his mouth with the sleeve of his shirt and nodded. "Yeah."

Minerva didn't like hanging around people who were drunk. She never could figure out how to act with them. Anytime someone yelled *I'm so wasted!,* it sounded like nails on a chalkboard rather than careless glee. She didn't understand the desire to end up kneeling in front of a toilet and puking up one's dinner. Besides, she couldn't afford to squander her evenings drifting into an alcoholic daze when she needed perfect grades.

Nevertheless, she tried to smile sympathetically at Noah. It couldn't hurt to be nice to Carolyn Yates's grandson, even if he looked like a buffoon right that minute. Hell, he probably looked like a buffoon all the time. She'd had to deal with many privileged, spoiled boys and girls at Stoneridge. Students who didn't show up to the language lab for their scheduled sessions and then expected the tutors to say that they had perfect attendance; residents who tried to roast marshmallows in their room and triggered the fire alarm at three A.M.; a whole league of bored, indifferent, rude youths who did not realize how lucky they were. Noah didn't speak, simply sipping again from his flask, and her smile withered. The music seemed to be getting louder inside. He sighed, grabbed his phone, and dialed.

"Hey, you can pick me up now."

He snapped the phone shut and gave her a sideways glance, but he still didn't talk to her. She wondered if she should walk back inside, if maybe she'd offended him. Then again, he didn't own the street, and if he was offended because she knew a few basic facts about English literature, that was his problem. She undid the knot of the flannel shirt tied around her waist and put it on again, pulling at the cuffs. He spared her nothing, not a look, not a word.

After a few minutes a gleaming white car rolled in front of the house. It was a smooth-looking vehicle out of the thirties, all chrome and elegance. It must have been parked nearby or circling the area to have made its way there so quickly.

"My grandmother's car and driver," he said, pointing at it. "You want a ride back to campus?"

"Sure," she said, surprised that he remembered she was standing there.

Once inside, she told the driver which dorm she lived in, and the car began rolling along. Noah sat with his head tipped back and his eyes closed. After a few blocks he spoke.

"Carolyn should be around tomorrow for brunch, if you'd like to come to the Willows. You can ask her about Tremblay."

The Willows was the Yates estate, an imposing mansion located a short drive from the campus. Minerva could walk it. In fact, she had walked by the house. Twice. She'd peered at its ivy-encrusted walls and wondered if she'd ever see the inside.

"You know where the Willows is? Because we have a good brunch. Better than any diner around here. It's not twenty-four hours, though."

He rattled off his address. Then he crossed his arms and remained like that until they reached her dorm. Minerva stepped out of the car.

"Thanks for the ride."

"Sure," he said, eyes still closed.

"What time for brunch?"

"Brunch is at noon."

She nodded. The car turned around and disappeared down the road.

She broke out in laughter. She had an invitation to the Willows. After weeks of dead ends, she would meet Carolyn Yates.

She looked at the Witch's Thicket. With only the porch light of Ledge House on and without the glow of the moon, the trees were smudges of gray sketched against a charcoal background.

On the night of the new moon evil witches liked to dance against the treetops; that was what her great-grandmother used to say. They'd slip out of their human skins and grow wings, turn into balls of light, and cavort in the sky. The teyolloquani, the most fearsome of all, drank the blood of their victims and ate their hearts.

Nana Alba talked frequently about that type of witch in the last months of her life; she kept repeating the story about her own brother's vanishing.

*That's what their name means, "heart eater,"* Nana Alba had said. *Listen, this story, you should hear it and learn how to fight them. About how to know them. Know the signs. A true witch is born, the day of their birth marks their path.*

Minerva had promised she would memorize her great-grandmother's tale. Maybe that's why she wanted to write about ghost stories, like Noah said. Some people might think it was silly to focus on horror fiction and the eerie disappearance of a girl in New England, but she'd grown up feasting on such narratives.

There were no warlocks haunting the treetops at Stoneridge, but there had been that curious feeling, the portent, and it had guided her to the party. Luck, perhaps, was at hand.

The night was deliciously calm as she stood looking at the trees. After the noise, the awful tumult of Patricia's party, she could finally breathe. She hurried up the steps and opened the door, slipping into the comforting lonesomeness of the old house.

# 1908: 2

AFTER THE MASS, SEVERAL friends of the family were invited back to Piedras Quebradas for a cup of chocolate, including Mr. Molina, his wife, and his daughters. The girls gave Alba their condolences while everyone stood outside the church.

"But then your uncle Arturo intends to remain here?" the older one asked. "I thought he never wanted to be around for more than a week, let alone a month."

"That's because last time he was here you tried playing the piano," the younger daughter said. "You destroyed the man's eardrums."

"I'll have you know he didn't complain about my playing, it was your silly flirting that irritated him. Tell her, Alba."

"You're both fine players," Alba said. "And, if you must know, my uncle is here to help us."

"My, Valentín looks handsome in his new hat today," the younger sister said, distracted and craning her neck to look over the girls' shoulders at the strong young man with glossy black hair and an effortless mirth. That day he'd donned his nicest jacket and his shirt was buttoned up to his chin, but he still looked like a rugged farm boy who'd taken a day off from rounding up the sheep and feeding the horses. He was no Paris wooing Helen, certainly no Cupid whose arrows might inflame the soul.

Valentín worked at the Molinas' farm. His uncle was Mr. Molina's overseer. Alba had known him since she was a young girl. Together with Tadeo, they'd played at skipping stones by the river, swum together, and even shot targets, either with a rifle or with her father's pistol. But it had been a long time since Alba's mother had allowed her to grab a rifle from the case and accompany the boys during their target practice. It was not ladylike, and she had become a lady.

Besides, now that their father had passed away, Tadeo kept the pistol in his room and didn't have time for practice shooting. Running the farm consumed his hours.

Valentín had a rich, full laugh and a pleasing-enough face, though Alba wasn't sure he could be called handsome.

"Now you're being even sillier," the older sister said. "Valentín is Alba's sweetheart."

"He is not!" Alba said, scandalized by such a bold proclamation.

"He would be if he could. Everyone knows he was going to ask your father for your hand in marriage, but then Mr. Quiroga died. Now the poor thing must wait a full year to speak to your mother; it wouldn't be proper to have a wedding when the family's still in mourning," the older sister said piously, and made the sign of the cross.

"Many things may happen in a year, especially if someone hasn't expressed their intent," the younger sister said, smiling coquettishly.

"Not when little chits go around flirting with every boy in town. Then no one proposes to them because they're too fickle."

"Who are you calling a chit?"

Alba adjusted her shawl while the girls bickered. Valentín smiled eagerly and walked their way.

"Miss Petronila. Miss Mariana. How are you, Miss Quiroga?" Valentín asked, taking his hat off to salute them.

"I'm very well," she said. Next to her, the Molina girls giggled.

"I thought you might like these," Valentín said, handing her a bouquet of pink roses.

Alba clasped it with both hands. "Thank you."

"May I ride next to you, Miss Quiroga?" he asked. His politeness, like his clothes, was awkward. Not that he was ever rude to her, but she realized he'd dressed and rehearsed his words hoping to impress her. Instead, she saw only a raw young man who wasn't quite sure of himself.

"You may," she said, muffling a little laugh, for it would have been cruel to greet him in such a manner, and she did like Valentín, even if he lacked polish.

In the months since her father's death, he'd scarcely stopped by the farm. She knew he did it out of respect, since they couldn't receive guests with such fresh mourning, but she'd missed him. Yet as they rode together, behind the wagon crammed with the younger children, she was quiet and did not know what to say to him.

Valentín smiled at her. "The black mare gave birth last week," he told her. "The foal has a white spot on its forehead. It looks like a star."

"Does it, then?" she replied.

The time of the harvest of the xoconostle approached, and Valentín talked about that, about the rains and the everyday happenings at the Molinas' estate. She was quickly bored by his chatter and looked at his face, wondering if she would be able to stomach long evenings conversing with him even if he wasn't displeasing to the eye. She was fond of Valentín, but playing hide-and-seek when they were children was different than picturing him as her husband.

She shook her head. He hadn't asked and might never ask. The Molina girls might simply be making stories up to fluster her.

When they reached the house, the first thing Alba did was herd the children up to the nursery so they could play there while the adults received the guests. Then she placed Valentín's flowers in a porcelain vase by her window and smoothed her skirts. She helped Fernanda take the chocolate into the parlor. This time, she did not bother with the mancerinas. They did not have enough of them to serve everyone, so she passed around simple cups and plates.

Mr. Molina's wife and his daughters sat on the pink couch while he pulled over one of the chairs that Alba had lugged into the parlor that morning for the purpose of this gathering. A few other friends of her father's who had attended the mass were also there. Fourteen guests in total, including Valentín and his uncle. It seemed almost like one of their reunions, before her father died, but there'd be no piano playing that day, only conversation.

After a couple of hours everyone began making their excuses and it was only the Molinas and the Quirogas who were left in the room.

Mr. Molina turned to her brother. "Have you thought about that offer I made you last month?" he asked.

"Yes, and my answer remains the same: I won't be selling this farm anytime soon."

"I do not speak because I wish to offend you, Tadeo. I speak because your father was my friend and I know that even before he passed away, he had money concerns. The situation can hardly be improving."

"If you came to talk about the sale of the land, then you made a trip for no reason, sir. It's rude to even broach the matter."

"It's logical to broach the matter," Arturo interjected. He was standing next to Alba's mother, resting a hand on the back of her chair. "I've done the math, no doubt Mr. Molina has done the same. The expenses at Piedras Quebradas are too high."

Tadeo stared at their uncle, his eyebrows knit in displeasure. "You did the math. Well, you are wrong."

"Do you wish to fetch your ledger?"

"There is no formula that can show you how much this land is worth. It's as much a part of me as my flesh and my bones."

Tadeo gave their uncle such a harsh, terrible glare that it made the Molinas quickly rise, uttering goodbyes. Then it was them, the family, left in the room, their merriment cooling like the ashes of a fire. Alba hoped that Arturo would let the matter be, but instead he spoke.

"In six months that man will make another offer, but a substantially lower one, and you will have lost money in the bargain," Arturo warned him. "It's stupid to let cash walk out the door like that."

"I have no desire to let Mr. Molina expand his holdings. In six months, I'll be here, watching over my lands."

"How will you do that? You have a large family, a large staff—"

"It's not a large staff."

"Large, yes, for what this place brings in."

"How can you know what it brings in? You spy on me. I won't have it."

"I am no spy. Your mother has shared her worries with me."

"Mother," Tadeo said angrily.

"Do not chide me, Tadeo," their mother said. She was looking down at her lap. "I have concerns, that is all."

"You don't think I can run the farm?"

"My boy," Luisa said, sighing. "You're strong and capable, but you should not be saddled at your age with the responsibilities of caring for six siblings and a widowed mother. You'll have no chance to make your own home if you must watch over us."

"But I want to watch over you! I don't mind the responsibilities. This is the land of the Quirogas, our land for generations. Do you think I could sell it and, what, run off to Pachuca? There's nothing to do there."

"In a city your younger brothers and sisters might have the opportunity for a proper education," Arturo said. "Your mother could spend her days in comfort instead of worrying about feeding chickens."

"A proper education, you mean like you?" Tadeo retorted. "What did you learn at that fancy school you attended?"

"French, Latin, poetry—"

"Poetry, yes. You've published three poems, Uncle," Tadeo said, raising that number of fingers and taking that many steps toward Arturo. "What else have you done? You play cards and bet on horses. You promenade with women down the avenues of Mexico City. Those are not accomplishments. When have you ever made your own supper? Chopped wood for a fire or fed chickens?"

"I am a gentleman."

"You're a useless fop," Tadeo said, his hands closing into fists.

Arturo's face looked flushed, as if he were suffering from a high fever. "How dare you talk to me like that, you insolent child," he said.

"Better a child than a leech."

Arturo's eyes narrowed like those of an animal preparing to strike. "I ought to teach you some manners."

They would come to blows, yes, they would. When Tadeo ran hot, he spoke nonsense and wouldn't think twice about breaking a fellow's nose. As for her uncle, she hadn't seen him pick a fight before, but she didn't doubt he could throw a punch.

"Stop it, you two," Alba said, stepping between the men and placing a hand on her brother's shoulder.

Tadeo opened his mouth but held his tongue. He threw his uncle one last furious look before turning around and stomping out of the room.

"My goodness!" Luisa said, wringing a handkerchief between her hands. "The way you boys talk! You'll give me a heart attack."

"He's foolish and pigheaded and prideful. Luisa, you know as much."

The noise of something crashing on the floor above their heads made Alba's mother wring the handkerchief even more. "Alba, go see what the children are up to. I'll be upstairs in a minute," Luisa said, waving her away.

Alba hurried up the stairs and slipped into the nursery where the children played together. Poor Fernanda had a mutiny on her hands. The twins were refusing to read in silence, and Magdalena had sided with them. Alba had to separate them, sending one twin to his room, the other to a corner of the nursery. It was only then that peace and quiet reigned in the house.

Uncle Arturo did have a point. At Piedras Quebradas, the children would never receive a proper education. Alba was no teacher, despite her best efforts. Besides, what would happen if she married and left the farm? Who would help look after the children then? Or would she be doomed to remain at home, watching her siblings struggle to thrive because no governess could be had?

Later, after the younger ones were tucked in for their naps, Alba ventured outside. She stood with her back to the house, surveying the land. It wasn't an easy, kind land for farming. Sudden frosts tended to stab the corn on their side of the mountain, and thus they depended on their barley, their pigs and goats. Her father had been neither a wealthy hacendado nor a poor peasant, but a ranchero, old-fashioned in many ways. He might have done better if he'd tried his hand at cultivating coffee, even sesame, or expanded his holdings by buying plots of land and having sharecroppers tend them, like Mr. Molina did.

Tadeo wanted to become their father, walking around the fields in his wide-brimmed hat, yet was that wise? On a previous occasion when Arturo had visited them, he'd said they were "petit bourgeois farmers." Alba didn't think he'd meant it as a compliment, but Tadeo had taken it as such. At least the farmer part. She imagined he didn't much care about the "bourgeois."

Perhaps her brother was being stupid and, like their uncle said, they'd be forced to sell anyway.

Alba walked back inside, into the deserted parlor. She heard footsteps, then Arturo's voice behind her.

"Did you wear the necklace after all? I didn't have a chance to ask," Arturo said.

"Of course I did." Alba whirled around and pressed a palm against her chest. "Discreetly, so my mother wouldn't chide me."

"Good."

He smiled at her, but she didn't return the smile, remembering the confrontation that had taken place before. "You shouldn't have quarreled with Tadeo," she said, her hand trailing down her dress, brushing the row of tiny buttons.

"He shouldn't speak to me with such impertinence. I know better than he about business matters."

She liked Arturo best of all the men in the world. She thought him intelligent, magnificent even. But Tadeo was still her brother, for all his faults and his hot temper, and Alba frowned. "He knows about farming, Uncle. He knows the land."

"I know it, too. I lived here for a few years. It's not good, fertile land."

"It's the Quirogas' land, though. Our inheritance."

"A poor one." Arturo walked past her and went toward the piano. He flipped the fallboard up, his fingers toying with a couple of keys. "Are you angry at me, just like Tadeo?" he asked with a smirk. "Would you like to see me gone? I will pack my bags tonight if you should wish it."

Quickly she stepped closer to him, the simmering irritation that had built in the pit of her stomach exchanged for surprise and anxiety.

"Of course not! I wanted you to visit us so badly! I even knotted a cord around a piece of yellow cloth so that you'd come to us."

"You did what?" he asked.

"It's a spell. It worked," she said proudly.

"Who taught you that?" he asked, his brow furrowed.

"Valentín. But everyone knows such tricks."

"That's the boy who works at the Molinas' estate, isn't he? The one who handed you a bouquet today?"

"Yes," Alba said, carefully touching a lock of her dark hair and glancing down at the floor. "He's my friend."

"You're a bit too old to be listening to the silly superstitions of the peasants. Those idiotic tales will rot your brain," Arturo said, snapping the fallboard of the piano shut with a firm hand.

"It's only stories. My father believed some of the same things. He'd put a bowl of salt by the door to keep witches out, or else a pair of scissors under the bed."

"And if the scissors rust it means a powerful witch is about," Arturo said, shaking his head. "I've heard such tales. That is why I left this place and why your brother should consider selling the farm. What can you learn on a farm like this except the uneducated nonsense the laborers repeat?"

"It's not always nonsense. I have portents, sometimes, when the light of the moon shines on my face. Even before you sent word that you'd be on the five o'clock train, I knew you'd come at that time."

"Portents. Truly, Alba."

"My father used to have them. And I remember when our great-aunt Guadalupe once visited us, how she'd talk to ghosts."

"Aunt Guadalupe was a senile old lady who couldn't remember what month of the year it was. If you believed her, then you must be sillier than I thought."

"Uncle, don't mock me," she said, wounded by his harsh rebuke. She supposed it was a bit silly to believe in such whimsies, but she blushed, fearing he now thought her crude. She shouldn't have told him anything, but then again, she'd been excited to share her secrets.

"Alba, dearest," Arturo said as he gathered her hands between his own and held them tight, his voice dropping, growing sweet, "in Mexico City a new century has dawned. There is no space there for such childish beliefs, not in this modern world of ours. Tadeo should most definitely sell this old tomb and rescue you from the perils of rural life."

"Those spells . . . they're games. You mustn't think I truly believe in it."

"I know, I know. Yet think of Mexico City. Wouldn't you like to settle there? Alba, it's a delight that you cannot even begin to imagine! You can walk through the Alameda and head to the Teatro Principal to listen to the opera. You can dance the latest dances and drink the best wines. I've attended parties where they dangle electric lights in the shape of stars, and they shine as bright as any celestial object. Everything is dull and drab here, and everything is alive there. There are palaces, carriages, even motorcars."

"Do you have a lover in Mexico City?" she asked.

He still held her hands and was looking down at them. He smiled the tiniest of smiles. "What a strange notion. You must have obtained it from my sister Julia, perhaps?"

"She wrote to Mother and said you must have a lover because of how quickly you go through money."

This was a brazen thing to repeat, but Uncle Arturo seemed amused rather than offended.

"I have used the meager allowance that my father provides to furnish a charming apartment with a balcony. But no woman has set foot in it."

"But you want one to set foot in it. I bet I can guess her name."

"Can you?"

"Yes, if I concentrate." She closed her eyes, felt his hands upon her own, and smiled. "Elena."

He abruptly relinquished Alba's hands and her arms fell leaden and useless at her side. She opened her eyes and looked at him.

"I've guessed right, haven't I?"

"You have not," Arturo said gruffly.

"Then Aunt Julia is mistaken, and you have no lady that you love?"

"I don't wish to discuss this," he said in a low, dry tone of voice that surprised her.

He stared at something over her shoulders, his eyes hard and unkind. The delight that had reigned in the room had vanished, leaving behind an icy, barren landscape. They were quiet, and then he shook his head and spoke, and his voice was changed, now charged with longing.

"There is a lady I love but cannot live with. Not for now, at least. Perhaps one day I might take her there, to the apartment with the balcony."

Alba thought of the woman with fancy perfumes and a hat with an ostrich feather whom she'd pictured before. She felt a stab of jealousy imagining that this woman would be able to walk arm in arm with her uncle down the street and attend the opera. But why couldn't he live with her now? Did she expect him to make a great fortune before she deigned to grant him her heart? Or was she entangled with another man? What if, God forbid, she was a married woman? Perhaps she simply didn't care about Arturo, even if he was handsome and charming.

"I suppose any romantic impediments will make an eventual union sweeter," Alba said.

"I would say we must endure the yoke of yearning, no matter if it be heavy," he replied.

She smiled. "You speak in verses, Uncle."

"Is that bad, from a poet?"

"I like it, but Tadeo would say it's silly."

"I'm sure he would."

Arturo watched her with careful, sharp eyes. There was an odd light in those eyes, a flicker of emotion she did not recognize.

Silence cocooned them. The stays of Alba's corset felt rather tight, and she fidgeted, one hand pressing against her stomach. At last Arturo spoke.

"Tadeo might belong here, but you don't. You're too pretty and clever, Alba, to be locked in one of the dusty cupboards of this farm."

She blushed at the compliment and, not knowing how to answer, said only, "Yes."

To which Arturo smiled, that languid smile of his that was as bright as the electric lights he'd described, dazzling and certain. There was a thumping upstairs and Alba looked at the ceiling, biting her lip and picturing the twins at war again.

"I must go," she said, and rushed to the second floor.

Indeed, civil war had broken out, and it wasn't until what felt like an eon had passed that Alba was able to slip back into her room. She tried to picture the city Arturo described, with vast theaters, magnificent shops, sumptuous houses. A place where ladies wouldn't have to be running to and fro, tending to children and plucking chickens for supper.

With a tired sigh she turned her head to look at her bouquet, seeking the beauty of this gift among her mundane surroundings, and was shocked to discover the flowers had all wilted. They'd dried up in a matter of hours. Confused, she pressed her fingers against a withered rose.

A petal fell onto the floor.

# 1998: 3

A TALL WALL SHIELDED the Willows from prying eyes. Minerva's general impression of the property was that this was a world delimited, the trees carefully obscuring the view, a path turning a tad to the right before one reached the front door, as if the house were hiding behind a decorous veil.

The Willows was a three-storied New England house with a flat-roofed columned portico and arch-framed windows, its façade painted a sedate beige color. The prominent, intricately decorated oculus on the third floor added a charming touch to the structure. It gave the impression of a lush grandness that had long gone out of vogue.

Minerva unscrewed the lid of her thermos, took a sip of coffee, gathered her courage, and rang the bell. She was admitted to the house by a confused man who had her wait in the entrance hall, then guided her to a bright and sunny solarium. Two wicker lounge chairs, two dainty end tables—each of them decorated with a white vase filled with carefully arranged dry flowers— a round white table, and matching white chairs served to create an elegant yet relaxing oasis.

An elderly woman with a gold-and-green turban wrapped around her head, the kind Elizabeth Taylor might have worn a couple of decades before, sat at the table. Her overplucked eyebrows were carefully penciled in and her mouth was painted a deep red. A tray and a pot of tea were set before her and she'd seemingly been nibbling on her toast, interrupted by Minerva's appearance. The woman now regarded Minerva with an arch, cold look.

Mrs. Carolyn Yates, née Wingrave, looked as imposing as she did in the brochures Minerva had spied around the college touting the renovation of Joyce House.

"Sit," Mrs. Yates said, and Minerva obeyed the command. "They tell me you are under the persistent impression that my grandson has an appointment with you."

"I'm sorry, I was trying to explain to the man at the door that Noah invited me."

"My grandson is very much asleep and won't wake for a few more hours. He came back tipsy last night and after shuffling around the house proceeded to open more bottles and make himself uproariously drunk, a situation with which I am familiar. When that happens, Noah tends to make certain promises he never intends to keep. So tell me, did he say he'd fly you to Paris? Did he promise you a car? You won't be getting anything, but I'm curious what lies he's been telling this time."

"He said I could pop over for brunch and meet you."

If Minerva was to be perfectly honest, she wasn't sure Noah would agree to such a thing in the daylight, once he'd sobered up, but she'd hoped Mrs. Yates might be merciful. That at least she'd get a few words with her. She ought to have had the guts to knock at her door months ago. No matter. Her meeting with Noah had provided her with an excuse to seek his grandmother out, or perhaps merely reignited her extinguished willpower.

"Meet me? Why would you want to meet me?" Carolyn Yates replied, punctuating the words with a disdainful smile.

"My name is Minerva Contreras. I've tried to speak to you before. I'm a student at Stoneridge and my thesis focuses on the work of Beatrice Tremblay. I've been told that you have the personal papers and diaries of Miss Tremblay. I want to examine them."

"Betty donated her archive to Stoneridge. Whatever materials I have are not meant for public consumption."

"That's the issue, Mrs. Yates. I think the personal intersects with the public in this case. Miss Tremblay said that *The Vanishing* was based on her personal experience, on the disappearance of someone she knew. It's that link that I wish to explore."

"Virginia's disappearance?" The disdain melted away; now she examined Minerva with guarded eyes.

"You know the girl who went missing?"

"We were classmates, the three of us. But I won't subject myself to silly inquiries or have you poking at Betty's old diaries. Off you go," Mrs. Yates said dismissively. She reached for the teapot and a cup.

"What was the missing girl's full name? Could you at least tell me that? I could look her story up in old newspapers if you do."

"I'm trying to have a bite, Miss Contreras."

The woman's pale hands shook, reminding Minerva of her great-grandmother in her frail final days.

"Please, allow me," Minerva said, quickly extending a hand and stabilizing Carolyn's wrist. There was a wide, faint scar that ran down the back of the woman's hand, an old wound peeking against the bluish veins and age spots. Gently, Minerva helped her hold the cup so she could fill it with tea.

Carolyn set the pot and the cup down, staring at Minerva. She seemed startled, then she rubbed her wrist with the other hand and smirked, composing herself.

"Growing old is terribly inconvenient," she said. "I used to practice archery and paint fine portraits, can you imagine?"

Carolyn carefully sipped her tea and looked at Minerva as if she were measuring her. The woman didn't ask her to leave again, and Minerva did not offer to get up. She sat with her hands on her backpack, waiting.

"I remember your name from a few months back when you tried to contact me. My secretary said you were one of the international students on a scholarship. And you work on campus, don't you?"

"I'm a resident director. I help in the language lab teaching Spanish and serve as a tutor."

"That's very industrious of you."

"It's necessary."

"It's a good quality to have. My grandson wouldn't know how to earn one cent if I kicked him out the door this second," the woman said, drumming her manicured nails against the table. "He can't even get decent grades, despite the tutors. Poor thing, he's useless. Grew up without a spine. It happens in the best of families. Some traits you can't acquire, you're simply born with the ability or not. It's all in the blood, you see."

Carolyn reached for a boiled egg that sat in a silver cup. She took a knife and tapped around the egg, cracking the shell until she was able to lift the top. Then she took a spoon and scooped out the contents. Her hand didn't shake this time; the maneuver was efficient and precise. Her moment of weakness had passed, and she sat as stiffly as a soldier as she spoke.

"Betty worked on campus. She taught French, though we didn't have a language lab back then. She grew up poor, like many girls in the Depression. We have some very wealthy international students at Stoneridge, but you're not one of those, am I correct?"

"No, I'm not," Minerva said, calmly looking at the woman. "I can't afford the tuition without my work on campus and my scholarship."

"Then you're like Betty, I imagine. An ambitious, energetic girl, struggling to climb up the ladder," Carolyn said as she scooped out another spoonful of egg. "Are Betty's personal papers really of any value to you?"

"They could have enormous value. One reason why we know writers such as Lovecraft so intimately—his prejudices, his predilections, the very essence of him—is because he left many written materials. Everything from his racism to his cosmological outlook is there in the letters, and it ties in with the stories in ways you don't at first imagine. To be able to peer at the mind of an early horror pioneer like Beatrice Tremblay, a woman writer like that, it would be an honor."

"Not everybody wants to be peered at. Besides, Betty published a few stories and her one novel, but she was never what one would call a truly famous author. She made her living copyediting. Is a minor figure like that really interesting to you?"

"She's not minor to me. And Beatrice might have published only one novel, but it gained something of a cult status and was reprinted twice. If you're worried I won't respect her legacy, I assure you I'm not going to do a hack job. Who was the girl who vanished? Please, Mrs. Yates, would you tell me about her?"

Carolyn dabbed a napkin against her lips. Once again, she seemed to carefully measure Minerva, as if trying to isolate a specific quality she possessed. Something must have convinced her, because she smiled.

"Virginia Somerset was wealthy and very different from Betty. That was her name, the girl who vanished. They were roommates."

"Virginia Somerset," Minerva said, repeating the name. It was almost like an invocation.

"Yes. But you won't find her in any newspapers." Carolyn tossed her napkin aside. "Her disappearance was not reported."

"Why not?"

"There was a boy from Temperance Landing whom she might have been involved with. Her family believed she'd run off with him. Betty disagreed."

"What did she think happened to Virginia?"

"Why don't we go for a walk, Miss Contreras? Perhaps you won't mind if I lean on you, I abhor the use of the cane, but I must admit I'm not my sprightly self anymore."

Carolyn stood up and Minerva offered her an arm. They headed into a living room that had clearly last been redecorated during the Jazz Age; the floor was a black-and-white checkerboard and the walls were a mint green. A crystal chandelier and a large glass mirror, a floor lamp with an emerald-green fringed shade, a lacquered folding screen and the black sofas with rosewood arms edged in brass, they all evoked the glitz and glamour of decades past.

"Betty assumed Virginia had come to a bad end. I suppose she always did have an imagination, and I also suppose Virginia was acting strange in the weeks before she went missing. I was convinced she'd reappear one day, telling us how she'd gone away and traveled the world. I hoped that would be the case. But she never returned."

"When did she disappear?"

"December of 1934."

Carolyn opened a door and they walked into what seemed to be a combination of an office and a library, with rows of bookcases and a massive table in the middle of the room. Two banker's reading lamps with their distinctive green shades were set atop the table and there were two chairs. A wall was decorated with paintings; most of them were large, portraits or floral compositions. Minerva stood in front of them, studying them with interest.

"These are very nice," she said.

"You like them? Those are mine. I studied fine arts at Stoneridge. I had several exhibitions in my youth," Carolyn said, an obvious note of pride in her voice.

Minerva's gaze drifted to a small painting. It was unlike the others; it lacked an ornate gilded frame and the subject matter was utterly different. It was abstract. Yellow circles upon a blue surface, painted by a hand that seemed to have proceeded at a furious pace; there was something wild about the strokes of the brush compared to the careful, methodical approach of the other paintings. Triangles and lines suggested rays extending out from the circles, as though she were looking at half a dozen miniature suns.

"This one's different. Were you experimenting with a new technique?"

Carolyn shook her head. "That is Virginia's painting. One of her Spiritualist images. Edgar kept it."

"Edgar?"

"My husband, Edgar Yates, was briefly engaged to Virginia. We all knew each other."

What an odd thing, Minerva thought. But then again, they were all members of the same social circle, and in those days especially, she supposed they would have been required to join the same country club, attend the same parties and gatherings, and marry each other.

"Did you also know the man she supposedly ran away with?"

"Santiago. He was a Portuguese boy. We had our fair share of them from the days when there was a whaling industry in Massachusetts. Of course, that was one major reason why Virginia's disappearance was not publicized. It would have been scandalous for people to learn that Virginia had rejected Edgar Yates and instead picked a handyman," Carolyn said, leaning forward and running a finger along the frame of the small painting. A heavy emerald ring decorated one finger, a golden wedding band another. "He did some work around our dorm. That is how we knew him. We used to tease Virginia about him."

"Why?"

"He stared at her. It was obvious he was infatuated with the girl. It all seemed rather innocent back then. Now, years later, who knows? Maybe Betty's suspicions about Virginia's disappearance were not unfounded. Maybe they eloped, then he hurt her."

Carolyn lifted her hand and stepped back.

"You said it's a Spiritualist painting? As in mediumship and ectoplasm?"

Carolyn nodded, the slightest bob of her head, pressing a hand against her chin. "It came back into vogue in the 1920s, after the Great War. People had lost loved ones and wished to contact them. Influenza had also killed many persons. Séances were popular, and there were numerous demonstrations of supposed mediums in action. Houdini debunked many of them. Then came the Great Depression and everyone had more pressing problems than ghosts.

"Virginia's mother had been a Spiritualist and she'd passed away in 1929. Therefore, it's not surprising that Virginia clung to ideas of paranormal activity and life after death. She believed in automatic writing and painted under the influence of spirits. I never understood her paintings or her drawings." Carolyn pointed to the little painting. "That is hardly art, don't you think? A ghastly, ugly scrawl."

"You didn't share Virginia's beliefs, then?"

"I'm afraid I believe in myself and myself alone. I always did, even when I was a young girl. I used to make fun of poor Virginia. I teased her about her ghosts in chains. No, I couldn't understand her paintings or her ghost stories."

"What about Beatrice? Did she believe in the supernatural? In witchcraft, for example."

The plot of Tremblay's novel, which was set in seventeenth-century New England, revolved around a circle of young women who begin to believe one of them is a witch. The novel culminates with the disappearance of one of the women. Her novella, "All Saints' Day," also involved witchcraft, and her short stories often starred young, unhappy protagonists who met tragic ends. The connection to New England, to witchcraft and the supernatural, was latent in all the tales.

Carolyn moved toward the other side of the room and slid open the drawer of a narrow cabinet. "Yes, she did," the woman said. "Help me with this."

Minerva hurried to her side and took out a green box. Carolyn gestured in the direction of the table and Minerva set it down. Carolyn lifted the lid, revealing a leather-bound notebook and beneath it a manila envelope that was tied with a wide green ribbon.

"Betty kept journals since she was in college and up until she was in her mid-twenties. I have them all, but this is the one you're probably interested in. It's her journal for 1934," Carolyn said, handing her the notebook.

Minerva carefully held the notebook and slid a hand against the button rivets on the front cover. She opened it. The words "Property of Beatrice Tremblay" were neatly written upon a lined page. She thumbed through it. The entries seemed mundane: scribblings about a dinner at the dean's house, a new movie playing in town, the weather. Then she looked at the manila envelope.

"Is that another journal?" she asked.

"No. You can open it."

Minerva set the notebook down. She carefully undid the knot on the ribbon and unwound it from around the envelope. Then she lifted a flap and took out a stack of pages tied with another green ribbon. The words "VIRGINIA SOMERSET" were typed in all caps on the top page and underneath them was written "Beatrice Tremblay, 1988." A year before her death.

She looked at Carolyn. "That is a manuscript, never published, in which Betty recounted Virginia's disappearance," the woman said. "I will make a deal with you, Miss Contreras. You may read Betty's journal and the manuscript, but you can only do so in this room. You cannot remove them from this house."

"Of course," Minerva said immediately.

"I also have a couple of other conditions. I will determine how many hours you can spend at the Willows, going over those pages. I don't intend to feed you or serve you cocktails, and I won't have you coming and going at any hour of the day, banging at my door and asking to be let in. You must make an appointment with me before coming over, is that clear? This is the one time you interrupt a meal of mine."

"I won't interrupt your daily activities and I'll abide by your conditions," she said very formally, mirroring Carolyn's serious delivery.

"Good. Then you may examine these pages for an hour. You may return after that at another time to read the rest."

"Thank you. I'm really very grateful."

Carolyn said nothing, merely touched the edge of the turban on her head, as if to ascertain that it remained in its proper place, and stepped out.

Minerva glanced at the diary, then the manuscript, and finally she peered in the box and looked in the envelope. She found two black-and-white photographs tucked in there. One was a shot showing three women dressed in costumes for a masquerade, though two of them had yet to put on their masks and their faces were bare.

She recognized Beatrice Tremblay in that picture, although she was much younger than she appeared in the publicity photo from the book jacket of *The Vanishing* that Minerva was familiar with. And even though Carolyn was wearing a domino mask and her hair was painted a platinum blond, Minerva easily recognized her. The way she stood, with a hand touching the string of pearls around her neck, had a sharpness to it that was unmistakable. Which left the third woman: that was Virginia Somerset.

The second photograph was a portrait that showed her more clearly, more closely, so that the viewer was able to appreciate the softness of her ringlets and the delicate curve of her mouth. She was smiling shyly in that portrait.

Minerva turned her attention to the manuscript. She'd brought a notebook and a tape recorder, on the off chance that she might be able to get a look at something of value. Now she slipped on her headphones and scribbled furiously, attempting to transcribe a few passages. She could have brought the laptop, but she preferred to take notes by hand, then type them into the computer. The process helped clarify her thoughts and her shorthand was well honed.

*Some moments return to us, intact and incandescent, undimmed by the passage of time. It is like that when I remember that December of 1934 and the night that Virginia Somerset went missing.* Minerva wrote that sentence down, and she kept writing until a loud tapping made her look up.

The tapping sound was Noah, his knuckles knocking on the table. "Time's up," he said. "You need to put that back where you found it."

Minerva shifted in her seat and consulted her wristwatch. She pressed a button on her Discman, pausing Los Amantes de Lola midsong, and slipped her headphones off. "It's been an hour already?"

He didn't reply. Instead, he yawned and stretched his arms. By the look of him, he'd woken up only a little while earlier. He was wearing a sweatshirt that said STONERIDGE COLLEGE on it and had a few stains to boot. There were dark circles under his eyes, and he was walking around in a pair of dirty-looking socks.

She returned the manuscript, the photos, and the diary to their green box and stuffed the box in the drawer.

Noah Yates leaned against the chair where she'd been sitting. "She said you can come back next week to look at this stuff again, but she wants you to call beforehand," he said, and pulled out a business card from his pocket. "Anytime after noon should be fine. Her private number is on the back."

Minerva took the card, which said CAROLYN YATES, PRESIDENT, YATES FOUNDATION and had a phone number beneath. It was the same number of the secretary whom she'd called before, but when she turned the card, she saw a different number written on the back.

"Thanks," she said.

"Thank her when you phone her."

She tucked her tape recorder, her notebook, the card, and her pen in her backpack.

"I didn't even remember I'd talked to you," he said as she zipped it closed.

"I thought you might not."

"But you still came," he said. There was a mocking edge to his voice.

She stuffed her Discman in the front pocket of the backpack. "I had to speak to her. You gave me an excuse to do it."

"Can't blame you for the initiative. That's what Carolyn said: you're a girl of great initiative. She appreciates courage," he said. He smiled, but the smile was sardonic.

She stared at him, surprised that he called his grandmother by her first name. Minerva would never have been able to get away with that. It seemed . . . well, Nana Alba would have said it was presumptuous. But people were different here. Times were different, too.

"Can I ask how old your grandmother is?"

"Eighty-three."

Eighty-three. She would have been nineteen in 1934, same as Virginia Somerset. Only Virginia remained undimmed by the passage of time, as Beatrice had written in her manuscript. Preserved like a rose that had been pressed in a book, all scent vanishing but the shape of the flower remaining.

"Did you ever meet Beatrice Tremblay?"

"Yeah, when I was a kid. But I didn't know her well, she dined with my grandparents sometimes."

"Did you ever hear her mention a Virginia Somerset?"

"Are you using me for your research now?" he asked, again with that faint trace of mockery. "Don't I have to sign a disclaimer or papers so you can interview me?"

"It's a casual question, Mr. Yates." She clutched her backpack with a firm hand and stared back at him.

He smiled openly, apparently amused by her response. "Beatrice called her Ginny. Do you want to see her drawings?"

He opened a drawer and handed her several sketches in charcoal. Minerva set them down on the table. Like the painting, they consisted of geometric shapes, sharp lines, with an energetic quality to the strokes. Abstractions.

"Carolyn doesn't like them. Never did. But Grandfather would have never let her throw them out," Noah said.

She looked down at the drawings again. "Then your family has had these for a long time?"

"Since before I was born. I think Ginny gave them to him."

"Of course," she said. "They were engaged."

"For a bit."

"Did your grandfather ever talk about Virginia?"

"Not to me. He talked to Beatrice about her. Carolyn hated it. They'd get all gloomy and speculate about whatever happened to the girl. My grandfather paid several investigators to find out where she'd gone."

"And?"

"Carolyn said it was a waste of money. They never turned up anything."

She looked up at the little painting on the wall and considered the manuscript she'd been reading. Beatrice had clearly been haunted by Virginia, so much so that decades after her death she'd typed up her memories of the girl. Edgar Yates must have been haunted too, carefully hanging a painting by his former fiancée, keeping her sketches safe and sound, paying private investigators to look into her disappearance.

Had Carolyn been haunted as well, in her own intimate way? Minerva's great-grandmother had also been haunted by a vanishing that had occurred decades earlier, a tale smeared with violence yet always out of focus because Nana Alba never provided a proper ending to her narrative. It always looped back to the beginning. Until the very end, until she was on her deathbed and whispered the final, quiet dénouement.

*Back then, when I was a young woman, there were still witches.*

# 1934: I

SOME MOMENTS RETURN TO us, intact and incandescent, undimmed by the passage of time. It is like that when I remember that December of 1934 and the night that Virginia Somerset went missing.

Any good writer must provide a setting for their story, and therefore before I speak to you about Virginia I must describe the time and place we inhabited. Certain details will be crucial for your understanding of this tale.

I must warn you that I will also narrate this story in my own voice, in my own way, and at my own pace, which may not seem like the way you might tell it, but it is important that I do it like this, for it will be the lone method that can perhaps render the truth of Virginia Somerset, or as much truth as I can approximate on paper.

We were in the midst of the Great Depression, a tragedy that seemed to have no end, though, I must admit, in the beginning I had not understood the extent of it. In 1929, when it all started, many folks shrugged it off. Who could blame them? People had been having a merry time for most of the decade. Women bared their knees and rouged them up, men parted their hair in the middle and tried to imitate Rudolph Valentino, and they all sipped illicit liquor and danced the weekends away.

Even as late as 1931 the papers were saturated with stories urging people to buy stocks at a bargain price. We thought things would turn around. But they didn't. Then, one morning, it was as if we all woke up from a spell, panic-stricken, and realized the ditch we'd rolled into.

My father had been a draftsman but lost his job. To make ends meet, he borrowed money on his life insurance policy and sold cardboard games where you'd punch a slot and try to win a prize. Everyone gambled; it was the chance to make a pile of cash with a little money, so he sold those betting games, which kept us from starving. My mother baked pies and sold them from out of our kitchen. Five cents a pie.

A lot of people used white-rabbit money instead of real cash, and lots of folks depended on charity to get by. I was lucky. Stoneridge College had accepted me on a special work-learn program, which meant I helped one of the French teachers, Mrs. Thérèse Audrain, and in exchange I received tuition and room and board.

Other girls back in my hometown in Ohio were washing laundry for pennies. When a manufacturer advertised for skilled workers at ten dollars a week, a riot started as people tried to get to the front of the line for a chance at the jobs.

It was hard on everyone, but harder for women. There were no flophouses for ladies. I met a girl from New York who said women would go into Grand Central and sleep in the waiting room, pretending they were catching a train. Where else could they go?

College granted me a place to live and study, plus hot meals. Best of all for my family, it meant they could take in lodgers and rent my room. They had three young men living at their apartment during that time, two sharing my old room and another rooming with my brother. My parents and my younger sister shared the third bedroom.

And what a place to live I had! Room 11 of Joyce House might not have seemed like much to other girls, merely a bed and a desk and a window. But for me it was a chance at freedom.

Because of the Great Depression, many women found it harder to secure work. If you were married, they wouldn't hire you. Men were supposed to be the breadwinners, and if you were married and working, you were stealing a man's job.

But I was single, and I knew that there were a few industries that hired women: retail and advertising. The trouble was those places liked to have college graduates. Macy's demanded it; you couldn't be a shopgirl there without a degree, it was a posh place.

If I could get a degree at a place like Stoneridge, with the excellent connections it might yield, I was sure I'd be able to land a job. If things went sour, I figured I could be a teacher and my English degree would still come in handy.

Otherwise I'd have to marry. That's what was expected of girls. We'd find a guy, pop out a couple of kids, and spend our days cooking and cleaning for them. Or else I'd be stuck scrambling to earn three dollars a week at a factory. Either way, I'd never get a chance to sit in front of a typewriter again.

Joyce House and Stoneridge were my one chance to secure a degree. Besides, Mrs. Audrain was a pleasant-enough woman and my work was far from exhausting, my room was comfortable, and my learning proceeded at a brisk pace. I was also making useful connections.

This is why I didn't contradict Carolyn when she found my new roommate, Virginia Somerset, "entirely insufferable," in her own words.

Carolyn Wingrave was beautiful, witty, and wealthy. Her father owned the Wingrave Manufacturing Company, which was a cotton mill that employed hundreds of people in Temperance Landing.

Everyone in the area knew the Wingraves; they'd been around for ages. I believe the Wingrave cotton mill was founded in the 1830s, when textile mills were popping up all over Massachusetts, Connecticut, and New Hampshire, but the Wingraves had lived in Massachusetts Bay long before that, and they were proud of their solid roots and outstanding lineage.

They had a grand house called the Willows, built in the Federal style and then altered to fit the whims of Carolyn's father. Carolyn might have lived there if she wanted and commuted to campus each morning, but she roomed at Joyce House because it allowed her more freedom than being with her parents. After all, our house mother was not a real mother, merely an employee who attempted to enforce the college's rules yet was often faced with a few dozen young women who smuggled their share of alcohol and cigarettes into their rooms.

This, then, was the world I inhabited, spending my days flitting between classes and my leisure time sitting by the pond reading a book, playing checkers in our common room, or joining the other girls for a movie night in town. This was an innocent world, insulated from strife. It was a world of light. After Ginny's disappearance I would know the shape of shadows.

NOW THAT I'VE DESCRIBED the setting, I must paint a portrait of the girl.

Virginia Somerset arrived at Stoneridge as a second-year transfer student. She came from California, where her father maintained a thriving medical practice. While many industries struggled, Hollywood kept on churning out films and Dr. Somerset had a clientele composed of studio executives, movie stars, and well-known entertainers. You might think this meant Ginny would be eagerly received among the other well-heeled girls who attended Stoneridge. But she was new money, and while I thought Ginny was effervescent, Carolyn found her gauche.

She was also a Catholic. Her mother had been an Italian beauty who'd met Dr. Somerset when he was touring Europe. Back then, affluent people still took a dim view of folks who embodied such traits—new money, foreign roots, and the lack of a good Protestant heritage would keep you out of the tonier country clubs—and Carolyn was more snobbish than your average girl.

Perhaps the biggest point against Ginny was her eccentricity. At a time when most women, Carolyn and myself included, were trying to imitate Joan Crawford or Jean Harlow, our eyebrows plucked, our eyelashes heavy with mascara, our hair bleached and curled, Ginny kept her thick, dark hair long and her eyebrows natural. While the girls at Stoneridge wore dresses with puffy sleeves and frilly bows, or else put on fur-trimmed woolen suits, Ginny sewed her own clothes and wore dresses that looked more like tunics, showing her slender arms, with colorful sashes around the waist. The hems often reached her ankles, and she looked more like a playful nymph than a proper lady. She liked to knit, using five different types of yarn to make gloves that left her fingers exposed. She went around hatless, weaving ribbons and beads into her hair.

She was, most important, a Spiritualist, which she revealed the first day we met as she was unpacking her suitcase and pinning her drawings on the wall on her side of the room. She was dressed all in green, with a silver belt around her waist, and resembled a sprite as drawn by Arthur Rackham.

She'd stretched out a hand and proclaimed, with a straightforwardness that caught me off guard, "I'm your roommate, Ginny Somerset. I like dancing and painting and designing my own clothes, I speak to ghosts, and I can draw your natal chart. I'm a Spiritualist."

"I'm Betty Tremblay," I said. "I'm an English major."

"And what do you do for fun?"

"I write stories. Excuse me, did you say you speak to ghosts?"

"Yes. What kind of stories do you write?"

"Stories," I mumbled, trying to utter a coherent sentence in the presence of such an apparition and managing only to stare at her. "I . . . ah . . . I write fantastic stories. I want to be in *Weird Tales*." When I spoke, I made a sound closer to the croak of a frog than words. "Spiritualism?"

"I'll tell you all about it over ice cream. I am deplorably in need of something sweet and I've been told they'll serve us sundaes to welcome us to campus this afternoon. I saw you have Poe's stories atop your desk. Who else do you like to read?"

That is how we met. Her communion with the dead struck me as odd, almost sacrilegious, but she dismissed my concerns with such good humor that I was utterly charmed. Soon enough it didn't seem strange to me that I had a roommate who would periodically sit at her desk and write down words dictated by a ghost.

Ginny did not go into a trance. It was none of the stuff you see in films. She'd simply sit and scribble. It did not bother me. But it bothered Carolyn. Their first meeting was frosty, the second was like we were living in Antarctica, and Carolyn didn't warm up to Ginny no matter how much I tried to convince her that the new student would make for a pleasant addition to our social circle. Carolyn called Ginny "a broad with a soft conk," and that was that.

Unfortunately, because Ginny was my roommate and because Carolyn and Ginny both happened to be arts students, they saw quite a bit of each other. I remember Carolyn ranting against Ginny's painting techniques. Ginny had said in class that she simply let spirits guide her hands, while Carolyn was a dedicated perfectionist, and she railed for an hour against the "frilly fool," as she'd nicknamed her on account of her eccentric fashion sense.

I quite liked Ginny's drawings and still have many of them, along with some of her Spiritualist "correspondence," as she called it. I thought her art was original and vibrant.

I couldn't tell Carolyn that.

It is difficult nowadays to understand the lines traced by someone's class and background, boundaries as rigid as iron. Traversing them was perilous. As the daughter of a working-class French Canadian couple, I was lucky that Carolyn had taken me under her wing, that she'd allowed me into her circle of friends. I couldn't jeopardize my standing by taking Ginny's side. I attempted to cool Carolyn's hot temper whenever she began bickering with Ginny, but these attempts were unsuccessful.

I was placed in an impossible position. I liked Carolyn and was grateful for the many times she'd given me a ride in her glossy white car and the occasions on which she'd let me borrow her shoes or a bracelet. For my birthday, Carolyn had given me an exquisite brand-new typewriter. It was the thing I'd dreamed of for months, and like a fairy godmother she'd waved her wand and brought it to my room, wrapped with a blue ribbon. Such generosity, such thoughtfulness. Carolyn was my friend.

Yet I loved Ginny.

At the time I was unable to recognize the nature of my feelings. I'd had schoolgirl crushes on other young women, yet I was struck quickly and suddenly with what amounted to true love when it came to Ginny. I loved the sound of her voice, the curve of her mouth, her long monologues at night while she brushed her hair and she told me about a book she'd read or a painting she'd seen.

This might be why she has lingered in my thoughts for so long: because she was my first love. It was a one-sided, silent love, and yet it was true. This might also be why I sometimes feel I understand Edgar's grief better than Carolyn ever did. Both of us were left brokenhearted and bereft. Both of us still cling to the hope that one day we might have answers, that we might be able to write an ending to this tale.

It would be much easier to know that Ginny died, even if it was in a terrible and brutal fashion, than to picture a nothingness, a void, darkness.

Forgive me, I am getting ahead of myself.

Suffice to say that September was a quilt knit of petty squabbles and spats, and there was little peace to be had around Joyce House whenever Carolyn and Ginny were in the same room. Most often it was Carolyn who instigated the disagreements and Ginny who'd storm off, but whoever caused the clashes, they were loud, and more than once the house mother was roused and spoke sternly to the both of them, with no discernible change. Carolyn was too proud to admit she'd done any wrong and Ginny too wounded to receive a half-hearted apology, if Carolyn should deign to speak it.

Peace reigned when Ginny and I were in our room, or when she spoke to other girls, but it was nothing but rows and arguments if Carolyn poked her head through our doorway or they chanced to bump into each other on the stairs.

In October, however, Carolyn evinced a drastic change in her attitude toward Ginny. She became more pleasant, less judgmental, and even began inviting Ginny on our outings. Bertha Trumbull, another member of our social circle, believed Carolyn's mind was altered after she learned that Ginny's father was a friend of an important Hollywood producer. Carolyn had mentioned once or twice that she'd like to act, and Bertha firmly believed Carolyn was courting Ginny's favor because she hoped to be screen-tested the next summer.

Mary Ann Mason said Carolyn had sweetened her tune after Edgar Yates stopped by one evening to drop off a few books for Ginny. He was a young law student in Boston, from a very good family, and rumor had it Ginny had transferred to Stoneridge to be closer to him. Further rumor was that he'd propose any day now, that he was besotted with her, and that they'd been writing to each other since they'd met a year earlier when he visited friends on the West Coast.

Carolyn knew Edgar through the intricate web of social connections around Massachusetts Bay and Mary Ann thought Carolyn's estimation of Ginny had increased greatly after she learned of her association with him. If Patrick Yates's son liked Virginia Somerset, then that must mean she was not a country bumpkin.

Still, there were other theories. If you believed the Gardner twins, it was Ginny's secret blueberry pie recipe that won Carolyn over.

I simply thought it was Carolyn being Carolyn, for she was mercurial and mutable, although that was part of her charm. One minute you'd be infuriated by one of her comments, the next you'd be delighted by a clever retort.

Whatever the reason for this change, I welcomed it.

I REMEMBER OCTOBER AS one long, pleasant succession of days filled with laughter and light.

We decorated the common room at Joyce House with harvest wreaths made with wooden beads and corn husks, went apple picking, and constructed a papier-mâché cornucopia for our dinner table.

Ginny did try to teach Carolyn and me her blueberry pie recipe. Even if Carolyn's valiant culinary effort turned out burned at the edges, we laughed and ate together. We headed to the movies, seven girls squished into Carolyn's car, all of us wearing hats and gloves except for Ginny. We flicked on the radio in the common room in the evenings and tried to learn the latest dances. They played "You Oughta Be in Pictures," "Cocktails for Two," and "All I Do Is Dream of You."

Ginny was a wonderful dancer. She told me that she'd met Edgar Yates at a dance thrown at a yacht club and that he'd been immediately smitten with her. I could believe this. You could be taken with Ginny at first sight, and you could certainly be hopelessly in love after a dance.

She was alive. I'd never met someone as alive as her. Every word she said, every motion of her hands, it was electric. She was a radiant creature. I was happy to bask in her warmth. Happy to be her friend, happy just to long for her if her heart was already taken by Edgar.

They were sugary sweet, those October days spent in Ginny's company.

The bright green of the trees at Briar's Commons turned to a flaming scarlet, as if scorching the sky, and then it was December and the beginning of a tragedy. Sweetness gone sour in a matter of weeks. December blotted out all joy and delight.

But perhaps it did not begin then. Perhaps evil had infected our world long before, the same way a worm awaits at the center of an apple. You take a bite, taste the concealed rot, spit out the awful flesh, and gaze at that pale, leprous worm wiggling at the core of the foul fruit.

Yes, when I think of it, it must have all started during the Halloween Ball, even before the séance. That was when I spotted that terrible darkness in Virginia's eyes. The seeds of tragedy had taken root by then.

# 1908: 3

HER BROTHER WAS DISTANT and ill-humored in the days after his confrontation with Uncle Arturo. When they headed into town for a trip to the market, he remained quiet and glum. Arturo accompanied them—he wanted to post letters and buy a few items he'd forgotten to pack—and as a result, Tadeo spent the entire trip mutely steering their wagon. Arturo responded with an equally stiff and pointed silence.

Alba wished she had ridden a horse instead of sitting between two taciturn men who resembled a couple of enemy fighters engaged in a brief truce before shots were fired again. Even as they walked into the church and listened to mass, which was expected during such an excursion—for the market and the weekend mass were always held on the same day—they both maintained their icy and disgruntled façades.

After mass, they walked around the plaza, looking at the vendors whose wares rested upon woven mats or blankets on the ground. There were men selling limes and chiles and firewood and eggs, women who knit rebozos and embroidered blouses, and a few people who offered cooked foods, like tamales. The arcade surrounding the plaza housed a handful of permanent shops, including the post office and the pharmacy.

Tadeo immediately began going down his list of necessary supplies and filling the canvas bags they'd brought. Arturo, on the other hand, asked Alba to accompany him into the pharmacy. The store carried dyes, soaps, syrups, hairbrushes, and perfumes. Arturo wanted eau de cologne. The pharmacist had only one brand, though he did sell three types of perfume for ladies.

"I should have guessed they'd never stock anything better," Arturo said.

He seemed cross, but Alba was pleased because the pharmacist told her she could try the perfumes if she liked, and her hands flew over the glass bottles. Tucked away in a corner of the store, next to the very end of the counter, they sampled the fragrances.

"Can't you inquire if they might bring another brand next time you come in, as a special order?" she asked, carefully dabbing a glass stopper against her wrist.

"I suppose. I'm simply used to having what I want at my fingertips. You can buy anything in Mexico City: French lace and silk, English linens, and Spanish wine."

"It must be costly to purchase all that."

"A life without luxuries would be terribly dull," he said. "Once in a while we must have a taste of what we desire."

"Catherine de' Medici perfumed her gloves. I think it might be fun to do that. But Mother would think me mad, and she would never let me buy French lace." She shook her head and sniffed at her wrist. "I don't think I like this perfume, it's too sweet. I don't understand why everyone likes roses—"

Arturo reached for her hand and lifted it, inhaling deeply. He threw her a self-assured smile that he must have practiced in front of the mirror, or at dozens of tertulias. A perfect smile. He was terribly handsome, he really was, and polished, too. A gentleman.

"What do you like, if not roses?"

"Orange blossoms, I suppose."

"You should try a violet fragrance. Not the cheap substitute made of ionone, but a true fragrance made of violet essence."

"They won't have that here."

"No, and yet you must have violets one day. Try this one," he suggested, and grabbed another bottle.

He pressed the glass stopper against her wrist, making her shiver at the sudden coldness, then raised his eyes as if noticing the jolt of her pulse. They looked at each other.

"Alba, you won't guess what I have!" Valentín said.

He emerged suddenly, intruding into the secluded corner where they lingered. Alba pulled her hand back, surprised. She looked mutely at Valentín while her uncle placed the perfume bottle back on the counter.

Arturo straightened the cuffs of his suit, giving Valentín a careless look. "Hello, Mr. Pimentel. I see you've forgotten how to greet someone properly. My niece is a lady."

"Ah, hello, Mr. Velarde," Valentín said, smiling at her uncle and looking chastised. Hastily he took off his hat, pressing it against his chest, and bobbed his head. "Miss Quiroga."

The bob of the head was quite funny, as if Valentín were doing an impression of a city gentleman, and Alba laughed lightly. The role did not suit him.

"I suppose you didn't think to wash your hands before stumbling in here?" Arturo said, glancing dismissively at him. Valentín wore no gloves and he had dirt under his nails. Then again, so did her brother. Arturo's scrupulously clean, neatly pressed suit and his fine gloves were wildly out of place in the shop, even if she liked the look of them.

"Don't torture him, Uncle," she said, smiling, and quickly stepped forward. "But you were looking for me?"

"Of course! It's market day. My mother said I needed to find you and give you a whole cargo of *pastes* she made," Valentín said, patting a basket that dangled from his arm. "If I may, I'd also like to talk to your brother. One of the horses has thumps and I've been scratching my head trying to figure out what to do with it."

Her brother was an expert horseman who could ride the wildest of stallions and understood their every illness. If there was someone to consult about such matters, it was Tadeo.

"Let's go find him," she said.

As they walked out of the pharmacy and stood under an arch, they spotted Tadeo. He was having an animated conversation with a woman who wore a dark red skirt and a white blouse. She was easily recognizable by the rebozo with the bright red stripe running down its length. It was one of the women of Los Pinos, a hamlet people said was inhabited by witches. There, someone could pay to hex a neighbor they disliked, or have a hot stone rubbed against their belly to cure ailments. The red stripe was like a badge, a marker that proudly identified the magic practitioners.

Tadeo brushed the woman aside and she grabbed him, pulling him back. He looked distraught and tried to peel her fingers off his arm. The woman suddenly looked in their direction. She stared at them, then her eyes narrowed. She spat on the ground and released Tadeo, hurrying off.

Tadeo rubbed his arm and walked toward them.

"What happened?" Alba asked.

"She was trying to sell me something," he said, grimacing. But then he smiled when he saw Valentín. "What are you doing? Do you have more flowers for my sister today?"

"No, I have *pastes* and a favor to ask about a horse."

"We ought to head home. You should have supper with us, you can tell me about your horse while we eat. It's been ages since you've come for a proper supper. It's so much better when you come alone than with Mr. Molina."

"Are you still angry at him because of the offer he made you the other day? Don't hold grudges, Tadeo. Mr. Molina didn't mean to insult you."

"Forget about Mr. Molina," Tadeo said, and threw an arm around Valentín's shoulder as they walked side by side.

Valentín took the reins of the wagon; Tadeo rode next to them on Valentín's horse. He chattered and laughed, talking about the farm, while her uncle held up his head and pressed his lips together.

At the dinner table Tadeo's mirth continued unabated. The children were also in high spirits and behaved glowingly after her brother promised everyone could have a sweet once supper concluded. Valentín joked with the twins and bounced Moisés on his knee. The boy giggled in delight. After the plates were cleared, the little ones ran back upstairs to eat their treats and the rest of them headed into the sitting room.

"I want you to thank your mother for the *pastes*," Luisa said. "It was very nice of her to send such a bounty."

"Yes, it wa—" Tadeo rubbed his arm and winced, growing quiet. His mother looked at him with concern.

"Are you feeling unwell?"

"It's that woman, she scratched my arm and it still aches," Tadeo said.

"What woman?"

"A woman at the market. From Los Pinos, I'm pretty sure. She talked about evil spirits and said she saw a shadow. She spooked me, I must admit, and then she held on so tight I did not know how I'd get her off me."

"Perpetua didn't mean any harm, I'm sure she was trying to sell you a charm against the evil eye," Valentín said. "It's what she does."

Arturo, who sat lazily on the couch with a glass of sherry in his hand, straightened up. "You know her?"

"She's sold us remedies. Bracelets with colored beads to drive off bad spirits. The people at Los Pinos are good at making those."

"Of course you'd know her, the countryside is full of superstitious fools," her uncle said, slouching a little, his face somber.

"It's not foolishness. I once saw a man whose soul had been trapped in a bottle. It took two healers to break that spell. Everyone respects the witches of Los Pinos, for good reason. Why, the tales I could tell you, sir! When someone is intent on evil, what they do is get a hold of a bit of hair, or a personal object, and then—"

Arturo stood up quickly, almost spilling his drink in the process. He clenched his free hand tight.

"This is why the countryside is such a cesspool. You have half the people believing in curses and curanderas as if we were still in the Middle Ages. They're a mob of stupid, superstitious idiots no smarter than a cow."

"Don't be rude, Arturo," Luisa chided him. "My husband had

his superstitions, too. In fact, I remember you listening with delight to his stories of spirits and witches and monsters when you were a child, especially the bloodiest ones. And I remember that we caught you going to Los Pinos with that Desoto boy on a couple of occasions, where you bought a talisman or a trinket."

"The Desoto boy bought the trinket," Arturo said dismissively. "And he dragged me there because there was a girl in that dirty hamlet that he fancied and wanted to talk to, but he didn't wish to go alone. He was probably too afraid her father would turn him into a pig. Such silliness."

"That may be true, and I don't like talk of ghosts and spells and devils, but there is no reason to antagonize a guest. The countryside is different from the city. We must tolerate a certain level of quaintness. Now, how about a little music? Alba, play a tune. Tadeo, you can sing that song by Melesio Morales. You know the one I mean."

"I'm a terrible singer, Mother," Tadeo said, but he sprang to his feet and laughed. "Valentín, come over here, if I'm to sing, you must sing with me."

"If you're terrible, I'm worse."

Alba played "Keep That Flower," and the boys were indeed as awful as awful could be, but they made her laugh. They sang several more tunes; Tadeo's ill humor had completely dissipated. He was, once again, the affable, teasing brother who grabbed Alba by the hand and twirled her around in an impromptu dance while Valentín clapped his hands. Then Valentín danced a few steps with her, but he was rather bad at it, and Tadeo made jokes about his inability to shuffle his feet in the correct direction. The young children joined in the merriment, lured downstairs again by the music and the noise, and Fernanda and Dolores poked their heads into the room. They smiled and clapped, too.

Arturo watched all this from his chair, subdued, though at one point he stood up and offered Alba his hand for a waltz. They swayed together and she gazed up at him, naked delight on her face, lips half open, amazed at how well he moved. But then he probably danced often, darting from party to party in the city.

Once their dance concluded, Valentín rushed back toward Alba, clasped her hand, and spun her around, making her laugh as her skirts flared. Valentín was not used to dances, his feet seemed baffled by the music, but she was charmed by his clumsiness.

Eventually, Valentín grabbed his hat and said he must head home. Tadeo promised he'd hurry over early in the morning to look at his horse.

Alba walked their visitor out. They lingered by the front door for a while as the sun was setting.

"It's nice to see you and Tadeo in better spirits," Valentín said. "I know it's been a difficult time for your whole family."

"Yes. Thank you again for the *pastes,* and for your company."

"I'll tell my mother you liked them. I'm wondering, Alba, if it's not too much of an imposition, might I stop by again next week?" he asked as he respectfully pressed his hat against his chest and looked at her.

"Tadeo will be happy to see you again."

"Well, I'm wondering if *you* would be happy to see me."

"That's very bold of you to say, Valentín. I ought to slap you."

"I hope not too hard. Then I'll see you next week?" he asked hopefully.

Alba felt like giggling but managed to compose herself, nodding instead. By the time she drifted back inside, the sitting room was half in shadow, lit by a couple of candelabras, and the one person left there was her uncle. He had a book between his hands but made no effort at reading it.

"Your beau has finally ridden away?" he asked.

"Valentín is not my beau," she said, her voice low. Yet the way her mother had smiled at him and Alba's smothered giggle and even Tadeo's laughter contradicted her words.

"Really? They think he's courting you."

She didn't want to dwell on it; the Molina girls had essentially said the same to Alba, but she refused to acknowledge it. Valentín was fun, that was all. She didn't want to make any more of him than that. Not yet.

"We're in mourning," she replied, though it was a flimsy response.

Her uncle pressed on, unconvinced. "Your brother was saying how good he is with children and your mother replied it was time he married. They didn't mention your name, but it was obvious, implicit. I imagine Tadeo would love it if Valentín Pimentel wedded you. He'd have another hand to help around the farm and a good friend to chat with."

Alba brushed a lock of hair behind her ear. "Tadeo has never said anything of the sort to me."

"He's thinking it."

"He may think it, but it doesn't mean he'd make my match without asking."

Arturo turned his head in her direction and looked at her sharply. "He's the man of the house. He'll say what bed you should slip into."

Her hands fluttered to her face and she blushed, both ashamed and startled by the crudeness of his remark. "You have no business discussing this matter," she said. "None!"

"Forgive me," he said coolly, and set his book down. "I thought you wanted me to read to you tonight, but I suppose it's not the best time for poetry."

"Certainly not."

She turned her back to him, eyes wide and bright as she stared at a painting without looking at it. Why did he have to speak of such things? Now all she could do was picture herself in bridal white, or married to Valentín, cooking his meals and darning his socks. It was a thought that should not have terrified her, seeing as she liked him, even found him attractive in his country-boy way. But she shivered nevertheless.

Arturo went toward the piano and began to play. It was dark in that corner of the room, and he played by memory, his fingers dancing on the keys. He was playing a piece she liked, and she recognized this as an effort at a truce. Alba hesitated, biting her lip, then she grabbed one of the candelabras and went to the piano.

When he concluded his melody, Arturo rested his hands against the keys.

"I am sorry, Alba, for wounding you. I shouldn't have spoken the way I did," he said, his voice steady and low.

"You are forgiven."

He gestured to the piano, but she shook her head. "No, you must play again. You're better than me."

"That can't be. You play wonderfully, and you sing like an angel. You have such long fingers," he said, and reached for her hand, carefully examining it.

She sat down next to him on the bench. "Tadeo has hairs on every knuckle. They look frightfully ugly. When he's old I bet he'll have hair growing out of his ears and nose. I hope you never have those ugly coarse hairs in your ears."

"I hope you never have hair on your knuckles," he said lightly.

They smiled in unison.

She gripped his hand now and examined it, as he had hers, first one side, then the other.

"Tadeo has dirt under his fingernails, and calluses. Even when he wears gloves, you can tell his hands are not a gentleman's hands."

"Well, he's a farmer," he said with a glib shrug.

"Valentín's hands are hard, too. Most of the time he smells like horse. The women in Los Pinos, they can read palms and tell you your future. But you don't believe in such things."

"No, I don't."

Her lips parted to make a quip, but she felt a spark strike inside her chest.

"I like your hands best," she said instead, the words hushed.

In the wan light of the candelabra the lines on his palm were faint, and when she looked at his face it was hard to discern his expression, though curiously his eyes seemed to burn bright. He looked down, shielding his gaze.

She shrank closer to him and turned her head. She thought she might put her lips against his ear and whisper . . . whisper what, she did not know. Her throat had been knit shut; her lips were parched. They had never been this close, this aware of each other.

She thought she understood, for the first time, what certain words in her books meant. How Leda could have yielded to the swan, Persephone to darkness.

Alba stood up, her face burning, grateful for the poor illumination that Arturo would not see the blush on her cheeks or the wildness in her eyes.

"It's late," she said as an excuse, and rushed away. As she climbed the steps, she heard the notes of the piano again, a plaintive melody.

She lay awake a long time, unable to find a comfortable position on the bed, and woke up several times during the night. At one point, she thought she heard a thumping against her door, but when she opened her eyes the house had gone quiet.

In the morning, she rose belatedly and had to hurry downstairs to help serve breakfast. Tadeo was not at the table. She imagined he had kept his promise and left early to meet with Valentín.

After clearing the plates, Alba went back upstairs and began gathering the linens that had to be washed. When she walked into Tadeo's room, she was greeted by a strange sight. The bed was unmade, although Tadeo was always tidy and made his bed early each morning. What was more, the bedsheets, the blanket, and the pillows were scattered around the room, as if he'd tossed them aside or stripped them off in a rush. The watercolor portrait showing Tadeo in his gray suit, smiling, lay flat upon the nightstand.

Alba slowly walked around the bed and saw that a pitcher had been overturned and broken. It lay in pieces on the floor. One of her brother's boots had been tossed by the headboard.

It disquieted her, as if it were a coiled viper or a dangerous spider, and she held her breath as she reached for it. When she lifted the boot, she noticed that there was a patch of red on the floor.

It was blood.

# 1998: 4

HIDEO WAS CAREFULLY STUFFING the homemade covers he'd printed into the plastic DVD cases. He planned to ship a dozen copies of a bootlegged *Bubblegum Crisis* original video animation the next morning. The big money, he'd told Minerva, was in hentai. He'd made a killing with a few fan-made VHS compilations of that kind.

Hideo's true passion was first editions of Henry James and the occasional anthology chock-full of horror stories, like that *Northern Frights* he'd gotten a hold of a few months before, but the bootlegs and Japanese manga he sold paid well. He'd considered getting into the toy collectible market, specifically the Beanie Baby niche—he knew a guy who smuggled them in from Canada, where the plush toys could be purchased at more attractive rates—but had found it both fiercely competitive and dull.

"I don't get why you're looking so glum," Hideo told her. He was spread out on the floor of his living room, with labels and scissors and cases, while Minerva perched on his futon. His goldfish swam in lazy circles in an aquarium that was tucked under an open window. "From what you're saying, it's all good. Tremblay's personal papers should make for one excellent thesis."

"It's fabulous stuff. I mean, an unpublished manuscript stowed away for years, just waiting to be read. It's like finding out Shirley Jackson left a whole novella tucked in a closet."

"Well, I'd think you would look less stressed, not more."

"I'm not more stressed. I'm getting organized, that's all." She sipped the Yakult she'd fetched from Hideo's refrigerator and toyed with the foil lid.

"Is it any good? The manuscript?"

"I love the opening pages. It's Tremblay, through and through. Although some of it reminds me of stories my great-grandmother used to tell. I flipped through it quickly, I couldn't read the whole thing, but she talked about lights in the trees. It's the same stuff they said about witches in Mexico."

"Collective unconscious," Hideo replied.

"Sorry?"

"You know, Jung. An ancestral memory shared by all of humankind. Patricia can tell you more about it." He stood up and stretched his arms. "Smoke break."

"Hideo, you should quit."

"I tried it. The nicotine patches didn't work," he said, fetching his cigarettes.

They went down the hallway and he held the door open for her. Hideo's apartment was located on the first floor of his dorm, but August Hall had been built in the seventies and possessed none of the charm of her beloved mansion. It didn't have the beautiful sight of Briar's Commons, either. In front of August Hall there was a lonely elm tree and a row of bushes.

Hideo leaned against the tree and took a puff of his cigarette.

"Quit cold turkey," she suggested. "I did."

"I don't have that kind of willpower."

"It wasn't willpower, it was self-preservation. Finances were tight, I didn't have enough money to buy lunch and smoke during my first year at university, so I skipped meals and picked cigarettes over food. I lost ten kilos that first year and by the second I realized I was crazy. I quit the whole stupid thing."

Although, in its place, she seemed to have picked up a coffee-drinking habit. She needed a cup. Too bad Hideo didn't partake of that beverage.

"Like I said: willpower. I have an addictive personality, so if I didn't smoke this, I'd be doing something much worse. It's in my nature."

"So said the scorpion to the frog," she replied. "It's a highly deterministic outlook on life."

"You don't believe in natures, then."

She stuffed her hands in her pockets and shrugged.

"When are you headed back to the Willows?"

"Tomorrow," she said, clenching her fists.

Although she'd told Hideo that she wasn't stressed, this was not entirely true. She was restless, which was not the same, yet it was also not a state of bliss and satisfaction. The sources of her restlessness were hard to pinpoint. Some of it was the constant thought of the thesis, the newly discovered manuscript she must copy and analyze. But there was also the campus itself, lonely at this time of year, with the few resident directors who remained and the skeleton crew doing maintenance or manning the library.

She did not mind loneliness, she embraced it at times, yet there was a strained feeling in the air. Something felt off.

*Just your usual fucking chronic depression,* she thought, and immediately tensed at the mere idea of diagnosing herself. Others liked psychology babble. Minerva did not.

"By the way, I talked to Hannah, and she said you need to move Thomas Murphy's boxes into your basement for storage. They should have never been left in his room."

"You're kidding me," Minerva said. "They're big boxes to be lugging there."

"We can take them together, tell me when."

"Can't Thomas come and pick them up and save us the hassle? The basement at Ledge House is full of junk."

Hideo blew a plume of smoke up toward the sky and held his cigarette with two fingers.

"Apparently Thomas went away after he dropped out. Hannah doesn't want to get rid of his stuff because last year they accidentally chucked a suitcase from a kid who transferred to Emerson and then the kid threatened to sue or something like that. If he doesn't come back for his boxes by the beginning of the new school year, then we can dump them in the garbage bin."

"Can't she phone him? Ask him to drive over? He was local, from Quincy or something of the sort."

"She didn't talk to him, she talked with his sister. The sister hasn't heard from him in months and doesn't have a number, so Hannah is following the campus housing guidelines: items not picked up from storage will be disposed of after three months. The problem here is the boxes were left in the room, not placed in storage, so the clock won't start ticking until you put them in the basement. She said your basement should have space left."

"Space where? She's trying to cover her bases. That way if there's any trouble, she can blame me for it. She should have phoned me and told me all this stuff herself."

"Classic conflict avoidance."

"The sister really hasn't heard from him in months?"

"Apparently not."

"I thought he transferred. To Northeastern, wasn't it?"

"I doubt it. If he'd transferred, Hannah would have said so."

Hideo asked her if she wanted to stay for dinner, but Minerva needed to keep working, so she declined and promised they'd watch a movie on the weekend. When she reached her dorm, Karnstein was waiting for her and she fed the cat.

She went for her first round at nine, taking the path that cut through Briar's Commons, and tried to remember the last time she'd seen Thomas Murphy. It had been late in December, before the break. He'd stopped lodging complaints against his roommate, so she'd imagined that they'd either come to a truce or he'd found a way to stomach Conrad.

In fact, now that Minerva thought about it, the last time she'd seen him had been on that very same path. Thomas had bumped into her, almost making her flashlight fly through the air—at night, and especially in winter, you couldn't do the rounds through campus without a flashlight.

She'd been alone. Although they were supposed to complete the shifts in pairs, she didn't mind covering for a resident assistant when they were studying for a final.

Thomas had apologized and continued on his way. It had been an ordinary encounter.

Although, hadn't he seemed rattled? And he hadn't been wearing a jacket. That detail, which she'd forgotten, now made her pause in her steps, clutching the same flashlight and frowning.

Why had she thought he'd transferred to Northeastern? Had she seen that in any of the paperwork from the housing department? Had she heard it at a meeting? Likely she'd simply assumed he'd transferred and picked a random school in her head to fill the information gap. She hadn't known the guy well, although she'd seen him in the tutoring center in the library, which was where the language lab was also housed.

She recalled politely nodding at him a few times late at night, when she'd spotted him on one of the green couches where some of the students caught a wink between study sessions.

They'd crossed paths quite often in November. He'd had a book under his arm every time. Her life was a hectic succession of classes and dorm duties and language tutoring. She understood what it was to have so many balls in the air and didn't inconvenience him with idle chatter.

Then in December he hadn't been there a single day, though it was the time of year when the tutoring center was stuffed with students desperate to pass a class and trying to cram in a few more hours of learning. All the tutors were booked solid. She was aware that Thomas worked as a teaching assistant for Christina Everett, in addition to tutoring students, so it could have been that he was busy helping prepare a course for her.

In January he had emailed the school—at least she thought he'd emailed in January—to say he was not returning. And yet he hadn't transferred. Thomas had been a good student. From what she recalled many of his conflicts with Conrad had taken place because Thomas needed to concentrate on his studies and Conrad was noisy.

Dropped out and didn't transfer or stay in touch with his sister. How odd.

When she stepped off the path and saw Briar Hall she recognized a car parked in front of the building: it belonged to Conrad Carter. Minerva tucked the flashlight in a pocket and went up the stairs to the third floor. She heard loud music coming from Conrad's suite long before she reached the door. She had to knock several times before a young woman opened it and almost stumbled to the floor.

"How much is it for the pizza?" she asked. In her right hand she was clutching a beer bottle.

"Sorry, I need to speak to Conrad," Minerva said, stepping into the suite. She immediately maneuvered toward the stereo that sat in the common area and turned it off.

"Hey!" the woman protested.

Conrad poked his head out of his room and looked at Minerva. "How's it going?" he asked casually.

"You have about three violations in one night, Conrad," she said. "Car parked in the wrong spot, alcohol, and a guest past eight P.M."

He didn't seem bothered by her enumeration. "Come on, Minerva, you're not going to enforce that silly shit, are you? We're all grown-ups here. We had one beer and it's barely nine."

"You knew the rules when you decided to stay on campus. I have to report the violations and your guest needs to leave." She turned to the woman. "I'll call you a cab."

"Seriously?"

"Seriously."

Conrad's expression changed, going from apathy to worry. "Minnie, don't do this," he said, quickly stepping in front of her and attempting to pull her aside. "If I get another write-up, then I can't live on campus in the fall, and the commute from my parents' place is a killer. Please?"

He smiled as if they were good pals, which they were not, but whenever Conrad Carter wanted something, he thought he could get it with a smile. She'd seen him wheedle his way out of multiple write-ups with a little charm. He'd even charmed her, once. She brushed his fingers off her arm and stood firmly in place.

"That's not my problem."

"Minnie—"

"Get your things," she told the woman while staring at Conrad's narrowed eyes. He reeked of booze. She had no idea how many beers they'd had, but it had clearly not been one.

"This is bullshit, Minnie."

"Don't call me Minnie."

"Fine, Minerva *Cunt*-reras," he said snidely.

She turned around and indicated the door to the young woman, who was clutching her purse with her mouth open, glancing at Conrad, then at her. She finally made up her mind and stepped out into the hallway.

Minerva began walking, but he followed her. Again, he tried to clasp her arm. Her hand slid into her jacket pocket, gripping the flashlight tight. She had that terrible split second of panic in which she did not know what shape a man's rage might take.

"I'm sorry," he whined. "I'm drunk, I'm sorry."

"Move your car first thing in the morning," she said, her voice hard, her grip on the flashlight not slackening.

Downstairs, she picked up the phone by the entrance and dialed the taxi company. They came quickly, thank God. After the taxi took off, she began walking to her dorm. She stopped before she ventured onto the path and turned to look at Briar Hall. The lights in Conrad's suite were all on and she saw his silhouette, standing by the window, facing in her direction.

She flicked on the flashlight and walked through Briar's Commons. A faint breeze swayed the branches of the trees. She shivered and thought that she should have called Hideo and asked him to walk her back to her dorm. For once it was unpleasant being alone.

Briar's Commons was merely a collection of old trees and moss, but as she breathed in the cool air, she felt uneasy and looked over her shoulder more than once to make sure she was not being followed.

Once back at Ledge House, she thought to organize her notes as she'd planned, but instead she curled up on a couch and sat quietly. Eventually, she phoned Hideo and told him about what had happened with Conrad and asked him to do the second set of rounds at eleven with her. Hideo instead told her to take it easy, he'd do the circuit alone so she could slip into bed early.

She slept well and, in the morning, fried an egg for breakfast. She put her tape recorder, the notebook, and her camera in her backpack. She was hoping to take pictures of Virginia's painting and her drawings.

Minerva stepped out into the summer morning to await the arrival of the taxi that would take her to the Willows, only to discover that someone had painted two long black lines on the front door of the house.

Minerva stared at the lines. *What the hell?*

It didn't look like paint. It was more like tar, sticky and with a foul smell. She stepped back a few paces, repulsed by the sight and scent of the marks.

"Fuck," she muttered.

She rushed into the house, phoned Hideo to tell him about the marks—maybe he could reach the handyman and have the mess cleaned—then ran back outside and stared at the door.

In October some kids had egged the dorm for kicks. But that mischief had not provoked the malaise that caused her to stare at the door. There was no writing, just the lines, and yet she tried in vain to make sense of them, feeling this was a message she ought to decode.

The sound of a klaxon made her whirl around in surprise, and the taxi driver waved at her. Minerva slipped into the cab but turned around in the back seat to look at the door as the vehicle began to move. The black upon the white door was like a cavity in a tooth: the announcement of decay upon a pristine landscape.

# 1934: 2

THE BOY SHOWED UP at our dorm two weeks before Halloween. The kitchen floorboards needed repairs and in came the burly, gray-haired handyman who worked on campus, followed by a lean young fellow in overalls and a flat cap.

Ginny, being a naturally friendly girl, offered the men a glass of lemonade and chatted with them, with the result that she learned the young man's name was Santiago. He was new to this job and had worked at a textile mill before being laid off.

For the past few months, the number of businesses with blue eagle signs from the National Recovery Administration on their windows had increased, giving us hope that the worst of the Depression was over, but the situation was still dire, and I imagine the young man was drawing barely a couple of dollars a week as an occasional handyman.

Santiago was no older than twenty and good-looking enough, in a dark, exotic way, that the girls in the dorm giggled when they saw him walking by.

I don't recall who began teasing Ginny about the boy. Perhaps it was Mary Ann Mason, but soon several of the girls were calling Ginny "Mrs. Ferreira," because that was his last name. Ginny rolled her eyes at them and said they were silly gooses and she was simply being polite.

Which I suppose was true enough, but in those days, and at a girls' college, it seemed very forward to be waving hello at the handyman and his assistant. Carolyn found it vulgar, but also amusing, and therefore kept her teasing to a minimum.

Later on, some said Ginny ran away with him.

Later on, others theorized that he'd killed her, but this in the lowest of voices.

What do I remember about him, about her, in those two months before her disappearance? Was there a dark gleam in his eye, a nervous tic, an indication of a monster lurking behind the pleasant façade?

No, there was nothing of the sort.

He was polite, but aside from that first conversation in the kitchen, they did not interact much. When it came to men, Ginny's heart was firmly set on Edgar Yates. He phoned every other day and Ginny rushed downstairs to the house phone and spent a good half hour talking to her boyfriend, no matter the glares from other girls who were expecting calls.

There were no "gentlemen callers"—that's what the house mother dubbed all men—allowed inside the dorms, so when Edgar Yates popped by on the weekends during visiting hours, Ginny had to come down the stairs and greet him in the foyer. Men had to sign in and out at the front desk and sit in the large parlor with their dates. A monitor made the rounds to ensure everyone behaved properly.

People were strict back then, and women were carefully policed. It's no wonder, then, that dances were monumental events. They provided the girls with a chance to have fun and to escape the nine o'clock curfew the dorm mothers carefully enforced. On dance nights, we might stay out until eleven.

We had the Freshman Hop, the Sophomore Cotillion, and all manner of dances, but the Halloween Ball was one of the biggest events of the year at Stoneridge, and that went on until midnight.

It was an electrifying time for all the girls, with everyone competing to wear the best costume and secure the handsomest date. I didn't have a large budget, so I dressed myself in a black bat mask and a black cape, and Ginny wore a shepherdess costume. She looked like a girl out of a nineteenth-century Romantic painting.

"What's Edgar's costume?" I asked.

"He wanted something original. I told him to come as the Red Death," she said as she adjusted the neckline of her dress and looked in the mirror. "Since you were reading Poe just a while ago, I had the image of it fresh in my mind. But you know Edgar, he's waited until the last minute and I'm afraid he's going to cut two holes into a bedsheet and pretend he's a ghost."

In the end, Edgar Yates was outfitted as a dashing highwayman, with a long coat and a tricorn hat. He'd offered to give a ride to the other boys who would be joining us, including Benjamin Hoffman, my partner for the event. He was a young would-be journalist currently employed as a copyboy, whom I quite liked for his acerbic wit. He was not the type of man who'd try to make amorous advances. Boys could get quite pushy after dances, emboldened by the music and the night air, and their kisses and embraces did not appeal to me.

Benjamin was the perfect young man to squire a girl around a party, because he had no interest in seducing one. For a while, I thought his desires might be focused on men, just as I was charmed by young women, but Benjamin turned out to be a confirmed bachelor who avoided all romantic entanglements.

Our dances took place at Cohasset House, a building in the Beaux Arts style where the dean resided, which had a ballroom and a baronial dining room that had both been decorated for the occasion, with many jack-o'-lanterns, orange and yellow crepe paper, and cutouts in the shape of black bats to provide the stately house with a festive air.

The Halloween dance was a brilliant, dizzying affair. The dean had hired a tireless band that played the latest tunes and everyone dressed themselves in extravagant costumes hoping to win a prize.

Carolyn was the star of the night, disguised as Marie Antoinette in a pink-and-white dress with a huge, heavy necklace around her slender throat. She'd come to the Halloween party with David Dundy, a medical student, but hardly spent any time with him, instead whirling around with a dozen other men. She even danced three dances with Edgar Yates, and her outrageous flirting raised an eyebrow from Benjamin while David looked at Carolyn with sorrow. He'd probably expected to spend the evening with Caro in his arms. His Don Juan costume, with the great plumed hat, was bitterly ironic.

"David, you have supper at the Willows every month, is it true what they're saying about Mr. Wingrave's cotton mill?" Benjamin asked him.

We were sitting together, sipping glasses of punch, watching the students laugh and twirl. Benjamin had taken off his skeleton mask and was toying with his long cape.

"What are they saying?" David replied.

"That he's in dire straits. That he must sell."

"Why would he be in dire straits?" I asked, shocked by Benjamin's comment. "Carolyn's family do very well for themselves. Their mill is magnificent."

Carolyn's entire life was magnificent. Not only did she own the prettiest shoes and dresses I'd ever seen, but she'd treated me to dinner more than once, bought me that new typewriter, and discussed her future plans, which included a long tour of Europe.

"The Wingrave Manufacturing Company has been in trouble for a long time. Wingrave hasn't updated the equipment in ages, they're running with outdated machines. The place is cold, you have the poor weavers working with their sweaters and their coats on because he won't provide heat or fix the drafts. Drafts in mills cause static electricity, it dries everything up and ruins the cloth. You can't keep the tension on the corduroy," Benjamin said. "Any weaver will tell you as much, but they cut their corners, pinch their pennies at that place. During the war Wingrave could get away with it because the army needed uniforms and such, so he had many orders, but those days are over."

"You seem to know a lot about the cloth business, Mr. Hoffman," Ginny said politely.

"Mills were numerous in Massachusetts once, Miss Somerset," he said. "Several people in my family worked as dyers and bobbin boys, although the business is lousy nowadays and folks like Wingrave fight tooth and nail to stop the workers from unionizing and improving their lot."

"Mr. Hoffman is a champion of the workingman," David said as he lit a cigarette. "No doubt he's thinking up a story about the plight of the mill workers. Well, you're not going to quote me about any of Mr. Wingrave's business dealings for some great scoop."

"I don't write stories, David. I haul copy from one room to the other," Benjamin said. "As I said, I have friends and family in the mill business, and the rumors around Temperance Landing are multiplying. I'm curious, that's all."

"You should ask Caro if you're curious," David said irritably.

*Fat chance,* I thought. Carolyn didn't like Benjamin. To her, he was a townie at worst, an upstart at best. She tolerated him because he was my date to several functions and because Edgar Yates got along with him.

"I think Mr. Wingrave is in trouble and that's why Caro is clearly turning into a boyfriend snatcher. She's hardly let Edgar out of her sight. Watch out, Ginny, Carolyn Wingrave is a mean competitor. She probably intends to be Queen of All Tuna," he said.

Among his assets, Edgar's dad had a canning facility in New Bedford, hence the cheeky reference to tuna. It was rather a cruel thing to say with David and Ginny both sitting there, even if it was true that Carolyn was playing the part of the coquette that night. But to essentially call her a gold digger, well . . . I figured David was going to punch Benjamin if he kept talking that way.

Ginny surprised me with a light laugh. "Carolyn may be mean, but she's no match for me, Mr. Hoffman," she said cheekily. "I'll tell you a secret: Edgar proposed over the phone yesterday and I've accepted. You are saluting the future Queen of Tuna."

The boys laughed. I stared at Ginny in surprise and felt as though I were the one who had been punched in the end. "But your studies!" I exclaimed.

"We won't get married until the summer and I still intend to complete my degree."

How likely was that? Not very, I thought. Once married, most women had to dedicate themselves to the upkeep of their home. Even if Edgar was a modern, liberal type who wouldn't begrudge his wife's studies, she'd live off campus. She'd commute. We would no longer share a room and we wouldn't have conversations late into the night. She would no longer be my Ginny.

I knew she loved Edgar, not me, and I had expected Ginny to marry him, but I had thought we'd have more time together. I felt as though she were being snatched away.

I muttered a cheery-sounding congratulations but could hardly keep the tears from spilling from my eyes, and at the first chance I said I was going to get fresh air and another cup of punch.

I sat down on an iron bench by the house's front door and stared listlessly ahead while the band inside struck up one merry tune after the other.

*I'll lose her, we'll never go to a party like this again,* I thought.

This, of course, was to be a chillingly accurate prediction. Soon she would vanish, slipping into the snowy whiteness, disappearing in the dead of night. I've spent years attempting to reconstruct that disappearance, to pierce the mystery of her vanishing.

Was it Santiago? Was it someone else? Did a stranger wrap his hands around lovely Ginny's throat and squeeze the life out of her, then drag her body into a grave?

But I am getting ahead of myself.

I was sitting there, feeling bitter and melancholy, when there came Carolyn's familiar laughter. She was walking arm in arm with David, who looked at her with renewed devotion. Benjamin and Edgar accompanied the couple. They smiled at me.

"These fine gentlemen want to drive us back to our lovely dorm before curfew strikes," Carolyn said. "I think we can all fit in Edgar's car if I sit on David's lap." She giggled and pinched her date's cheek.

"Where's Ginny?" Edgar asked.

"Ginny must be inside," I said.

"She went out looking for you," Benjamin said. "She's been gone for a good half hour."

We figured she'd drifted back inside, but when we walked into the ballroom, we didn't spot her. Out we went again and circled the house, thinking maybe she was chatting with someone, and then walked in again and looked around the dining room. It was late by then and most of the girls were heading back to the dorms. We stepped out once more and began calling out to her.

Quickly everyone's high spirits were doused, and I felt the chill of the night against my skin, wrapping tight the long black cape that was part of my costume. We yelled her name. I strained my eyes trying to spot her.

Then I saw her running toward us. Even in the darkness and at that distance I sensed something terrible had happened to her. Her mouth was open as if she wished to scream, yet no sound came out.

I dashed in Ginny's direction, and she sobbed when I reached her and threw my arms around her. I held her tight as she shivered.

"Ginny, what's happened?" I asked.

In a few moments the others were next to us. Ginny turned her face toward Edgar and reached for him, disentangling herself from my embrace and hugging him.

"Ginny, darling," he said, pressing a kiss against her brow, "where have you been?"

"I went to look for Betty, but then I saw you walking ahead, Edgar, and I followed you. At least, I thought it was you," she said. "It seemed like you from behind, but when I called out you didn't turn toward me and you kept walking. I thought maybe you were playing a game."

"I was inside," Edgar said.

Ginny didn't seem to hear him; her eyes were bright and large as she spoke. "Then there was a bend in the road, and you were gone. I figured I'd mistaken someone else for you and began walking back toward the dance. I was alone, yet after a few paces I felt as if someone was looking at me.

"I turned around thinking it was that guest from the party who I'd confused with you, but there was no one there. I kept walking and soon I had that same feeling that I was being watched and followed. Again I turned, and again there was no one.

"I began to walk at a quicker pace, but the feeling of being followed became even worse. I could hear the crunching of leaves and twigs, and a pebble being kicked, but then I turned: there was no one.

"I finally saw the lights of the house. I felt someone, *something,* a few inches behind me, breathing down my neck with a terrible, hot breath and moving like an animal, not like a man, though it must have been as tall as a man because its breath was next to my face. But there was nothing, Edgar! I could see nothing, yet it was there!"

She began to weep. Edgar hugged her tight and murmured soothing words while the rest of us stared at her in astonishment. David was clutching his hat between his hands and Carolyn twisted her necklace with nervous fingers. I looked at Benjamin and he stared at me, both of us baffled, unable to speak.

"It must have been a prankster," David suggested. "A local boy trying to cause mischief."

"Yes, that's right," Edgar said, quickly seizing upon that explanation. "Benjamin was telling me that the boys in Temperance Landing are always trying to scare the girls this time of year."

"They're awful!" Carolyn said. "Why, one boy who danced with me tonight said there's a headless ghost that haunts the local cemetery."

Ginny clutched Edgar fiercely but eventually she began to nod, mutely agreeing with the explanations that were offered to her. We walked to Edgar's car and by the time we drove back to our dorm we were all laughing.

"Gin-gin, are you going to keep the lights on tonight in case a ghoul crawls inside your room?" Carolyn asked as she opened the car door and slipped out. "Or should we sneak Edgar into your bed to keep you safe and sound from monsters?"

"Carolyn, the things you say!" Ginny replied, but she was smiling.

"Fine. Shall we see if we can sneak David in, then?"

"I wouldn't dare with that brute of a house mother that you have," David said. "She's scarier than any ghoul."

Our laughter turned even more uproarious, threatening to really get us in trouble with the house mother if we didn't rush inside, which we did.

Yet now, when I think back to that night, I wonder if the laughter was not hollow. I think we were all terrified children attempting to shield ourselves from true horror, and that we recognized the indications of a great evil, a terrible darkness, stretching out like a gnarled, clawed hand that scratched the back of our necks.

# 1908: 4

"YOUR BROTHER OBVIOUSLY CUT himself when he broke that pitcher. That's why there is blood," Alba's mother said as she carefully threaded a needle. "If his horse is not in the stable, he must be with Valentín. There is nothing to worry about."

"Something is wrong," Alba insisted. "I want to speak to him. I'll take a horse and be back—"

"You, alone?"

"Yes, I can ride faster on my own."

Alba's mother put down the stitching she was working on and looked at Arturo, then at Alba. She sighed. "I say it's silly to go there when there's a great deal of work to be done around the house today."

"It won't take long," Alba assured her.

"Arturo, might you accompany her?"

"Gladly," her uncle said.

Alba hurried out of the parlor. Arturo laughed, rushing after her. "You are going to gallop to that farm, aren't you?"

"Yes," she said. "Can you keep up with me if I do?"

"Are you afraid I'll fall off my saddle?" he asked.

"Perhaps."

"I don't like to ride, but I can. Sometimes I used to ride up the mountains with the Desoto boy when I was young, up all those narrow trails. I'll keep up."

Belisario saddled their horses and Alba climbed onto her mount. Then off they went toward the Molinas' lands. When they arrived at the stables, she spotted Valentín, who waved at her with an eager smile.

"This is a nice surprise," he said. "What brings you here?"

"Can you fetch my brother? I need to speak to him."

Valentín frowned, his bright smile fading. "Tadeo hasn't been by this morning."

Alba clutched the reins tightly and stared at Valentín in surprise. "His horse isn't in the stable. He should be here."

"He must have changed his plans and gone somewhere else," Arturo said, then gave Valentín an apologetic look. "She's needlessly worried."

"He'd send word that he wasn't coming," Alba persisted. "He wasn't in his room this morning and there was blood."

"Blood?" Valentín echoed.

"He broke a pitcher, or perhaps he cut himself shaving," Arturo said.

She shook her head. "It was too much blood for that."

"Alba—"

"Something terrible has happened. I know it," Alba said, her voice strained. An awful fear was spreading down her spine, a fear she couldn't explain, yet it chilled her body, threatening to make her teeth chatter.

Valentín had seemed hesitant a moment earlier, but something in her face or her voice changed his mind. "I'll gather a few men and have them look around the area, see if we can find him. You get Belisario and Jacobo and see if they can locate his horse's tracks and follow his trail. I'll stop at your house later and let you know what we discover."

When they returned, Alba asked Belisario and Jacobo to look for her brother. This irritated Arturo, who kept insisting it was silly to raise such a fuss. Alba's mother also shook her head, especially when Alba proved no help in the kitchen. She kept dropping wooden spoons or bumping into things; she was too distracted to do anything but sit at the table while Fernanda threw her worried glances.

When she heard the clopping of horses, Alba immediately rushed out to the front of the house. She watched Valentín riding his own mount and pulling Tadeo's horse behind him. She'd intended to greet him but instead froze by the door, the cold dread that had spilled down her spine now knotting in her stomach, becoming a lump of ice that weighed her down. She thought she might faint.

Valentín gave her a worried look. Alba's mother and Arturo had stepped out too and they greeted the visitor.

"We found Tadeo's horse by the river, but he wasn't with it," Valentín said.

She clutched her hands together and listened as Valentín spoke to her mother and Arturo. He explained that he'd been heading back to the Molinas' farm and fetching more men to help him search for Tadeo. Belisario and Jacobo had not returned, and her uncle theorized that Tadeo might have met the men and already be on his way back home, but Alba squeezed her eyes shut, bile coating her tongue.

Belisario and Jacobo returned later and there was still no sign of Tadeo. Valentín stopped by the house near nightfall. He had no news to share but promised they'd resume the search in the morning. By now everyone in the house had been overcome by nerves and they sat as quiet and still as stones during dinner.

A WEEK PASSED. MR. Molina had sent more men to help in the search, and neighbors from other farms were also on the lookout for the young man. No trace of him had been found, nothing but his horse.

Alba stood at the doorway of Tadeo's room each morning. She'd cleaned the room and made the bed so that everything looked as it normally did. Yet everything was amiss.

They went to town, finally, she and her mother and Arturo and

Belisario. They went for supplies, but also because Luisa wanted to advertise a reward for any information about her son's where-abouts. Arturo thought it would attract riffraff looking for easy money, but Luisa would not be dissuaded.

It was strange walking through the town square. Many people stared at them; a few whispered. News of their misfortune had spread like wildfire. Arturo and her mother headed to the mayor's house, hoping he might help them advertise the reward and assist them in their search for the missing young man.

Alba made an excuse about needing something from the pharmacist and hid under the arches of the town square, unable to imagine sitting in the mayor's stuffy house, having to hear him say how sorry he felt for them. Everyone was sorry and no one could do anything for the Quirogas. She stood there with her head lowered until she heard a familiar voice.

"Good afternoon, Alba," Valentín said as he approached her and took off his hat.

"Good afternoon, Valentín."

"I hear your mother and your uncle are over at the mayor's house."

"How fast gossip travels in this place," she said, adjusting the shawl around her shoulders with a brusque motion of her hands.

She glanced toward the vendors and the shoppers in the town square. A young girl pointed at Alba and she turned around, resting her back against a column.

"They're all talking about us."

"It's big news what's happened, yes," Valentín said, scratching his head.

"What do they say happened? I caught Belisario talking with Jacobo, and they think bandits kidnapped my brother."

He looked apologetic and traced the rim of his hat with one hand. "Alba, there's no need for me to repeat gossip."

"I want to know. I'd rather know than guess the lies they're spreading throughout town. Tell me."

"Are you sure?"

"Tell me," she demanded, her voice sharp.

"Very well. Yes, they say he was kidnapped and they'll ransom him, or perhaps he was killed in a struggle when someone tried to rob him. Other folks say he's run off, that he couldn't take the pressure of handling the farm, or he fell in love with a girl and headed to the city."

She shook her head. "He'd never leave us behind, and he has no girl to lure him away."

"He might have fallen from his horse and lost his memory."

"That's silly."

"I know."

"What else do they say?" she asked, for it was clear by his expression that there were other tales.

"Nothing important."

He was guarded, his eyes fixing on his shoes, and this in turn made her want to know even more. "Please," she said. "I'd rather hear it than make up stories of my own."

Valentín hesitated, but she clutched his hand and finally he nodded and relented. "They say it was witchcraft. That some evil person from Los Pinos put a spell on Tadeo and killed him."

Luisa prayed the rosary each night, asking for the safe return of her child. Alba prayed, too. Neither one of them had yet acknowledged the possibility that Tadeo might not return home, that he had perished.

"He's not dead, I know it. We were born ten months apart, Tadeo and I. We're practically twins. I could always tell when he was up to mischief even before he committed it. I could almost feel his sorrows before he spoke them. And I can feel him now too, even if he's not here. It's like his heart keeps beating in tandem with mine."

"I also hope for the best, and yet—"

"No, you mustn't tell me he is dead. He lives," she said, yet her voice was as brittle as glass, threatening to break into a thousand shards.

"Perhaps. But I fear he may be bewitched."

The word made her tug again at her white shawl, her fingers

tangling in the delicate scallop pattern of the lace. Valentín looked at her, his face grim and weary.

"How?"

"I don't know. But such things have happened before."

"People going missing?"

"Pitch-black luck following someone. First your father died, then Tadeo disappears and there is blood in his room and his horse left behind. It's strange and I fear it'll grow stranger still. Unless—"

"Alba, have you made your purchases?" her mother asked, then, noticing Valentín, she gave him a tired smile. "Hello, Mr. Pimentel. I hope you're well."

"I am, thank you," he said, politely inclining his head first at Alba's mother, then at her uncle. "You've been to the mayor's house, I think?"

"Yes, we were there," her mother said. "He's promised to assist us as best he can."

"We ought to hire a private investigator from Mexico City," her uncle said. "The men of this town don't know how to conduct any police work, and that reward money will merely be a means for every fraudster to earn an easy coin."

"Arturo, how much would that cost us, and how would we find a reputable investigator?" Luisa asked.

"If I may say so, perhaps you should consider a cleansing before you think of city investigators," Valentín suggested.

"A cleansing," Arturo repeated, turning toward Valentín, his brow furrowed. "You mean we should head to the hills and ask one of those crude fools to rub an egg against our bodies?"

"The hueseros heal sprained legs and the yerberos cure coughs. And when it comes to matters of another sort, yes, there are those who'll cleanse you of evil influences. At Los Pinos you will find many who can do the cleansing."

"For a price," Arturo said. His voice was a freshly sharpened knife.

"Well, yes, sir," Valentín said. "But it wouldn't be that much, I imagine."

"You speak nonsense. I won't have you talking to my niece if you're going to place insane ideas about cleanses and the evil eye into her head. You'll give her nightmares."

"Mr. Pimentel, thank you for worrying about us," Luisa said, her face severe, "but I agree with my brother. A cleansing won't bring Tadeo back to us. We must consider the investigator, I suppose."

Valentín nodded. They said their goodbyes. Arturo offered Luisa his arm and they walked at a quick pace.

"What a foolish boy that is," Arturo said. "What silly stories was he sharing with you, Alba?"

"Nothing much. He fears that Tadeo might be bewitched," she said.

"Ridiculous. Next he'll claim he was eaten by el coco."

"People around these parts have their superstitions," her mother said. "He probably meant well."

"He is an idiot."

"He is my friend," Alba said, and she rushed ahead of them.

During the journey back home Alba's mother and her uncle discussed the matter of an investigator while Alba toyed with her shawl and remained silent. She remembered her father's stories of monsters and witches and how they had amused her and Tadeo when they were little. These were nothing but folklore, and yet Alba herself believed in portents.

She recalled the tales of witches that sucked the blood of their victims, and how they flew through the air on stormy nights, bent on mischief. And other stories of those who stripped off their skins and became animals when the moon was high in the sky. Could Tadeo have been bewitched by one of those beings? For Alba, magic was the spells she'd learned from other children: spells to coax someone to visit you, like the one that required the knotting of a cord around a piece of cloth. These were games, innocently played, and carried no dire consequences.

She wasn't quite sure she believed in other forms of magic, in darker things, in real power. Or that she should even consider that the terrors from her childhood tales could be true. Ghosts did not truly roam the mountains and the fields, but she was troubled.

When they arrived back at the house Arturo took her aside and they sat on the sofa of pink damask.

"I'm sorry I called Valentín an idiot. I know he is your friend."

She removed the shawl and folded it carefully as she spoke. "He's trying to help."

Arturo was tense and his voice was hard. "No amount of bracelets against the evil eye are going to bring Tadeo back to us. If you put your faith in folk remedies, you'll only be disappointed."

She hesitated, knowing he was correct. She did not wish to sound like a fool. "Uncle Arturo, sometimes the remedies do work. My father himself believed in them, and he was a wise man. He chased ghosts and devils away so that they wouldn't haunt the roads near our farm."

"I'm aware that country folk have their superstitions, but do you really believe a cleansing will be more effective than an investigator?"

"No, not really, and yet—"

He sighed and shook his head, looking disappointed. "Alba, you start thinking of ghosts and devils and soon you won't be able to go to sleep without imagining a thousand terrible monsters lurking in the bushes. You're a clever girl, well educated, not a peasant who will fall in the claws of a charlatan. That is what the people of Los Pinos are: charlatans. Do you realize how they work?"

He held her hands tightly and looked into her eyes. "You visit those people once and they promise to rid you of your troubles, but then they say you'll have to come a second time for their remedy to work. You pay them twice, then thrice, and soon you're giving good money to toothless fortune tellers and frauds. Your mother doesn't have money to spare on such silliness."

"But an investigator will cost money, too."

Arturo let go of her hands and scoffed. "You think an investigator and a fortune teller are the same?"

"I know they're not."

She began to tremble and broke into tears. Arturo's face softened; he pulled her into a tight embrace.

"I want him back," she said, trying to blink back the tears, but they flowed freely and her voice turned into a sob.

He cupped her cheek, held her even tighter as he spoke. "I'm sorry," he said.

She closed her eyes, tried to speak, but no words came. She hung her head and clung to him until her eyes stung and she felt spent. Arturo's hand trailed down her hair, brushing it with gentle fingers, and then at last she moved away from him, feeling embarrassed at both her wild display of feelings and the press of his body against her own.

"Mother must be needing me in the kitchen by now," she said, quickly rubbing at her eyes, which were still bright with tears.

Arturo's eyes were bright too, though not with tears. A mysterious light illuminated them, fueled by a strong emotion that she could not pinpoint. He looked down and nodded. When he glanced up at her again his gaze was distant, concealing his thoughts.

Alba helped devein chiles in the kitchen, her hands clumsy and her work slow. Afterward, she spent the rest of the day with the children, watching them play in silence. Dinner was a quiet affair, and once she'd made sure all her siblings were settled in bed, she proceeded to slip into her nightgown and began brushing her hair.

The motion of the bristles reminded her of Arturo's hands as they'd trailed against her hair. The oil lamp on the table burned bright, returning her reflection in the oval mirror. She set the brush down, one hand against the necklace he'd given her, which she made a habit of wearing. She undid the clasp and placed the necklace back in the wooden jewelry box.

Now her fingers trailed against the neckline of her nightgown as she leaned forward and looked at her reflection, fancying that the glow of the oil lamp made her look like a Baroque painting. She wondered, if Arturo were to see her like this, whether he might agree with her assessment.

Alba recalled that he likely had a lover in the city, a woman who rouged her lips and cheeks. She smiled, thinking that the woman in the oval mirror looked more like a courtesan than a country girl. That the woman was not Alba but someone else, and that this someone else knew the taste of champagne and the softness of exquisite furs and all the wonderful things that Arturo talked about. On other nights she had imagined similar things, imagined herself walking in the company of her handsome uncle to the opera, decked in jewels. His letters, filled with information about the big city and its wonders, inflamed her imagination. But now these fantasies seemed altered, rendered in a different hue.

She remembered the pressure of his arms around her, the feel of his navy suit under her fingertips. Did he hold his secret lover like that, or closer yet?

She quickly lowered her eyes and looked at her hands, blushing and thinking it was wicked to even begin to imagine that.

A long, shrill whine made Alba turn her head and drop her brush with a gasp. She sat still and waited until she heard it again, then she stood up and moved to the window, trying to peer into the darkness. Was it a coyote? A dog? She could see nothing.

Alba fetched the oil lamp and opened the window, leaning out and breathing in the fresh night air. She held the lamp up and squinted. The whine came again, this time hoarser, lower, coming from somewhere below her window, and Alba looked down. There was a scuttering and she thought something darted between some bushes.

The noise repeated itself; this time she thought it wasn't in the bushes but that it drifted from the branches of one of the peppercorn trees to the right of the window, though she was certain no animal could have climbed so quickly up its trunk.

It shrieked once again. When barn owls cried out, they might sound like a gasping person, and sometimes like a screaming one. But she knew that cry and this was a different sound, something she'd never heard before, even though she recognized the noises of many animals, living as she did in the countryside. Yet it was not an owl of any type, not a dog, not a person, but perhaps all three. It was a whine and a growl and a yelp, thick and rough.

Dread whipped her body, making her mouth go dry, and she

stood with her hand trembling by the window, her eyes fixed on the outline of the tree, which was a smudge of gray. The oil lamp did little to illuminate it, and she could not tell what crouched there in the darkness.

She was sure that the creature that had cried out was still there and she waited, holding her breath, for its luminous eyes to glare at her.

The wind stirred the branches of the peppercorn tree. She hastily shut the window and turned her head away, extinguishing the lamp. She feared that the creature in the tree might look into her room and wished that it would scurry away.

Hurriedly, she closed the curtains and placed the oil lamp back on the table, saying her nightly prayers as she walked around the bed. She forgot what she was saying and had to start over again.

The cry did not repeat itself as Alba lowered herself under the bedsheets. By the morning, she'd forgotten about the animal outside the house, until Jacobo came rushing into the dining room as they were breakfasting. He whispered into her mother's ear and Luisa stood up quickly, excusing herself.

Alba followed them outside. Jacobo and her mother headed into the stables, and Alba slowed her pace the closer she moved to the building. The dread was bubbling up again, gathering in the pit of her stomach and then coating her throat.

She stared at one of the stalls, where Tadeo's horse lay on the ground, dead, its eyes open as a fly crawled upon its eyelashes.

# 1998: 5

IT WAS NOAH WHO greeted Minerva upon her second visit to the Willows. He was neatly dressed—even overdressed—in slacks, a shirt, a vest, and a herringbone jacket with broad shoulders. He looked alert, quite different from the drunk frat boy or the sleepy young man in a dirty sweatshirt she'd met on previous occasions.

"Are you going out?" she asked.

"No. Why?"

"The clothes."

"Carolyn thought I should look proper today, since we have you over."

He guided her to the library. The journal for 1934 and the manuscript had been set upon the table, ready for her to continue her work. She began by taking out her notebook and pen. Noah hovered on the other side of the table, watching her. Minerva wondered if he would stay the whole time she was scheduled to use this room, guarding its contents.

"Why are you interested in Beatrice Tremblay?" he asked. "She wasn't a famous writer."

"Precisely because she wasn't famous. It means nobody has written the definitive account of her life."

"Maybe, but she wrote horror stories."

Minerva smiled. She'd heard such comments before. People

were keen to assign Poe's "The Raven" or Shirley Jackson's "The Lottery" in class, but not so keen to allow the rest of the horror authors a place in academia.

"I would think someone who is part of the Yates Foundation would appreciate all kinds of literature and art," she said, attempting to be tactful, to moderate her temper.

"Have you been reading the brochures? My name is in them simply to fill up space and to ensure they don't kick me out of this fucking school before I'm done with my degree."

Clearly tact was not Noah's strongest quality. Well, he was wealthy enough to say whatever he wanted, she supposed. Minerva had to mind her words. She was a woman, a Mexican woman at that. A brown girl on a scholarship.

"You don't care about economics, then," she said as she took out her battered paperback copy of *The Vanishing* and set it next to Tremblay's journal.

"No. But Carolyn wanted me to be a law student or study economics like my father. Join the business world."

"Where does your father work?"

"He doesn't. My mother and father are dead, but he used to work for the Yates Foundation. Vice president of development. Whatever that meant."

"I'm sorry, I didn't know."

He shrugged. "It's fine. It happened a long time ago. I've grown up healthy and coddled, as my grandmother can testify. What about it, though?" he said, reaching for the copy of *The Vanishing* and examining the cover. "Why a horror writer?"

"I like horror stories, always did. I think Beatrice Tremblay is a horror pioneer and deserves to be remembered."

She brushed a strand of hair behind her ear and watched as he began thumbing through the book.

"What about the witchcraft connection that you mentioned before?"

"I thought you didn't remember our conversation. You were too drunk."

"I remember a bit of it. I remember I didn't think you'd have the balls to come here."

She wanted to rip the book out of his hands and cradle it like a child, upset at the way he was turning the pages, his fingers careless upon the yellowed paper. It was a cheap paperback, but it was hers.

"Then you shouldn't have invited me," she replied dryly, despite her desire to maintain a pleasant façade.

He smiled. "Don't get angry. I thought it was funny that you would mention witchcraft."

"Funny how? It seems pertinent. From Rockport to Pepperell, New England's chock-full of stories about witches. Beatrice Tremblay distilled those folktales into her work. Maybe all you see is pulp fiction when you look at her stuff, but it has deep roots."

"Carolyn doesn't like horror stories." He handed her back the book. "She never liked Betty's novel, either."

Minerva threw him a perplexed look. "She arranged for the college to preserve her manuscripts and business correspondence."

"That was my grandfather. He promised he'd do that. I think he was doing it for Ginny. You know, because Betty and Ginny had been friends. That's why that painting's there and those papers are sitting on that table." He checked his watch. "Carolyn said you can have two hours in here. See you later."

Once Noah stepped out, she shook her head, put on her headphones, and quickly set to taking notes while she played Robyn Hitchcock's "Raymond Chandler Evening." Although she needed to hurry, eventually she found herself staring at the painting Noah had pointed at earlier, her mind wandering. It was funny how certain elements of Beatrice Tremblay's narrative echoed not only her horror stories—people going missing, a feeling of being watched or followed, unexplained animal deaths or illnesses—but Nana Alba's tales of witchcraft.

Collective unconscious, like Hideo had said. Well, perhaps, and there was no doubt that stories migrated and were shared by different groups of people. Stories of werewolves in Canada had been imported by French colonists and mixed with local folklore, creating the rougarou. Such connections were logical.

Yet there was a feeling of déjà vu that almost made her skin itch, uncomfortable.

The black marks on the door—which she'd be able to wash off with soap and water should the handyman be difficult to locate, thank God they were grease and not paint—added to that feeling of unease. She'd told Hideo about it, and they both agreed it was probably the work of Conrad. Vandalism would be well within his skill set. Yet that petty act seemed more sinister considering her recent reading material.

She slid off her headphones and took photos of the painting, then opened the drawer that Noah had showed her last time and placed the charcoal sketches on the table. She photographed the drawings, then stared pensively at them.

"Carolyn wants you to have tea with her," Noah said.

She hadn't even heard him walk into the room. She helplessly checked her watch. Two hours and fifteen minutes. She'd accomplished little.

Noah guided her into the living room with the black-and-white checkerboard floor and sofas with arms edged in brass.

Carolyn Yates sat in a black armchair with a high back. A portrait of a gray-haired man hung on the wall behind her, and by his looks Minerva took him to be Carolyn's father or another relative on her side of the family. They had the same eyes, the meager smile.

Carolyn's head was wrapped with a red turban this time. A black tea set with gilded edges had been placed upon a table.

"Are you going to paint afterward?" Noah asked. "The easel is set up already. Should I—"

"I don't know. I'll make up my mind about it later. You can serve the tea, Noah," Carolyn said, motioning at the cups. "Milk, lemon, or sugar?"

"Sugar," Minerva said.

"How many lumps?"

"One."

Noah picked up a cup and a pair of silver tongs, tossed a cube into the cup, and handed it to her. Then he poured milk into another cup and passed that to his grandmother.

"Sit with us. You look perfectly presentable, for once," Carolyn said, giving her grandson a half smile of approval.

Noah replied with a half smile of his own, plopping himself down on the other end of the couch Minerva was occupying.

"How does your research proceed?" Carolyn asked.

"Very well, Mrs. Yates."

"Any deep insights you can share with me?"

"I'm afraid not yet. I do have some questions. In one of Beatrice Tremblay's short stories, 'A Wisp of Fog,' she seems to parallel an incident after a party you attended on Halloween."

"I'm sorry, dear, I'm not very familiar with her stories."

"There's a masked ball and a stranger slips into the party. The protagonist keeps looking in his direction because he's wearing a carved mask with horns. The stranger is concealing a knife—"

"Oh, I'll have to stop you." Carolyn shook her head. "I never shared Beatrice's love of the macabre. I suppose you like those strange, dramatic stories of ghosts and ghouls?"

"I do. I think the stories are beautiful."

"Well, I don't, and I didn't bother to read more than a page or two of her works. I don't enjoy being frightened. Do you have any other questions?"

Minerva looked down at her notepad, shifted direction. "In her manuscript, Betty mentions that she kept many of Ginny's drawings and Spiritualist correspondence. Noah showed me a few sketches, but I'm hoping to look at more of them. And I haven't come across her correspondence."

"There are no more. This is what she left behind when she passed away. Many things were lost when she moved to Boston with Benjamin Hoffman."

"Her date for the Halloween party?"

"Yes, he was her date for several functions," Carolyn said as she took a sip of her tea. "Benjamin was a good friend, there was no romantic connection there. He took her in. The cancer wiped out most of her savings and Betty was not exactly wealthy in her last few years. It's really a pity, Betty could have married well, but she chose to ignore the good prospects that came her way."

"I thought she liked women," Minerva said. "She was a lesbian."

"What a bold way to put it!" Carolyn raised a thin eyebrow and sipped her tea. "You mustn't judge me closed-minded, but we tended to be more discreet back in my day and didn't discuss our love lives, especially when they veered in certain directions."

"She means it's not polite to say it out loud," Noah said cheerfully. "There are many things you're not supposed to say around these parts."

Carolyn gave her grandson a pointed look before speaking again. "When she moved, she took her things to Benjamin's apartment, and whether he has any of those drawings or letters somewhere, I do not know," Carolyn said.

"Grandfather would have known," Noah said. "He wanted to preserve those scraps of paper and old documents. But he died a couple of months after Beatrice, and dear old Granny has never bothered much with memorabilia, have you?"

"Perhaps there is something else that might help your research?" Carolyn asked, ignoring her grandson and focusing instead on Minerva. Clearly those two did not get along well. Minerva thought to simply mumble an apology and step out quickly, but she did need help.

"In her manuscript Beatrice says that you were trying to get Santiago, the young man who worked around the dorm, a job at your father's factory. I'm wondering if the employee applications from that time would have been kept somewhere?"

"Yes, I believe I told Ginny I'd help him. But you must understand these people were flighty. Workers were always changing jobs, jumping from one place to another for something better. They'd leave you without any remorse, especially the immigrants like him. Or they simply were no good for the job and we had to let them go."

"There'd be no paperwork? Nothing we could use to find Santiago? Beatrice thought he might have been connected to Ginny's disappearance, and you said the same."

"I said they probably ran away together. Betty was the one who always made it into a complicated mystery when it seemed like a simple story."

"But if he didn't have a stable job or much money, how far could they have gotten?" Minerva replied. "I feel if we can connect him to her, we'd get somewhere."

"You're starting to sound like my late husband. Theories and theories, but nothing solid," Carolyn said with a smile. "Well, there's little we can do about it now. What's left of the factory is a ruin and the records are probably powder in a drawer."

"I'm sorry, I didn't know about the factory," she said.

"It hardly matters. I want to turn that old site into a high-tech hub. Optical fibers and communications. It's the future. The next leap for the Wingraves. My father would have wanted it that way," she said, looking over her shoulder at the portrait of the man with the gray hair. "My great-grandchildren will have something better than a musty old factory. Noah can show you the old site sometime."

"That would be wonderful, Mrs. Yates. If I might bother you just a minute longer, would you be able to tell me anything about the day Ginny went missing? Did you see her that morning?"

"I didn't see her. I went skating early that day. When I came back everyone was looking for Virginia. What an awful day that was. We were all so worried. Betty could hardly stop trembling. She was pale, like she'd seen a ghost. Such an awful, awful day." Carolyn turned to Noah, and her voice had a hitch to it. "I don't think I'll be painting today; you can put everything away later."

Carolyn held out her teacup with all the majestic bearing of a Roman empress. Noah stood up and took it from her hand, placing it back on the table. He sat down again.

Carolyn rubbed her wrist and smiled at Minerva. "Arthritis," she said. "It flares up. My right foot can be terribly annoying, but the hands ache, too. I still try to paint occasionally. The doctors insist it's good to stay busy and nurture such hobbies. But now I must rest. Since my grandson is looking the part of a gentleman, perhaps he might play the part, as well. Noah, can you drive the young lady back to her dorm?"

"Gladly," he said.

INSTEAD OF SLIPPING INTO the gleaming white car that had driven them last time, Noah guided her into a red Jeep.

"What happened to the other car?"

"It belongs to Carolyn. She always owns a white car. It's her favorite color, though she also likes green. I'm not allowed to recklessly drive it. That's a 1934 Cadillac V-16 Phaeton. Only four thousand were ever made. Joan Crawford had one. Carolyn was very partial to Joan. What do you think of her?"

"She was a good actress."

"Come on. You know what I mean."

"She's interesting," she said.

He smiled a little. "You don't need to be polite."

She did not reply, instead fixing her eyes on the road.

"What do you think of me?" he asked.

"I don't know you."

"General impressions."

*You're a rich boy who does as his grandma says, even putting on a tie and shiny shoes when she demands it,* she thought. His smile grew and he gave her a sideways glance, as if he could guess her uncharitable opinion.

"I think you want me to say the wrong thing."

"You speak like you're a fencer, parrying blows. Want to see the factory?"

"Can we?" she replied.

He turned the wheel as an answer. They sped in the opposite direction from where they had been heading. Before long, they parked in front of a large building surrounded by a chain-link fence.

She'd seen ancient remains of buildings poking out through the

New England landscape, like the bones of dinosaurs left to fossil-
ize in the sand. There was a cemetery with seventeenth-century
graves right behind the Hollywood Hits multiplex, and the abandoned State Lunatic Hospital at Danvers, which had long ago inspired Lovecraft's Arkham Sanitarium, loomed large above a hill,
close to the bustle of a highway and the glow of the signs of fast-
food restaurants. But she'd never peeked at the skeletal remains of
the Wingrave Manufacturing Company.

It was a three-story mansard structure of dark red brick. Many
of its windowpanes were broken and crude graffiti had been splat-
tered along its walls.

"I used to play here as a kid. Come," Noah said. He lifted a corner of the rickety fence that seemed ready to crumble into dust,
slipping across the perimeter and holding the fence up politely so
that she could follow him.

They walked around the building. She snapped several photographs and saw pigeons staring down at them from the windows.

"When did it close?"

"Oh, like 1980. It held on longer than the other textile mills. By
the fifties all the work went south, and then abroad, where manufacturing is cheaper. They tried bringing in Colombian workers in
the seventies to handle the machines, but it did no good."

Noah kicked an empty glass bottle, sending it rolling into a
patch of yellow grass.

"What did your grandmother mean about a tech hub?"

"There's a software company that she wants to buy. The head-
quarters would be moved here. My grandfather owned a cannery,
but Carolyn says textiles and fish are old-fashioned. She'd like to
build a new empire made of zeros and ones."

"How do you feel about that?" she asked.

"I go to the same school Carolyn attended and study what she
wants me to," he said, tossing her a sharp smirk. "Do you imagine
it matters how I feel?"

For a second his mask of indifference cracked. He was vulnerable, just as he'd seemed the night of the party when she'd helped

him find his cellphone. He took out a cigarette and lit it. When he offered her a drag, she shook her head and began walking again, rounding the building.

"What's your family like?" he asked.

"Small."

"How small?"

"My parents divorced when I was five years old. My mother worked in sales and traveled a lot, so my great-grandmother basically raised me."

"What was she like?"

"Tough. She lived through a revolution."

*She met a monster and survived,* she thought. She pictured the countryside, long ago, the mountains of Hidalgo with their thick canopies of fir, oak, and juniper. That had been Nana Alba's world, a countryside still steeped in folklore and superstition, in tales of witchcraft, devoid of fax machines and cable TV. Once again, Minerva found herself thinking of Beatrice Tremblay and her musings on witchcraft.

Minerva took more pictures of the building, then paused to lower her camera. The day had been warm, but the building shadowed them and the evening had brought with it a cool breeze. Shadows stretched and grew as the sun descended.

"What did your grandfather think happened to Virginia?" she asked.

"Everyone said she ran away with that man."

"Santiago."

"Yeah." Noah contemplated the façade of the factory, with the graffiti running up and down its padlocked doors. "That one."

"He really thought that?"

"One of the detectives he'd hired said maybe it was a serial killer. It's not like murder is a modern invention. They might still be alive now."

"That would be a really old serial killer if they were around in 1934," she said.

"Monsters don't age. They live forever."

"What do you mean?"

"My grandfather thought maybe Betty was right. That there had been a supernatural occurrence. When Betty still came over, before she got too sick, they used to sit together and talk about Briar's Commons, how it was haunted. It irritated Carolyn when they'd carry on about it—you heard her; she can't stomach horror stories. My grandfather and Betty spent whole evenings sharing ghost stories and local legends. I learned a lot about headless horsemen and demonic black cats by overhearing their conversations."

"I learned about similar stuff," Minerva said as she slipped her camera into her backpack. "Is it possible to look inside?"

"Carolyn would have the keys. We could come back another time."

"It's fine," she said.

They walked back to the car. When they ducked under the fence, she held her hand at the wrong angle and a bit of wire sliced her palm. Minerva let out a loud *ouch*.

"Are you okay?" he asked and turned to look at her.

"I cut myself."

"Let me look," he said.

She showed him. He took out a handkerchief from a pocket and tied it around her palm. "That'll have to do for now."

"Thanks."

They jumped inside the car. In a few minutes they were back at her dorm. Minerva opened the back door of the house and motioned for him to come in. In the bathroom she peeled off the impromptu bandage and inspected the cut. She had iodine somewhere.

"If you want a soda there's Diet Pepsi in the refrigerator, or you can make coffee," she called out. "There's a can of Yucatec coffee above the microwave; you don't have to have my usual shitty cup of Folgers."

"You're a coffee snob."

"Can't afford to be. But I do have that one can of good coffee."

"I feel privileged sharing in your bounty."

"You get one cup. I need to ration it."

She washed her hands and the shallow cut. When she was almost done bandaging it, he leaned against the bathroom's doorway. "Can't find your good coffee," he said with a shrug.

"Hideo must have moved it. Thanks for that. I hope it's not silk or anything too fancy." She handed him the handkerchief.

He stuffed it in the pocket of his jacket. "Let me see if I can find the coffee," she said.

He followed her across the bedroom and back to the dining room but paused to look at the pictures above her dresser. "Is that you?"

Minerva looked at the photo he was pointing at. It was a girl with her hair in two braids. A gray-haired woman sat next to her. "Yeah."

"Then that's your great-grandmother."

She nodded. "Nana Alba. That's my mom," she said, pointing at another picture.

"Only child?"

"Yes."

"Same," Noah said. His eyes drifted to another photo. "Boyfriend?"

"Hideo, a friend. He works at another dorm. No time for boyfriends."

He smiled. "There's always time for a boyfriend or two."

"How many do you have?"

"One girlfriend, recently turned fiancée. Chelsea. If my grandmother has her way, she'll be my wife by the end of the year."

He inspected her bookcase, looking curiously at the titles. She had three collections by Amparo Dávila, Stephen King's horror compendium *Danse Macabre,* a couple of Michael McDowell novels, a Lugosi biography, Carol Clover's *Men, Women, and Chain Saws: Gender in the Modern Horror Film,* and Faye Ringel's *New England's Gothic Literature: History and Folklore of the Supernatural,* among other books.

They walked back into the dining room. She found the can of coffee behind a box of cereal. While it brewed, Minerva stacked the books and papers that were spread over the table. For weeks she'd let chaos creep into the house and now with a guest sitting in her kitchen she could see how disorganized everything looked. Her reading materials were haphazardly balanced upon random chairs and surfaces, telegraphing her lost impetus and energy.

"What happens when you graduate?" he asked.

"What do you mean?"

"Are you going to get a doctorate, a postdoc, all that bullshit?"

"I hope so. You don't want to continue your studies?" she asked as she poured the coffee into two cups.

"I'm twenty-four and if I can get my bachelor's before I'm thirty it'll be a minor miracle."

"Someone said you went to different schools before this," she said, remembering what Rose had told her. She'd called it a merry-go-round, to be exact. "But you're a senior now, aren't you?"

"Come September, yeah. Nevertheless, graduating with a slew of C's despite multiple tutors is no accomplishment. My grand-mother said you're extremely smart. She called a few people, asking about you."

Minerva set the cups down on the table and passed him the jar with sugar cubes. She had no tongs and Noah had to scoop the cubes with a spoon. He stirred his coffee and took a sip.

"Was she trying to vet me?"

"Obviously. She's a huge snob. But you passed whatever test she administers. She even said I should be nice to you. She must like you. You don't know how rare that is."

"I'm flattered."

"No, you're not. You're too levelheaded for that," he said as he drummed his hands against an old cup with faded flowers painted on it. "I'm still not quite sure what you think of me."

Before, when she'd spotted him across campus, he'd simply been one more blue blood asshole to contend with, and maybe he was still a blue blood, but he wasn't the worst kind. Maybe he was okay. But she offered no reply.

It was growing dark outside. She flicked on the lights in the dining room. His cellphone rang and he answered it while he contin-ued to sip his coffee.

"Yeah?" he said. "Ten minutes." He slid his cellphone away and pushed his chair back. "That was Carolyn, summoning me back to our ancestral seat. Thanks for the coffee."

"Thanks for the ride."

He stepped out onto the porch. Minerva followed him and stood with one shoulder against the doorway.

"If you want to really know about Beatrice, you should talk to Benjamin Hoffman," Noah said. "They were best friends. I don't know where he lives, but he used to write for *The Barker Bulletin.*"

"I will. Thanks."

"See you around," he said.

Instead of watching him walk off, Minerva glanced toward the steps that led down to the beach and the barberry bushes below, then went back into the house.

THE MOLLY TANZER LIBRARY at Stoneridge College was likely the most iconic building on campus. Its double doors at the main entry were set within a concave apse with a richly decorated ceiling whose fleur-de-lis pattern gave it an air of solemnity. The library had been expanded with an annex in the 1950s and renovated again in the 1970s, and the result was that the interior was a dark web of study nooks and wooden shelves that defied logic, leading to dead ends and shuttered windows. The basement was labyrinthian and housed the college archives, periodicals, special collections, and movable stacks.

Normally, the head librarian and her staff sat at the reference desk by the entrance, busy checking out books or assisting students, but with the summer lull there was a sign directing patrons to the secondary desk located in the back of the library, where a single bored graduate student sat guard over the main floor. The rest of the skeleton crew was holed up in the offices located on the second floor.

Temperance Landing had its own newspaper, *The Temperance Voice,* with its old issues kept on microfilm at Stoneridge College. Minerva made the jaunt up to the second floor and hunted down the filing cabinet she needed, pulling out a box containing issues from 1934 to 1935.

She pushed the microfilm roll onto the peg and loaded it in. Her headphones blared "Down by the Water" as she gently turned the knob, forwarding and focusing the film until she found the front page for December 21, 1934, two days after Ginny went missing. But the front page had a story on the Santa Claus Parade that had been held in town a few days earlier, nothing on a missing girl that week, or the week after.

She returned the microfilm to the filing cabinet and sat down at one of the old pine desks that were arranged along a row of windows. It had a hole for an inkwell. She took out her thermos from her backpack and had a sip of coffee, staring at one of the portraits hanging on the wall. It was a man in a brown suit, Dean Adam Donahue, who had presided over Stoneridge's English department from 1940 to 1949. The portrait must have been intended to make him look imperious, but instead he seemed stuffy. Next to him were portraits of other ancient department heads, their names engraved on bronze plaques: Stephen Graham Jones, Philosophy; Nicholas Mamatas, Classics; and so on and so forth.

Minerva headed downstairs into the basement. They had a section with college materials, including yearbooks and college publications. Ginny Somerset did not appear in the yearbook, but Minerva was hopeful that she might have made the *Stoneridge Gazette.* The college newspaper had not been established until 1952, but before that there had been a sporadic two-page newsletter focused on school events. Minerva had already scoured this periodical for information, but she'd been focused on Beatrice.

Space was highly valuable in any library, and to make way for more books, Stoneridge had set the bulk of its stacks in the basement on a rail system. Students would operate a hand crank to roll a stack open and fit between the rows of books, using a locking pin to keep the carriage from moving. There was a notice by the hand cranks that read BEFORE MOVING THE STACKS, CHECK TO MAKE SURE THERE ARE NO PEOPLE OR STOOLS BETWEEN THEM.

For a dose of humor, a student had printed a cartoon of someone being squeezed inside an iron maiden to better illustrate the situation.

Minerva spun the crank, set the pin in place, and went down the row. Old issues of the newsletter had been bound up and sat on the shelves, offering a plethora of information on cotillions and gatherings of years past. She saw Carolyn Yates featured prominently in several of these issues: Carolyn smiling at a spring formal, or posing with the members of the tennis club. Ginny, however, appeared only in one 1934 story about art students at work in the studio. There was a picture showing her at an easel, smiling. You could see Carolyn in the background, and another unknown girl.

An issue from January 1935 had something more substantial. A short story cautioned students against rumors and innuendo, saying:

> Although it may be tempting to speculate on the reason behind the departure of second-year student Virginia Somerset, students should be reminded about the pitfalls of conjectures and dramatic theories. Even though Miss Somerset has not been in touch with her old friends and associates at Stoneridge, this does not mean that she has been harmed in any way. Miss Somerset may in fact resume her studies at Stoneridge at a future date.

Minerva returned the volume to the shelf and considered whether it was worth thumbing through more issues.

The stacks groaned as a crank turned, and Minerva slid the headphones down to rest on her neck. Someone must have lifted the locking pin.

"Stacks!" she called out, which was the usual warning any student uttered when a bozo began turning the crank without doing their due diligence.

The stacks continued to roll closer to her. "Hey, I said I'm here!"

she yelled again, but quickly began walking down the row toward the safety of the aisle.

She tripped and landed smack on her face. For a moment Minerva lay there stunned, the pain too sharp to elicit more than a groan. Then she scrabbled up and out of the stacks. She tumbled into the aisle as the stacks clapped shut. She'd almost been squeezed between two metal shelves. Minerva rubbed her jaw and furiously stomped down the aisle looking for the culprit.

"Hey, are you stupid?" she yelled out.

But the aisle was empty. She checked the next aisle. No one was there. She wandered back to the row where she'd been working and looked at the crank. The safety notice above it had been defaced. Someone had blacked out the words, leaving only the cartoon of the iron maiden visible.

# 1908: 5

ANOTHER HORSE DIED ON Friday. There was no reason for these deaths, no illness that marked the animals' last days. Alba's mother told the men to bury the corpses and grimly surveyed the land. They prayed no other evil would befall them, but four days later two goats were killed by a wild animal. No one, however, could determine *what* wild animal. The goats had been savaged, their heads practically torn from their necks. Her uncle said it was the work of mountain lions, or perhaps a wild dog. Whatever it was, it struck again.

Every night, Alba stayed up trying to listen for the sound of howling, but there was only the music of crickets or the soft stirring of the wind. Whatever had killed the goats was clever. It left no tracks and did not announce its presence.

She had a dream in which Tadeo ran out of the house, naked, and collapsed in the field of barley. He screamed but no sound came out. He clawed at his face and rolled against the stalks, snapping them with a loud crunch. When she woke up it was not yet dawn and she spent an hour shivering under the bedsheets.

Valentín stopped by the farm the next afternoon. She saw him approaching the front door of the house and rushed outside to meet him before he could be intercepted by her mother or her uncle. They'd take him to the dining room or the sitting room, and she did not wish to be inside. She felt stifled and anxious; she could not possibly sit in a chair and converse. They walked away from the house, quiet, quick, and wary.

"I heard about the dead animals," he told her.

"A mountain lion killed a few goats," she said.

"Jacobo said you've had two dead horses and some goats."

She nodded and carefully adjusted her shawl. Valentín slid his hands into his trouser pockets. They followed the path that cut through the green fields of half-grown barley. There were years when the spring and summer were too hot and then the rains too heavy, and the crops were blighted by chahuistle. To avoid such fate, her father went into the fields each May and spoke loudly among the crops, warning any nahuales and evil sorcerers to leave their fields alone. It was part and parcel of the superstitions her uncle dismissed as nonsense.

Ironically, this year, with her father dead and her brother gone, no one had bothered with such speeches, and yet the barley would soon ripen into a bountiful crop. She could feel it, as in previous years she'd had portents and could tell when the chahuistle would emerge simply by gazing at the fog kissing the sides of the mountain.

"I know your family doesn't believe in such things, but I'd say it's a bewitchment. What's more, I bet it's the work of a teyolloquani," Valentín said, looking serious.

There were all sorts of witches in the stories their father used to tell. Some of them could conjure hail to blight the crops or change into the shape of animals. But the most dangerous were the witches who sucked human blood and devoured the hearts of men, for in the heart resides the life force of all creatures. The teyolloquani was formidable, the kind of being you spoke about in a murmur for fear of summoning it.

"My mother and my uncle will be angry if they hear you discussing such things," she said.

"But it makes perfect sense. All this bad luck you've been having, and now the dead animals! It's a bewitchment, all the signs are there. I know they'll tell me I'm crazy, but it worries me. I can't keep quiet, can I? And you've sensed it, haven't you? There's a foulness here, almost like a stench."

She looked back at the house. She ought to walk back inside and tell Valentín to stop speaking nonsense. But she couldn't. Something deep inside her body made her stare at him instead.

There *was* a foulness. Ever since that day when Tadeo went missing, something felt askew inside the house, as though the walls in each room were crooked. The air itself felt heavy, charged, like a cloud pregnant with rain. She'd noticed cracks that had not been there before in the kitchen tiles, or a broken piece of pottery by the back door. In her room, any flowers she cut withered with incredible speed. The house, warm and familiar, was now like a house she'd never visited before. A stranger's house. All these things she'd seen and felt but could not speak clearly about. How to put into words the nameless dread that assailed her when she climbed the stairs? Or the fear of her window at dusk?

When she did try to tell the others that something was amiss, her uncle asked Alba not to trouble her mother. If her father had been alive, he might have taken her portents seriously, but he'd died. Her brother was gone. Alba's mother was too burdened by grief to pay attention to Alba's misgivings.

She had no one to speak to, yet she hesitated, unsure, not because she thought Valentín would dismiss her worries, but because then she'd be admitting that she was indeed afraid.

"I heard something the other night," she said, her voice low, and she hugged herself as she spoke. "There was an animal outside my window, but it was no creature that I could recognize. It did not sound natural. And I dreamed of Tadeo last night, only it felt real. I don't know what to do, something terrible is happening but no one seems to realize it."

"Have you told your mother?"

"She doesn't want to hear it. My uncle rails against superstitions. But something lurks near our home. I can almost feel it watching us sometimes. Whether it's the teyolloquani or another dreadful creature, I can't tell."

They stood in the middle of the fields of barley, which were not hedged by any fence or rocks, spreading freely, with the river in the distance to mark the contours of the Quiroga farm. To the west, behind the house, there were the fields of corn, which were also ripening. A grove of poplars and willows provided shade to the farmworkers in the warmest weeks of the year, and many times Alba had seen her father standing there, under the trees, waving back at her.

This was a land she understood, yet it had grown alien to her. She gazed at each tree and each clump of wildflowers with unease; the swaying and rustle of the barley made her shiver. She feared something hid behind the curtain of greenery. Valentín could feel it too, she was sure, but when he spoke his voice was firm.

"Alba, you know how a witch acquires power over someone, don't you? They grab hold of their victim's nails, their hair, a personal item. Then they can cast spells and tease their victim, and the more the bewitched grows fearful, the more pleasure and power the witch derives. So what we'll do is we'll remain calm," he said. "You must have heard about that old trick of placing a pair of scissors in a bowl of water under the bed to ward off evil."

"I've never done it, but yes."

"It'll keep any witch away," he said, and with careful fingers he took a chain from around his neck and handed it to her. "That locket is blessed, there's a picture of the Holy Virgin in it."

Alba opened the locket. "And your picture, too."

He blushed. "Yes, but you can toss my picture and keep the Holy Virgin by your heart. She'll watch over you."

The necklace with the single pearl that her uncle had given her was what rested by her heart, but now Alba contemplated the locket.

"Thank you. But this still doesn't tell me who's bewitched us, if that is the case, or how the bewitchment might be broken."

"Sometimes there's no real reason for wickedness. But the people at Los Pinos might have remedies against such magic, I'll have to see about that."

"We could ride there together next week," she suggested. "I could say I'm going to visit the Molina girls."

"Your uncle won't chaperone you?"

"On Tuesday he's going into town to post letters and talk to the mayor again. My mother still wishes to bring a private investigator here."

"Then we'll sneak out together that day."

She looked again at the house and spoke in a hushed voice. "I should go in. They'll be looking for me soon."

"I know. Alba, one more thing, and I do not mean to frighten you with this, but in every story I've heard about these creatures, once they drink the blood of their victim, the situation becomes dire. The more blood they drink, the more powerful they grow, and the deeper their victim falls under their spell. I advise you to protect your room with the scissors, but also look for your brother's pistol and keep it by your pillow."

"Tadeo kept Father's gun in his room," she said. "I don't think it did him any good. Besides, you said we should remain calm."

"We are calm, and calmly, you should find the gun. Please do it," he said, and indeed he did sound composed.

"I will," she said.

"Be careful, Alba."

Valentín took her hands between his own and kissed them, then bowed his head, blushing again. She remembered how the Molina girls thought he was her sweetheart, which was not true, for no word of romance had passed between the two. However, something about his young, pleasant face struck her that day. Maybe it was the confidences they were sharing, or the way he spoke, resolute but also kind, which moved her deeply, as she hadn't been moved before.

She clutched the locket he'd given her against her chest with one hand and stood on her tiptoes to kiss him on the cheek. He smiled at that, and she blushed in turn, feeling silly. She walked ahead of him. When they reached the house, she bade him a quick goodbye.

He waved at her before heading to the stables, where he'd left his horse tied up, and she lingered by the door to see him ride away. Then she rushed back inside, into the kitchen, where her mother was baking bread.

"Have you finished mending the buttons on your brother's shirts?" she asked.

"I'll do it today."

Alba's mother shook her head. "You can't avoid your responsibilities."

"I'm not, I promise," she said, even though she was sure she'd pinch each of her fingers with the needle; she was terribly flustered and anxious. Valentín's warnings mixed with the sweetness of his smile in her memory, making her want to blush again and making her feel warm.

At dinner, the warmth of her heart transformed into a cold lump in her throat. Since Tadeo had disappeared, the children were glum and quiet. The feeling of desolation around their table had increased with the death of the animals around the farm. They hardly spoke, but after Alba took the little ones upstairs and was returning to the parlor, she heard her mother and her uncle conversing.

"You can't stop people from being superstitious, Arturo. Fernanda and Dolores might speak of monsters and witches, but they're loyal to the family."

"I simply worry about what the children might think if they hear such idle prattle," Arturo said. "It's not good for them. If I were you, I'd fire them both."

Alba wondered what idle prattle Arturo was referring to. Perhaps he'd caught Fernanda and Dolores discussing the possibility of a bewitchment, same as Valentín had done that day?

"I don't have money to hire new workers. And as I said, they're loyal to the family."

"You're too soft."

Alba quietly headed back up the stairs and went to Tadeo's room and held his gun in her hands. They'd shot targets with this when they were smaller. She knew its weight, its recoil, the way to clean it. But she'd never actually shot a living creature. Her father hunted, as did her brother. Deer had been served at their table on more than one occasion. But Alba did not hunt.

She stared at the watercolor portrait of her brother on the nightstand and took it with her, along with the pistol.

The gun made her wary. She did not place it by her pillow, as Valentín had suggested, instead tucking it into a drawer, next to the portrait. Then she contemplated the drawer and wondered if she was being stupid. Simply because she had not recognized the cry of an animal did not mean it was a supernatural creature, and her feeling of unease might simply be grief.

She was suddenly afraid not of witches and enchantments but of what her mother or her uncle would say if they should discover that she believed a witch was the reason for their misery. Her uncle, especially, would have unkind words for her.

Arturo was so urbane, so sophisticated, so clever. She dreaded looking like a stupid country girl in front of him. He'd mocked Valentín viciously, and she suspected he'd pronounce an equally harsh judgment against his niece should he know she was planning to go to Los Pinos.

Nevertheless, she knelt by the bed and set down a bowl. Then she dropped a pair of scissors into the dish and filled it with water. She tucked it under the bed and said her prayers.

She slept soundly. In the morning, with the light streaming through the curtains, she reconsidered her behavior. How silly she'd been the previous day, convinced monsters roamed their farm.

She stretched her arms up, opened the window, and contemplated the green fields. The air was fresh and when she knelt under the bed and grabbed the bowl, it was with the intent of throwing the water out the window and forgetting about such ridiculous stories.

But she dropped the pewter bowl and stood with her hands pressed against her mouth to muffle a scream.

The scissors had rusted overnight. They were crusted with brown and red flakes, as if they'd been left out in the rain for many months.

# 1934: 3

WE HELD A SÉANCE three days after the dance. Some might think it odd to be attempting to communicate with ghosts following the disturbance at the Halloween Ball. But for Ginny, ghosts were not frightful apparitions dangling their chains in the air. She believed in communion with the departed and found comfort in her writing and her sketches, which were supposedly influenced by invisible hands.

When you are frightened, whom do you turn to in your time of need? Who is the first person that springs to mind? For many of us, it is our mother, and it was no different for Ginny, even if her dear mother was dead and buried.

The séance required four people. Carolyn was skeptical about the venture but agreed to join Ginny and me. Our fourth participant was Mary Ann Mason, who could hardly stop giggling about the whole idea. After some shushing, however, we all gathered around the table and waited.

We sat in our room in semidarkness. We didn't have a Ouija board or any spectacular contraptions—spirit trumpets, spirit slates, or the like—to assist us. Ginny asked us to clear our minds and remain open to any communication. We held hands.

Carolyn and Mary Ann had fortified themselves with sips from a hip flask, and by the time we were to begin they could hardly act quiet and solemn.

"Spirits, are you with us?" Ginny asked.

There was no reply. No sepulchral voice spoke to us. In the dim light, I could see the sharp curve of Carolyn's smirk. Mary Ann was trying hard not to burst into laughter. I was a bit bored, to be frank. We had spent much of the morning studying and reading, and now instead of heading out we were stuck in our room, with only a candle for illumination.

After a few minutes, I began to wonder if I shouldn't have agreed to go with the other girls instead. Several of them had departed toward the cinema. I'm sure our companions were of a similar mind. Indeed, I could almost swear Carolyn was about to suggest that we all pile into her car and head out for a drive when a soft knock on the table startled us.

"Spirits, we welcome you," Ginny said, sounding serene. "Please knock once for yes and twice for no."

"That's no spirit knocking, that's Mary Ann's knobby knee bumping against the table," Carolyn said.

"It is not!" Mary Ann replied, offended.

There came another knock on the table, this time louder. We looked at one another, confused.

Ginny smiled. "We welcome you this evening and hope you might share your wisdom with us."

The knock was repeated. I'm no credulous fool, but I could not tell where it came from. It wasn't someone's knee bumping against the wood, as Carolyn had suggested, and it wasn't a tapping against a table leg. If you had asked me to pinpoint the source of the sound, I might have said it seemed to come from within the walls. The others must have had a similar thought, for the girls suddenly seemed unsettled.

"Ginny, stop teasing us," Mary Ann said.

"Do not be afraid," Ginny said calmly. "The spirits come lovingly, without quarrel."

The candle flame trembled and bent. We held our breath and clutched one another's hands.

"Spirits, might we seek your counsel?" Ginny asked.

A loud knock reverberated across the room. We looked around, nervous. Then there came two knocks in quick succession. I gasped.

Before any one of us could ask Ginny what was happening, the knocking had grown so violent it made the table vibrate. It was as if someone was punching the surface. I was not holding anyone's hands anymore; I was pressing down on the table to keep it from being toppled. I thought the wood would splinter under my fingertips.

"Ginny!" Mary Ann yelled.

The knocking ceased. All was still and quiet. Ginny sat stiffly, palms pressed against the table. Her eyes were wide open.

"You are in deadly peril, Virginia," she said.

The words were odd. They didn't sound as if they came from her mouth. Her lips hardly moved, and the voice seemed to rise from her chest rather than her throat. These words were between a whisper and a croak, coarse and spoken with difficulty.

It didn't sound like Ginny at all.

Somehow, during this whole mad ordeal, the candle had remained in place, burning bright. Ginny bent forward, her forehead almost touching the table, and the candle blew out.

Mary Ann screeched. Someone flung a chair aside. I heard a thumping and a scrabbling, and the door opened. One of the girls rushed out.

I reached out blindly, trying to grasp Ginny's hand, and the electric lights turned on. Carolyn stood next to the light switch.

"I better find Mary Ann," she said. "You almost gave her a heart attack, Gin-gin!"

Ginny did not reply. She stared at Carolyn in surprise and Carolyn shook her head before stepping out. Slowly, almost dreamily, Ginny turned to me.

"I'm very sorry," she said.

My heart was beating fast. I struggled to speak. "What happened?" I asked at last.

"I don't know."

She clutched my left hand and pressed her lips tight together. She seemed drained. Her beautiful dark hair hung upon her like a shroud. After a couple of minutes, she stood up and headed to the bathroom. I heard the water running. She spent a long time in the bathtub, and after she emerged she said she wished to go to bed.

The next day was Sunday. On Sundays, Edgar Yates normally made the trek to campus to visit Ginny. But he'd been detained with business back in Boston and sent a bouquet of red roses, which Ginny arranged by the window. While the other girls sat in the parlor of Joyce House with their boyfriends and admirers, Ginny was alone in her room. I intended to stay there with her, but Carolyn caught me as I was heading up the stairs.

"You must help me keep David distracted. He's too keen lately and it bothers me," she said. "He bores me to extinction at times."

"Why are you telling me that instead of *him*?"

"I have my eye set on a new beau, but if that shouldn't turn out the way I want, I can always keep David. In the meantime, I can't have him looking at other girls and getting ideas about them. You simply must sit with us, or Kathleen Kelley is bound to flutter her lashes at him."

Carolyn had a ruthless charm that I'd long since grown accustomed to, and I had served in a similar capacity for her on several previous occasions.

"I planned to spend my day with Ginny. She hardly slept last night, and I'm worried about her," I said. "Don't you remember what happened?"

"You're worried about her ventriloquist's act?"

"You think it was an act?"

"Of course. She does it to get attention. I can't understand why Edgar Yates wants to marry a girl who could be working at Coney Island reading palms. It's vulgar."

"I don't think she was doing it to get attention."

"Don't tell me you were scared! I can believe it of that silly goose Mary Ann, but not of you. She was tapping her knee under the table the whole time. How spooky!" Carolyn said, and rolled her eyes for dramatic effect. "Mary Ann's still angry at Ginny over it, you know? She doesn't want her going with us to the pictures next week."

"Is Mary Ann really that upset?"

"Well, yes. I'm sure she'll get over it. Now you simply must sit with me and David."

"Caro, maybe it would be better—"

"No, it wouldn't be better," she said firmly. "You'll come with me because I want you to. This is my final word."

Carolyn was used to high-handed proclamations. Her money, her position, had ensured that she possessed a tremendous expectation of being obeyed. At times she acted like a tiny tyrant. I was used to doing what she wanted. That same money and position were things that I envied and admired, keys to a different kingdom. With her connections, Carolyn could greatly assist me after graduation. But only if we remained on good terms. She knew it, I knew it. And there were moments like this when that knowledge stung.

I therefore spent a couple of hours sitting awkwardly between Carolyn and David, acting the role of duenna. Eventually, I was able to extricate myself from my duties when Carolyn determined she wanted to spend a few minutes alone with David.

I rushed up the stairs and back to my room. Ginny was not there. I was immediately deflated. However, when I looked out the window, I saw she was standing no more than a few feet from our dorm.

She wore a dark gray coat that favored her greatly. She was not alone. Santiago was rolling a cigarette and talking to her.

This is one of the keys to the mystery of Ginny's disappearance, one of the moments I've replayed in my mind ever since, trying to recall the angle of the light outside, the feeling of the glass upon my fingertips as I pressed them against the window, the soft ticking of a clock, the scent of the roses that were tucked in the white porcelain vase.

This moment matters because it's one of the only occasions when I saw Ginny and Santiago speak to each other alone. Or, at least, speaking when they thought they were alone. Every other time he turned his eyes toward her, or she nodded at him in greeting, there were other girls nearby. The house teemed with activity.

But there they were, outside the dorm as he lit his cigarette, talking.

I could see Ginny's beautiful face clearly, but the drops of rain that had begun to fall quickly marred the old glass pane, distorting the view. I rubbed my hand against the glass and thought of opening the window, but like everything else in the house, it was ancient and could not be easily operated.

Santiago stood with one hand in the pocket of his trousers while he held his cigarette with the other. He pointed at something in the direction of Briar's Commons. Ginny crossed her arms and they kept talking. He was nodding, he smiled. Then she turned away and walked back into the dorm.

I heard nothing of their conversation, and their gestures did not strike me as odd. I've tried hard to rack my brain, attempting to recall if at any point Santiago touched her, or she touched him, if they shared a small gesture of affection. Or else, if Ginny stepped away frightened, suddenly anxious.

Ginny came bounding up the stairs a few minutes later and walked into the room. She unbuttoned her coat.

"Betty. I thought you were downstairs," she said.

"I came up to see how you're doing." The porcelain vase with the roses was by the window and I toyed with the petal of a flower.

"I went for a walk."

"In the rain."

She smiled. "It's not much rain yet. More of a drizzle."

"You were speaking to Santiago."

"Yes. The poor boy needs a stable job. He has family back in Portugal depending on him, you know? I think I might ask Carolyn if she knows of any positions at her father's mill."

"He's hardly a boy. He must be older than us."

"He's twenty-one and a Pisces."

"It sounds like you know him fairly well to have memorized his zodiac sign," I said.

"I know you're a stubborn Taurus," she said, and laughed her light, delightful laugh. With one hand she shook off the droplets of water in her hair, then she leaned down and smelled the roses.

"Isn't Edgar wonderful?" she asked, and she smiled, glowing with joy. "He never forgets my flowers."

"It's a nice touch. How are you feeling now?"

She grabbed the basket with her knitting supplies, placed it on the bed, and pulled out a ball of yarn, twisting a piece of thread. "Much better."

"You haven't told me what happened last night."

"I'm still not quite sure. Most spirits are kind and gentle. I can't explain what happened. The spirit, it was agitated. Something frightened it. . . ." She paused, deep in thought; her smile dimmed like a flame under glass. "I apologize if I disturbed you. I know Mary Ann and Carolyn are angry at me and both think I was playing a prank on them."

"Don't worry about them. I want to make sure you're well."

"I'm fine. Although I suppose this won't do much for my reputation. 'Eccentric' Virginia Somerset. My father will be livid if he hears I terrorized my housemates."

"I'm sure no one will talk about you."

"Back in California they did."

"What did they say?" I asked with interest. Ginny didn't talk much about California, even if she'd lived in a swanky neighborhood full of movie stars. "Did you do something scandalous?"

"Well, there was this one boy, a couple of years ago, before Edgar. Terry was his name. He was adorable and he stole his cousin's car and we—" She shook her head and laughed. "No, I'm not going to tell you that tale, you can't keep a secret."

"I can!"

"Never, Carolyn wheedles it out of you in seconds. I've seen it."

"No. Come on, tell me."

"I won't. It was an affair of the heart, my first boyfriend. He was wild, very different from Edgar. My father didn't like him," she said, and she looked down at the floor thoughtfully. "My father says I embarrass him. I wear the wrong clothes and I make a mess of things. That's why he's happy I'm here, far from him."

"Ginny," I said.

She smiled. "Don't feel sorry for me. I'm quite glad to be away from home, working on my art. I have you and the other girls. I suppose I worry sometimes that things might change. After my mother died, I was terribly sad and lonely. I'm different now and I'm so glad. I'm in love with Edgar. I'm engaged, which is terribly exciting. Did I tell you what he said when he asked me to marry him? He said he'd make me perfectly happy."

"You think you can really be perfectly happy?" I asked.

"Yes. With Edgar. I wasn't happy in my father's house after my mother passed away. We stopped being a family. But I'll have a new family now, a new home."

"Yes, you will," I said, and the words were jagged in my mouth.

She rose and looked out the window. I looked, too. Santiago was still downstairs, smoking. He must have felt our eyes on him, because he looked up. He gave us a wave; Ginny gave him a nod in return. Santiago looked away, crushed his cigarette under his shoe, and walked off.

That is what I saw, that is what I remember, that is the cornerstone of the theory that she loved Santiago. Yet, when you analyze it, it means nothing. I saw two people talking, I saw a girl coming back to her room. She revealed no breathless affair to me; instead she talked about her boyfriend.

The other evidence that bolsters the idea of a secret relationship between Santiago and Ginny comes from Mary Ann. She said she'd seen a young woman standing outside in the snow with her arms wrapped around Santiago. The woman wore a coat that might have been Ginny's gray coat. Except it was late in the evening, and Mary Ann wasn't sure the coat was gray. Nor was she sure the girl was Ginny, because she had a scarf and a hat.

Although it was common practice in those days for all women to wear hats, Ginny eschewed such fashions. She preferred to walk around bareheaded, her long hair streaming down her back. Then again, it wouldn't have been difficult for Ginny to grab a hat if she wanted. I had hats, Carolyn had hats, Mary Ann had hats. Even in the cold of winter, when it would have been more advisable to be wearing earmuffs and a warm beanie, it might have made perfect sense to don a nice hat.

It might have been some other girl with Santiago that day. It didn't even have to be one of the students who roomed at our dorm.

But let's pretend for one moment that the couple is Ginny and Santiago. Mary Ann gets but a glimpse of them. She thinks the woman has wrapped her arms around the man's neck and is pulling him down for a kiss.

Let's assume they are indeed lovers. Why have I no notion of this? We share a dorm room, we share meals, at night we talk. In the days before her disappearance Ginny is strange, but she is not racked with the anxiousness of a young woman thinking of elopement. Instead she lives in fear of unseen forces, of evil lurking in shadows.

She speaks of black magic and curses. She's not receiving letters from a secret lover. In those final days before her disappearance, she's terribly isolated.

I want to believe that the meeting I saw through my window was the meeting of a boyfriend and girlfriend. I want to believe that the couple Mary Ann saw hugging in the snow was Ginny and Santiago. I want to construct a simple, ordinary answer to this puzzle that has haunted me all these long years. Yet there are too many threads that remain unresolved.

For you see, that evening when Mary Ann notices the couple, she yells at them playfully.

"Ginny, you're a fast one!" she yells.

But Ginny doesn't answer, she doesn't turn to look at Mary Ann. Instead, the couple walk away, giving their backs to her, without acknowledging the intruder. Mary Ann huffs, she thinks it very poor form for Ginny to act like that, and she hurries into the dorm. It's starting to snow again, and the couple are walking away. Snowflakes cling to their coats. They take a turn and disappear around the corner of the house.

At no point does Ginny react to her name being called and at no point does Mary Ann see her face. So even though weeks later

Mary Ann will say that Santiago and Ginny were probably having a love affair, her evidence is scant. And even though I saw them speaking outside that day, I can only replay the memory without arriving at a definite conclusion.

Was it a prosaic dime-store romance that drew Ginny away? Or were there darker forces at work? The séance is but one of the eerie unexplained elements that haunt my narrative. Further mysteries occurred.

Thus, when I think back about that snowy meeting, I cannot, even though I wish it with all my might, picture Ginny turning her head and smiling at Mary Ann in recognition. No, when I picture that moment all I can see is the figure in the gray coat with the hat, and when she turns her head toward Joyce House, she has no face. There is but a void. A woman grasps Santiago's arm, but she is not Ginny, she is a terrible darkness.

I am trapped next to that window, with the rain distorting my view, always looking out, and never able to see the face of the woman I love.

# 1998: 6

MINERVA LISTENED TO VERUCA SALT on her Discman as she walked to town, thinking the trip might lift her spirits, but the peacefulness of the streets did little to soothe the nervous twinge that had invaded her waking hours and that she was unable to either explain or wave away.

She supposed it was the stillness of the summer that caused this discomfort. In the daytime—with commuters off in Boston or at some other workplace location, with the town devoid of students to patronize its two cafés and its one bookstore—there was a sense of melancholy enveloping the brick buildings that lined the core of Temperance Landing. Its yellow-and-white city hall building, with the date 1667 proudly engraved above its doors, and the imposing library in the Beaux Arts style lay quiet and forlorn.

She thought the town was charming. It looked like the towns they depicted on Christmas cookie tins. A place like she'd never visited except in old Hollywood movies where Cary Grant played the hero. But now she perceived a forced cheerfulness embedded in the wood and brick and mortar, and behind it the shape of something sharper and unpleasant. The campus too had begun to shed its elegant appeal, like paint that is peeled away by the elements.

She had thought the summer, alone by the sea, would provide

her with a chance to focus on her work, but instead the silence of Stoneridge lay heavy upon her shoulders. The incident in the movable stacks added to the feeling of malaise. Well, no matter. She needed to keep going through Beatrice Tremblay's papers, needed to coerce herself back into a semblance of order.

She dropped off the film she needed developed and bought herself a cup of coffee, then walked back the way she'd come, glancing at the houses with the plaques that testified to their venerable history. There was a gray house with a yellow door and a plaque that read ROBERT THORNDIKE, MARINER, 1723. A pink house with its oval plaque that declared this had been the home of JEREMY LUTTER, BRICKLAYER, 1806. Charming tidbits of the past.

ISAIAH MARSH, 1887, LOST AT SEA.

She paused before that red house and gazed at the plaque, wondering how exactly Isaiah had been lost. A freak storm, or a trip from which he never returned? Had he fallen overboard or been murdered by a resentful crewmate? Minerva hefted her backpack from one shoulder to the other.

When she arrived back at the dorm, she took a nap for far longer than she'd intended and woke up feeling wrung out rather than refreshed. Hideo arrived soon after.

He helped her carry Thomas's boxes into Ledge House. They dumped them in the old library, under the shadows of stuffed ducks and owls, instead of dragging them to the basement. In the end, someone in the residence office had phoned Thomas's sister and the sister had promised she'd call back and see about picking up the boxes. It made no sense to drag the boxes up and down the basement stairs, so they'd stay in the library for now.

"You could write him up, you know," Hideo said when they were back in her kitchen.

She took a can of Diet Pepsi from the refrigerator and handed it to him before she prepared her second coffee of the day. "There's no proof he drew on my door, even if it's obvious it was him. He'll become more insufferable if I say anything and they're not going to boot him out during the summer."

"If you don't get it down on paper, you'll never get rid of him."

"I don't want to talk about Conrad," she said, and flicked on the light in the kitchen. It was getting late and soon Karnstein would come by to have its dinner. The glow of the kitchen enticed the cat during the evenings.

"Did you tell Hannah what he said to you?"

"Yes, I told Hannah about him. It'll be added to his file and in the fall we'll have a mediation session."

Hideo poured himself half a glass of soda while he shook his head. She grabbed her cup of coffee and sat across from him.

"So what's Carolyn Yates like?" Hideo asked. "Did she actually speak to you when you went to her house?"

"Sure, we've spoken. She seems to have been a former artist and a debutante who married well. In Beatrice Tremblay's diaries she paints a picture of a fashionable, privileged woman."

"And her grandson, that Noah, what's he like?"

"He's the grandson of a privileged woman."

"I mean, is he cute?"

"How would I know?"

"You have eyes."

He was a bit vulnerable behind the bluster, she thought. She had a fondness for stray animals and slightly damaged things—the chipped frame of a mirror, the weathered pages of a book that has been kissed by the rain, the sweater that has been nibbled by a troublesome moth—which primed her to look kindly on a man like him. But she ought not to. Strays bit sometimes, and certain old books were suffused with pernicious mold.

"My eyes are busy," she said. The coffee was too hot. It scalded her tongue.

"Sometimes I think you want to play at being Emily Dickinson, secluded in a brick house and feverishly writing by candlelight."

She didn't. She admired, even envied people like Hideo, who could swiftly navigate the world, smiling and laughing and making friends while she was coiled tight inside her head. These days, she felt even more removed from everything, the silence of the dorm and the summer heat that spread across campus lulling her into a restless half sleep.

"I should get the Chinese food now," Hideo said. "Do you want to come with me? I need to go to Stop and Shop, but it won't take long."

"No, I'll wait for you here," she said. She feared he'd ask her more about Noah or Carolyn. She didn't want to discuss them. Nor did she relish the idea of listening to Hideo's loud music while they drove, the notes like sandpaper against her ears. She was raw and prickly these days; perhaps it was another side effect of this lonely, hot summer.

After Hideo stepped out, Minerva fiddled with her notes, underlining a word here and there. She took a final swig of her coffee, then walked back into the library and looked at Thomas's two boxes.

Once again, she recalled the last time she'd seen Thomas Murphy, when she'd cut through Briar's Commons and bumped into him in the middle of the night. It had been quite dark, and she'd hardly noticed him before they almost collided. He'd looked frightened, hadn't he? He'd stared at her with wide, alarmed eyes before shuffling away.

Minerva opened one of the boxes and took out a book, then another. She set them aside without really looking at them. Thomas hadn't been wearing a jacket that night, and now that she thought about it, he hadn't been wearing a hat or mittens, either. He couldn't have gone far dressed like that, without a coat or any other clothing to protect him from the elements, like the protagonist in *The Vanishing* couldn't have gone far.

The protagonist who was modeled after Virginia.

Minerva shook her head and grabbed the two books she'd toyed with, ready to pack them away again. A single piece of paper slipped from in between the pages of one of them and she picked it up.

It was an ordinary piece of paper. On it, Thomas had drawn a few idle doodles with a black pen. They were nothing special.

Except that Minerva had seen drawings like those at the Willows: the drawings resembled the charcoal sketches she had photographed.

Minerva stared at the page. Quickly she began looking for another loose page tucked inside the two volumes. When she didn't find one, she began pulling out other books from the box without any luck. Finally she opened a notebook, and its pages were lined with more and more of those drawings that inexplicably resembled Virginia's sketches.

That flower! She'd seen that flower pattern in the archive at the Willows. Circles and more circles. And the markings on the side, almost like letters but not quite. There they were, and other drawings too, as she turned the pages, drawings that resembled in their mood and style Virginia's artwork.

It was like he had photocopied the three sketches she'd found, only these were drawings made with a pen—the eerie similarity made a shiver go down her spine. Because essentially Thomas had vanished, like Virginia had vanished, and she had not seriously thought about this coincidence until now.

Perhaps she was exaggerating. Perhaps the drawings were not that similar. She couldn't be sure until she compared them to the photos she'd taken at the Willows, and yet her heart was beating fast. She felt a dread she could not name.

She clutched the notebook and raised her head, listening intently. The dorm was quiet, no steps were heard on the floor above, there was no opening or closing of doors. The house remained sensibly still and silent, the windows locked, the curtains pulled tight. Yet she thought she'd heard something, and even if she hadn't, perhaps it was that old feeling that her great-grandmother used to call a portent. It was like a thorn under your skin, jabbing you and making you pay attention.

Minerva thrust the notebook aside and stood up. She went to the kitchen and lingered by the table, attempting to peer at the darkness that extended outside but keeping her distance from the windows. When Hideo had left it was still dusk, yet night seemed to have fallen suddenly, blanketing the house with an oppressive blackness.

There was no porch light, so she couldn't see who was standing outside. But she knew there was someone even if no silhouette lingered at the edges of the kitchen windows.

That someone wasn't Hideo, nor any of the other resident directors who might be making their rounds. Not that they would venture to this sector of campus, since Minerva was supposed to keep guard over these buildings.

Then she began to hear it: shoes upon the path, then upon the steps that led up to the porch. She'd anticipated the visitor, yet the knock on the door startled her so much she held on to the back of a chair.

"Minerva? Are you there?"

That was Conrad Carter's voice. She pressed her lips together and stepped forward, opening the door a tad.

"What is it, Conrad?" she asked.

"I'm dropping by to talk about the other night. You know, to apologize," he said.

The young man smiled at her with his friendliest, sunniest smile. Conrad could be fun and pleasant when he wanted to. She'd seen him crank up the charm with his fellow residents. In the beginning, when she'd first met him, he'd tried to seem likable. All throughout September and late into October he'd greeted her with a warm hello.

"Thanks. But I've filed my report already," she said, returning his smile with a wary stare.

"I know you did."

"I can't delete the report, if that's what you're thinking."

"I was thinking I'm bored tonight, the cable's all fucked up in my room, and the campus is deserted. Want to go to Bailey's to play pool? You like pool."

Minerva crossed her arms. She'd gone to Bailey's twice, both times with Hideo and a few of the other resident directors. She'd bumped into Conrad Carter that second time, and they'd played pool and chatted. Well, he chatted. She'd been quiet, as she often was in bars and loud, chaotic places like that. Then, when she'd excused herself, saying she was going back to campus, he'd told her they could walk together.

It was a nice walk in the crispness of the October night and

Conrad Carter had kept talking and she'd answered his questions and their rapport was pleasant. Then they'd reached the edge of Briar's Commons and there was the path he needed to take back to his dorm, so she prepared to bid him goodbye.

Before she turned away, he'd kissed her. One fleeting kiss as the wind blew and made the tops of the trees sway. Back home, she'd seldom gone out with anyone, so busy with her studies and part-time jobs. She was quite hopeless with people, anyway, barely could muster the courage to attempt a romantic encounter. She'd had one boyfriend in high school, a relationship that amounted to a single season. There had been Jonás in university, who detested the idea of her going abroad the moment she mentioned it, who accused her of being lukewarm about him during the whole year they dated, which was true. Then in the States she hadn't ventured beyond message boards—the guy from Brookline whom she'd met a few times had connected with her that way.

She really had no idea how to navigate hookups, and dating was an equally confusing equation. Besides, Conrad was a student at one of the dorms she supervised.

She'd mumbled a quick good night and hurried into the house, leaving Conrad Carter looking surprised and Minerva befuddled. When she hinted to Hideo about an interesting grad student she'd met from a nearby dorm—was it ethical to go out with someone in a dorm that was technically under your watch?—he laughed and asked which guy she was talking about. Minerva shook her head, unwilling to reveal more.

She'd seen Conrad in the following days and smiled at him when they crossed paths, thinking perhaps she'd ask him if he wanted to catch a movie or head to Bailey's on the weekend. But when the Halloween weekend came, chaotic and interminable, she stumbled onto him smoking pot with a junior who was dressed as a sexy witch.

She wrote both of them up. She was doing her job, although she suspected he interpreted it as a petty attempt to get back at him for hooking up with another girl instead of her.

Anyway, she was glad she'd been cautious around him. He was a brat, a spoiled boy. Noah Yates was probably more of the same.

"I'm doing rounds with another resident director in a bit," she said.

"Well, then, I guess I tried," he replied with a shrug, stepping back.

She glanced at Briar's Commons, the dark trees smudged across the sky like charcoal. She wanted Conrad to leave, but a question tumbled from her lips.

"Did Thomas tell you where he was going before the winter break?" she asked.

He paused and frowned. "Why would he tell me anything?"

"You were roommates."

"We didn't get along. And it wasn't my fault. I know that's what you think, but I wasn't always antagonizing the guy. He found weird shit to freak about."

"Like what?"

"He said I stole things from him or moved them around. Then he had this insane idea that I was staring at him at night."

"Staring at him?"

"And following him. Our last blowup was because he said I followed him down a path but that I erased my tracks. I mentioned this to you, it's in one of your reports."

"No, you didn't," she said. Hannah must have written that up, or maybe another resident director. She'd been trying to avoid Conrad in the winter, so there might have been an incident that she'd passed on to another staff member. Or the admin office had simply handled that one by themselves. The campus was chaotic at the end of term.

"He was a freak. And he should have been written up, not just me. He lit candles in his room, you know? Talked to himself. Weird shit. All I did was play a few CDs at night."

"Do you remember what he was doing in December, during finals?" she asked.

"Skipping classes."

"You're sure about that?"

"He was locked inside his room and complaining about any noise I made."

"When was the last time you saw him?"

"I don't know. Before Midnight Breakfast. I knocked on his door to ask if he wanted to go to the cafeteria together and he didn't answer."

Midnight Breakfast was one of those campus traditions left over from the old days when Stoneridge had been a women's college. The girls at Stoneridge had gathered the first Friday in December in the dining hall, where eggs, bacon, and toast were served to hungry students cramming for exams. It remained a popular activity, an event that signaled the impending end of term.

Minerva tried to remember the exact day she had last seen Thomas. It must have been after Midnight Breakfast. Perhaps the weekend after? Damn it, she wasn't sure.

"Why are you asking about Thomas?"

"His sister is picking up his stuff and it came to mind."

Conrad nodded. Minerva didn't say anything else, but he remained by the door, looking at her.

"You filed the report?" he asked.

"Yeah."

"I didn't just come to ask about that, you know? I really did want to head to Bailey's."

Maybe he did, maybe he didn't. He was an opportunist, and she didn't think he'd be above throwing her a few lines with the hopes of having the report modified. But she had no intention of doing that. She knew enough about him now; she knew better.

She shook her head. "I have to work on my thesis."

"It's okay to relax occasionally. Otherwise you'll burn out."

*Witches burn,* she thought. At least in the stories, in cheap horror films. Not in real life. In real life they had been hanged at the rocky outcrop called Proctor's Ledge in nearby Salem.

"I'll take that into consideration," Minerva said.

He gave her one of his trademark shrugs accompanied by a smile and hurried away. Minerva closed the door and returned to the library. She looked at Thomas's boxes with weary eyes. Once again, she felt that oppressive anxiousness that seemed to keep her company more and more these days. Slowly she bent down to look at the paper with the drawings, which she'd left on a couch.

*Isaiah Marsh, lost at sea,* she thought. Lost like Thomas, who did not return to his room one evening? Or lost like Virginia Somerset, who walked out of her dorm one cold December night? How many people were lost that way, people who slipped into darkness, never to be seen again?

A noise made her raise her head. Had someone knocked? Had Conrad returned? Or was it Hideo carrying the bag with Chinese takeout? She walked into the kitchen and stared at the door.

"Hideo," she said.

But there was no reply. There was someone outside again, though. She knew it. Her fingers rested upon the doorjamb and she yanked the door open with her other hand. Darkness greeted her, a faint breeze caressed her hair, and she heard the rustling of the trees nearby.

Behind the membrane of normality of this summer evening lurked a foulness that she could not pinpoint, yet she sensed.

"Witches," she said.

The moon, drifting across the sky, seemed to grin at Minerva, like a ferocious beast that shows its teeth.

*I'm going mad,* she thought, and she wondered if she shouldn't have accepted Conrad's invitation. Or perhaps she should have jumped into the car with Hideo. Then she wouldn't be alone with her nerves and the shadows of the house for company.

Karnstein meowed and ventured toward her. Minerva bent down to pick up the animal and clutched it against her chest. The cat purred while she squinted and looked at the tops of the trees before spinning around and slamming the door shut.

# 1908: 6

ALBA HAD NOT VISITED Los Pinos before. Why would she? It was but a dusty hamlet up a narrow road that wrapped around the mountain. A waterfall dashed down a ravine, sprinkling moss-covered rocks, and the pines grew straight and tall, shading their path. It was a beautiful landscape, lush and rich with vegetation, but there was little to attract her to that rugged place. It had its dangers too, for sometimes the fog descended from the mountains and carpeted the road, making it impossible to divine what lay ahead.

They said that the witches at Los Pinos turned into balls of fire when the fog came, luring unwary travelers to their doom. She remembered spooking her siblings with such tales, but now these harmless stories made her tug at the heavy coat upon her shoulders, wishing to suppress a shiver that was not entirely the fault of the chill that reigned upon the road that morning.

She'd found out what Fernanda and Dolores had done that had irritated her uncle: they'd started sporting a pair of charms against the evil eye and wore them on their wrists. He considered this both pagan and silly and railed at them.

"I didn't mean to offend your uncle," Fernanda told Alba, wringing her hands and sniffling. "But it's been strange around here, Niña Alba. And it was my sister who came by to give me the amulets, I didn't ask for them."

"Don't worry about it. I'm sure he's forgotten," Alba said.

Which might have been true, but it meant that if her uncle or her mother found out about this expedition with Valentín, they'd be furious. Should she have set off on this journey? Charlatans abounded in the world; she knew as much. Valentín was her friend, but he might be leading her into the hands of a huckster who would merely take her coin and laugh at her naïveté.

By the time they reached the town, the sun had broken through the clouds. There was no central plaza in Los Pinos; its houses were grouped along chaotic dirt paths, and they all looked the same to her eyes, painted a white that had been dirtied by the elements and time. But Valentín seemed to know where he was going, navigating the labyrinthine roads with ease until they reached a house with a scratched yellow door.

Valentín helped her off her mount and then tied the horses to a post while Alba glanced around. She could hear chickens clucking nearby, but otherwise the town was oddly quiet. A few houses away, an old woman sat by the door on a stool, mending a shirt. A child darted into a house. These were the only people they'd seen so far. In the distance, a dog barked.

"Most of the men and women work on the farms nearby during the day," Valentín explained. "There is little to do here otherwise."

"Except read palms and sell charms," Alba said.

Valentín nodded. He knocked on the yellow door. An old woman opened it and stood squinting at them. Her gray hair was tied in a messy braid and around her shoulders she wore the black rebozo with the red stripe that identified the witches of Los Pinos. There were always witches in every town, people who knew how to make poultices and love potions alike. Here they clustered together at the edge of a mountain. Had they been chased there? Had they joined forces in an ancient pact? No one knew, but as far back as the people of the neighboring towns could tell, there had been Los Pinos and its witches.

"Mrs. Jovita, I've brought you a gift," Valentín said. He reached into the leather pack hanging from one shoulder and handed her a blue bottle. "May we come in?"

Jovita nodded and opened the door wide, letting them into a small, dark vestibule. A horseshoe and an image of San Martín Caballero hung above a doorway, along with crosses of ocote. They followed the woman down a hallway.

There were many shelves in this hallway, all crammed with jars and flasks. Some contained dried plants, herbs, and mushrooms; others seemed to be filled with the ground bones of coyotes, the wings of moths, desiccated toads, the skins of snakes, carefully ground obsidian, and powdered grasshoppers.

They walked into a room that smelled faintly of mint. A large window let in a good amount of light and this area looked less crowded than the hallway that they'd passed through. Still, little bundles of ocote sticks tied together with thread were tucked on shelves, boxes with neat labels and more jars arranged around them. Ribbons of different colors had been nailed under a niche with a plaster statue of the archangel Gabriel.

Alba and Valentín sat down at a table. The old woman wrapped her hands around the bottle and was looking at it with interest. She did not sit. Alba peeled off her riding gloves.

"This is the girl I told you about, Mrs. Jovita. We've come for your counsel," Valentín said. He gestured to Alba.

She slid a pouch across the table. It contained the pocket money she possessed.

Jovita set the bottle down on the table, then shuffled out of the room. When she returned, she had a wooden bowl in one hand and an egg in the other. She sat down. With trembling fingers she cracked the egg and let its contents fall into the bowl. Then she took a sip from the bottle and smacked her lips, but she didn't say anything as she stared at the bowl.

Alba began to wonder if the woman was capable of speech. She again questioned the excursion. There she was, shivering, doomed to catch a chill from the early-morning ride up the mountainside, and for what? Her uncle was right. She'd find no answers in this place.

"There's a shadow upon you," the woman said. "A teyolloquani haunts your family."

Valentín must have mentioned the creature he believed afflicted the Quirogas, just as he had arranged this meeting, yet the word still filled her with dread.

Jovita took another sip from the bottle and looked down at the dish. All Alba could see was the egg yolk, but the woman seemed keenly interested in it.

"Such a witch is dangerous. No ordinary mischief interests a teyolloquani. You must watch your step. They can turn their enemies into animals, into things."

"What things?" Alba asked.

"There once was a young man from a nearby village. He was handsome and all the women liked him, and he liked all the women. But he made a mistake when he angered a girl from our town. She hexed him, turned him into a stool, and sat on it. There she sat, on her stool, by the door of her house, smiling. She still does."

Alba recalled the woman nearby, sitting on a weathered stool, mending her shirt. She clasped her hands tight.

"There have been deaths, haven't there?" the woman asked. "Horses. Goats."

"Yes," she said.

"Folks are talking about it."

Folks were indeed. She realized that even without Valentín, the woman would have guessed the purpose of her visit and easily rattled off a remedy.

"It's a bewitchment. We'll need to make a talisman. Something tough, something to keep you safe. It'll cost you more than a bottle of rum and a few coins. Much more."

"I see," Alba said.

She was beginning to feel foolish, a country rube who was about to be duped by tricks learned from a carnival sideshow. She wondered what her mother would think if she could see her now. Her uncle would be appalled. At best, he'd laugh at her gullibility. At worst, he'd forbid her from ever seeing Valentín after this.

"How much?" Valentín asked.

"The ring on the lady's finger," Jovita said.

Alba looked at the ring with the green stone, the one her father had given her, and shook her head.

"This is nonsense," she said, turning to Valentín. "They make up stories in places like this and fleece people who visit."

"Alba, you must listen," he urged her.

"No, I don't want to. Take me home."

"Please, she is a wisewoman."

"Valentín, I do not want—"

"You have portents," Jovita said calmly, interrupting them.

Alba looked at the woman and clapped her mouth shut. She hadn't told Valentín about her portents. She'd spoken about them only to her uncle Arturo. She feared her mother would dislike such silly blathering. Perhaps her father might have lent her a friendly ear, since they were both more attuned to the folklore and stories of their community, but she'd felt that these were private matters. Secrets that must be shared sparingly.

She had spoken to Arturo about portents because he was a special soul, the one person who understood her nature. He was a poet, a dreamer. Even Tadeo, who'd been her confidant and playmate, could not comprehend Alba as deeply, for they were made of different substances. Tadeo was almost her twin, but not her double.

"You dream and you glimpse things that will be, and sometimes you see things that have happened," Jovita said. "It's a gift."

"A gift?" Alba toyed with one of her riding gloves, tugging at it gently as she spoke. She was unable to remain still.

"Some people have a good ear for instruments, others can run fast. We are born with certain quirks in our souls and in our bodies."

"It sounds like you're saying I was born to be a witch, or a fortune teller at the very least," Alba said, and scoffed at the thought.

The woman shrugged. "Is someone born to be a musician? Those who have gifts may have an easier time walking certain paths, but it doesn't mean they will."

Alba took a deep breath. "Very well. I have dreams and sometimes I see things that will happen. What of it?" Alba fell silent. She twisted the ring around her finger.

"What a teyolloquani wants is to feed on the blood of its victims. It'll get hold of a bit of hair, or a few nail clippings, and use them to bewitch the person. It'll make it hail in the summer, or cause restless dreams. It'll send its minions, like the owl and the serpent, to roam near houses at night. Its victim grows fearful. That is what makes the blood sweeter, the pain and the fear. The teyolloquani ate your brother, that's what it did. He's bones in a field somewhere. It'll devour you too if you're not careful. Show me your wrists."

Alba hesitated but offered her hands. Jovita looked at them and nodded. "You have no bite marks. On your neck, there is nothing either, is there?"

"No," Alba said, and reflexively touched her neck.

"Good. It means it hasn't fed from you. Once a witch drinks the blood of its victim, their room can't be warded, and the more it drinks, the stronger the witch becomes and the deeper the victim falls under its spell. But we can chase it off, with the proper charms."

"I'm not sure—"

"If you're not sure, then off you go," the woman said, although she did not sound exasperated.

Once again, Alba twisted the ring around her finger, feeling the coolness of its stone beneath her fingertips. She slid it off and handed it to Jovita, who pocketed it and nodded.

The woman stood up and walked around the room, pulling a bundle of cloth from one of the shelves. She placed it on the table and unwrapped it. Inside was a dead dove that had been stuffed and stabbed with seven long pins.

Alba gasped at the ghastly creation. "What is that?"

"This you will place in your room. It'll repel any evil thing that tries to crawl through your window."

"She placed scissors under the bed and they rusted in one night," Valentín said.

"This is stronger, better," she said as she carefully slid out a pin from the dove's body. "Stab your finger with it and slide it back in."

"Why would I ever do that?" Alba replied, disgusted.

"Blood has power. It's why they drink it. The blood of someone who is gifted like you is even more powerful, better than that of others. There's magic in it. Prick your finger."

Alba brushed the wings of the bird, feeling the smoothness of the feathers. The pins were like thorns sticking out of the bird's back, and these she did not dare touch.

Her father would have believed in a bewitchment and would surely have consulted someone in Los Pinos. But Alba's mother and Uncle Arturo were not governed by such superstitions, and she was still dithering, trying to determine which was the correct course of action.

"It's no good thing to be caught in the snare of a teyolloquani. If it drinks from you, you'll be doomed. Death will surely follow. There is no remedy, after that."

The woman was silent. Alba thought of poor Tadeo, who had been missing for weeks, and of that dream she'd had in which he screamed in the fields of barley. Perhaps it had been just that: a bad dream. The noises outside her window were the product of a wild animal, the same one that had killed their horses and their goats. But what if it was something else? What if that odd feeling running down her spine, that fear and restlessness that filled her to the brim, was the product of darker forces?

She looked at Valentín, then again at the old woman. She hesitated.

"Will this be sufficient? If I take this charm with me, will it leave us be? All of us?" Alba asked. "It's not enough to keep it out of my room. What of my mother? My siblings? If it already took my brother, why wouldn't it take another? If I could know who this witch is and destroy—"

"It's no simple matter to do such a thing. Besides, most of them are opportunistic, fearful of being discovered. Should it sense opposition, a protective charm, it might let you be and seek easier prey."

"And if it shouldn't?"

"Then another remedy must be procured, but I tell you, it is no simple matter, not even for a girl who has portents."

Alba cupped the bird between her hands. Carefully she slid out a needle and held it up.

"My father spoke of evil witches. He said they eat the hearts of people because that is where they get their power. And to kill a witch you must cut off their head or carve out their heart."

"Your father was right."

The needle glinted. She pricked her finger quickly, staining the tip of the needle with her blood and then sliding it back into the bird's body. The sting of it made her wince and Valentín gallantly handed her a handkerchief.

"Take the talisman. Keep it close. Make more of them, like this, hide them around your home," Jovita told her.

Alba pressed the handkerchief against her finger. "You mean dead doves?"

"Hummingbirds are the best, but doves will do."

"But make them how? Don't you need an incantation, special powders?"

"You need belief, is what you need. You need to clutch the dead bird and stab it with six needles, and at the seventh you tell it, *Keep me safe, keep any evil away,* and offer your blood, like you did. That's the crucial ingredient. You've cast spells before, have you not?"

She looked at Jovita and opened her mouth. She did not know what to say. There had been a few spells, the kind one learned in the countryside. The one with the cord and the yellow cloth to make someone visit you, for example. But those were nothing; those were games. She'd heard of other, more elaborate spells, like cutting dolls out of paper and offering them alcohol, copal, and the blood of a black hen to dispel illness, but she'd never dared try them.

"One or two," Alba said, twisting the handkerchief around her hand. "For luck and such."

"Then you understand. It's not about powders or birds, girl. This is the physical shape magic takes."

She remembered when her father had gone out into the fields and warned nahuales to leave their crops alone, sometimes dragging an old iron pot with him to frighten them away, for they detested certain metals. But he didn't always employ the pot. She supposed it was the ritual behavior that mattered most.

"Very well," Alba said. They stepped out, the yellow door closing behind them.

Alba placed the dead bird in the side saddlebag and Valentín helped her onto her horse. She put on her riding gloves. They rode side by side. As they were about to leave Los Pinos behind, she spotted a woman walking down the road and reined in her mount.

The woman was dressed in a white shirt and a red skirt. She wore a black shawl upon her head.

"What is it?" Valentín asked.

"I know her," Alba said. "It's that woman, from the market. Remember? The one who quarreled with my brother."

The woman turned her face toward them. Her eyes fixed on Alba with the certainty of an arrow. The witch's mouth was curled with displeasure.

"We must go," Valentín said, urging her on.

"What if it's her? What if she's the witch who killed Tadeo?"

"We must go," he repeated in a gruff, low tone.

The woman looked at the ground and shook her head.

Alba spurred the horse forward and they began moving again. The woman watched them as they passed by her. Her eyes were dark as obsidian, deep and sharp. Alba swallowed. A few times she looked over her shoulder, fearing the witch was following them, but the only person they met as they made their descent was an old man carrying a bundle of sticks on his back.

They rode in silence to her home. When they reached the edge of the field of barley, he spoke.

"Perpetua wouldn't bewitch you," he said. "She's a widow who sells charms, but I've never known her to broker in other kinds of spellwork. Her mother made charms before her, and before that her grandmother. People talk and you learn who does certain kinds of work and who doesn't."

"Then she's a good and decent witch who happened to accost my brother before he disappeared?"

"I can't explain that. But I don't want you to rush to conclusions. Even if you were correct, you should never confront a witch openly."

"Why not?"

"Because it's dangerous. Even if Perpetua was behind all of this, it would be reckless to accuse her of any wrongdoing."

"How well do you know her?"

"I told you; she sells charms. She used to go with her daughter to the Molinas' and the Desotos' to visit the workers there."

"Then who is hurting us? Tell me, who?" she demanded.

He shook his head. "I don't know," he said, and his serious, sad face felt like a slap, something in his distress stinging her. She wanted him to fix everything, to put things back together the way they were. To bring Tadeo back.

"You don't care about me!" she exclaimed.

Valentín let out an exasperated grunt. "Alba, I care the world about you!"

"Liar!"

"Alba," he said in turn, and clutched her hand with such vehemence that she almost gasped. Then he leaned down to kiss her.

She was too surprised to react at first, but then she parted her lips and kissed him back. She felt his hand on her cheek as she tipped her head to the correct angle. She understood then that he could not provide her with easy answers, but he was there nevertheless. She held him tight.

The horses grew restless, shifting, and they finally separated. Alba blushed. Valentín simply smiled.

She tucked a stray lock of hair behind her ear and remembered how the Molina girls had teased her about Valentín. They'd never let her be if they suspected she had kissed him. And Alba's mother would be furious if she knew. She glanced toward the house in the distance and then back at Valentín.

He was a pleasant-looking man, and kind. She'd complained to Arturo, telling him Valentín had hard hands, farmer's hands, but when he'd kissed her and pressed his palm against her cheek, she hadn't cared that it was calloused and firmed by manual labor.

Nevertheless, Alba ought to tell him he shouldn't be taking liberties with her. Instead, she ducked her head, attempting to maintain a decorous expression on her face.

"I should go. Thank you for helping me and for the hand-kerchief," she said, and held it out to him.

He shook his head. "You may keep it. It's only a cheap square of cloth, not fancy silk."

"Thank you."

"Be careful, Alba."

In response, she kissed him quickly on the lips. They looked into each other's eyes and perhaps he might have shared another kiss with her, but she urged her horse forward. It trotted down the path that led to the door of her house and she smiled.

# 1934: 4

SNOW ARRIVED EARLY THAT November, dusting the tops of the pines and frosting the windows. With the colder temperatures Ginny's mood grew somber. While the rest of us were eager to skate on one of the ponds or build a snowman, Ginny kept to our room. Often, I found her looking out the window, in the direction of Briar's Commons.

She seemed to be eternally ducking between the library and our dorm. A pile of books formed by her bed. These weren't the tomes on art and design I'd grown to expect. I spotted *The Superstitions of Witchcraft, Old Paths and Legends of New England, The Wonders of the Invisible World, The History of Witchcraft and Demonology,* and many other books, all dealing with matters of ghosts, witchcraft, and things that go bump in the night.

New England is rife with narratives of the uncanny. Almost every town in Massachusetts boasts a tale of devilry and witches. Some of the protagonists in these stories are innocents sent to the gallows and others are agents of evil. There's a witch rock in Rochester and another in Peabody, and even though these may be merely boulders left behind when glaciers retreated in distant ice ages, they mark the land in unusual ways. More than one girl in our dorm liked to share legends of strange haunts, sending her roommates shrieking out the door. And, as evidenced by our own séance, sometimes the girls were willing to dip their toes into the world of the supernatural. Myrna Whitemyer, for example, had a fondness for tarot cards.

Which is to say that Ginny's interest in matters of witchcraft was by itself not an odd trait, not when you considered her automatic writing or her spirit paintings, but I felt that this was fundamentally different from her other pursuits. There was no joy in this quest, simply a grim determination.

There were other changes in Ginny's behavior as the days advanced. More than once while we were walking together, she looked over her shoulder or turned quickly around as if expecting to find someone behind us. She grew distracted and sometimes I'd have to call her name twice to get her attention. In the mornings she looked tired and dark circles formed under her eyes. She scribbled incessantly in her notebooks.

Two incidents stand out from that November, one before Thanksgiving and the other shortly after our return to the dorm from the holiday, which in those days took place on the last Thursday of the month.

Edgar had promised to pick Ginny up and take her to Boston for Thanksgiving dinner with his family. I, on the other hand, had plans to enjoy dinner with Mary Ann Mason and a few other girls at her home in Gloucester.

The evening before our departure, when I was packing my suitcase, Ginny ran into the room, practically breathless, her hair in disarray. Before I could even open my mouth, she pushed me aside and rushed to the window and looked outside.

"Ginny? What's the matter?" I asked.

She did not reply. I went toward her and gently clasped her shoulder until at last she shook her head and turned to me.

"I thought someone was following me again."

"Again?"

"It happened twice last week, and two days ago there was someone watching our window."

"Where?"

"Below, pacing there and looking up. I thought it might be him again, following me."

"What does this person look like?"

"I don't know. I thought I caught a glimpse of a man in a blue overcoat, but I couldn't get a good look at his face. And there have been other things, Betty."

"What things?"

"Lights in the trees. Hovering there," she said, her hand brushing the curtain gently.

"It might be fox fire. Mushrooms can glow as bright as jewels in the dark."

"Hovering, Betty. Up in the trees."

"An owl, perhaps? With moonlight reflecting on its plumage? Or else it's a will-o'-the-wisp. I read an explanation about that phenomenon in a book."

"No. It's not natural."

I looked out, in the same direction she was staring, toward the path that cut through Briar's Commons. Suddenly Ginny gripped the curtain tight with one hand. There was a figure coming down the road. We held our breath.

Two, three more people dashed down the path and toward Joyce House. We quickly saw that these were three fellow students, laughing merrily and carrying their books in their arms. Ginny closed the curtains and sat on her bed, looking weary.

I kept on packing and shortly afterward we turned off the lights and went to sleep. Ginny woke me up early the next morning.

"Betty, come quick," she said.

Edgar was not supposed to stop by until noon and Mary Ann Mason wouldn't be driving us to Gloucester until at least one o'clock, so we didn't have to rise early, but it must have been scarcely past six in the morning when I opened my groggy eyes.

"What happened?" I asked.

"Get dressed, we need to head outside. Quick."

I stuffed my feet into a pair of boots, found my gray woolen dress, and pulled my coat over my shoulders as fast as I could. We rushed outside Joyce House. Ginny took me by the hand and excitedly pointed to the ground.

"See? Footprints! Someone was standing outside here yesterday and looking at our window."

I leaned down and looked at the snow. The imprints of shoes had been preserved, but all I could tell by the size of them was that these had probably belonged to a man. It didn't mean anyone had been looking up or pacing under our window. It could have been one of the other girls' boyfriends or any number of other people.

"Someone is following me. This is the proof."

The expression on my face must have revealed my skepticism.

"Betty, it's proof. See?" she insisted. "Footprints."

"It's the outline of someone's shoe."

Her eyes shone bright and large and wounded. Ginny stomped back into the house. I followed with a sigh. By the time I reached our room, Ginny had bundled herself under her blankets. I did the same, hoping to catch a couple more hours of sleep.

I did manage to sleep a little more and then went about my morning routine. I showered, dressed, had a quick breakfast. I chanced upon Carolyn and her father in the parlor.

He was an imposing man, with a steely look in his eyes and his temples streaked with silver. He was always impeccably attired and that day he wore a heavy navy coat that almost brushed the floor.

"You must increase the pace," she was telling him. "It'll do no good next season."

"You can't hurry such things," he said, and tapped his cigar against an ashtray. He had a fondness for those. Whenever I'd visited the Willows, he'd been smoking a cigar, with a cloud of smoke around him.

"It's becoming dire and the tuition for the next term is due by January."

"You know well it's not an easy situation. I have creditors yelling at me each week. I would love to solve it all tomorrow, but there is nothing that can be done, not yet."

"It'll be a miserable Christmas if you don't do something soon.

I've done my bit and there's nothing to show for it. It would be a lot easier if it was one. Why do we need two?"

"You know why two. Symmetry. Don't try to teach me how things are done, girl."

I was surprised to hear that the Wingraves were experiencing any economic turmoil, despite what Benjamin had told us during the Halloween dance. They seemed flush with cash and Carolyn had never hinted at any financial deprivations. Not that she would have confided in me about such matters, but I thought I would have suspected something was amiss. What did they need? Two loans, perhaps?

At that moment they spotted me. I gave them an awkward smile and felt embarrassed to be caught snooping around.

"Mr. Wingrave," I said. "How do you do? Have you come to fetch Caro yourself?"

"I'm fine, Beatrice," he said, clasping my extended hand with both of his strong, large ones. He had a grip that could crush bones. "And yes, if I didn't drive to campus myself this girl might spend another hour primping before the mirror. I'm attempting to stop her from bringing ten pairs of shoes back to the Willows."

"Daddy, you exaggerate! Come on, help me get packed," Carolyn said, and swiftly took me by the arm.

We went upstairs to Carolyn's room, where she proceeded to slowly go through her wardrobe, pulling out a dress and discarding it, then another. Because Carolyn lived in a single, probably the most spacious single in the whole dorm, she had enough dresses to outfit two girls.

"I should see how Ginny's doing," I said. "This morning she was awfully nervous."

"She should be. She's about to have Thanksgiving dinner with her future in-laws."

"No, she wasn't nervous about that."

"Blue or green? I can't decide," Carolyn said, and held up a couple of sweaters for me to inspect.

"I think there's something wrong with her. She complains someone's following her."

"There's always something wrong with Gin-gin. She's such a melodramatic child." Carolyn lowered the sweaters, tossing them aside. "Betty, you really need to do my hair, Mother's maid never gets it the way I like it."

"What if she's right, Caro? What if someone's been spying on her? I know it sounds strange, but—"

"You worry too much. Ginny has butterflies in her stomach from staring at Edgar, that's all. Maybe she feels a bit out of sorts, but a love affair does that sometimes; it drives you mad for a season. My hair, Betty, you must work your magic on it."

Carolyn sat down at her dressing table—another benefit of having a single was the extra furniture she could fit in there—and looked at the mirror with expectant eyes. I'd brushed and curled Carolyn's hair plenty of times and didn't mind being something of a handmaiden to her, but I felt exasperated that morning. Carolyn wasn't paying attention to anything I was saying.

I was about to begin brushing Carolyn's hair when Ginny's scream reverberated through the walls of Joyce House. I immediately dropped the brush and ran back to my room.

When I stepped inside, I found Ginny pointing at her bed, her eyes wide. A dead rat lay upon the bedsheets. It was on its back, its feet curled tight.

"Someone put it there," Ginny said. "Someone put it."

Carolyn had followed me and looked over my shoulder. She shook her head. "All this fuss over a rat? Virginia, it must have swallowed poison and crawled into your bed. By Jove, don't cry, I'll ask the house mother to clean it up. Virginia? Gin-gin?"

Ginny did not react to Carolyn's words. She looked as if the life had been leached out of her body, just a husk of a girl leaning against the doorway.

Other girls were beginning to poke their heads into the room, asking what was wrong. I grabbed Ginny's hand and walked down the stairs with her as she blubbered about the rat. I hoped Mr. Wingrave hadn't heard the screams; the house mother would be furious if she found out a parent was around while one of us was causing a commotion. It reflected badly on her; it meant she had a lax hand with the girls. In turn, the house mother might administer a punishment, or be stricter with us. I simply did not want trouble and needed to calm Ginny down.

We stepped outside. Ginny took a gulp of fresh air and crossed her arms.

"Caro's right. It must have ingested poison and crawled onto your bed," I said, although as far as I knew the handyman used traps, not poison, to deal with any vermin. But rats nibbled on everything. It might have chewed the wrong type of morsel.

"I've found several dead flies by the windowsill. Two dead moths. Everything is dying in this house," Ginny said, her breath curling up like smoke in the cool November air.

She clutched my hand tight and more than that, she clutched my heart. I wished to throw my arms around her and hold her, but then a car came up to the front of the house. Edgar stepped out of it and Ginny rushed to greet him.

She practically leaped into his arms and Edgar laughed happily. I went into the house and climbed the stairs back to Carolyn's room. I did her hair as she liked it, my fingers slow and mechanical. Afterward, I stood at the doorway of our room and looked into it. Someone, likely the house mother, had gotten rid of the rat and taken away the linens. Ginny had apparently left with Edgar without saying goodbye to me. Her swift departure dampened my spirits.

Yet Thanksgiving was a merry affair, with enough cranberry sauce, mashed potatoes, gravy, and delicious turkey to feed an army. I did think about Ginny, wondering how she was doing, but the small hurt she'd caused me faded like a bruise. I longed to see her again.

Our recess lasted five days.

I returned to campus on Saturday and was surprised to find Ginny was already back. Most of the girls would try to extend their holiday until the very last minute and head back on Sunday evening, especially the ones who had family in the area. I figured Ginny would want to be with Edgar. The reason why I'd hurried to Joyce House was the work-learn program: I needed to finish preparing a few lessons in French.

When I opened the door, Ginny was sitting on the floor with a pocketknife in her hands. She looked up at me and smiled. I was caught off guard and merely stared at her, my joy at her reappearance mingled with apprehension.

"Betty, how was Gloucester?" she asked.

"It was fine," I said cautiously. "Is there something wrong?"

"Not really." She stood up and brushed her hands against her skirt. "Well, maybe yes, but it's hard to explain. Betty, if I tell you, you mustn't be upset with me, please. Edgar is already angry."

"Why? What happened?"

"Lately I've felt as if something is amiss. I've told Edgar about this, but he doesn't seem to understand what the trouble is. While I was staying with Edgar's family, I wrote a little and the spirits provided me with answers. I've placed protective charms around the room."

"What do you mean, protective charms?"

"I spoke to the spirits about it, and I looked it up in this book," she said, eagerly grabbing one of the volumes on the pile by the bed and handing it to me.

"*A History of Witchcraft Lore,*" I said, reading the words stamped on the cover. I picked up a second book, then a third. "*The Witch-Cult in Western Massachusetts.* Ginny, what is all this?"

"It'll keep me safe. But Edgar is convinced it's my interest in Spiritualism that has me upset, that this is the root of my problems. It isn't."

"Then what's the root of it?"

"Witchcraft. I am now sure of it."

I laughed. It was a thin, nervous laugh. I didn't mean to mock her. But at once Ginny's face grew guarded. It was as if someone had turned a light off. She took the book from my hands and tossed it on her bed, then she picked up the pocketknife.

"I should return this to Santiago," she said. "He's downstairs, fixing something in the house mother's apartment."

"Ginny, I'm sorry," I said.

"It's fine, Betty. I realize how ridiculous I must seem to all of you. No wonder Edgar is tired of me."

"You're not ridiculous. Never!"

She sighed. We walked downstairs. The door to the house mother's apartment was open and we called her name. Instead of the woman, Santiago greeted us, rubbing a rag between his hands and nodding.

"Miss Price is at Ledge House," he said. "She said she'd be right back."

"I wanted to return this," Ginny said, handing him the pocket-knife. "Thank you."

Santiago tucked it in a pocket of his denim overalls. "You're welcome, Miss Virginia. Oh, thank you for telling Miss Carolyn about me. She might've found something for me over at her father's business."

"That's wonderful, Santiago," Ginny said. I bit my tongue. If the conversation I had heard between Carolyn and her father indicated anything about their finances, I doubted they'd be taking him on. But I supposed Carolyn must be attempting to maintain appearances.

The young man smiled and looked down. He stuffed the rag in another pocket. Ginny and I went to the kitchen and made ourselves two cups of tea.

"You quarreled with Edgar, didn't you?" I asked. "That's why you came back sooner than expected."

"Yes. He thinks I'm a fool." Ginny carefully picked up her cup of tea and took a sip. "But I saw him again, Betty. While we were in Boston. Standing outside Edgar's house."

"The man in the blue overcoat?"

"The same."

"Perhaps you would be able to describe him to the police. He might be a criminal who targets young women like us."

"He's not a criminal. Don't you see, Betty? There's evil out there. I can feel it, like I can almost feel the cold beyond that glass pane," she said in a low voice.

I looked at the landscape outside. Trees and the soft whiteness of fresh snow, and beyond the trees the dormitories, the two ponds, the library, and the classrooms that constituted Stoneridge. A picture-perfect college that deserved to appear on postcards. What evil could reside here? Yet as the snow fell, and even with the kitchen warm and cozy, I had to suppress a shiver.

"Anyway, I didn't see his face this time, either. I knew it was him, though. It's always him. The dead rat, the dead flies and the moths, the lights in the trees, they're simply symptoms. He is the disease."

"Did you tell Edgar about this?"

"Not quite. But he thinks I'm a madwoman nevertheless. My father telephoned Edgar while I was there. Someone wrote to him saying my nerves are frayed, that I need help. They spent a good half hour discussing my 'mental stability,' or lack thereof. I couldn't help it. I broke down in tears and Edgar held me in his arms, but he doesn't believe me."

She quickly set her cup down and clutched my hands, anguish ravaging her beautiful face. "Betty, whatever happens, you must believe me. Promise me, please. Even if the rest of the world yells that I have gone mad, please believe me."

"I will," I said.

My words soothed her, and she picked up her cup again. A few minutes later we saw Santiago trudging through the snow in the direction of Briar's Commons. He wrapped his ragged winter coat around his shoulders and pulled a cap down over his dark hair.

It was the first of December. On December 19, Virginia would go missing. We had less than three weeks left together, though of course I could not know that. Or perhaps I did know. After all, a terrible, restless darkness had been inching toward her every day. I had sensed it, I had almost tasted it, yet I had dismissed it as nonsense.

In the end, I had not believed her, despite my steadfast promises. In the end, I left her to face that terrible, hungry darkness on her own.

# 1998: 7

MINERVA CAREFULLY TOOK OUT Thomas's books and notebooks from the boxes, spreading them around her. She found two books on legends of New England and what appeared to be a bibliography that further expanded on that subject, likely for use in a course taught by Christina Everett, since her name appeared on several documents, including a syllabus and some of his time sheets. She noticed that *Bell, Book, and Candle: Witchcraft in the New World* was among the titles in the bibliography and had been circled with a red pen, the words "crucial to find" written next to the title. Other books with similar themes also made an appearance: *A History of Witchcraft Lore, The Witchcraft Delusion of 1692, The Witch-Cult in Western Massachusetts,* and many more. These titles matched ones Ginny had been reading in 1934, before her disappearance, and which Betty had noted in her manuscript and her journal.

She drifted into the library and sat on one of the couches. As she dialed a number, she contemplated the stuffed birds and the shadow boxes with butterflies decorating the walls of Ledge House. She thought of Nana Alba when she sat by the window and talked to a parrot that was dead, her mind gone dim. Old age could wreck the human brain, but perhaps insidious thoughts could ruin it in one's youth, chipping away at one's sanity.

"Hello?" a woman's voice said.

"Hi, is this Emily Murphy? I'm Minerva, one of the resident directors at Stoneridge College."

"Stoneridge. Right. Someone already called about my brother's stuff and my car is in the shop right now so I really can't say when I can drive there to pick up the things he left behind."

"That's fine. No rush." Minerva paused and fiddled with the spiral binding of a notebook. "Actually, I wanted to ask you about Thomas. Has he been in touch with you? The last email we had from him was in January."

"Yeah, that's when he emailed me."

"He hasn't talked to you since then?" she asked, sitting back on the couch. She placed the notebook aside.

"No."

"It doesn't worry you? It's been months."

The woman sighed. There was a brief silence. "He did this before. He dropped out after the first year, he said it was too much. He moved in with a girl I'd never heard about and three months later he was back in Massachusetts. He dropped out like that, in a heartbeat. I thought he'd figured out his life this time around, but I suppose I was wrong. He's a smart guy, but he's high-strung. He doesn't take pressure well."

Minerva twisted the phone cord between her fingers.

"Look, we weren't the best of friends, especially after he took that time off to figure what he wanted to do with his life and basically mooched off me for months. He's my brother, but it's a small apartment and he's a little difficult, you know?"

Minerva recalled the constant quarrels between Thomas and Conrad Carter and pictured a similar situation.

"He didn't even come home for Thanksgiving. It's an hour away and he preferred to have dinner with that buddy of his."

"What buddy?"

"Noah something. He tutored him, I can't remember what subject it was. Probably art. Yes, art. That's what Tom was interested in."

"Noah Yates?" Minerva asked, clutching the phone close against her ear.

"Maybe. Listen, I gotta run. I'll pick up his stuff next month. Maybe he might even be back by then, who knows?"

"Yeah, who knows," Minerva muttered.

She hung up the phone, then began poking into the boxes again, pulling out more books, marked papers, a few CDs. She found a planner and tucked in it there was a printout of Thomas's tutoring schedule.

"Noah Yates, Tuesdays and Thursdays, six P.M.," she whispered. "AMS 513."

She fished out a course catalogue from under a pile of books and flipped through its pages. AMS 513 corresponded to a special seminar titled Religion in Puritan New England, taught by Christina Everett. It hadn't been art at all.

A folder containing Thomas's tutoring paperwork and class materials also had the syllabus for AMS 513, which matched a few, though not all, of the books she'd found on the sheet with the bibliography. Robert Derie's *Bell, Book, and Candle: Witchcraft in the New World,* which he'd seemed so keen on, was not listed as required reading.

"Crucial," she said, looking at that sheet again. "Crucial for what? What were you researching?"

She grabbed her laptop and plugged it into the Ethernet port. She jumped onto the NOBLE Libraries page and typed the title into a search box. There was a copy of the book at Stoneridge, but it was checked out. She tried a few of the other titles. *A History of Witchcraft Lore* was nowhere nearby. She switched to the Boston Public Library page and the title popped up on the screen. The book had been published in 1928 and one copy was available at the Central Library branch. *Bell, Book, and Candle: Witchcraft in the New World* was also quite old—1925—which was probably why the books were proving elusive.

She tapped a pen against her notepad then unfolded an MBTA timetable and phoned Noah.

"Yeah?" he said.

"Hey, it's Minerva. I was wondering if we could meet today."

"My grandmother's not in right now. I'm guessing you want to look at papers, but if you need to talk to her, you'll have to wait. Does that work for you?"

"No. I mean, yes. Yes, I want to look at the papers. And I'm wondering if I could talk to you. I need to take the train into Boston, but I should be back after . . ." She paused, looking at the timetable. "After six. Is that too late?"

"That's fine."

She hung up and quickly dialed Hideo and asked him for a ride to the station. He arrived a few minutes later. Two air fresheners in the shape of palm trees swung back and forth from his rearview mirror.

"Jump in!"

"You're a lifesaver," she said, and tossed her backpack onto the back seat. "Thanks."

"I need to go into town anyway. I'm out of soda. You can't write a thesis without caffeine and bubbles. What time should I pick you up?"

"I'll be on the five-fifteen train."

"That's great. We can have dinner and do the rounds at nine."

"Actually, would you mind dropping me off at the Willows on the way back?" she asked.

"Are you going to look at documents again?"

"Yeah. I can't do dinner, and don't worry about the rounds, I'll handle it."

"I don't mind going over there," he said in a tone that indicated it would be easier if she simply agreed to it.

"Okay, I'll call you when I get back into the house, how's that? And I got you a little something for your efforts," she said, holding up a CD case between two fingers.

"Is it the Sneaker Pimps I wanted?"

"No. But you might like it."

He pressed a button and the CD player sprang to life. Molotov played as they headed to the train depot. Hideo tapped his fingers against the steering wheel.

She hadn't been in Boston in a while, and it was strange to step out of North Station and into the city with its chaotic traffic and knotted web of streets. After the silence on campus, it was a cacophony of sounds that made her pull out the Discman from her backpack and put the headphones on. Music, even when a singer was screaming their head off, was easier to process than random people in the streets or the honking of horns. You could get lost in music.

She took the subway to Copley Square and bounded up the library's stairs while Babes in Toyland blared in her ears. She found *A History of Witchcraft Lore* and walked toward Bates Hall. The great reading room of the BPL resembled a Roman basilica, with a soaring, ornate ceiling and light filtering through its tall windows. Upon the dark oak tables sat green glass-shaded lamps, and patrons read their books in reverent silence. She pulled out a chair and snapped the book open.

From a glance at the table of contents, it didn't seem to be a particularly interesting compendium, and she couldn't quite figure out why Thomas and Virginia would both have been so keen on it. She noticed that a corner had been turned down in the book, as if to mark a page, and opened it to that section.

A quote by King James from his 1597 book, *Daemonologie*, appeared at the top of the page. It read: *For some of them sayeth, that being transformed in the likenesse of a little beast or foule, they will come and pearce through whatsoeuer house or Church, though all ordinarie passages be closed, by whatsoeuer open, the aire may enter in at.*

"Thresholds and witch marks," she said in a low voice, her finger running down the page. "An apotropaic mark, also called a witch mark, is a symbol or pattern scratched on the walls of a building to protect it from evil spirits. The word 'apotropaic' comes from the Greek word for 'averting evil.'

"The marks were usually scribed onto stone or woodwork, particularly near doorways, windows, and fireplaces. They have many forms. In England, they often have flowerlike patterns or overlapping circles."

She turned the page and looked at a drawing that was labeled as a medieval apotropaic mark from a church in Suffolk. It looked eerily like the sketches Virginia and Thomas had made.

"Apotropaic marks could also take the form of mazes and diagonal lines. Shapes and repeating patterns could be used to fool evil spirits. In Ireland, the burial of horse skulls under the floor may have served a similar purpose."

Minerva looked at another illustration showing more symbols that had been carved on a fireplace lintel.

Her great-grandmother had spoken about things like this, amulets to ward off evil. Her amulets had been made of pins and the body of a bird, but the purpose was the same, to cordon off a dwelling from witches. In the vast majority of cases, her great-grandmother said, witchcraft of the malicious kind does not amount to great harm. Witches may toy with a person, sour a day or two of their life, then move on to other matters. Their magic is often slight. A few witches, the ones born on a propitious day, who descend from a lineage of powerful witches, might attack in more nefarious manners. Yet they are often opportunistic creatures—stealing a hog to get back at a neighbor who slighted them might be the most they would attempt.

But a bewitchment, that is a different tale. It is a campaign, a siege. Thus, other measures must be taken. How do you bewitch someone? Hexes come in myriad shapes. A witch could make an effigy of their enemy, stuff a bottle with nails, or simply draw a sigil on their property. That's what Nana Alba had said, and now Minerva's mind drifted back to the black marks she'd found on her door.

She checked out *A History of Witchcraft Lore* and another book on witchcraft in medieval England then stepped out of the library.

HIDEO PICKED HER UP at the train depot at the appointed time. He played "New Music Machine" and offered her konpeitō from a tin. She popped one of the candies into her mouth while he bobbed his head.

Hideo stopped in front of the Willows and whistled. "Wow. That's a big house. These people are loaded."

"I know," she said as she unbuckled her seatbelt.

Noah opened the front door himself before she was able to step out of the car. He had reverted from the too-formal outfit he'd worn last time to a faded T-shirt. He waved at her as he stood by the doorway.

"Is that Noah Yates?" Hideo practically stuck half his body out of the car, trying to get a good look at him.

"Yep."

"He's kind of cute. Terrible haircut, though. You would think with all that cash the man would find a decent stylist. Hey, do you get invited to dinner when you come over here?"

"I've had tea with Mrs. Yates."

"What do they serve with the tea? I mean, do you have caviar? You know, I went to the Master's Tea in November, and they don't give you proper drinks nowadays, but someone told me back in the fifties they had wine and martinis and—"

"Master's Tea?"

"Yeah. You know, the reception they throw in Walden Hall. It's part of a lecture series."

"That's not the name of it."

"What's it called, then?"

"I have to go," she said as she snatched her backpack from the back seat.

"Well, do they feed you caviar or not?"

"Bye," she said with finality.

Hideo shrugged and adjusted the volume of the stereo. "You're no fun, Minerva."

He drove away and she hurried to the door. "Sorry, my friend is chatty. Thanks for agreeing to see me."

"No problem. Come in. Carolyn's off in Boston getting examined for every illness known to mankind, so if you have questions about Betty Tremblay you'll have to return another time," he said. "She won't be back until tomorrow."

"Is she okay? Are her hands giving her trouble?"

"She's fine. She loves to get her checkups every six months. She adores it when she goes into the hospital and the doctors hover around her. She says she plans to live to over a hundred."

"My great-grandmother lived to a hundred and one."

"Is that so?"

They walked into the room where they'd had tea the previous time. Noah plopped himself down on the high-backed chair that his grandmother had used. Behind him loomed the portrait of the gray-haired man.

"My great-grandfather was also long-lived," Noah said. "Lived to be ninety-eight, which is probably why Carolyn wants to beat him at the longevity record."

"That's him behind you, right?"

Noah looked over his shoulder and nodded. "Mr. Wesley Noah Wingrave, after whom I'm named. Not that my grandmother thinks me worthy of the name, mind you. Carolyn painted that portrait." He turned to look at her again. "Anyway, you said you wanted to talk about something?"

"Yes. I heard you're Thomas Murphy's friend. I was his resident director."

"Thomas was my tutor," Noah said. "He came over sometimes to help me with my papers. I'm not sure I'd call him a friend, though."

"But you invited him over for Thanksgiving dinner."

"My grandmother did. She felt sorry for the guy. His sister was mad at him because he owed her money, and he didn't want to have dinner with her. His dad lives in Miami, and he wasn't going to fly there. He spent most of the time talking with Carolyn, not with me. I was busy drinking myself into a stupor. Why are you asking about him? He dropped out."

"Paperwork," Minerva said. "He left a couple of boxes behind at the dorm and I need to get them back to him. His sister doesn't know where he is, but she mentioned your name. Have you talked to him lately?"

"No. All we ever talked about was homework and class bullshit. I didn't like him much and he didn't like me, either. He chatted with Carolyn about art. I couldn't care less about painters and sculptors."

She didn't know what else to say and was grateful when Noah offered to take her to the library. He left after a few minutes, and she quickly pulled out Virginia's drawings and set them on the table. Then she took out Thomas's drawings and her copy of *A History of Witchcraft Lore*. Thomas's and Virginia's drawings were almost identical. They had an eerie similarity to the apotropaic marks in the book.

Christina Everett taught AMS 513, which likely meant that she knew Thomas well and might even have been his adviser. The page with the bibliography might have been for a paper for a class she taught, or research for Thomas's thesis. Minerva decided to email her and ask her if she knew anything about Thomas's work, because she couldn't let go of the idea that there was something to be found if she continued poking around. A dark thread wove everything together.

But for now, she needed to concentrate on her research, not get dragged away by flights of fancy. She grabbed Beatrice's manuscript and began diligently scribbling her notes. Noah came by later carrying a tray with two plates and two glasses of milk. She slipped off her beaten-up headphones and paused her Discman, silencing Bowie in the middle of "Strangers When We Meet."

"The staff has the day off since Carolyn's not around, so you get a baloney sandwich," Noah said. "It's what I used to make when friends came over to the house when I was a kid."

She laughed.

"What?" he asked.

"My friend asked if you were serving caviar."

"I fill the pool with it every Sunday."

This elicited another laugh from her. She stretched her arms and rubbed the back of her neck before grabbing the sandwich. She'd spent two hours bent over the table and her body felt stiff and uncomfortable.

"It's hard to believe it happened, isn't it?"

"I'm sorry?" she replied.

"Salem," he said, and pointed at her book on New England witches. She'd left it open to a page showing men in Puritan outfits undressing a woman and pointing at her back, presumably at a birthmark or wart that would be used as evidence against her. "Salem's a carnival nowadays. Witch Town USA. All they do is sell memorabilia with cartoon witches sitting on brooms or cute black cats nestled between pumpkins. But back in the day, people took this stuff seriously."

"There's a theory that it was moldy bread." He stared at her. She took a bite out of the sandwich. "Linnda Caporael theorized that there was an outbreak of ergotism. Basically, there's a type of fungus that can grow on crops and cause hallucinations in people who consume it."

"When I was a kid, I was terrified by stories of witches and demons."

"You said you spent a lot of time overhearing stories of headless horsemen and evil black cats."

"Sure. And they scared me silly. I suppose you liked those stories? Horror tales. Movies like *The Amityville Horror* and *Poltergeist*."

"In a way," she said, her voice growing cautious.

He laughed. "You don't want me to know anything about you, do you? What do you do for fun, can you tell me that?"

She slowly tore off the crust from the sandwich and shrugged.

"I thought I saw a ghost one time at the factory," he said, and she looked up at him. "Ah, now I've got your attention."

She smiled at that. He seemed pleased with the reaction. She supposed he was used to people finding him charming and expected her to behave accordingly. Not that she knew how to behave with charming people. And there was always the danger that all those charmers were assholes in disguise, like Conrad Carter.

But she figured she could at least answer his question honestly.

"I've always been concerned with the idea of absolute evil. There's cruelty in all those stories. Witches committing terrible deeds to get their kicks—but then if you spin it around and look at the witch trials, you have innocent people who are being accused of something simply because their neighbors have a petty grudge against them."

"A petty grudge, and they ate moldy bread."

She nodded and checked her wristwatch. "Yeah. I need to head back to campus. I have rounds at nine. Thanks for the sandwich."

"You have rounds? There's no one there."

"There's a few people and it's part of the job," she said as she placed her books and notebook in her backpack.

"I'll give you a ride. It's better and faster than walking back in the dark."

"Thanks. I appreciate it."

He drove the vintage white car that day. When he held the door open for her, she raised an eyebrow at him.

"I thought you were not supposed to borrow your grandmother's car."

"Are you going to tell on me?"

"No," she said, and hopped in.

During the short drive, she chewed on the cap of a blue pen, hoping Hideo hadn't arrived and been waiting for her. Soon the silhouette of Ledge House appeared ahead. Hideo's car was not there yet. She'd returned on time.

Noah parked and turned to her. "Door to door."

"Thanks again."

"Well, you didn't complain about my lousy baloney sandwich, so you deserved a prize. By the way, if you want to visit the inside of the factory, we could do it tomorrow, before Carolyn gets back. We can grab the keys and pop in and out. It's not the same as swimming in the caviar pool, but what can I say?"

There really wasn't much that interested her inside the factory, but she supposed it was a chance to talk to him again, and she wanted to see if she could get more information from him. Granted, she wasn't quite sure *what* she was even after. One moment she felt like asking him about Thomas, the next she figured she should focus on Beatrice, then she considered discussing Carolyn.

"Okay, how about eleven?" she replied.

"Sounds good."

He drove away and she climbed the steps up to the back door of the house. She tossed the backpack on the floor and turned on the lights. God, her neck ached. She had terrible posture. Her mother said she was going to end up a hunchback at forty because of the way she bent over her books. Maybe she was right.

Minerva closed her eyes and rubbed the back of her neck. She opened them again. On the kitchen table she noticed a dark lump and stepped closer: it was a dead rat, with its feet sticking up in the air.

# 1908: 7

SEVERAL OF THE CHICKENS had stopped laying eggs even though they were young and healthy. Her mother accepted the news with stoic practicality. She said they would butcher them and have them for supper.

The butchering always made Alba flinch. Her mother would grab a chicken by the legs, lay its head against a chopping block, and cut it off with one sure swoop of the axe. Then she'd tie its feet together and hang it to prevent the headless animal from thrashing around on the ground.

Alba despised everything about this process, from the boiling of the water to the cutting of the chicken meat. That afternoon, her mother chopped off the heads of two birds and hung them, and Alba shoved a bucket beneath the animals to collect their blood.

They were supposed to scald and pluck the animals next, but Alba kept thinking about Tadeo and how he always made fun of her when she had to handle the animals. He called her "princess," mocked her for her squeamishness. One time, when she'd cracked an egg and found blood at its center, she'd shrieked in horror and Tadeo had teased her about it for a whole week.

He mocked her and they fought, but she mocked him too, and in the end their quarrels ended with a hug. But he wasn't there anymore; he wouldn't smile during dinner and ask if Alba had fainted this time around.

Alba's mother said a woman should not fear blood. Blood was a woman's destiny anyway, each month there was blood between her thighs, so blood from a bird should not frighten her.

Alba removed the viscera of one of the birds, which shone like jewels against the palm of her hand, and wondered if the witch had carved her brother open like this and pulled out his ruby-red heart.

She began to cry. Fernanda and Magdalena, who were helping her mother in the kitchen, stared at her in surprise.

"What is it?" her mother asked.

"We are cursed and Tadeo is dead," she said, unthinking.

Fernanda almost dropped the pot that she was carrying, and Magdalena looked at them in confusion. Her mother grabbed Alba by the arm and pulled her out of the kitchen.

"Don't you say that, especially in front of one of the servants," she chided, in a voice that was almost a hiss. "I don't need them thinking of phantoms when they're working."

"It's true, Mother. We've been bewitched."

"What is true is that people are superstitious, and if you frighten them, they'll leave, and then who will help around here? Don't be silly, Alba. You're no use to me like this. Go wash yourself and come back, there is more work to be done."

She hurried up the stairs and washed her hands in the porcelain basin, tinging the water pink with blood. When she ventured downstairs, instead of returning to her mother's side, she slipped into the parlor. She rubbed a hand against her eyes.

"Are you unwell, Alba?" Arturo asked.

She turned around and shook her head. "I was cutting onions," she lied.

He stood at the doorway and looked at her skeptically. "It must have been a large number of onions," he said as he walked past her, moving toward the piano.

"I suppose the kitchen is not my place."

"Very likely not."

He pulled out the piano bench and tapped his fingers against the keys, wringing a lovely melody from the instrument. She edged closer to him, mesmerized by the music.

"Do you like it?" he asked. "I played it at a salon in Mexico City. It's a waltz by Waldteufel."

"Oh, it's beautiful, but you should play 'Over the Waves.' I love that one. I'd like to dance it at a big party one day."

"Will you wear a pretty dress?"

"Yes, a watered-silk pink taffeta dress," she said, and smiled, brushing her fingers against the hollow of her throat. "And diamonds in my ears and around my neck."

Arturo turned his head and looked at her. "I might have thought to buy you diamonds, except that you don't seem to like my gifts."

"I don't know what you mean."

"The necklace I gave you." He pressed a key and then repeated the note. "You seem to have switched it for a cheap locket."

Her hand wrapped around Valentín's locket, she glanced at the floor. "I was in the kitchen butchering chickens, Uncle. I can't wear pearls there," she said, for she didn't want to tell him the locket was blessed and she feared removing it lest a terrible evil befall her.

"No, I suppose not."

His face was stiff and the notes he drew from the piano this time seemed harsh. He began slapping the keys, his fingers flying up and down.

A creature of passions, a weather vane, that's what Arturo was. She'd heard her father say as much. He had not meant it as a compliment, but Alba found the image enticing. To be able to turn and be swept away by one's heart as swiftly as a leaf is carried by a current, rather than taking root like an oak: this seemed to her exciting and commendable.

Yet his frenetic energy was different from his anger, and this strain of darkness, of sharp rage that spiked beneath the notes, was not something she enjoyed.

Arturo's hands stilled on the keys. The room was quiet. Alba's body had tensed as much as piano wire; his swiftly changing mood filled her with trepidation.

"You're a talented player, Uncle," she said, to try to dispel whatever dark cloud had intruded into his thoughts. "They must like you very much in the city."

"I suppose they do," he said. The compliment seemed to have the desired effect. His face relaxed. He loved when people spoke of the city, loved to describe its streets and its sights.

"You must miss it, I'm sure. All the people and the parties there and—" *And your lover,* she thought. She practically covered her mouth with a hand to stop herself from speaking.

"And what?" he asked, looking at her with curious eyes.

She shouldn't talk of illicit affairs; her mother would be appalled to learn she'd been inquiring about such things. But Alba bit her lip and sat down on the piano bench next to him. She spoke in a soft voice.

"And the lady you love. The one you can't live with. Does her family dislike you? Is that why you can't be together? Is she married?"

He laughed. "Is that the image you have of me? I'm a dissolute cad who seduces married women?"

"You're handsome, and all ladies must find you pleasing," she said. He also liked to be complimented about his looks, his charm, and she knew her words would win another laugh from his lips.

"Even married ones?" he replied.

"Yes. The lady in question must be beautiful, but her husband is bound to be horrid. He would chase you down the street with a pistol if he knew about you."

"You have a wicked imagination."

"Have I guessed right?" she asked.

Arturo leaned forward, his lips close to her ear. "I won't tell you."

He lowered his eyes. Arturo's eyelashes were as long and sharp as daggers and the slant of his mouth as he smiled made for the most delightful of portraits.

"*You* are the wicked one," she said, and smiled in turn. "Confess! I wish to hear about your sins and follies."

"No."

He glanced up at her suddenly, his eyes serious, the smile receding.

"Suppose I really am sinful, what would you do then, Alba? Your opinion of me matters greatly. I cannot afford to have it diminished," he said.

He spoke with a heartbreaking sadness and his melancholic expression turned his appealing good looks into something that edged on the hypnotic.

"Nothing you'd say would alter my feelings," she replied, matching his low, mournful tone.

Such was the closeness of their faces and the angle of their bodies that in one tilt of the head their breath might mingle together. Her pulse fluttered like a bird, and she knew well enough that there was indeed something wicked in her blood.

"Perhaps," he said, and a dangerous eagerness flashed in his eyes, as fast and ferocious as lightning, but he lowered his gaze once more.

Arturo stood up, stretching with the nimbleness of a cat. He was smiling again, politely, and she realized he wore that cordial smile like a mask, and now his voice was disguised too, flatly pleasant like his expression.

"I'll tell you my lover's name, but not today," he said with a joviality that was false, and she laughed at him with an equally false humor. Why, they were playing! Why, it was but a little teasing!

Then he strode out of the room.

Alba stretched out a hand and touched the piano keys where his fingers had rested before quickly standing up, brushing her skirts, and running outside. She needed air. She needed to breathe. She ran until she reached the bank of the river, and there she stumbled and lay down upon the grass.

She rested by the river, on a bed of green, for an endless expanse of time, staring at the dappled sunlight streaming through the branches of trees. She lay there, racked with shivering sighs, and closed her eyes.

Her thoughts strayed, wild and unfettered, back to Valentín. She remembered his kiss and the pressure of his rough hands against her cheek. She had not imagined herself fancying a man like him. She had always wanted a refined man, a cultured man, a man who was more like . . . well, more like Uncle Arturo.

For one second, she imagined that she had recklessly tipped her head forward when they'd been at the piano and kissed him.

She opened her eyes wide.

She propped herself up on her elbows and anxiously looked in the direction of Piedras Quebradas.

She ought to run back to the kitchen. Her mother would be angry if she didn't. But she feared Luisa would look into her eyes and discern her sinful nature. The grass had stained her dress and the sun had begun to drift low.

With a flutter of skirts, she rushed into the sitting room, where her mother was bent over a piece of cloth, needle in hand. Her sister Magdalena was also busy stitching something. By their mother's feet, Lola and Moisés played quietly with a pair of wooden horses. On the piano, the twins practiced their scales.

It was a charming show of domesticity. Quickly she sat down and began to embroider the handkerchief Valentín had given her. She had thought to gift it back to him, monogrammed. The steady work of the needle soothed her, and she was able to keep her eyes down, busy with her work, so that her mother had no chance to look into them.

"Where did you go earlier?" her mother asked.

"For a walk, by the river," Alba said simply.

"You were out for a long time."

"Was I?"

She sensed her mother's heavy gaze, but Alba did not look up. She felt that if they'd been alone, she might have been questioned more thoroughly. But surrounded by her siblings, Alba was able to shield herself with silence.

She had trouble going to sleep that night. She tossed and turned in bed, rearranging the pillows, hugging them tight and then shoving them away. She lay on her back in the dark. A beam of moonlight slipped in between the curtains and Alba turned her head toward the window.

The light filtering into her room, however, was odd. It had a greenish tinge that made her frown. She stepped toward the window and tugged at the curtains, looking out.

The light did not come from the moon. It seemed to drift down from one of the peppercorn trees as if someone had hung a lantern among its branches. Unlike the light of a lantern, this greenish glow had no source—it was diffused, as hard to pinpoint as mist. It was, in fact, so faint you could hardly see it, and for one moment Alba thought it was an optical illusion.

Yet as Alba looked at it, the mist seemed to coalesce, its color growing stronger, from a faint green to a brighter hue closer to the shade of an emerald. It looked now like a sphere, trembling in the tree branches and burning like an ember.

The phantasmagoric light made Alba think of diseased flesh, of rot and decomposition. She stepped back from the window, recognizing this strange light. She'd never seen it herself, though she'd heard about it enough times growing up to name it: it was the glow of a witch, outside her window, like a hideous, gigantic firefly.

The ball of light let out a long, doleful cry, an ululation that resembled that of an owl. Except she'd heard owls all her life, knew their hoots and the noise of their wings, and this was different.

The branches of the peppercorn tree drooped, as if pressed down by a great weight.

She backed away from the window, one hand wrapped tight around the medallion that hung from her neck. The glow seemed to strengthen, bathing her room with tones of emerald that crept upon the floor, like long fingers stretching in her direction.

Alba felt fear like she had never felt before. Terror clawed at her throat as fiercely as a tiger, stopping her from uttering the softest of cries, and her heart beat so quickly, her breathing accelerated with such violence, that she felt dizzy and almost faint.

She managed to stumble against her door and with clumsy hands pawed the doorknob. For a second her eyes were awash with such bright green that it was like staring into the sun or a searing flame.

Alba managed to pry the door open and stumbled into the hallway. Flecks of green danced before her eyes and she hurried toward her mother's room, slamming her hands against the door.

"What is it?"

"There's something outside," she said.

Alba's mother opened the door. She held up a brass chamberstick in her right hand with a half-burned candle.

"You must come with me," Alba said before her mother could ask another question.

She pulled her by the arm, and they went as quickly as they could, but when they stood at the doorway of Alba's room, it was all in shadows.

"It was here," Alba said, and pointed at the window. "In the trees. It was floating there. It woke me. It screamed."

"An owl?" her mother asked.

"No, although it was noisy as one. It glowed. It burned."

They looked out the window. There was no wind to make the branches of the tree shiver, no whisper from the treetops. The moon lay hidden behind clouds. It was so dark outside that even if someone had been holding a lantern it might have been difficult to glimpse the trees.

"You've had a nightmare," her mother said.

"It was real. It's a witch. It's taunting us," Alba said, breathless, the words a jumble.

Her mother sighed. "Alba, I told you not to speak nonsense. If the servants or the children should hear you—"

"But there's something out there," Alba insisted. "It took Tadeo."

"Tadeo was probably kidnapped by bandits."

"What bandits? They'd have returned him by now. A witch killed him and ate his heart."

"Hush," her mother said sternly, and she drew the curtains closed tight with a harsh motion of her wrist. "You had a dream."

"It's true. It could break through a window tonight and take one of the little ones, it could—"

"Stop it," her mother ordered. Her eyes were narrowed in steely fury.

Alba stared at her mother. The light of the candle, held up with her steady hand, deepened the hollows and lines of her high-boned face.

"Do you think it is easy living like this, Alba? I am a widow. I've lost a son. I must take care of my younger children and be both mother and father to them on a farm that is beset with debts and misfortunes. By God, Alba, there are mornings when I can barely summon the strength to rise from my bed.

"You don't help me. You're an indolent child who shirks her responsibilities and spends her time daydreaming. Do you think I can afford to think of ghosts and witches? Maybe you can. You run out of the kitchen so you can fret with your hair and your dresses. I can't!"

Alba shook her head and looked down. She'd have no sympathy, no answers, from her mother. Her uncle could not provide any solace, either. They did not believe in curses or sorcerers. They could not see what she saw, shielded by their mundanity.

Her mother sighed. She pressed a hand against Alba's cheek. "I'm sorry, Alba. We're all exhausted. Go to sleep."

Alba kept her eyes on the floor. She heard the soft groan of the door as it closed. Slowly she slipped back into bed. She turned toward the window, which was a black rectangle, a void.

# 1998: 8

STEPPING INTO THE FACTORY was like slipping into the belly of a dead whale and roaming through its carcass, for this place had once been alive and now was nothing but a lonesome shell of itself.

They peeked inside workrooms where circular knitting machines lay covered under a fine layer of dust. The green walls of the building were peeling, and tools resting on benches had rusted. There were shelves piled with wooden boxes containing brightly colored threads that contrasted with the gray grimness of the surroundings. A pile of dyed fibers, left behind in a corner to be spun, was an orgiastic shade of red.

She'd woken up with a funny feeling that morning, that old itch in the back of her skull that her great-grandmother used to call a portent. The sight of the red fibers made her want to recoil; something in the color triggered a sense of revulsion she could not explain.

"Did you really play here when you were a kid?" she asked, looking at Noah instead of the corner.

"I did."

"It doesn't look very safe," she said, glancing dubiously at the ceiling. "You say it closed in the eighties?"

"It's always been pretty run-down, even when it was still open. The good years of the business were probably the 1940s. They manufactured uniforms for the war. It brought the factory back from the dead, but it was downhill after that. For a while Carolyn had dreams that my father or my uncles would turn it all around, that they'd resurrect it."

She imagined the factory filled with the clanging and churning of hulking, well-oiled machinery, the rhythmic snapping and rattling of the looms, and the voices of the workers as they gathered for their lunch break.

She glanced once again at the red fibers, and she had the unpleasant sensation that she was being watched. What the hell was wrong with her these days?

She slipped out of that room, walking quickly. Noah followed at a more leisurely pace.

"My dad didn't have the knack for it. My great-grandfather, the beloved Wesley Noah Wingrave, he was a shark. But his sons and grandkids didn't cut it. My uncle Roy, he's a womanizer and an alcoholic who knows how to draw a monthly allowance and nothing more. Uncle Timothy is a nervous mess and even more incompetent. Dad, he had the smarts but hated the business. For a few months in the sixties, he became a hippie, joined a commune."

"Really? A hippie?"

"Not for long. Carolyn found him and dragged him back home. He was the oldest, the heir, and she wasn't letting him run off. He came back, got married, had me, and continued to be a great disappointment to my grandmother. Shortly before my parents died, he wanted to move us to Vermont and open an organic food store or something like that. Carolyn hated the idea, of course. She forbade him to even think about it."

They were standing in the middle of a long, empty room with tall windows. Two of the panes had been replaced with colored glass: yellow and green. She leaned down and looked through one of them. The world outside became a shade of emerald.

"What was your mother like? Was she also a hippie at one point?"

"No. She was a Cushing, of the Cushing Manufactory. My grandmother has always been strategic about marriages. You marry someone for the cold wads of cash, not for the love. My parents spent many miserable years together before they were buried in two nice plots, side by side. It's a family tradition, you know, to stay together with someone you can't stand."

She glanced down at the worn floorboards, then at him. "How did your parents die?"

"A freak accident. A truck driver had a heart attack and plowed right into them," he said simply.

"How old were you?"

"I was eight."

"I'm sorry."

"Yeah, you've said that before," he replied, and for a moment she thought he was irritated with her, but it was that veneer of indifference being peeled aside, showing the raw edges of the man. He shrugged. "Anyway, after that I moved in with my grandparents. Then Grandfather died, and it's me and Carolyn now."

Carolyn. The name was spat out, not really spoken. Noah stuffed his hands in his pockets with a smirk.

"Did you get along with your grandfather?"

The smirk still danced on his lips, but he took a breath, and the corners of his mouth trembled.

"He was okay, I suppose. It's funny being raised by old people. The thing they talk about is the past. How good it was, how much they miss it. I guess that's why I liked it when Betty would come over and talk to my grandfather. At least then they were talking about ghost stories, even if they scared me a little. It was something different. I still remember most of them. Want to hear one?"

"Which one was the scariest?"

"It would have to be the story of Anya Martin. She was a girl who was lured into the ocean by a mysterious singing voice and drowned. They say you can see her ghost walking around Glass Cove. It wasn't an especially gruesome story. I suppose it's because she was a kid that it frightened me much more than the other stories they told."

Noah leaned down next to her to look out the dirty yellow glass pane.

"It was a bit morbid, how they sat in front of the fire and swapped ghost stories. Carolyn hated it, but I liked it, for the most part. The only thing that bothered me was the Black List."

"What was that?"

He looked away from the window and stood up straight. "Come get a coffee with me. I'll tell you about it."

"You said you'd tell me about the time you saw a ghost in this building."

"I'll tell you about that over coffee, too," he said breezily.

They stepped out of the building, he locked the door through which they'd let themselves in, and they headed to Temperance Landing. There was one coffee shop on the main street—P. Jessup's Java Hut; the logo in bright yellow letters looked like it had been designed in the swinging sixties and never updated—and it was reliably packed with students during exam season. But in the summer the place seemed as deserted as the factory they'd visited. The corkboard, which was normally covered in notices advertising tutoring services or local events, had one lonesome sheet of paper promoting a reading club for children at the library.

They sat by the window. The furniture and décor inside were also of a dated psychedelic variety, from when students walking into this joint would have said "dig it" and "groovy" and found the yellow-and-orange wallpaper fashionable and vibrant instead of hideous.

"My grandfather figured we were living near the Bermuda Triangle because of the Black List. It was a sort of scrapbook. Betty and my grandfather kept a tally of missing people. Not just people near Temperance Landing: in all of New England."

She carefully measured a spoonful of sugar while he tipped the sugar dispenser with abandon. "How long was that list? I bet there are hundreds of disappearances every year, between people who run away and crimes," she said, sipping her coffee.

"The list had certain criteria, so you'd be disqualified if it looked like it was a run-of-the-mill teenage runaway or something that strongly indicated a crime. There had to be a certain element of the uncanny. I think that's how Betty defined it."

"Uncanny how?"

Noah shrugged. "I don't know. The stories were weird. Made a chill go down your spine."

"Give me an example."

He tilted his head back and tapped his fingers against the table.

"Jean Welden in Vermont. She was a student at Bennington College in the forties. She went for a hike, people saw her turn a corner of the trail, and then she vanished. Or Danny Williams, a Harvard student who was involved with Warhol's Factory in the sixties. He went back home to Rockport, borrowed his mother's car for a drive, and was never seen again, but his clothes were found by the ocean. Those were the stories that interested them the most, the ones that happened in Massachusetts, and the closer to Temperance Landing the better."

"How many disappearances happened near Temperance Landing?"

"I don't remember all of them. Five, maybe six in modern times? There were cases that went back a couple of centuries. Susan King, she's the one I remember the most. She lived in Temperance Landing sometime in the 1960s. She'd had a stroke and could only walk with the aid of a cane. She was confined to her home. Two nurses and her niece watched over her.

"One morning one of the nurses shows up, ready for her shift. She finds that there's a teapot and a warm cup of tea on the dining room table. But Mrs. King isn't inside the house. Since the old lady can't walk without a cane and is slow on her feet, and since the cup of tea is still hot, the nurse looks outside the house, reasoning that she can't have gone far. But she's not there and she never reappears. All she leaves behind is that cup of tea."

"What happened to the scrapbook? I haven't seen it in the papers I've looked at. Does your grandmother keep it somewhere else?" she asked.

"I don't know what happened to it. Maybe Benjamin Hoffman kept it. Have you talked to him?"

"No, I'm trying to get in touch with his former editor."

"Well, if he has it, he can keep it. It was creepy. Anyway, are you spooked yet?"

She pictured the New England house, with its white shutters and its cozy kitchen, and there, on the table, the cup of tea sitting on a saucer with no one to drink it. The image was more disturbing than any skeleton or hideous monster featured on the covers of pulp magazines, for it was not the presence of evil that drew the eye, but the absence of something.

"The disappearances sound creepier than stories of headless horsemen."

"Definitely another level of morbid," he agreed. "But I suppose Betty and my grandfather found joy in such stories."

"Maybe they felt they had to tell them. That it would be dangerous if they were forgotten," she said, and thought about her great-grandmother in her last few days, rambling about Piedras Quebradas. An old secret, whispered in Minerva's ear. The ending to a story she'd never fully told before.

Noah looked at her with curiosity. "Dangerous?"

"Every fairy tale has a message hidden in it, a moral that you'll figure out. Maybe not," Minerva said, tracing a knot in the wooden surface of the table.

He kept his eyes fixed on her and smiled. "Do you think there's a hidden message in Beatrice Tremblay's writings?"

"There's probably a hidden message in the work of all writers," she said, and brushed a strand of hair away from her face. She was beginning to grow restless.

She crossed her arms. She didn't like talking to people that much. Characters in books she could understand, and complicated academic arguments in papers were no problem. But people . . . they were a puzzle she couldn't quite crack. Too much time talking with others took a toll on her.

Besides, she figured he was the type that always made her nervous, a person who liked to ask questions, to lift a veil and peek beneath it. She was confined; the table felt too small. She wanted to step out for a breath of fresh air, but people always took it the wrong way when she said that. They assumed she was annoyed, or that they were boring her.

There was also that nagging feeling she'd had since the morning. The portent. Maybe she was having a nervous breakdown. The damn dead rat certainly hadn't helped her nerves, and that book on witchcraft and her stray wild thoughts made her dizzy with anxiety. She clutched the teaspoon, then let go of it and pushed it away.

"What?" he asked, laughter bubbling in his throat.

"You haven't told me about the ghost in the factory," she said, because she didn't want him to know what she was really thinking.

He leaned forward, resting his elbows on the coffee table. "I saw someone standing outside one time. It was a young man in overalls and a flat cap, staring at me through a window. He freaked me out. I stepped out to yell at him and tell him he was trespassing and I'd call the cops. But when I walked out, he was gone."

"That's not much of a ghost story. It could have been someone else who was sneaking around the factory."

"I didn't say it was a *good* story."

"It's sad, the factory," she said, and she carefully lifted her cup of coffee to her lips.

"What do you mean?"

"The fact that it's run-down and closed. Doesn't your grandmother miss it?"

"You heard her, she's going to make a high-tech hub out of its bones," he said dismissively. "Maybe she'd care if we were in financial trouble, but my family's always managed to dodge any money issues. We're terribly rich."

"And you don't care what happens to it, either."

"Is that reproach I detect in your voice?" he replied, but he sounded pleased.

"No."

"You know, Thomas Murphy liked ghost stories."

"Oh?" Minerva said, looking at him with interest.

"Yeah. It's the only thing I know he liked. He mentioned it one time, you know, that he believed in ghosts. Or he was compiling ghost stories. I don't know, he was the studious type, he probably slept by the stacks."

"Not really the person you'd hang out with."

"Nope." He shook his head and smiled.

Thomas Murphy had been like her, she thought. A quiet, studious fellow more comfortable roaming the library than nightclubs. Gone missing, Thomas Murphy. Unnoticed, unobtrusive Tom. Minerva rested her chin on the back of her hand and looked at Noah thoughtfully.

"Why did you sign up for Religion in Puritan New England?" she asked.

"I needed an elective, and it wasn't early in the morning. Plus, my adviser recommended it. I got stuck with Thomas as my tutor after I did horribly on the first exam. Carolyn is determined to have me pass the courses, so I guess I'll keep having to stumble my way through this degree."

Despite a dash of frivolity, Noah was amusing. His cynicism served to buff the edges that she might normally have found exasperating. She smiled at him.

They finished their coffee and Minerva went next door to pick up the film she'd dropped off. Noah gave her a ride back to campus.

"Want to stop by tomorrow and look at more of that archival stuff?"

"Sure," she said. "Is noon okay?"

"Should be fine."

She was about to step out of the car when he spoke again.

"Can I ask you something?"

"Sure."

"Did you always know you wanted to be a scholar?"

"Yeah, I think so. Even if I don't feel like much of one these days. Sometimes it seems pointless. Why write papers that six people are ever going to read about a person who is long dead? How does that benefit the world in any way? I could be doing something more practical, more tangible."

"Then why keep on with it?"

She thought about giving him a canned answer and glanced down, looking at her lap. Instead, she spoke earnestly.

"The romance of it. It's as if you're conducting a secret, passionate love affair. You know every detail about someone, their every word and thought. When you look at their writing, you swoon over a sentence fragment or a turn of phrase. It's as if, through the mists of time, someone reaches out and touches your hand."

She looked up at him, wondering if he'd find her words strange or just plain perplexing. But he seemed intrigued, not daunted.

"If someone had explained college to me like that, maybe I would have made more of an effort," he said.

"It makes it harder to notice people in the real world. Difficult to make friends, all that stuff."

She glanced at Ledge House, which faithfully guarded the books and papers that constituted her entire existence.

"Music," she said.

"Sorry?"

"The other day you asked what I do for fun: I listen to music."

"What kind?"

"I'll burn you a CD," she promised.

He waved goodbye as he drove off. She didn't wave back, clutching the straps of her backpack instead. Then she hurried up the steps and pulled out the key to the dorm.

After dropping her backpack on a couch, she checked the back porch and saw that the cat hadn't eaten the food she'd left outside. She normally waited for Karnstein to appear, but that morning she'd been in a hurry.

She carried the dish inside, then she sat in the shadow of the stuffed library birds and turned on her computer. There was still that nagging, unpleasant feeling scratching at the back of her skull, though it had become a dull throbbing after the coffee.

She looked at the pictures she'd taken of Ginny's drawings. Staring at them, she was struck again by the similarities they bore to Thomas's doodles. She arranged them side by side and opened *A History of Witchcraft Lore,* paging through the section on witch marks. The book she'd picked up on witchcraft in medieval England also mentioned these symbols and other methods of protection.

*Dried cats might be found under roof spaces and floors, often posed as if they were hunting for mice. Margaret Howards indicates that the cats were used as luck bringers or as sacrifices to protect against magic and pestilence.*

Her finger slid across the page. *Written charms are often found in gaps between timbers. Sometimes they might be placed in bottles and hidden behind the walls. An iron nail, wrapped in red wool, was also reckoned to offer protection against witches. A significant amount of ritual might have been involved in the creation of these charms.*

Ginny had basically been imitating people of four centuries before who might have consulted "cunning-folk" to help them deal with their problems. By creating repetitive patterns in her drawings to dispel evil, Ginny was engaging in a type of folk magic. Of course, Betty wouldn't have been able to understand this kind of behavior, but in the context of magic practice it made perfect sense.

Minerva sat at her desk, working through her notes. It was hot inside Ledge House and she opened the windows, sipping her third cup of coffee that day. Her mother said warm drinks cooled you off on hot days. She had no idea whether this was true, but she drank her coffee all the same while she typed an email to her mom, emphasizing her progress, glossing over any troubles, ending on a cheery note.

When night fell, she opened the back door and called for the cat. She stood at the doorway and crossed her arms, waiting. It didn't come.

She had rounds to do and grabbed the flashlight and carried the clipboard. She followed the path through Briar's Commons, heading to Briar Hall. The dorm was mostly in shadows. There was a light in the foyer that turned on automatically at night and the one floor that was in use—Conrad's floor—also had automatic lights, but the rest of the house remained dark to conserve energy.

She paused in front of Conrad's closed door. He didn't seem to be in. She went down the stairs, inspecting each floor and the common areas. When she was done, she checked off the list on her clipboard and wrote down the time and date.

As she stood in front of Briar Hall, she had the sensation that someone was watching her and lifted her head. To her right was Joyce House, shuttered and awaiting renovations. There was no one there. In front of her was Briar's Commons and its clumps of trees.

She raised her flashlight, but the beam of light revealed nothing out of the ordinary. Minerva waited for a minute, frowning, trying to figure out what exactly was bothering her, before she shook her head and stepped forward.

The night had grown cool and pleasant, chasing away the uncomfortable heat of the day, and she'd worked for a good three hours that evening. Maybe she'd be able to work another hour as soon as she finished her rounds.

She smiled as she stepped on a twig, snapping it with her weight.

Behind her someone kicked a pebble down the path.

She turned around, flashlight in hand.

"Hello?" she said.

The path was empty. A faint breeze rustled the branches of the trees. She held the flashlight still, craning her neck, before shrugging and continuing down the path.

She took six steps and then she heard the weight of a shoe against the ground.

Minerva turned around fast. Again, she had the sensation that she was being watched. Again, she saw no one. Minerva picked up the pace. It wasn't as if the path through Briar's Commons was long. People used it for exactly that reason: it served as a shortcut. Yet it seemed different now, as if it had been stretched.

Minerva walked briskly, with the flashlight clasped tight in one hand and the clipboard in the other. She should have stepped out next to her dorm by now, she was sure of it. She followed this route every day. She could practically walk it blindfolded.

Yet the path went on and on; the trees were a sea of green that did not end. The tops of the pines seemed higher, the canopy was like an ebony lid blotting out any moonlight, and the flashlight in her hand provided but a trickle of faint light. She shook it, as if she could force it to shine brighter with that motion.

*Witches trick you*, that's what her great-grandmother had said. They make you follow the wrong path until you tumble into a ravine.

She shook her head.

Behind her there was the shuffle of feet. She looked over her shoulder and still there was no one.

Yet she was being followed. She felt a burning, insistent gaze fixed on her.

Minerva rushed down the path while behind her someone rushed, too. The flashlight was like a flickering firefly, practically useless as she tried to see what lay ahead.

As she turned a bend of the road, her foot caught in the protruding root of a tree and she stumbled onto the ground. The flashlight slipped from her hand and rolled away.

"Fuck!" she yelled.

A hand settled on her shoulder and she let out a hoarse cry. She shuffled back, swatted her hands madly, trying to shove whoever was reaching for her away until she bumped her back against the trunk of a tree and a man spoke.

"Minnie," he said.

She looked up into Conrad's face.

Her breathing was ragged, as if she'd been running a marathon instead of simply walking a few meters between two dorms. She brushed the hair away from her face and stared at him openmouthed.

"Are you drunk?" he asked. "Do you want me to take you to your dorm?"

Her heart beat wildly; the itch in the back of her skull was now a loud throbbing, like a drum. He leaned down, his hands found her arm, and she pushed him off. He looked at her with wide, aggrieved eyes.

"Hey! What's the matter with you?"

"You've been following me, you creep! That's what's the matter!" she yelled, and clumsily pulled herself to her feet.

"Are you nuts? I saw you on the ground and thought you were in trouble."

She snatched up the flashlight she'd dropped and pressed the clipboard against her chest. She shone the light at him and felt a trickle of sweat slip down the collar of her blouse.

"I'm fine," she said.

"You're nuts," he declared firmly.

Minerva stepped away from him and ran back to Ledge House. This time she got there quickly, stomping onto the porch and unlocking the door with trembling hands. Once inside she dashed toward the phone and called Hideo. She could feel him smiling when he answered. She cut him off.

"Someone followed me from Briar Hall," she said.

"What do you mean? A student?"

"Maybe." She walked back and forth in the living room, pulling the long cord of the phone along the floor. "I bumped into Conrad."

"Then it was Conrad?"

She closed her eyes and clenched one hand into a fist, pressing it against her mouth.

"Hello?"

She snapped her eyes open. "I don't know. Someone followed me from Briar Hall, I fell, and then there was Conrad."

"Look, if someone's bothering you, we can call campus security."

She pulled the curtains aside and looked out the window.

"Minerva?"

"I'm not sure it was Conrad," she said as she looked at the trees outside.

"I'm coming over."

Ten minutes later he was in her kitchen. He began boiling water for tea while she sat at the table and examined the dark smudges on the palms of her hands. She'd dirtied them when she stumbled and fell.

"You don't have much of a selection of teas," he said as he set a mug before her.

She wiped her hands with a napkin. "I prefer coffee."

"I don't think you need caffeine right now. What happened?"

Minerva tugged at the piece of string from her tea bag. "Something strange. Something bad. I woke up and I had this feeling that something would happen today. My Nana Alba used to call it a portent, and it's when I get this feeling, this jolt, like something important will take place. But it was different today and then someone followed me even though I couldn't see them. They were invisible."

"Invisible?"

"Like they were invisible to Ginny," she said, remembering that incident after the dance when Virginia had said someone had followed her.

"You've lost me."

Minerva took out the tea bag from the mug and set it atop the napkin she'd used. "It doesn't matter."

"Minerva, don't bullshit me."

She shook her head. "I don't know what happened, Hideo. I thought someone was following me. But I don't think it was Conrad."

"Okay, maybe not. We should still tell campus security."

"No. Look, I'm tired," she said, rubbing her hands together. "I'm . . . I think it's my anxiety spiking, you know? Everything is so fucking hard lately. I can't write properly and my adviser is going to be pissed off if I don't . . . it's hard."

She pressed her hands flat against the table. Hideo patted one of them.

"I know that thesis is kicking your ass, but you're going to figure it out. Look, you're too cooped up here. Why don't we catch a movie with Patricia? Or there's that party she's planning."

That wasn't going to solve anything, but Minerva knew she'd never get rid of Hideo if she didn't agree. She said yes, they could go to the movies, and Hideo headed back to his dorm.

She walked to her desk and warily contemplated the notes she'd been working on, her eyes fixing on the collection of Tremblay's short stories that lay by the computer. She picked up the book and looked at the cover. This was a newer edition of *Wicked Ways and Other Stories,* printed in the mid-eighties, when horror was in its paperback heyday, and the artist had decided to paint a garish picture of a woman running toward the reader with her mouth wide open.

Minerva shoved the book away and went to bed.

# 1908: 8

RAIN DRENCHED THE FIELDS and in the evening the fog descended from the top of the mountains, nuzzling the trees, painting the land with wispy shades of gray. Outside, the world seemed
wrapped in gauze, and she beheld the fog with wary eyes. She'd
had a portent that morning, a feeling that something would go
wrong. After all, her father had told her that days of rain and wind
were propitious for casting spells.

All day Alba had gone about her chores with the utmost care.
She watched over her siblings, looking at the letters they traced on
a slate or listening as they read out loud from a book. All the while
she wondered what doom might befall them.

The mysterious glow outside her window had not returned, but
that did not mean Alba felt any safer. Perhaps the inside of their
house was a haven, but who knew what lay in the trees, in the
fields?

"What are you looking at?" her mother asked.

"Nothing," Alba said, and sat down quickly. She adjusted the
wooden ball inside the sock she was supposed to be darning.

"I'm thinking of inviting Father Aguilera to the farm next week
to have a cup of chocolate. Jacobo and Belisario have also been
muttering about curses. Father Aguilera's presence should calm
everyone down."

"You think they'd leave the farm?"

Her mother wove the thread back and forth, skillfully handling her darning needle. "No. But we'll need to hire workers for the harvest, and they won't come if they think something is awry here. And I won't risk Fernanda taking off. She hasn't been long with us, and if anyone might leave, it would be her. We don't have enough people as it is." Her mother sighed. "Arturo is right, Piedras Quebradas is a hopeless endeavor. Without Tadeo we can't possibly oversee—"

Alba stared at her mother, who seemed close to tears. Yet the tears did not come. Luisa pressed her lips together. Within an instant the woman composed herself, her capable hands once again tugging at the thread with stubborn determination.

"However the twins manage to make such holes in their socks, I cannot imagine," she said.

They continued working under the fading light. The day was at an end, night drawing upon them. Alba's unease had not abated, but she was careful to tuck it away while she continued her work, unwilling to let her mother discern it. She had enough troubles.

Alba changed into her nightgown, carefully washed her face, and brushed her hair. From time to time, she peeked out the window until, at last, she drew the curtains tight together. In a corner of her room, she'd hidden the talisman the woman from Los Pinos had given her, and around her neck lay Valentín's medallion.

Valentín, who'd kissed her in the field of barley. She giggled at this. The memory was sweet. Then her thoughts strayed back to the piano, to Arturo playing that waltz by Waldteufel. Sweetness was replaced by impudence as she thought about kissing him instead.

What a wicked idea, although the same wickedness was what made it enticing. She blushed, ashamed of herself. How silly she was to be thinking these things. The next morning, she must read the Bible and repent.

She said her prayers and slept.

Her dreams were usually bursting with color. She dreamed of the city, of its sights, of wearing pretty dresses and attending lavish parties.

Her dream that night was different.

She felt that someone sat at the head of her bed and extended a hand, gently caressing her face. She was not afraid. The presence was soothing, the caresses as soft as silk.

That shapeless someone lay beside her and drew her close, running a hand down her neck.

A mouth pressed against her lips. One kiss, and then another, and another, but all of them butterfly soft. The dream lover who sought her company was knit from darkness and fog. The room around her was blackness and shadows and patches of gray. She could not see him.

Vaguely she remembered the story of Cupid and Psyche. Vaguely too she recalled Valentín's kiss. Yet the memory of the field of barley and the skies above their heads seemed distant, as if that were the true dream.

A voice murmured in her ear, deep and steady. It spoke in a language she did not know, or perhaps in the drowsiness of sleep the words became jumbled. She sensed the meaning, though, for it was love that was spoken to her, and she responded with the same whisper of words, echoing the voice.

She sighed and languidly reached up, grasping the face of the phantom that sought her embrace, and wrapped her arms around a body that was solid and strong. Fog he might be, but his breath tickled her skin. He pulled her arms above her head with the same languor she'd displayed, and she smiled.

Her hair was spread upon the pillow, her body taut as she arched her back and her fingertips brushed the carved headboard. He lay upon her, yet he was weightless, insubstantial, and not, for she could sense the power of his muscles, his hands tight around her wrists.

He kissed her beneath her ear, kissed the hollow of her neck, rested his lips upon her breast, and she twisted and shuddered, wanting to drag him closer to her.

The lips against her flesh were suddenly two needles that pierced her skin, digging deep into her chest. The stinging pain spread down her belly. She cried out loudly and attempted to fling the phantom away, but the needles sank in, pinning her down, and the body above her was now like a block of iron.

She could not breathe and opened her eyes wide. The room had turned into a splash of vermilion, the color suffocating her.

How cold she felt. Her limbs were frozen stiff and the breath of the phantom who had invaded her room was like a gust of icy wind. She pressed a hand against flesh, felt the quick beating of a heart before it melted away and she was holding on to nothingness. This, she thought, was the tale not of Cupid and Psyche, but of Persephone dragged into the depths of the underworld. This was a chthonic sacrifice.

An eon passed and the presence shifted and slid away, receding slowly, nails raking her torso and her legs before lifting from her body.

She breathed in and turned her head. In the darkness Alba caught a glimpse of two hungry, large eyes, fixed on her. The eyes had no face; they belonged to a shadow that had the outline of a body, yet she could discern none of its features. No nose, no mouth, no teeth.

Only the eyes, enormous and terrible, unblinking, were clearly visible. She opened her mouth, raised a feeble hand, trying to shield herself from the gaze of the apparition, and when she looked again the shadow slipped down upon the floor, like a river of tar, and slid under the bed.

She tossed her head from side to side, the bedsheets tangling around her limbs like a shroud. Then the bedsheet slipped from her fingers and the bed below crumbled into dust. She was flung into an abyss.

Alba woke up with a start and stared at the ceiling. It was morning and light filtered under the curtains. She tossed the sheets aside and stood up. She was forced to sit down immediately. Her limbs felt like wet paper and the dream still made her heart race.

She touched the sheets, alarmed, suddenly afraid something might slink from under them and seep onto the ground. She kicked the sheets away with one quick motion and held her breath.

She wanted to peek under the bed, but the thought of doing so made her heart beat even faster.

"Hail Mary, full of grace, the Lord is with thee; blessed art thou among women and blessed is the fruit of thy womb, Jesus. Holy Mary, Mother of God, pray for us sinners, now and at the hour of our death. Amen," she said, speaking hastily and making the sign of the cross.

After a minute she knelt by the bed with her hands resting on the mattress, as if she were about to say her prayers. Then she looked under it. But there was nothing there to see.

Alba let out a shaky sigh. What a strange dream she'd had. Although she had to admit that in the beginning it had been rather pleasant. But then it had turned horrid, and she pressed both of her hands against her medallion, feeling the cool metal under her fingertips.

She stood up and opened the curtains. The motion of her arms made her wince; a stabbing pain extended through her body. She looked down and saw the nightgown had a maroon splotch upon the chest. It had not been there when she went to bed.

Quickly she pulled the gown off her body and stood naked in front of the mirror. Above her heart there was a cut, as if she'd nicked herself with a knife. The skin around the cut was bruised and purplish. Alba leaned forward, her fingers brushing the cut and pressing down on it.

In horror she stepped away from the mirror. Her mind was in chaos. She wanted to yell for her mother but knew it would be futile. She would be disbelieved. If she told her uncle, he'd say she'd listened to too many silly folktales. Perhaps they'd think she was going mad and was harming herself.

Alba managed to dress herself and pin her hair up, then descended the stairs quickly and found the maids in the kitchen.

"Will you let my mother know I've gone to visit the Molina girls?" she asked them, and did not wait for a response.

She rushed to the stables and grabbed a sidesaddle from the harness room. When Tadeo had been with them, he'd often readied her horse for her. Now she had to complete this task alone.

She'd lost her brother. Evil had dragged him away and might snatch her, too.

"Are you going for a ride?" Arturo asked, startling her with his question.

He stood at the doorway of the stables and peered at her curiously.

Alba adjusted the stirrups. "I want to see if the Molina girls have those new magazines that were supposed to come in sometime this month."

"It might rain," Arturo said, turning to look at the sky outside.

"I won't be long," she said, trying to seem careless and calm, even though she feared he might want to accompany her. But then again, he didn't like to ride. He preferred the wagon, which was the closest thing they had to a carriage.

"Very well," he said.

He helped her onto her mount. Alba thanked him, but Arturo held on to the bridle, looking at her with interest.

"You seem tired, Alba. You're not falling ill, are you?" he asked.

"I'm fine."

He bade her goodbye and she proceeded at a leisurely pace, but once the stable was out of sight, she spurred the horse forward.

As soon as Alba arrived at the Molinas' estate, she sought Valentín. He walked toward her with his wide-brimmed hat on his head and a smile on his lips, but then, as he noticed something was amiss, the smile vanished and was replaced by a look of concern.

"Is something wrong?" he asked.

"Can you accompany me to Los Pinos?"

"Now? I must—"

"It was in my room," she said, looking at the ground. "The witch came into my room and it bit me. I don't know what to do, Valentín. I'm afraid."

He took her hand and held it between his own. Then he nodded.

THE PATH TO THE town was swathed in mist and the scent of wet earth; the pleasant, fresh smell of the resinous ocote enveloped them, soothing the senses. Soon their horses were clopping through the quiet village and they reached the house with the yellow door.

The old woman opened the door before they knocked and looked at them with grave eyes. Valentín handed her a bottle that he'd brought with him. Jovita grabbed it with a nod, although she seemed displeased.

"Come inside," she said.

Jovita took them to the room that smelled of mint and they sat at the table. Despite the light streaming in through the windows, Alba shivered as if she'd caught a chill.

"You've come back quick."

"I thought your talisman was supposed to keep me safe. I thought it would work. It hasn't and I need another remedy."

"It works. Of course it does. You place the pins in the body of the bird and tell the witch to stay away."

"I've been bitten."

Jovita was quiet. She looked at Alba, then at Valentín. She shook her head. "If it has caught your scent and tasted your blood then it will not let go of its prey."

"There must be a way," Valentín said. "There are stories, about how one can trap them. The knots—"

The old woman turned piercing eyes in the direction of the young man. "Hush. Don't talk foolishness," she said, and then she looked again at Alba. Her expression changed; a trace of pity appeared on her face. "There are no happy endings when you face such a creature. Run. If you run far away perhaps it will not follow. Let it find another victim."

"It might kill someone else from my family," Alba said. "If it got my brother and then went after me, who's to say it will not attack my mother? Or my younger brothers and sisters?"

"That may be the case. But the danger is too great. You cannot face it."

"You will not help me?" she asked.

"I can sense it," the old woman said, and she lifted her hand carefully, grimacing. "It's too powerful, stronger than I thought. It might come after me if I say anything more. You must go. That is the answer."

"And let my family die," Alba said.

The old woman did not reply. She did not need to. Her silence was the answer. For a second, Alba considered it. She thought about boarding a train, with a bag by her side and a handful of coins in her pocket. She considered leaving Piedras Quebradas behind.

Abandoning her kin to face the wrath of a witch.

Alba bolted up from her seat. She ran out of the house and stood by the door, hugging herself.

"Don't worry. We'll fix it," Valentín said, rushing after her and placing his hands on her shoulders.

She closed her eyes. Alba's mouth tasted bitter; it tasted of bile. "How can you fix it?" she asked, but her voice was a pitiful croak.

"We'll do as the stories say. We'll lure it and trap it."

She looked at him. Valentín was nodding.

"Yes, like in that story my grandfather used to tell. We wait until night falls, skin an animal, and lay its dead carcass upon the ground. Then we wait in the shadows until the scent of blood draws the teyolloquani out. When it approaches, we take a cord and tie a knot, then say some words. Then tie another knot and say more words. Once you've tied twelve knots it will be trapped. Then you can kill it."

"What words?"

"The first word is 'earth.' You tell it that you're holding it with earth. Then you say you're holding it with water, then with fire and air. You say it again until you reach twelve. Once you've begun tying the knots, you can't stop speaking. That's the trick. It might try to scare you or trick you, but you must keep going."

"What if your grandfather forgot something? Or he made it up? Wouldn't Mrs. Jovita have recommended this to us? Why do you know this story and not her? Or maybe she does know it, but it's as she said, it's simply too dangerous."

"You've heard stories like this, I know you have."

"I've heard of witches who control the wind by tying it with knots."

"There, you see? And think hard, you'll remember a few others, I know you will."

"There's a risk to it. No, no, no. It's foolish," she said, shaking her head.

"Alba, you must trust me," he said. "I'm sure it will work. We can ask the priest to bless my bullets, to make sure they hurt the teyolloquani. If the bullets are blessed, there is no way it can survive."

"The medallion was blessed. It did no good," she said, and now she pressed a hand against her neck. Beneath it was the piece of metal, but next to that was the bruise with the tiny cut. The creature had simply slinked into her room as if it were made of smoke.

Alba looked off to the side, blinking away tears. "It'll kill me if we fail," she said. "I know it. You have no idea what it is like, the fear I feel. Last night, I saw its eyes, and they were such terrible eyes. I cannot forget them. Even if I live a thousand years, I will not."

She meant it. The terror was what made her shiver like a leaf, she was sure of it. It was caught inside the marrow of her bones. She could not shake it off, nor could the coat around her shoulders warm her, for the chill of the grave was what she'd felt as she laid in her bed.

"Alba," Valentín said, and put his arms around her.

She slipped her arms around him in return. Valentín stroked her hair gently.

"Don't let it catch me," she begged him. "Oh, don't let me remember its eyes."

She turned her face toward Valentín and kissed him. She wanted to clutch someone real, someone who was warm flesh and blood, not a shadow that crept into her bed and kissed her with lips of ice.

When she pulled away, she carefully brushed his temple with her hand and looked into his eyes.

"In a few nights we'll trap it and kill it," Valentín promised, and he quickly pressed his lips against the back of her hand. "I'll have the priest bless my bullets and we'll catch it. I'll run into town this very evening, as soon as I get you back home."

They rode together and once again Valentín stopped by the edge of the field of barley. He helped her dismount. They stood in front of each other, her hands pressed flat against his chest.

"Be careful," he told her. "I'll come and see you soon and we can discuss how we'll go about setting that trap."

"Thank you, Valentín," she said. "Thank you so much."

They embraced. Her face was close to his neck, and she kissed him there before he turned his face down and kissed her on the lips. She smiled and he blushed. "I ought to start courting you properly," he told her.

"I suppose so," she said.

He grinned at her, as happy as could be, and she twirled away from the young man, grabbing her mount's bridle. As she led the horse back toward the stable a light rain began to fall. Once again, she recalled how her father had said rainy days were good for casting spells, and she quickened her pace, afraid of remaining out in the open.

# 1934: 5

TIME IS A TREACHEROUS mistress. In our youth it flows slow and deep; the days stretch out endlessly. When we are children, a summer lasts for a century. As we age, the flow of time speeds up. Suddenly, a year vanishes with the snap of one's fingers. How quickly time eludes us, how easily it tricks us.

When I think back to the end of 1934, I picture an unending, bone-chilling whiteness. That month of December seems to have taken place in slow motion, as if our lives had been as frozen as the pond where the students skated.

Certain sentences, certain words, suddenly leap to my mind, and I can recall with a startling clarity a moment I thought long faded. Tiny details surface, as if revealed by the spring thaw. I can remember, even decades later, the timbre of Ginny's voice, the sound of her footsteps on the stairs, the embroidered vines adorning the cuffs of her winter gloves.

After Thanksgiving break Ginny's melancholia and anxiousness worsened. It was a few days into December that she had a row with Edgar over the phone. I didn't hear what was said, but Mary Ann Mason, who made it a habit to eavesdrop on anyone who used the house phone, hurried up to tell Carolyn and me about it.

"Ginny hung up on Edgar," she said, installing herself at the edge of a couch while I was busy combing Carolyn's hair. She was going out that night and I was to be her handmaiden again.

"Mary Ann, you should be ashamed, snooping around on us," I said, even though I'd eavesdropped on Carolyn and her father recently.

"What? I was getting a book I forgot downstairs and happened to overhear them," Mary Ann said. "Anyway, she's mighty strange lately, don't you think?"

"She likes melodrama," Carolyn said. "She's probably trying to seem more interesting."

"I don't think she's doing this for attention," I said.

"Betty, I know you're fond of her, but you must admit she's an odd one and getting odder. If she's not doing it for attention, then she clearly has something wrong up there," Carolyn said, and tapped her forehead with her index finger for emphasis before fiddling with her jewelry box. "Mind you, Gin-gin can be a sweetheart at times, but she's also a handful."

"You're absolutely correct," Mary Ann agreed eagerly. "That's a pretty necklace. Where are you going tonight, Caro? Don't tell me, are you heading out with David Dundy?"

Carolyn pressed a pearl necklace against her neck and looked in the mirror. "It's not David."

"Who, then?"

"Someone or other," Carolyn said.

"A secret lover?"

"Mary Ann, if I tell you, then it's no secret."

I joined Mary Ann in her cheery teasing. I was eager to move us away from the subject of Ginny's behavior. It was not something that could be discussed with Carolyn, who'd never understood Ginny's personality in the first place and seemed now even less likely to comprehend the delicate state of our mutual friend.

But did anyone understand her? Did I? Decades later this question still haunts me. Did I even know Ginny? If I had known her, wouldn't I have been able to save her?

The day after that fight over the phone, when I was working on a paper, I heard the sound of a motor and looked out the window to see Edgar's glossy car coming down the driveway. It stopped in front of the dorm. He stepped out of the car and waved up at our window. I waved back, put on a sweater and my gloves, and hurried downstairs to greet him.

"Ginny's in class," I informed him. "She won't be back until three o'clock."

"I know that. I was wondering if I could talk with you," he said.

"The house mother is not here right now, so you can't come in."

"Understood. Can I interest you in a brief ride instead?"

Edgar had a light, effervescent quality, yet that day his face seemed sallow and serious. Whatever he wanted to discuss must have been important. I suspected, by the way he looked over my shoulder, that even if we could have gone together into the dorm, he wouldn't have liked that. There would be no guarantee of privacy, not with people like Mary Ann around.

We drove down the road that they called the scenic route, which ran parallel to the sea. Winter had transformed the land, lending it a melancholic quality. We parked by a desolate cove and stood by a wild blackberry bush, its brambles weighed down by snow, looking out at the water. In September, at the beginning of the school term, several of the girls, including Ginny and me, had stopped there for a picnic.

The cove was dead and quiet, and the December air was cold. I was wrapped in my ugly sweater and had gloves on my hands. Edgar's coat seemed expensive and warm. We both stared at the ocean.

"I'm worried about Ginny," he said. "I need to know if she's told you anything about . . . well, about hurting herself."

I looked up sharply at Edgar. "No. What has she said to you? Has she—"

"She hasn't said anything. . . . She hasn't been *explicit,* but she has talked about death and dying."

"What?"

He crossed his arms and shook his head. "I can't even explain what she's said, only that from several allusions and comments I have the impression that death is constantly on her mind. And she's very different lately; Betty, you must have noticed it. How anxious she seems, how every noise seems to startle her? Did she tell you what happened over Thanksgiving?"

"You were upset at her because she spoke of ghosts."

"Not just of ghosts. Of faceless men who lurk outside the windows and peek into her room. Those mad scribblings of hers! Have you looked at her notebooks? She spent two days trying to commune with the dead and writing down their laments."

What could I say? Of course I'd noticed her drawings, her scribblings, the stacks of books on witchcraft and the occult multiplying around her bed. Her evasiveness, her tense face, how each creak of the boards of the old house made her sit up expectantly, how her eyes darted across the room. I'd heard her speak of men who followed her, men who paced below windows, and vague worries that became incoherent murmurs. She was like an orchid that wilts in a pot, yet I did not like to discuss this, not with anyone, not with him.

"I fear she may be going mad. I think it would be best if I took her away. Perhaps a sanatorium might be the best place for her."

Those words were like a blow to the temple. I felt as if I might lose my balance and looked at him in wide-eyed surprise. A sanatorium! Did he mean the State Lunatic Hospital at Danvers, that grand old building perched like a vulture upon a hill? Would they place Ginny in a straitjacket? Would they make her take one thousand pills and tinctures and remedies? I pictured him dragging Ginny by the hair up to an attic where she'd be locked away.

"Ginny has certain eccentricities. But madness! No!"

"Madness. Nerves. I have no idea what to call it."

I moved away from him, my feet stomping upon the fresh snow. This landscape of white and cold was like a knife to my throat. My voice was hoarse and pained.

"How can you say such a thing! You who are supposed to love her."

"It's because I love her that I'm talking to you."

"You probably have cold feet. Maybe you don't want to marry her anymore," I said. I had a sudden hope that this would be the case, that he might leave Ginny and me alone. That I wouldn't have to part from her side. I'd take care of her. I would. I wouldn't abandon her.

Edgar shook his head vehemently. "I do want to marry her. More than anything in the world. But you can't tell me she hasn't changed. You can't tell me everything is fine with her."

No, I couldn't. I opened my mouth and sighed, letting out a puff of warm breath. We had drifted away from the car and now turned around, retracing the steps we had left in the snow.

"Betty, I'm afraid she'll hurt herself, that's what it is. She won't listen to me, but perhaps she'd listen to you. A doctor is not the end of the world, is it? At least if she had a chat with one . . . I want her to stay with my family during Christmas break, and then afterward it would be easy to see Dr. Landis while we're in Boston. You're her close friend, if anyone can talk to her, it's you."

"Me, Edgar? What would I say? I wouldn't know how to bring it up."

"At least promise me you'll keep a careful eye on her, Betty. I call each day but still I worry. Please watch over her."

His anguish was obvious and when I nodded he smiled that great big smile that Ginny adored. Poor Edgar! Ginny's disappearance robbed him of his youth and easy joy; that smile seldom adorned his lips afterward. It robbed me of something, too. Innocence and ease. I can never look at the darkness outside without wondering what lurks in the corners. When the lamps bloom on the street, I peek through the curtains and gaze at shadows.

Who goes there, I wonder. *What* goes there.

The winter season also changed for me. When I was a girl, winter was the season of snowball fights and sleds. After Ginny vanished, winter became the season of death and sorrow. For a few years I lived in Arizona, lived with a woman whom I loved dearly, and escaped those New England winters. But eventually I returned, drawn back to northern latitudes. Drawn back to the questions and the incertitude.

Winter brings with it too many memories; the warmth and cheer of a fireplace give way to painful recollections when I turn my head and contemplate the snow. I remember that night when Ginny vanished. I did not see a person outside, an intruder who might have been lying in wait for her.

Yet I've never been able to shake off a feeling that, as I pressed a hand against the trunk of a tree, I was not alone that night. That something watched and hungered and waited in the dark.

The older I grow, the shorter the days seem to become, and I'm certain that what I sensed that night was the shadow of death. But I'm getting ahead of myself. I'm proceeding too quickly.

For now, let us return to the car, where Edgar toys with the radio and I look out at the trees covered in snow. Let us return to those first days of December, when my heart is still whole and Edgar's smile spreads across his face. Let us remain there, one second longer.

# 1908: 9

THE RAIN DID NOT summon any horrid phantoms. The sun
rose, set again. Peace reigned inside the house. The memory of the
terror that had attacked Alba grew dimmer and dimmer with each
passing hour. Yet a shapeless fear gnawed at her heart. She looked
warily out the window, eyed the shadows in her room at night
with suspicion.

On the fourth night after she'd spoken to Valentín, she woke up
sobbing in her bed.

She could not remember what she'd dreamed. It had not been
the same dream as before, of the creature that bit her and drew
blood. For one thing, there was no fresh mark upon her skin, and
for another, the quality of the dream was different. She was sure of
this, even if the dream came back to her only in blurred snatches.

She remembered the redness of blood and the way her hands
shook. She remembered an awful sorrow that made her cry when
she awoke even if she did not understand why she wept.

SHE WAS HELPING WITH the laundry. The sun had come out
from behind the clouds, thus Dolores and Alba hurried to pin the
bedsheets to the clothesline before the weather changed. Nevertheless, the sun didn't warm her head; instead Alba felt as if it
chilled her limbs.

Her fingers were slow, clumsy, as she scooped the wooden clothespins from a bucket.

She had that funny feeling inside her skull again, that portent. She lifted her arms and stretched the bedsheet upon the clothesline. Two of her siblings were playing nearby, their squeals of joy interrupted when Dolores warned them not to touch the laundry.

She bent down to pick up a pillowcase and when she looked up the world turned into a dark splash of red. The bedsheets hanging from the clotheslines were scarlet and the clouds that drifted in the distance were tinted crimson. It was like gazing through a pane of colored glass in a great Gothic cathedral. Even her hands, when she looked at them, were painted a terrible shade of vermilion, as if she'd squeezed rotten cherries and let the juice drip down her arms.

Alba dropped the pillowcase she was holding and stepped back.

"Niña Alba?" Dolores asked, looking at her curiously.

Something terrible was going to happen. She could feel it. The dream, the tangled snatches of it that still lodged in her memory, now seemed to reassemble themselves like jagged shards of pottery.

*Valentín,* she thought, and she blinked. The redness faded. She turned away and headed back into the house, rushing into the laundry room, where Fernanda was bent over a stone washboard, her hands wringing a hypnotic rhythm from the fabric as she scrubbed a shirt clean.

Alba went past the maid; she flung open the door that led to the kitchen.

Alba's mother was making soap that day. She used ashes and lard, and as a girl Alba had liked to see the concoction boiling in a pot and her mother adding grease or lye depending on what was needed, looking in wonder at the frothy mass as it solidified. Such alchemy was more suited to her tastes than the strong scents of blood and guts coming from the kitchen.

"Mother, I must ride to the Molinas' ranch today," she said.

Her mother, with a kerchief tied around her head, was busy by the stove and did not look at Alba as she spoke. "Whatever for? You were just there."

"Yes, but when I was there Valentín said he'd fetch me a tonic to help me sleep and I want to get it."

Her mother did turn now to look at her and shook her head. "For those dark circles under your eyes, the remedy is chamomile tea, I told you this, and I can make it tonight."

"But I would be quick, I promise, and I've helped Dolores with the laundry already."

"Let the girl take a holiday," Arturo said. "I'll accompany her."

She had not seen her uncle standing by the doorway and was startled by his voice. Alba's mother sighed and wiped her hands with a rag. She shook her head and looked at her brother, then at Alba.

"Fine. But don't eat a thing while you're there. Otherwise you'll peck at your food in the afternoon."

"We'll go immediately and be back quickly," Alba promised.

"First we must change into proper clothes," Arturo said.

"I see nothing wrong with your clothes," she told him. Her uncle took a terribly long time to ready himself and she feared he might even want a bath drawn before stepping out of the house. She must go quickly.

"I see plenty wrong with yours. Alba, you can't possibly head out in that dress and with your hair like that," her mother said.

Alba looked down at the old brown housedress with its dirty cuffs, which was fine for chores but obviously the wrong choice when it came to visiting friends.

"What am I going to do with you, Alba? You're awfully scatterbrained these days."

"I'll change," she told her mother, and rushed to her room.

She pinned her hair up and slipped into another dress as quickly as she could. Then she knocked on the door to Arturo's room.

They went to the stables. Alba found her horse and turned to her uncle, trying to keep her tone casual, trying not to let anxiety infect her throat.

"I know you don't like to ride, Uncle, so you need not go with me," she said.

"I've told you I can ride," he replied, and stretched out a hand, tipping her chin up as if to take a better look at her. "Besides, fresh air will do both of us good." His thumb brushed her cheek. "Your mother is correct: you have dark circles under your eyes."

"An owl has kept me up at night," she lied. She did not want to speak of the dream that had made her weep.

"We must chase that naughty bird away, mustn't we? Otherwise sleeplessness might mar this beautiful face."

She looked down, bit her lip, and busied herself with the saddle of her horse, wishing he would have left her alone. She might have moved faster that way. Besides, she wouldn't be able to talk properly to Valentín with Arturo standing at her side. What a mess this was. Yet she needed to see Valentín that day.

They followed the wide road that led to the Molinas' farm. Her uncle kept a leisurely pace and more than once she tried to hasten him, only to be told there was no rush. Finally, they reached the farm. Arturo offered to take the horses to the stables and Alba quickly dismounted and knocked on the front door of the house. She was surprised when Mrs. Molina opened the door. The woman let out a soft sound that was not a word.

"Mrs. Molina," Alba said, smiling. "I'm sorry to come uninvited. Valentín was supposed to procure a tonic for me and I'm here to fetch it."

Mrs. Molina clasped Alba's shoulder. Her mouth trembled and then she spoke. "I am so sorry. He passed away half an hour ago."

Alba's smile melted like hot wax. She stared at the woman. She was invited inside and numbly stepped into the sitting room. At some point, Arturo walked in, and an explanation was offered, but Alba did not hear the whole of it. Mere fragments reached her ears.

*A wild animal. Alone. Out riding.*

BELISARIO DROVE THE WAGON into town. As Arturo helped her up into it, she thought, rather somberly, that at least they all still had proper mourning attire.

Valentín's kin looked at Alba and her family with wary faces as they walked into the church. So did other people from town. There already had been rumors involving the Quirogas flying around. Now they multiplied. People whispered as they sat down.

Behind the black veil, the same one Alba had worn for her father's funeral, her eyes were wide and dry. Sorrow had manifested as a bitter silence. She had not cried, though she feared that this stoicism would not last.

Alba took her seat, bowed her head, trying to keep her mind blank, trying not to sob. She looked at the Christ on the cross behind the pulpit, at her gloves, at the Bible between her hands.

When the priest spoke Valentín's name, she stood up and stepped outside through a side door.

Outside it was no better. She felt breathless and peeled her gloves off. Valentín's medallion hung heavy around her neck and in her right hand she clutched his handkerchief.

She heard Belisario's voice and that of a groom of the Molinas'; both of them were lounging against the wagon and had not seen her.

"A mountain lion wouldn't have clawed him like that," the groom said. "You should have seen it. His guts were nearly outside his body."

"Then what could it have been?"

"You know what. It's witchcraft, plain and simple. The Quirogas' land is cursed."

"He wasn't that close to Piedras Quebradas."

"He was on the road that leads to it. Where else would he have been going? There's nothing that way except Piedras Quebradas."

"What would he have been doing there at night?"

"Maybe he was going to see Alba. The poor devil was in love with her."

She pressed the handkerchief against her mouth to muffle a sob and hurried away from the church. She ran down an alley, down narrow streets with houses that had flowerpots at their windows, past a plaza with a broken fountain until, breathless, she stopped in front of the gates of an old, abandoned house. She tossed the handkerchief away and might have pulled off the medallion from around her neck and also flung it aside, but as soon as her hands touched the locket she slid down to the ground and lay there sobbing.

"Alba!" a voice cried out. "Alba!"

She looked up. Arturo was standing at the other end of the street. He saw her and hurried to her side whip quick, kneeling in front of her.

"How did you find me?" she asked, and roughly wiped her tears with the palm of her hand.

"It wasn't that hard. Come, Alba. We must head back to church."

"No," she said, and pushed his hand away when he offered it to her. "No!"

She shoved him. Her hands landed on his chest. It was a hard blow, but he did not flinch. Arturo stroked her cheek with the back of his hand and looked into her eyes.

A scream caught in her throat and became a low whimper. She wrapped her arms around his neck, hugging him tight.

"I can't stay here. It's cursed, yes, this land is cursed. I want to go away, please, we must go away."

"My darling," he said as he held her. "We'll leave this place, yes, we will. I swear it."

"How? Where might we go?"

She turned her face and they stared at each other. She exhaled hard, couldn't draw an even breath as she looked at him and his hand rose again to touch her cheek, this time with an open palm.

"We'll sell that wretched farm and head back to the city. The Molinas can have it, it's a useless mess anyway. We'll be much happier in the capital. We can buy a house and a proper carriage. I'll take you to the opera and buy you pretty things. You mustn't cry, Alba. It will be fine in the end."

"In the end," she repeated. He smiled, nodding.

*Yes,* she thought. *Yes, I want to sell the farm and run off.* But then she imagined the difficulties of such a transaction. Even if performed quickly it might take too long.

Assuming their safe departure, what would happen to the people left behind? The Quirogas might escape, but the Molinas and their other neighbors would face a hungry evil that would kill and maim.

She had not seen Valentín's corpse; the coffin was mercifully closed. Yet somehow a picture had formed in her mind of his death. Perhaps this was the product of her imagination, or perhaps it was as the old witch from Los Pinos had said: that one could dream and glimpse things that would be, and others that had been already.

Either way, it amounted to the same result. As she sat there with Arturo at her side, she knew exactly how Valentín had perished. He'd been riding toward Piedras Quebradas, heading to meet with her. At a bend of the road there had been an assailant, unseen, protected by the cover of shadows.

It shrieked, and its cry was not the cry of the barn owl or the coyote or a human being, but of all three chained and bound together. Valentín reined his horse. For one second he saw it, and then it was gone. Darkness in the shape of a person, feathers, teeth, claws, there and gone and then—

She could trace the arc of the first blow, hear Valentín's anguished screams as he tried desperately to escape the clutches of the creature. He was tough, Valentín; his hands dug into the thing's flesh, squeezing a sturdy neck—tendons, scales, an unholy mixture of bird and reptile and wolf that snapped at him. But it was stronger and its teeth were sharp, and when it bit into Valentín's arm all was lost. It savaged him from elbow to wrist, and then, as Valentín tried to kick it, the monster began to gnaw at his stomach.

Much blood seeped into the ground, staining the roots of a poplar red, and she knew that as Valentín heaved and wheezed, his hands scrabbling at dirt and stones, as he looked up at the sky and the moon above, he'd been thinking of her with his last two breaths.

Alba squeezed her eyes shut. Behind her lids everything was crimson again and then it was black. Her heart was also crimson and black, wounded so deeply that it could hardly beat inside her chest. Yet beat it she must and live she must and fight she must.

The witch would be destroyed. She'd kill it, even if she had to vanquish it all alone, all by herself. To do anything else would not only be cowardice, it would also be the most terrible betrayal of the memory of Valentín and of her brother, both of whom had perished at the hands of a monster.

A bell tolled. The service was at an end. She blinked and stood up, wobbly, like a moth that emerges from its cocoon.

She'd dropped her gloves, and now she retrieved them. She picked up the handkerchief too, folding it into a perfect square. "Let us walk back to the church."

"We might stay here longer, so that you could rest," he told her, and his hand found her cheek once more.

She shook her head. "No, I'm ready," she said.

Arturo offered her his arm and they slowly made their way back together.

# 1934: 6

DECEMBER BROUGHT US FINAL exams and term papers, but also plenty of social activities on campus. There were gift exchanges and faculty parties aplenty. On a chilly night, after drinking too much punch that had been vigorously spiked with gin from a hip flask, I arrived at Joyce House feeling tipsy and merry. I went into the parlor where four of the girls lounged and chatted.

"Boy, it's late. We thought you were going to miss curfew," Mary Ann said.

"I have fifteen minutes to spare," I told the girls cheerily as I took off my gloves.

"Where's Ginny?" Bertha Trumbull asked.

"What do you mean?" I replied.

"We thought she'd be with you."

"Yes, I imagined you were both at Enfield House," Carolyn said. "Weren't they having a raffle for a turkey or a ham or some other funny thing there this evening?" She was sitting on a couch and leafing through a magazine. She didn't raise her eyes to look at me when she spoke and turned to Mary Ann, showing her a picture of a dress.

My merriment drained away with the tick of the stately grandfather clock in a corner of the room. Ginny hadn't said anything about going out that evening. I was certain that if she'd been invited to a party, she would have asked me to tag along with her. The library would be closing soon. Could she be there, working on a paper? Or else might she be at another dorm studying with a friend? Though, to be frank, she seemed rather friendless lately, and I couldn't picture her engaging in an impromptu end-of-year celebration.

When the clock struck the hour, we went upstairs before the house mother chased us out of the parlor, settling in Carolyn's room. Carolyn and Elizabeth Gardner sat on her bed and continued flipping through magazines. Bertha had commandeered the couch and Mary Ann and I were left standing.

"Do you think she's with Edgar?" Bertha asked. "Maybe they went for a ride and his car broke down."

"I bet you if she's out with anyone, it's with Santiago," Mary Ann said, smiling slyly, pleased with herself.

"No!" squealed Elizabeth.

"Yes! I saw him a few days ago, outside the dorm. He looked like he was waiting for someone, and when he saw me he turned red as a tomato. It's not the first time he's been around. I saw him on Monday, hugging a girl who must have been Ginny."

"Must have been? Monday we walked back and forth together from Joyce House to our classrooms and then had dinner together. She was here all evening long," I said.

"It was late, and I couldn't quite see her face, but she was wearing a gray coat like the one Ginny has with the upturned collar. Who else would it be?"

"That's a fairly common coat. Carolyn has one with the collar upturned," I said. "I'm sure other people do, too. Elizabeth has a gray coat."

"I hope you don't think Elizabeth or I would be downstairs with that Portuguese boy," Carolyn said disdainfully.

"He did stare at her quite a bit when he was working on the repairs in the kitchen," Bertha mused. "Wouldn't it be crazy if she'd rather pick a nobody than Edgar Yates?"

They laughed. I felt irritated by their baseless accusations.

"You shouldn't be starting silly rumors," I said, and my voice was rather sharp and curt. "What if she was in an accident? What if something bad has happened to her? You're cruel to be speaking like that about a friend."

The girls stared at me, their laughter and smiles dying on their lips. Carolyn raised an arched eyebrow at me and tossed her magazine aside. "Don't be silly. We're having a little fun."

"It's not fun to me!"

"You're not angry, are you?"

I was too upset to reply and my hands were shaking. Carolyn stood up and took me aside, worry now replacing blitheness.

"She'll be here any second now. She must be at Enfield House and walking back. Maybe she even won the raffle. Gosh, we're only teasing, Betty. If we thought anything could happen to her—"

"What if something did happen? We wouldn't know, would we? She could be bleeding out in the snow."

Carolyn opened her eyes wide, startled by my words. "My, that's ghoulish! Betty, if you're really worried we can talk to the house mother. Let's give it a few more minutes, shall we? It's not that late yet."

I nodded and spent the next few minutes chewing my fingernails. It wasn't long before Lily Gardner came running into the room, eyes bright and mischievous. "Ginny is back! I heard the house mother giving her a talking-to."

"I wonder what her excuse'll be," Mary Ann said.

I rushed to my room and let out a sigh of relief. Ginny was standing by the window. She'd taken off her coat and her knit hat and she was peeling off her gloves. The snow that had flaked off her shoulders was melting and creating a puddle by the radiator.

"Thank heavens," I said. "We were worried. What happened?"

"I told Miss Price I was at a party."

"Were you?" I asked, because both her face and the wording of the sentence gave me pause. She looked pale, bloodless. Neither the flush of alcohol nor romance colored her cheeks. I was certain she had not been at a party, nor had she entertained a lover, whether that be Edgar or Santiago.

No, she seemed frozen stiff, like an explorer who had been wandering atop a high peak rather than a young woman who had left a late-night celebration.

She sat on her bed and began unlacing her boots. "You won't believe me if I tell you the truth."

"Tell me."

"Why?"

"Ginny, please."

She was quiet. "I was at the library and lost my way." She pulled a boot off, then began working on the laces of the other. "The path changed."

"What do you mean?"

"I mean exactly that. I was on the path and suddenly it was different, and I wasn't sure where to turn. It was dusk by the time I left the library, but it took forever to find the path to Joyce House. It kept getting darker and darker and I went around and around."

Ginny grabbed the boot and placed it on her lap. Her fingers traced the contour of its heel. She tossed the boot aside with a sudden, furious motion and sat stiffly with her hands closed into fists resting against her legs. Then she rose and sat at her desk, where she began drawing on a piece of paper.

I approached her cautiously, the same way someone might approach a wild animal.

"Maybe you should talk to a doctor," I said as gently as possible. "I'm worried."

Ginny laughed. She ran a hand through her hair, which was damp from the melting snow. Her eyes were on her drawing. Circles connected to other circles. "Why would you be worried?"

"Ginny, all you do is scribble in those notebooks of yours, and the things you're reading, they're terribly odd!" I said, and rested a hand on one of her books on witchcraft. "And then you talk about ghosts and claim to speak with them. . . . Of course I'm worried."

She immediately pulled the book away and pressed it against her chest, as if she were cradling a baby. "I do speak with them. I've explained it to you. I talk to my mother. It keeps me sane. It keeps me safe."

"Ginny, if you would speak to Dr. Landis, maybe you'd feel better."

She looked up at me with sharp, angry eyes. "How do you know about Dr. Landis? You've been chatting with Edgar, haven't you?" She pushed her chair back and stood up.

"He came by, yes."

"How many times have you talked about me with him?"

"Once. He came by once. He's afraid you're suicidal. You talk about death—"

"I don't want to kill myself, Betty! It's the exact opposite. You don't understand. Neither of you understands!"

She shoved her papers and books and pencils off the desk. The mad clatter of the items against the wooden floor gave way to a painful silence. We stared at each other.

"Ginny," I said, and extended a hand.

She shook her head and sat on her bed. Shoulders slumped, she gripped a blanket and closed her eyes. "Each day I feel an evil, like an invisible noose around my neck, tightening an inch," she said, and held both hands up, placing them around her throat. "Something terrible is chasing after me. It's magic. I'm under a spell and can't escape it. I don't know who cast it. If I knew . . . I've asked my mother, but she can't see, and I'm afraid . . . but if I don't discover the answer soon, it'll be too late."

She opened her eyes wide. I knelt in front of her and grabbed her hands, clutching them tight between my own.

"Nothing is going to happen to you," I said. "I wouldn't allow it."

"I'm not mad, Betty. A doctor would do no good because I'm not mad. If they take me away, I won't be able to protect myself. Don't you see? At least here I'm a bit safe, but in a sanatorium they wouldn't let me speak to my mother, they wouldn't let me draw. Betty, don't let them take me away."

"No, no, they won't," I promised. I meant it. If ten orderlies had arrived, I wouldn't have let them get to her.

Soon after I convinced her that we must ready ourselves for bed. I quickly fell into a fitful sleep and woke up to the noise of footsteps and the creak of a floorboard. I raised my head, blinking, and caught a glimpse of Ginny standing by the doorway.

"Ginny?" I said.

She didn't respond. Instead, she slipped out of the room. I sat up in bed and quickly shoved my feet into a pair of shoes and followed her.

"Ginny," I said as I descended the staircase, gripping the banister tight. The house was in shadows, and I feared I would tumble down to the first floor.

When I reached the foyer, I saw that the front door was open and snowflakes were lazily drifting inside, landing on the carpet. I wasn't properly dressed, all I'd done was put my shoes on, and the cold nipped at my skin as I poked my head outside.

Ginny was standing a few feet from the house with her back to me. I hurried to her side as fast as I could. My feet felt clumsy and heavy in the snow.

"Ginny, we must head back inside," I said.

But when I reached her, she did not look at me. She was staring in the direction of Briar's Commons.

"It's there. Between the trees," she said.

"What is there?"

She raised a hand and pointed, but all I could see was a fallen tree trunk half submerged in snow. I sighed and crossed my arms, trying hard to keep my teeth from chattering.

"I tried to see its face, but it hid in the shadows. Wait and you might see it."

Her words made me shiver, for they were low and quiet and had a cadence of suppressed panic, as if she were gazing at a horrible sight rather than a simple fallen tree covered in snow. This, more than anything, hinted at madness. I pictured the stately asylum in Danvers with its red brick walls and pretty gardens. I pictured her there and shook my head.

"There's nothing," I said, and tugged at her arm. "Let's go back in. I'm freezing."

We walked back to the house together and slipped into bed. I didn't see anything that night, nothing hiding between the trees.

When Ginny's breath was slow and steady and she was fast asleep, I stood up and pulled the curtains aside. I looked at the alabaster whiteness blanketing the trees and again tried hard to see something, anything out of the ordinary.

My eyes perceived nothing. Yet as I stood at the window I heard a high-pitched noise, which I took to be the wind making the branches of the trees rattle. After a few seconds I realized that the snow was falling straight and steady, with no strong winds to bend the trees. The realization startled me, yet I couldn't begin to dwell on the true source of the noise, for it had ceased.

Had it been an owl or some other bird crying out? Yes, most likely. As I stood by the window, I heard Ginny speak.

"It's out there again," she said. "Don't tell Edgar. They'll throw me in a madhouse, Betty. Don't tell him about tonight."

Her tired eyes fixed on me for a moment, then she turned her back to me and faced the wall.

I didn't tell Edgar. I've wondered what might have happened if I had. What would have been the result if I had phoned him the next morning? If not him, then perhaps I could have spoken to Ginny's father. Would he have whisked her back to the warmth of California? Would I have spoken to her ever again after that?

Yet most of the time, I fear nothing would have changed. That Ginny was condemned, and it was as she said: an invisible noose had fastened itself around her neck. Each hour it grew tighter. The evening of December 19, the last time I would ever see her, was fast approaching.

# 1998: 9

SHE'D LEFT FOOD OUT for the cat on two consecutive days. It hadn't bothered eating it. Minerva called for Karnstein half a dozen times before admitting defeat. In the end, she plopped another can of cat food into a dish and placed it next to the back door.

She had a headache and did not look forward to spending hours bent over a table, looking at Beatrice Tremblay's papers. But she went to the Willows and soldiered on, her pen quickly moving across her notebook, eyes on the manuscript one second, on a journal entry the next. Her Discman spun music by Gustavo Cerati and she tapped her foot to the rhythm of "Amor Amarillo."

At one point, she opened *A History of Witchcraft Lore* and stared at the page showing apotropaic marks, then kept flipping through the book until she landed on an illustration showing several animals—a toad, a cat, a dog—that functioned as servants of witches.

"Familiars were thought to do the bidding of witches. When associated with cunning-folk, they had a more benevolent purpose," she read out loud. "While they often manifested as animals, they might also appear human. Such demonic familiars could remain invisible to everyone but the witch."

Minerva tapped her foot faster and stared at Ginny's painting across the room. She stood up and slowly made her way toward it, her fingers brushing its frame. She sighed and whirled back to her seat, feeling utterly lost.

When Carolyn Yates sent word that she wanted to have tea with her, Minerva stretched her arms and shoved her belongings into her backpack.

Carolyn was having her tea in the solarium, like the first time they'd met. The sun blazed through the windows as she tucked a silver bookmark into a slim volume and smiled at Minerva.

"One lump, isn't that right?" she asked, plopping a sugar cube into a cup before Minerva had a chance to reply.

Minerva set her backpack down and sat. "Yes. Thanks."

"When we were young, we'd have our beaux over for tea in the dorms. They'd file into the house under the eye of the house mother and we'd serve them tea. That horrid Benjamin Hoffman held a sugar cube in his mouth while drinking it. Such terrible manners!" Carolyn sipped her tea. "Incidentally, how is your exploration of Betty's manuscript going?"

"I'm finding my way through it," Minerva said with a smile, which was an outright lie. She wasn't sure what she was doing anymore. "It's always complicated, the whole thesis process."

"I imagine it is. You seem tired."

"Late nights and sleepless hours," she said, and raised her teacup to her lips. "I wanted to ask if you noticed anything strange back when Ginny disappeared."

"Strange? How so?"

"There are plenty of strange things that Beatrice talks about in her manuscript and in her journals. Ginny feeling someone was watching her, that she was being followed. I'm wondering if you ever saw someone around the dorm, or perhaps on campus—"

"A prowler? No. I didn't see any ghosts, either," Carolyn said. "I know what happened to Ginny and it's no great mystery: she ran away with the Portuguese boy."

"But no one saw her with him."

"Our good friend Mary Ann saw them together."

"It couldn't have been her. In her manuscript Beatrice makes it clear that she was with Ginny the day Mary Ann thought she saw

Santiago with a woman. Plus, Mary Ann never got a look at the woman's face."

"Don't start going down the route of horror stories like Edgar and Beatrice used to do, Miss Contreras. You'll waste your life chasing phantoms. There are other possibilities, but the odds are slim."

Minerva guessed it was sound advice. After all, her increasingly strange, paranoid ruminations were not exactly assisting her research. What had happened the other night, when she'd bumped into Conrad, for example?

She felt deflated and squirmed in her chair. Carolyn adjusted the turban around her head, the rings on her fingers sparkling in the bright sunlight. "I was looking at your file, the one we get for the scholarship recipients. You're an only child, aren't you?"

"Yes. That's right."

"Your mother can't help much with your expenses, can she? That's why you work on campus."

"No, she can't," Minerva said simply.

"I suppose your situation is very much like Betty's. Poor thing, they used to work her raw on campus, teaching French."

Carolyn looked her up and down, her sharp eyes cool and steady. Minerva had the uncomfortable sensation that she was being dissected like a frog, her innards carefully exposed with a scalpel.

The old woman shrugged. "Then again, money is not always the solution. Look at Noah, for example."

"I'm not sure what you mean."

"He's lazy, like his father. Like my other children. There's a certain ambition that runs in the blood, but it can easily skip a generation or two. Take my father and me: both of us determined, vigorous specimens." Carolyn set her cup down firmly. A little tea spilled over the rim and pooled in the saucer. "Then look at my Noah. The best tutors, the best opportunities, and the boy can't graduate from college or even set a wedding date. He's twenty-four, can you believe it?"

Minerva set her own cup down with careful fingers. "People

don't get married as young as they used to," she said, and thought about Jonás's accusation that she lacked the capacity for intimacy, for commitment.

"Marriage is a crucial step to ensure our legacy, yet he can't manage one easy task. It brings me to despair!" Carolyn said, throwing her hands in the air dramatically. She smiled. "You, on the other hand, maintain perfect grades despite competing deadlines and responsibilities. A model of maturity."

"I'm not sure how well I'm juggling my responsibilities these days, Mrs. Yates. But I keep trying," she said.

Her mother hadn't wanted her to study in the United States. Because it would be too onerous, too demanding. Even now there were recriminations in her emails. Minerva was too far away, Minerva wouldn't visit during the summer break. But Minerva had desired New England very badly, even if she had been warned time and time again how stressful her studies might be.

"I'll make you a deal. I'll pay for your room and board in the fall, plus living expenses. That way you don't have to be working two jobs and can focus on your thesis," Carolyn said breezily.

Too shocked at first to say a word, Minerva simply stared at the woman.

"Well? What do you say?"

"I couldn't . . . that would be very generous," she managed to say, and she remembered what Betty had written about Carolyn waving a wand, like a fairy godmother.

"It's nothing. I've done it before, for other young people of limited means. But you must promise to focus on your work. I know how difficult it can be to bring a project to fruition. All the long months and uncertainties piling up around you. My paintings, have you ever paused to look at them? How many months do you think it takes to perfect the brushstrokes, to capture someone's smile, the curl of their hair?

"I was painting since I was a young girl, and by the time I started school at Stoneridge, I still didn't know enough. It's more than holding a brush that makes the artist, and more than typing words that makes the scholar. You have something, I can see it. You must not give up."

"Thank you."

"Thank *you,* Miss Contreras. My grandson is not much for tea and conversation. You do me a service by chatting with me."

Carolyn smiled and patted her hand.

MINERVA PRESSED A HAND against her temple and closed her eyes. Her fingers brushed the knob on the car's stereo, turning the music down. It was her own CD she'd popped into the player. A compilation of the Pixies.

"Are you okay?" Noah asked.

"My head is killing me."

"Was Carolyn grilling you about something?"

"No. I've had a migraine all morning."

"She has those. Terrible ones. When I was little, I thought she had a tumor and her head would explode. You should try chewing peppermint. It works for her. Better than an aspirin, she says."

She opened her eyes. What she needed was a nap. She wasn't getting enough sleep. Discordant thoughts rattled inside her head until dawn and there was the rising tide of anxiety.

The previous night she'd dreamed of her great-grandmother in those last few days before she died. *You simply live through it,* she'd said.

The words had followed her through the morning, like a melody that had wedged itself in her brain.

Noah gave her a sidelong look. "Anyway, if Carolyn said something nasty, you should ignore it. She can be a real piece of work, but it's not worth thinking about it."

"She wasn't being nasty. She offered to pay for my room and board. I don't know how that would work, but she did."

"It should be easy enough. She set up something like that for Thomas, so the university must know how to funnel the money."

"For Thomas Murphy?"

"Yeah, when he was tutoring me and came to the house they got to talking. Art, like I said before. Then, during Thanksgiving, I was mostly wasted, so it was Carolyn and him chitchatting. She thought he was a 'promising young man.'"

Minerva frowned and turned to look at Noah. "Why would he drop out if all his expenses were being covered? I mean, he had a full ride."

"Maybe he was tired of academia. It can happen, you know."

Maybe. Burnout wasn't out of the question. Minerva herself was probably smack in the middle of an existential crisis.

Noah slowed the car down. "Did she talk about me?" he asked.

"Somewhat."

"Come on, if she was discussing her band of prodigies, she must have mentioned what a great disappointment I am. She loves to do it."

"What do you mean, her band of prodigies?"

"The underprivileged kids she's given scholarships to, or grants or whatnot. The Yates Foundation is 'dedicated to fostering the brightest young minds of their generation.' She enjoys going through all those files with their pictures, reading about the spelling bees they won or the trophies on their shelves. Fine little prodigies like yourself with their high IQs and their empty bank accounts."

"She implied you were immature and said you should get married," Minerva said bluntly, but then again, he'd been equally blunt.

He snorted. "Of course she did."

She crossed her arms and glanced at the ocean. Noah drummed his hands against the wheel of the car and sighed.

"I shouldn't have said that about the empty bank accounts."

"It's true," she said simply.

"It's dickish."

"Well, yeah, you are."

"That's true, too," he said, smiling.

Minerva shook her head and smiled back.

"Do you really have a fiancée?" she asked as the car slid onto campus.

She regretted asking the question immediately; it was a bit too personal and open. He laughed. "You think no flesh-and-blood woman would date me?"

"I didn't say that."

"There's always subtext in your words."

"What's that supposed to mean?"

"You speak with footnotes tacked onto every sentence." He laughed again, cheeky and good-humored. "Carolyn picked her for me. She even picked the ring. Another Boston Brahmin to join our illustrious family. What, are you shocked that they still arrange marriages in this day and age?"

"You're very melodramatic, do you realize that?" Minerva replied, flustered by the exchange.

"Part of the charm," he said, and parked the car in front of her dorm. "You're not offended, are you? Because—"

"No," she said quickly, and the sight of Ledge House, which she normally thought beautiful and stately, suddenly struck her as uncanny, even treacherous. She flinched in her seat. "Did Thomas ever tell you what kind of research he was working on?" she asked. "I know you said you only talked about class stuff, but this would have been class related. Something to do with witchcraft and New England, maybe?"

She really didn't want to spend so much time thinking about Thomas Murphy; frankly she wasn't even sure why she kept dwelling on him. Yeah, there was something that eerily reminded her of Ginny when she thought about him, and he also reminded Minerva of herself, but she was probably creating connections that were not there. Her depressed, anxious mind was conjuring mysteries and puzzles.

"Not really. He might have told my grandmother the specifics. I don't have anything to do with the foundation and who she picks for the scholarly grants. He had a different major, we weren't in the same crowd. Why do you ask?"

"I think his research interests overlapped with mine," she said as diplomatically as possible, scooping up her backpack. She opened the door. "Thanks for the ride."

"Happy to help. Hey, you're friends with Patricia, right?" he asked, pressing the eject button and handing her the CD.

She tucked it back in its case. "Yes."

"She's throwing a party Saturday."

"Patricia is always throwing a party. Or a luau. Or something."

"Are you going?"

"It's not my style," she said, although she could already imagine Hideo badgering her about it. Minerva had narrowly avoided heading to the movies the previous night, but only because Hideo had an unexpected date with a philosophy student from Harvard.

"I'm planning to attend. And not puke in the bushes this time."

He looked as if he expected them to continue this line of conversation, but Minerva had no idea what else she was supposed to tell him. She had no intention of partaking in Jell-O shots, beer pong, and Ace of Base playing on repeat. What she needed was to rest.

"Thanks again. For the ride."

"No problem. It's wicked good, you know?" he said, pointing at the CD case she was holding.

"Yeah. Fuck. I forgot to . . . I'll burn you a copy later. Or some other music. I give my friends music all the time, but I've been distracted," she said as she stuffed the CD in her backpack.

"Am I being upgraded to friend?"

She zipped the backpack closed, looking at his amused face. "Trial friendship," she said.

Minerva hurried up to the front door rather than rounding the building. She went straight to the bathroom and looked for the bottle of aspirin. She wandered into the kitchen and washed the pills down with a few sips of coffee.

God, her damn head was bursting! It was stuffy inside the house, which made things even worse, so she opened the back door and promptly gazed upon the corpse of the orange tabby.

Its neck had been twisted and broken in such a violent way that at first she did not register what had happened to the animal. It looked like a towel that had been wrung tight. She bent down and touched its head.

She felt a violent twitch on the nape of her neck, as if she had been hit with an object, and leaped back. She locked the door and stood in the middle of the kitchen, breathing fast.

Minerva rushed to the phone and dialed Hideo. She got a busy signal, which echoed as loud as a dynamite blast in her ears. She slammed the receiver down and fell back on the couch.

The pain seemed to be radiating down her back and she curled up on the couch. She felt exhausted and squeezed her eyes shut.

*You simply live through it.* The refrain invaded her mind.

When she opened her eyes, it was dusk. Someone was knocking. She shuffled into the kitchen and flung the door open. Hideo smiled at her.

"Ready for rounds?" he asked.

Minerva looked toward the corpse of the cat. It wasn't there.

"You didn't forget, did you? I brought the car so we could cover our dorms faster."

She pulled her hair away from her face with both hands. "Where is it?"

"Where's what?" Hideo replied.

"Someone killed Karnstein and left the body. It's gone."

"The cat you like to feed?"

"Yes." Minerva moved quickly past Hideo and walked down the back steps of the house. She looked around the bushes.

"The animal that killed it probably dragged the carcass away."

"It wasn't an animal. Someone snapped the cat's neck. It was right there."

Hideo looked in the direction she was pointing. "Are you sure?"

"Yes, I'm sure! They left it for me to find, they . . . fuck!"

She stared at the house. Hideo walked toward her slowly. "Okay, did you call campus security?"

"What?"

"If someone played a sick prank on you, you need to report it. Is it Conrad? The other night you said Conrad—"

"Un embrujo," she said, switching to Spanish in her disquiet.

"Sorry?"

"Bewitchment. The dead animals, the feeling of being followed . . . I bet flowers would wilt inside the house."

"Minerva, what are you talking about?"

"Hexing, curses, whatever you want to call it. My great-grandmother used to talk about this, and Beatrice Tremblay wrote about the exact same thing."

"Beatrice Tremblay . . . wait, you're talking about your thesis?"

"Not my thesis. The real thing. The real deal. What if witches do exist, Hideo? Have you ever wondered about that? Not like in *Bewitched*, not the funny witches with pointy hats. Spell casters who follow ancient, well-known patterns. Universal concepts. Physics is universal, isn't it? It doesn't matter if you're in Japan or Mexico or Salem, the apple will fall from the tree. What if it's like that for magic? You find the constants; you make them work. You alter reality."

"What about . . . what about when you told me about inugami. Remember? They're similar to familiar spirits and they're created by sorcerers by killing a dog. My great-grandmother told me a story about something like that, about creating a minion—"

"Those are very old stories," Hideo said, interrupting her. "No one believes in that now."

"Maybe they should. They should believe in familiars and spells and curses and witch marks."

The lampposts by the path that led to the dorm turned on automatically with the coming of the dark and she was able to clearly see Hideo's worried expression under the stark light.

"Minerva, I know you've been stressed lately. Maybe you should contact health services."

He thought she was losing it, but she wasn't going to call health services. It would go in her file and her adviser would give her a call, and what if they yanked her scholarship or took her campus jobs? Sure, Carolyn Yates had said she could have a full ride, but if she was too loony to attend classes, she wasn't going to be a student for long. They would take her visa, too. She'd have to go back to Mexico with a half-completed degree, babbling about witches and familiars.

"Yeah." She watched a moth flutter close to the bulb of a lamppost. "Yeah, sorry, I haven't been sleeping much. I'll email health services."

"In the morning?"

"First thing in the morning," she said. "Let me get my clipboard."

"I can do the rounds alone."

"No. Are you kidding me? I'll grab the clipboard."

She rushed back inside and closed her eyes, breathing slowly. When she snapped them open, she picked up the clipboard and went back out. Hideo looked at her funny during their whole route. Once they returned to her dorm, she asked him if he wanted to have a soda or water or anything. He relaxed considerably once they were in the kitchen.

"You sure you're okay?" he asked before he left.

"Yeah, I've been living off coffee and pretzels. I swear, I'll call health services and go to bed early."

"Okay. But I'm dropping by to see how you are tomorrow. And you're going to go with me to Patricia's party."

"Sure," she said, sliding her hands into her pockets.

"You mean it?"

"I'll go. Noah Yates will be there. I'd already planned to meet him," she lied.

"That's great," Hideo said, and he smiled, looking perfectly pleased. Shit. She'd have to show up to the party after all.

As soon as Hideo's car was out of sight, she locked the back door and headed into the library. She looked at the collection of stuffed birds staring at her from the walls. She grabbed a canary that had probably been preserved a hundred years before. She pulled a sewing kit from the back of a drawer. Then she went into the bathroom.

She held the canary in one hand, as if testing its weight, and looked in the mirror. On the sink she had placed seven pins from the sewing kit.

All this time she had been clinging to rationality, avoiding slipping into superstition and fear. No more.

"One," she said, and pricked her thumb, then slid the bloodied needle into the bird's body.

# 1908: 10

*FOLLOW THE PLAN, SIMPLY follow it,* she thought. This refrain, repeated with each step, helped to numb her brain so that she did not rush back to the safety of the farm, to her bed, where she would be if she'd let reason guide her.

She held the lantern up with her left hand to light the way, paying attention to all the sounds of the night: the wind in the trees, the crickets chirping, the snap of the twigs under her shoes.

The burlap sack felt as if it were filled with lead. Her palms were sweaty, and her grip seemed to slacken every couple of minutes, as if her body conspired against her, wanting Alba to drop this burden and rush back home.

*Follow the plan.*

It was awfully late. The moon's light barely grazed the ground, and the glow of the lantern was subdued, making the darkness almost impenetrable. She walked slowly, each step deliberate and careful.

When Alba reached the clearing by the river, she took a deep breath and placed the lantern on the ground. She'd surveyed this area in the daytime, paced up and down the river, determined how she'd proceed until it all seemed like a play and she an actress performing a part. But at night the landscape had morphed, and strange shadows crisscrossed the ground, making her wince.

She opened the burlap sack and reached inside. She took hold of the rabbit she'd grabbed from the hutch and struck with a hard, quick blow to the skull. A fresh kill: its body was still warm.

She reached again into the sack and pulled out the handkerchief, the rope, and the knife. The items were laid next to the rabbit. She contemplated them as she rubbed her arms.

Finally, she knelt next to the rabbit and placed it flat on its belly. She pinched the hide near the neck and made a cut, then pulled with one hand toward the rear and with the other toward the head. The skin began to tear and separate.

It had always amazed her, when she performed this task in the kitchen under her mother's watchful eye, how easily the skin would slide away, like tissue paper being ripped, revealing muscle and fat, a sharp reminder of the frailty of all living creatures.

This time, she trembled so much she feared she'd be unable to complete the skinning, yet at last she removed the entire hide and the exposed corpse lay before her.

Alba wiped her hands with the handkerchief and stood up. She hung the oil lamp from the branch of a tree that practically dipped its roots into the river. Then she picked up the rope and rested her hand on her brother's pistol, which was tucked in the gun belt around her waist. The belt had also belonged to Tadeo. She'd never had a gun belt of her own, but then, she'd never had a pistol. When her brother or Valentín took her target shooting, she used their weapons. She didn't hunt.

Would it be different from shooting a target? she wondered. How easily did a bullet pierce flesh rather than a tin can? Could a bullet that had not been blessed kill a witch?

Valentín was dead and she had no one to mentor her through this task. All she knew about trapping a witch was murmurs and half-forgotten tales, which might be wrong even if she had been able to remember them clearly. All she had was what Valentín had spoken, and he was dead.

She had nothing else, nothing but that pistol and the rope and the skinned rabbit. But she'd made up her mind that day; she'd loaded the gun and promised herself she would not return home until the witch was dead.

Alba had never wondered about the source of her portents. To her, they seemed like the mole on her neck, simply a part of her. Now she felt that whatever quality allowed the portents to manifest also gave her an instinctive clue to what words to say and how to proceed.

She cleared her throat and spoke. "I bring you an offering of flesh and blood!" she yelled.

She stepped away from the rabbit's corpse and clutched the rope. She waited.

The tree under which she stood was a few paces from the river, so that in case of an attack she might jump into its current and swim away. There was no guarantee the water would shield her from harm, and yet it was the one escape route she'd mapped. Besides, she knew this area, knew the riverbank. Tadeo and Alba had skipped stones there, jumped rope, drawn figures in the mud with a stick.

The feeble light of the moon drifted between the branches of the tree and the wind stirred her hair, tugged at her skirt, but no blood-thirsty creature sought her.

She rested her back against the trunk of the tree and waited some more.

A cry made her quickly raise her head. It was the strange cry she'd heard once before, outside her window, almost a growl, and it seemed to come from far away, though when it rang out again, it sounded dangerously close.

Something was approaching fast.

She brushed a hand against her lips and looked around, trying to discern any movement in the distance. The night yielded no clues as to the source of the noise. The wind toyed with the grasses by the river; it rustled the cattails softly. A leaf fell from the tree and lodged in Alba's hair.

Then she saw it, slipping into the edge of the clearing. It was as if a ripple sliced through the blackness of the night, as if someone had thrown a pebble into the dark and the dark had awoken. Forward slid a shadow and the shadow was a thing that had the body and the head of an enormous dog, with a long snout and pointed ears.

As the thing inched closer to the dead rabbit, sniffing and hissing, it seemed to drag with it a veil of shadows, so that she could not see it clearly even as she noticed certain details of its anatomy. She saw the line of feathers running down its bony spine, the talons like those of an owl, the slick skin of an eel, for this was a creature of impossibility, neither mammal nor bird but something in between that moved with the gliding smoothness of a snake.

The creature began to bite into the rabbit's carcass, and she heard the sharp snapping of a bone, the slobbering of a rabid, ravenous animal.

Her heart beat madly and for one moment she considered jumping into the river, letting the current carry her. *Follow the plan, simply follow it.*

She tied a knot and spoke.

"I bind you with earth," she said, her hands working quickly as she spoke. "I bind you with water. I bind you with fire. I bind you with air."

It was when she tied the fourth knot that the thing in the clearing threw back its head and she noticed its eyes: they were of a glowing green and there was an emptiness to them, as if the skull of the creature had been hollowed out and a candle placed inside it.

"I bind you with earth," she said, beginning the sequence again and tying the fifth knot.

The monster kept chewing. Blood dripped from the creature's mouth onto the ground. When she tied the seventh knot it growled and flashed its teeth, growing restless. Its feathers shifted; it arched its back and spat out whatever was left of the carcass it had been gnawing. Its ears lay back flat against its skull.

"I bind you with air," she said, and tied the eighth knot.

It began moving toward her. Slowly. It lowered and raised its head, and when she tied the ninth knot and spoke the ninth phrase it let out a screech that was the sound of a knife being sharpened, metallic, strident.

The creature opened its mouth and out slipped its long, forked tongue, and then it fixed its unearthly green eyes on Alba. She felt as though it was grinning.

Alba took a step back, her fingers working the tenth knot.

"I bind you with water," she said.

The thing stood on its hind legs. It was as tall as a man and for a moment looked no longer like a dog, but like something else, something almost human, its skin wet and smooth, as if smeared with tar or blood. It spoke.

"Alba, stop," it said, and her fingers stilled. She grew mute.

Because that was her brother's voice. It was Tadeo speaking.

She stared at the creature, at its eellike flesh and its glowing green eyes that burned bright and eager.

It couldn't be him.

She backed away from it. Her hands were shaking. *Once you've begun tying the knots, you cannot stop speaking. You must keep going.* That was what Valentín had said. But her throat was dry, and the rope was heavy in her hands.

"Alba, you must stop," it said again.

"I bind you with fire," she said quickly, and tied the eleventh knot.

The creature gritted its teeth. The sharp sound made her wince. She froze in place, her eyes wide. It sounded like Tadeo, it did, but witches always tried to trick you. Her brother was dead, Valentín was dead, and this fiend was not her kin. She shook her head.

"I bind you with air," she said, and tied the last knot.

The thing in the clearing crouched low and began scratching the ground with its claws. It heaved and opened its jaws.

She slid the pistol out of the holster while clutching the rope with her other hand. She lifted it. "Father, give me strength," she said.

"Alba," the creature said, and fixed its green eyes on her.

That look, it stopped her. Her hand shook. Although she had

planned this, although she'd thought herself brave enough, fear and confusion now overwhelmed her. Alba let out a sob.

As if it were echoing her, a sound came out of the creature's throat, and it sprang forward with such speed that Alba was unable to respond, not even to cry out. She was simply shoved against the ground and the thing pressed hard against her chest, holding her down. It opened its mouth; the whiff of carrion made her want to retch.

The creature threw its head back before staring into her eyes again, that green glow so bright it was like a searing flame. She could not scream, though she wished dearly to shriek in horror, and mutely looked back at it.

The thing inhaled and grunted, but it did not bite her.

"Alba," it said.

Slowly it lifted away from her, and she was able to shift her arm, to angle the pistol. Yet that subtle motion caused the creature to hiss; it slammed her against the ground again, her skull thumping against the root of a tree with such force that this time she did cry out in agony.

She felt its fingers against her neck—the wicked claws drew a thin line of blood—and then it grinned and snapped its teeth in the air before bending its head down, ready to devour her.

The pistol was slipping from her hand, for she was half-dazed by the blow to the head.

She pulled the trigger and the charge exploded. At first she thought she'd accomplished nothing. The thing kept staring at her, its teeth a breath away from her neck, but suddenly it rolled aside, its limbs flailing wildly.

It contorted in agony, its whole body pulsing; the eellike flesh seemed almost liquid. For a moment it was able to regain control of its muscles and stood up. Alba also scrambled to her feet. She stumbled and through eyes clouded by tears pulled the trigger again.

The monster reeled backward with a groan and lay on the ground.

Alba stood still until she regained her breath. Pins and needles ran down her spine.

The creature's breathing was loud, laborious, and she approached it slowly. Her left hand hurt from clutching the rope so hard, for she had not let go of it for a second. She looked at the thing on the ground, which shivered and opened its mouth, and shot it a third time in the chest. The green glow of its eyes grew dim.

The sleek eel skin dissolved and the claws sloughed off, revealing hands and then quickly a bare chest, and there, on the ground, was her brother. He coughed and spat blood.

And she knew in that moment, with a certainty that almost smothered her, that this was indeed Tadeo. He'd been wrapped in black magic and transformed, turned into a horrid beast that the witch could command.

Alba had been tricked.

The gun slipped from her fingers as she knelt and touched his face.

"Alba," he said.

Frantic, she helped him sit up. "I'm sorry, Tadeo. My God, I didn't know."

She clutched his hands, which were icy cold to the touch. He coughed, blood as black as ink spilling down his chin. "You must live, Alba."

"You also must live. Tadeo, please."

Tadeo smiled, clutching her hand back. For a moment he was the boy with the mischievous smile she'd grown up with, who teased her and could ride the wildest of horses, and the torment of dark magic that had twisted his body and the pain of the bullets inside his chest seemed to vanish.

Then he closed his eyes and went limp. His body began to melt, slipping through her hands like hot wax. Alba tried to hold on to him but was left clutching a few black feathers and staring at a dark stain on the ground.

She wept until she could not cry any longer, all sorrow wrung out of her, leaving her drained.

# 1998: 10

"YOU LOOK TIRED," HIDEO said as soon as she stepped into his car.

Minerva snapped her seatbelt in place, opened the thermos, and sipped her coffee with a shrug. "Late-night reading."

It was half the truth. She had been busy reading and working on the computer. But she'd also carefully carved witch marks by the windows and the doors of the house. Wood and plaster now bore the imprint of her handiwork, though the circles she'd drawn were tiny and inconspicuous. In several spots, she'd lifted a board and placed a slip of paper with the witch marks below instead of carving the wood.

In her backpack was the bird she'd skewered three days before, a talisman that now accompanied her wherever she went, although she hadn't strayed far from the dorm. The previous afternoon she'd finally succeeded in obtaining Benjamin Hoffman's phone number and he'd said he'd be happy to meet her in person. This meant a trip to Boston.

"Did you get in touch with health services?"

"Yep."

She'd left a message on their voicemail, knowing they wouldn't get back to her until September, and the message had been vague anyway. A request to speak to the counselor when they had the time; it wasn't urgent. But Hideo didn't need to know those details.

"The guy you're going to visit, he knew Beatrice Tremblay?"

"He knew her very well. They were friends since they were about our age."

"That's a great find, then. Your thesis should be in pretty good shape with all the info you have from Carolyn Yates and now this guy."

"I'm getting closer to something."

"Be careful, okay? You were kind of weird the other night."

"It's steam building up. It'll be fine as long as I let it out, and I think I've figured out how to do that."

He parked the car by the train depot and turned to her. "Are you sure?"

"Uh-huh."

"Okay. But we're going to Patricia's place tomorrow, don't forget. It'll give you a chance to let out some of that steam."

She sighed. "I'll go with you, sure."

"What time are you heading back into town?"

"I haven't figured it out. Maybe I'll walk back to campus."

"Okay. Dinner, then? You can save me from spending the rest of the day working on my bibliography."

"You cooking?"

"Yeah, soba."

"I'll give you a ring before I head back," she promised.

On the train she drew circles in her notebook and pondered her great-grandmother's stories. She'd loved those fantastical tales of people transforming into animals and balls of fire flying through the night sky, but they always took place in what was to her an alien world. Long ago, far up the mountains. She'd never thought you could have a modern witch story. It was as if the glass and steel of office buildings repelled them. But in her backpack there was the talisman, and between her hands the notebook with her idle circles.

Iron and glass might not be enough.

She walked from the train station to Hoffman's apartment,

which was in the North End, above an Italian deli. Several of the brownstones and apartment buildings were undergoing renovations, giving way to luxury developments, but Hoffman's building looked untouched by the changes.

Two old ladies sat in plastic chairs on the sidewalk across the street, fanning themselves, and looked at her curiously. She rang the bell and was buzzed in, climbing the dark, narrow staircase until she reached the third floor.

Hoffman wore small, round glasses, a hearing aid in his left ear, and black slippers on his feet. As soon as she walked into his living room, he offered her a cup of tea. Unlike Carolyn Yates, he didn't have a proper tea set and handed her a mug that said BOSTON ATHLETICS ASSOCIATION while he held one with a picture of Snoopy at the typewriter. The pictures on the walls were ocean views, photos of shells, a dock. An upright piano, tucked in a corner, had more photos above it, perhaps of family and friends.

"I was glad to hear from you. Betty would have been thrilled to know people are interested in her work. You said you wanted to look at some papers I might have?"

He handed her a hexagonal coaster and she set her cup down atop the coffee table. "Carolyn Yates gave me access to Betty's journals and a manuscript she was working on. But she said you might have a few other things of hers."

"I do. Three boxes."

She took out her tape recorder and her notebook. "Do you mind—"

"Go ahead, go ahead."

She pressed the record button. "You met her when she was a freshman at Stoneridge, correct?"

"I did. I was a friend of Edgar Yates and other young men who frequented Stoneridge. They held many social functions there. It was an easy way to get to dance with a nice young lady. You'd simply ask a friend of a friend to get you an invitation to the formal dances. The girls were always looking for dance partners. Do you still hold your dances at Cohasset House?"

"We don't really have formal dances anymore."

"A pity. I liked dancing," he said wistfully.

"You and Betty seem to have been close, but it wasn't the typical relationship you might expect."

He smiled. "No, it wasn't the college romance most people were looking for. We connected because we stood out among the others. Betty was a poor girl trying to move up in the world and I was a Jewish boy from Brighton. And there was the fact that she liked women, and I didn't find anyone attractive, so that put us in a different spot than others. We bonded, kept in touch through the years. I went to Chicago once and met Irene, her longtime girlfriend. When they moved to Arizona, they made sure to invite me to spend time with them there. Eventually Betty came back to the East Coast."

"Is Irene still in Arizona?"

"I think she passed away a few years ago. But I can see if I have contact information for her friends and family."

She lifted her cup. The tea tasted black and bitter. Minerva made a face.

He chuckled and slid a dish with sugar cubes in her direction. "Place one between your teeth and then sip the tea. It's how we drank it."

She took a cube and imitated him.

"Better?"

She nodded and smiled.

"She spent her last two years here, with me. I was the only one left. Irene and Betty had broken up long before that. She had a brother who died during World War II and a sister who passed away years before. No other family to help her at the end, and she never did make a great living. Copyediting. That's what she did. Her stories, her novels, she worked on those in her free time, and she never wrote for the slicks, so there wasn't much money. You can go through the boxes if you want, look at pictures of Betty when she was young."

"That would be amazing."

"Well, and what else do you need? Any other questions I can answer?"

"I was hoping to learn more about Virginia Somerset. *The Vanishing* seems to be inspired by her disappearance. You knew her too, right?"

There was a brief pause before he replied. "Ginny Somerset cast a long shadow over Betty's and Edgar's lives."

"They used to talk about her, didn't they? At least I have the impression that they spoke often."

"They did, eventually. Betty and Edgar were not in touch for several years. When she moved to New York, they reconnected. Betty would come up, stay with me for a few days, and pay Edgar and Carolyn a visit. Such a sad case that was, Ginny's disappearance."

"I'm told the most popular theory was that Ginny ran off with a boy."

She was getting used to the taste of the tea and drank more.

"Santiago, yes, I heard that. I never believed it. It didn't add up. Not when you looked carefully at the timeline."

"What do you mean?"

Hoffman clasped his hands and leaned forward. "I was working at a newspaper when Ginny vanished. Naturally, I tried covering her story. Santiago Ferreira lived in a rooming house in Temperance Landing. Like most of the young men there, he had trouble finding employment. We were in the middle of the Great Depression and folks were bouncing from gig to gig. He had little money and no car.

"This means that if Santiago and Ginny ran away together, they would have had trouble getting around. Of course, they could have walked to the train station and taken the train, but no one saw two young people walking down the road that day. Nor did anyone remember seeing them on the train. The men who had cars hadn't given them a lift."

"I suppose someone outside the rooming house could have given them a ride," she said, trying to picture the scene. A secret rendezvous, then a swift getaway in a borrowed vehicle. It was unlikely, but she did not feel at liberty to voice more sinister theories.

"Yes. But here's the problem: How could Santiago be arranging an elopement when he had been missing for five days?"

She shook her head. "I don't understand. Santiago went missing before Ginny?"

"When I talked to his housemates, they said he hadn't been seen since December 14. Ginny went missing December 19. Did he go away and come back for Ginny? If so, why didn't he also pick up his clothes, his money, his correspondence? Those were all back at the rooming house. Besides, he'd landed a full-time job at the Wingrave Manufacturing Company. First couple of days in December he started at the company.

"One of the other men in the rooming house also worked there. He and Santiago walked to the factory and back together. I wanted to talk to more factory employees, maybe find out if Santiago might have left a clue to his whereabouts in his locker, but Mr. Wingrave wouldn't hear of it. He didn't want anyone associating his company and personnel with Ginny's disappearance. Bad press and all that, especially if it turned out the man had done something to her. He phoned my editor, and my editor told me to forget about Ginny and Santiago. I was a copyboy trying to become a journalist. I did as I was told."

"Did you tell the police about any of this?"

"I spoke to an officer and told him Santiago's belongings were all back in his room and he hadn't given any hints he planned to go anywhere. I doubt they investigated it."

"I would have thought Edgar would have asked them to look into it."

"He probably asked, but I got the impression Ginny's family didn't want people poking too hard at the case. I heard she'd run off with a guy a year or two before. Her father dragged her back all the way from Chicago. They thought she was up to her usual high jinks."

"I understand that. But didn't anyone investigate Santiago's disappearance?"

"The police didn't care what happened to folks like Santiago; he was just a mill boy, a nobody. They didn't push too hard with Ginny's case, and she was a wealthy girl. Do you think they would even bother to open a case file for someone like Santiago?"

It was her turn to grow quiet. He stood up. "I'll get the boxes."

The boxes were labeled BETTY in black marker and Minerva opened the flaps with careful, reverent fingers. Inside, she found a scrapbook that didn't contain any photographs or family memorabilia. Instead, newspaper stories had been pasted on each page, along with passages photocopied from old books. *Missing since November 1, 1979. Last seen in 1954. Vanished 1960.*

"The Black List," she said. "They tracked missing persons stories and told each other ghost stories."

"It was their way of coping. Death hurts, yet the wound heals. But when Ginny went missing, it left a void. No scar tissue could be formed."

"How did it begin? Telling ghost stories, keeping the Black List."

He refilled his cup of tea and motioned to her. She nodded and he poured more tea into hers, too. "I suppose it began in the summer of '66. That's when Betty went to New York. After Irene, her other girlfriends were short-lived affairs, and then, when she did try moving in with someone new, that girlfriend cheated on her. She was feeling lonely, nostalgic. She was finalizing her novel."

He meant *The Vanishing*. It had come out in 1969. The first reprint was three years later, when Gothic romances were all the rage, and it was packaged as one of those books, with a woman running away from a castle on the cover, even though there was no castle anywhere in the novel. The second reprint was from the eighties, during the horror boom.

"She contacted Edgar and they got together, started reminiscing. After that, they made an effort to see each other every year and they played 'the game.' That's what they called their ghost stories."

She pulled out several black-and-white photos: a young Beatrice Tremblay holding a tennis racket between her hands, Beatrice with Benjamin outside a movie theater, a group of young women by a dock, a handsome man laughing at the camera.

"That's Edgar, when he was young," Benjamin said, pointing at the snapshot she was looking at.

The next photo was of Carolyn, in a snappy dress and a chic hat. "Did Carolyn ever play the game?"

"No. I don't think she enjoyed Betty's visits; frankly I think she would have preferred if Betty didn't come to the Willows, but it was the one time Edgar put his foot down. He wouldn't stop speaking to her."

She looked at Benjamin in surprise. "Carolyn and Betty were friends. Why wouldn't she want to see her?"

"Sure, Betty considered Carolyn one of her great friends. She was always grateful to her. It was Carolyn who helped get her a job in Chicago after graduation, and she never forgot it. You'd never hear Betty say a bad word about Carolyn in public."

"But you might have something to say, in private."

"Perhaps I might speak my mind by the time we are done looking through these items," Hoffman said, but he did not elaborate on the subject. Instead, they looked at Betty's yearbook. He opened a thin volume of poetry where Betty had pressed a flower within the pages, spoke of Betty's time with Irene and of another girlfriend whom Betty had lived with for three years in Brooklyn, before settling in an apartment on Beekman Street near what used to be the Fulton Fish Market.

She dug into the boxes again, pulled out postcards, a couple of theater programs, letters with faded ink on the envelopes. More photos.

"Well, that's too bad," she said.

"I'm sorry?"

"Carolyn said you might have some of Ginny's drawings, but I don't see any. She has a few at home."

"The college might have more of them in its archives. Edgar wanted them exhibited, just like he wanted to preserve Betty's work."

"You know, I always thought Carolyn had funded Betty's archive, but her grandson told me the same thing: that Edgar was the one who collected her papers."

"That's correct."

She found a few handwritten pages that didn't match Betty's handwriting. They were dated 1934. Could that be Ginny's spirit correspondence? She set them aside and came upon another cache of photos.

There was a snapshot of Ginny hugging Edgar. Another of her sitting pensively at a desk. Minerva set them down on the coffee table next to the pages. Then, almost incongruously, there was a snapshot of Carolyn and Edgar together, posing for a wedding picture. His face seemed harder, older than that of the man in the previous photos.

"It must have been strange when Carolyn married Edgar, considering all of you had known Ginny."

"I imagined how it'd go quick enough. Carolyn didn't waste any time giving Edgar a shoulder to cry on. He married her August of 1935."

"I guess he wanted a shoulder pretty badly."

Hoffman frowned. He grabbed Edgar's photo, the one where he was alone, looking merrily at the camera. "He was a wreck and Carolyn knew it. I'm not saying she took advantage of him, but it was a bit unseemly how fast she sailed into his harbor, so to speak. Yes, yes, he was a grown man. Still, I found it distasteful. I don't know, maybe I just liked Ginny a whole lot more than her."

He stared thoughtfully at the photo, his fingers gently gliding across its surface. "He never laughed like that again. Spent the rest of the decade drunk, stumbling home. It wasn't until his first child was born that he sobered up, but only for a while. He cycled through sobriety and heavy drinking binges. A few years fine, a few more in a haze of booze."

"What about Betty? How did she do?"

"Betty was anxious. Brittle. Doubts always circled in her mind. She loved Irene but was so afraid of losing her that she ended up pushing her away. Like I said, when Ginny disappeared it left a void. A black hole. Neither of them could ever hope to fill it."

A clock struck the hour. Hoffman turned his head to look at it. "I'm afraid I need to cut our meeting short. I have another appointment. But you're welcome to come back and visit me."

"Thank you. Could I borrow this?" she asked, pointing to the scrapbook. "And these pages, too?"

"Of course. I hope they'll be of some help to you."

He walked her to the door. She shook his hand. "You haven't spoken your mind about Carolyn, and I'm about to leave."

Hoffman sighed and took off his glasses. "I'm afraid I don't have a good opinion of her, although she didn't have a high opinion of me, either. I was the Jew boy who had sneaked into her social circle and since she didn't bother keeping up appearances with me, I got a good look at her. She was a user of people. Her father was the same, a slippery, awful man who treated his employees like dirt. I was hoping his stupid business would go under, but the Wingraves always come out all right."

"It did go under, though."

"Yes, even if Edgar's money kept it on life support. But when the place closed down, Carolyn and her family were still rich. Now, I know the mills were always hard, it didn't matter if it was in Lowell or Temperance Landing or Ludlow. Union busting, supervisors taking advantage of immigrant workers or sexually harassing the women, that's what you'd find at many mills. The Wingrave Manufacturing Company was an excellent example of these tactics."

"I suppose Edgar didn't care how the place was run or how his money was spent."

"It was Carolyn's family business, that's how he saw it. He wrote checks when necessary and left it at that. And he was sick, the alcohol preoccupied him more than business matters. He passed away less than a year after Betty died. I knew it would be like that."

"What was his relationship with Carolyn like, if I may ask?"

"He was troubled, and that trouble spilled into his marriage. It was at times . . . tempestuous."

"Then she didn't love him?"

"Oh, no. I didn't say that. Carolyn adored Edgar. She loved Betty, too. I'm not trying to imply she didn't. And everything was nice and cheery as long as things were going Carolyn's way, and she made sure things went her way, whether you liked it or not. I never could stand passive-aggressiveness. I like things to be open and straightforward. Carolyn didn't. Maybe I'm a sour old man nursing grudges, huh?"

"I think you're very nice, Mr. Hoffman," she said.

"Keep in touch. I want to see what you write about my Betty in the end," he said, and when he smiled she could almost glimpse the young man who had danced the evenings away at Stoneridge.

They shook hands again. She put on her headphones and pressed play on her Discman. It was a nice day and she'd always enjoyed her walks around Boston, especially when she had music to keep her company.

Soon after leaving the apartment, she felt that someone was following her. She turned around a few times but couldn't say who was watching her. The feeling went away and then returned, much stronger than the first time, when she reached Causeway Street.

Minerva stopped and slid off her headphones, letting them rest on the back of her neck. The Green Line train running overhead made the elevated tracks rumble, and that prickling feeling in the back of her skull that never boded well began to emerge.

On the other side of the street there was a pay phone decorated with colorful graffiti. Two construction workers were standing outside a bar chitchatting. Ahead of her a businessman hurried by, clasping a briefcase.

The Cardigans were still playing, music spilling from the headphones.

She walked faster, hurrying to the train station, and sat down. On the bench next to her someone had left a copy of *The Phoenix* open to the section with all the adult personals. She grabbed the newspaper and pretended to read, lifting her eyes a couple of times, trying to see if she could spot the person who was following her. Because there definitely was someone after her; someone was staring even if she couldn't pinpoint who it was.

Then the sensation dissipated and it was time to board. She clutched her backpack all the way back to town, sometimes unzipping a side pocket to brush the feathers of the talisman tucked inside.

Rather than phoning Hideo, she stopped by the liquor store and purchased a bottle of wine and a six-pack of beer. She stuffed them in her backpack and walked to campus. She wanted more time to wind down.

By the time she reached Hideo's place she felt much better.

"I come bearing gifts," she said, and pulled out the beer.

"As long as you're not Greek," he said cheerfully. "Go sit down. Shove the books away. I'll bring the food."

The dining table was covered in papers and books. She piled them in a corner.

Among Hideo's books and comic books, with the shelves crammed with CDs and DVDs and the gurgle of the fish tank, she realized how much she'd missed spending time with him. She'd truly been neglecting her friends that summer.

Hideo reappeared with two bowls and chopsticks. They sat down to eat.

"Were you working?" she asked, motioning to the books she'd pushed aside.

"Trying to fine-tune the bibliography and instead wasting time with video games. At the end of the day, I'm probably going to do a boring, tried-and-true analysis of *Turn of the Screw*. I was toying with pairing 'The Romance of Certain Old Clothes' with the 'Black Hair' segment of *Kwaidan,* but I don't think it works. So what were you up to today?"

"Listening to ghost stories of a different type."

"How poetic. Hey, I was on a message board that had a story you might like. Apparently, *The Necronomicon* is hidden at Bradford College. Lovecraft dated a coed there and they entombed it somewhere in the tunnels beneath the college."

"That's a funny one. Lovecraft would have been more afraid of coeds than of nameless horrors from beyond the stars."

"You never know. Sometimes there's some truth in all that fiction. Hey, wasn't Shirley Jackson into witchcraft?"

Minerva nodded. "I think she said it was a way of channeling female power." She tapped the chopsticks against the bowl. "If you're looking at *The Turn of the Screw* you should borrow my copy of *An Anatomy of 'The Turn of the Screw'* by Cranfill and Clark."

Hideo had made matcha cheesecake to go with the meal. They ate it while watching a videotape with episodes of *Aeon Flux,* then talked further about James and the non-apparitionist view versus the supernatural interpretations of Peter Quint and Miss Jessel. Afterward, Hideo drove her to her dorm.

Minerva placed the bottle of wine underneath the kitchen counter and headed to the library. She looked at the stuffed birds in the room and two shadow boxes displaying a collection of moths and butterflies.

She pictured the house as it would have been in Beatrice Tremblay's day, when the students would have flitted in and out of the library and a house mother enforced curfew, back when there were formal dances and Benjamin Hoffman and Edgar Yates might show up in freshly shined shoes with their hair combed back for an evening of merriment.

Darkness approached and she turned on the lights. A sense of placid normalcy reigned after her evening with Hideo; phantoms and hauntings were merely academic exercises as she sat on one of the couches and leafed through the Black List. Like Noah had said, all the news clippings and stories concerned disappearances. The time periods and circumstances varied and the locations were spread mostly across the United States. There were a few exceptions. A handful of stories reached into Canada, near the valley of the South Nahanni River, where prospectors moiling for gold had disappeared more than a century ago. But the bulk of the disappearances were on the East Coast.

The names and circumstances began to blend together after a while. Alice Corbett disappeared in 1925 from her residence hall at Smith College in Northampton. Dorothy Forstein vanished from her Philadelphia home in 1949. She'd left her purse, money, and keys behind. The front door of her house had been locked.

Most chilling, there was Joan Risch, a housewife from nearby Lincoln, who vanished in 1961 from her home, leaving a trail of blood behind. A woman matching her description was spotted later walking down the highway, blood dripping down her legs. Risch had been researching missing persons cases before she herself vanished.

Not included in this narrative was Ginny, who had vanished during the month of December, long ago, yet her story remained in the blank spaces between the pages of the scrapbook, for this was ultimately a futile quest for a clue regarding her whereabouts. Now a question lingered in Minerva's mind, this one about Santiago. They were linked, the two of them, but not as lovers. No, Minerva felt it was something else.

She turned from the scrapbook to the handwritten pages. She compared the handwriting to the photos she'd taken of Betty's journal. Indeed, it wasn't her penmanship. These letters were beautifully elaborate, while Betty wrote with a sloppier hand.

Despite the gorgeous penmanship it was difficult to make sense of the writing. There were sentence fragments and interrupted paragraphs.

One bit struck her as interesting: *Beware. Beware. Place wards, lock windows, beware. This room is safe. They're after you. They're here—*

A blotch of ink hid the rest of the words, and a slash ran down the bottom of the page, as if the pen had been pressed too firmly against the piece of paper. She pictured Virginia Somerset at her desk, madly scribbling, the ink staining her fingers.

A car was approaching, its bright headlights intruding on Minerva's solitude. She raised her head, wondering who it might be. Then she realized the light was not the right color: it was a soft green.

Minerva brushed the scrapbook and the pages aside and went toward the window.

There was no car. Instead, a wispy mist drifted toward the house, wrapping it like the silk of a spiderweb tightens around a helpless fly. It glowed, and that glow seemed to intensify as the mist coalesced, became thicker, concentrated in one spot until there was a floating green sphere perched in the air, looming close to the window.

She held her breath. Her hand was frozen stiff upon the windowpane. The greenness pulsed and she had the thought to run, to simply get out of the house and run away. Normalcy had been annihilated. Now the uncanny pierced the night.

"No," she said, and shook her head.

Slowly, she lifted her hand.

She closed the curtain and stepped away from it, looking around the room, counting the wards she'd placed in this section of the house: tiny scratches by the doorways, and others hidden under boards she'd carefully loosened. They ought to hold. Unless she was wrong about all of this and witch marks were useless. That might be the case, after all.

The phone in the library began to ring and she fumbled with the receiver, but the line was dead. She slammed the receiver down and it began to ring again, louder and louder, like discordant cymbals. It almost seemed to be shrieking at her. Minerva tugged at the cord, disconnecting the phone.

She reached into her backpack and pulled out the bird talisman. The light was growing steady now, its emerald glow spilling eerily under the curtains and across the floor.

She stepped back, avoiding the light, which slithered like long fingers that stretched into the room and threatened to grasp her ankles. She bumped into a couch and almost lost her footing.

Something knocked against the back door and knocked a second time, louder, until it wasn't knocking, it was like the pounding of fists. Then it moved to the right, scratching under a window, scratching against another. Its nails slid upon glass, raked against shutters.

The noise changed again; it seemed to be moving all around the house. Above her, the wood squeaked and groaned, like the pipes sometimes groaned in the winter, rattling with the cold. The floor vibrated under her feet and then more strongly, as if this were an earthquake that was gaining in force, but she'd never felt a quake like this before, and she'd grown up in Mexico City and weathered the big one in '85.

She pressed herself against a doorway, grasping the doorjamb for support.

Dimly, she heard the tinkling of crystal: she realized it was the grand chandelier near the staircase, which now shivered like a tree touched by an icy wind. In the kitchen, the spoons and forks were rattling in their drawers, and pots clanged against one another.

The lights were flickering. On the shelves, her books slid to the side. Her alarm clock in the bedroom started beeping. One of the shadow boxes on the wall tumbled to the floor. Its glass shattered; minuscule bright shards spread onto a rug, the delicate bodies of butterflies and moths pinned a century before now lying upon the floorboards.

She clutched the talisman tighter. One of the pins scratched her hand, drawing blood.

The curtains fluttered and a chair toppled over, crashing violently against the floor, but then, just as suddenly as it had begun, the movement ceased and the house was still. The glow had receded.

She carefully made her way to the window and peeked outside. There was a green glow above Briar's Commons, but it was quickly dissipating, and within two blinks of the eye it was gone. There was nothing but the summer night sky outside. She could have dreamed the whole incident.

Except she was wide awake and there was blood dripping down her left hand.

She sat on one of the couches for a few minutes, not knowing what to do next. Eventually she went to the bedroom and turned off the alarm that was still blaring. Then she washed her hands and looked for a bandage.

When she returned to the library she began picking up items from the floor. She grabbed the pages she'd been reading and stared at the words scrawled there: *Beware. Beware. Place wards, lock windows, beware. This room is safe. They're after you. They're here—*

# 1908: 11

SHE WAS A GHOST for three days. She moved through the house in silence, tending to her chores, her eyes downcast, her steps slow. Grief clouded her sight. Twice she almost broke out in sobs at the dinner table.

"You're too idle, girl," her mother said as they climbed the steps to their bedrooms.

Alba expected to be viciously chided about her listlessness, but instead her mother brushed a strand of hair away from her face with a gentle hand.

"I understand, Alba. I lost my mother when I was about your age. Now I've lost a husband and a son. There's a darkness that wants to swallow you, but you must not let it."

She thought about her brother, about the viscous mass of feathers and cartilage that she had pressed against her chest and which had dissolved into nothingness. They reached the top of the stairs and she stopped and stared at the floor.

"Valentín was your sweetheart, wasn't he?"

Alba did not speak, for it would have been too difficult to explain what she'd felt for Valentín. It had, perhaps, been the beginning of love, which had been cut off before it could truly bloom.

"Mourn him. But do not try to follow him to the grave. You'll make yourself sick if you continue like this."

"I know," she said.

They were quiet for a couple of minutes. Alba rested a hand against the iron banister.

"Tomorrow, your uncle and I are headed to see the mayor and perhaps to speak with Father Aguilera. I need you to help Fernanda around the house and assist with the cooking. Fernanda is a darling girl, but she has not discovered the importance of salt and Dolores complains she's more trouble than help in the kitchen."

"I will, Mother," Alba said, even though her mind was filled with disordered thoughts and her mother's visit to town conjured a dangerous idea.

On the fourth day, as she was cleaning the irons with wax and preparing to tackle the week's ironing with Fernanda, her mother walked into the room and bade her a good day, promising to return in a few hours.

Alba nodded. After her mother and her uncle left, she brushed aside the basket with the damp clothes that she was supposed to lay flat before they were pressed, and went to her room. With shaky hands she removed the apron around her waist and changed into a different set of clothes. She'd spent half the night thinking what she'd do once her mother and uncle were away, once she had a chance to step out of the house without being noticed. She headed to the stables.

Once she was atop her horse, her purpose and her strength returned; her hands held the reins without the slightest twitch or shiver. She rode without fear or hesitation. Grief crystallized into rage as she followed the path up the mountain.

Los Pinos was quiet and lonely as she guided her horse down its streets. Next to a well she saw two teenage girls filling jugs with water and spoke to them.

"Do you know the way to Perpetua's home?" she asked.

One of the girls gave her directions and Alba thanked them. Soon, she was standing in front of a house that was shaded by a great gnarled tree. A withered vine encroached on the building, wrapping itself up the walls. The house was assembled more roughly than the others in the village; the stones of this building seemed haphazardly piled together and its windows were small and shuttered tight.

She pushed the front door open and walked in, holding her brother's pistol in one hand.

She slipped into a room with an old curtain barring further passage and easily pushed aside this piece of cloth. She stepped into a bedroom that was a nest of darkness crammed with half-glimpsed jars upon rickety shelves, much as in the home of Jovita. On the floor there was a pile of blankets.

She pointed the pistol at the woman sleeping under the blankets and when she did the witch opened her eyes and stared at Alba.

"I've come to ask you why you hate my family and then to kill you," she told the woman. Her voice evidenced no fear. She'd sloughed it off during the climb.

But the witch didn't seem surprised or frightened by her presence, either. Even in the semidarkness Alba could tell she remained unperturbed. "Light a candle," Perpetua said, motioning to a table, "unless you want to speak in the dark."

On the table there were a box of matches and a candle. Alba lit it. The woman sat on a large chest and Alba pulled over the one chair available.

"You should put that down," Perpetua said.

Her long black hair fell down her back and she wore a dark-colored dress and around her shoulders she'd knotted a shawl with a red stripe. Her hands were hidden in the folds of her clothing. They stared at each other.

Alba shook her head, pointing the pistol at the woman. "Not until you speak."

"If I hadn't wanted you to walk inside, you'd never have been able to open that door. I won't harm you, even if it's what you want."

"Yet you've harmed my family."

"Not me. There's more than one witch in these parts."

"I saw you talking to my brother."

"You saw me trying to warn him, but he wouldn't listen. He

didn't believe in curses. But you do. You've come to die, haven't you? Silly girl. Well, I won't kill you. I have no grudge against you."

Yes, she'd come to die. She'd recklessly ventured into that house not with the hope for retribution, but with the desire for oblivion. Now the woman denied her this. Instead she looked at Alba with composed, steady eyes. She had the stillness of a painted icon; Alba sensed no menace, no darkness.

Alba slowly lowered the pistol and set it on the table, close enough to her hand that she'd have no trouble shooting if it became necessary.

"If it wasn't you, then who cursed us? Where is the witch?"

"I thought you'd know by now, with your gifts. You have them, same as him. I can tell. They've always had them, the Quirogas, and maybe his family also carries the gift."

"Who?"

The woman shifted her head and the silver of her temples caught the light. She was not old, not truly; perhaps she was the age of Alba's mother, though the two lines bracketing her mouth were severely etched. "When he was little, he used to come to town with that friend of his. Wealthy boys wanting to buy amulets, wanting to woo a village girl and steal a few kisses, they always make their way to Los Pinos. Bored boys, stupid boys. We sold them trinkets. And he was clever, and he asked smart questions. Many, many smart questions."

"Who?" she asked again. Her fingers slid upon the pistol, not grasping it, merely touching the metal of the barrel, reassuring her that it was there.

"He came to Los Pinos with that Desoto boy."

Alba's mouth had gone dry. The words were croaked, not spoken. "Who?"

"Arturo Velarde. He's the warlock you seek."

She grabbed the pistol and pointed it straight at the woman's face. "My uncle is no warlock, you liar."

"You don't believe me? Set a test for him. Place a flower against his lips while he sleeps, watch it wilt."

"If it's true, then it's all your fault. You cursed him and made him into an evil creature, that's what you did."

"I didn't put that ambition in his blood. He made his own path."

"Liar!"

"I warned your brother. I warned my daughter. If you want to pull that trigger, do it. But I'm no liar. You know it. You feel it. He killed my Elena."

The name—it was the one she had tried to guess, and she recalled how upset Arturo had been at the guess. Alba stared at Perpetua and slowly lowered the pistol. The woman remained still—her lips moved, but her body was that of a statue. Her face was serene.

"She was a year older than him. They played together. He knew a few tricks, she knew others. I'd taught her, and she shared my teachings with him. He'd come with his coins and ask me questions, he'd fetch ingredients, he'd listen and write in a notebook. So I taught him too, some things I knew. Others he found himself."

"You taught him black magic."

The woman chuckled; a flicker of emotion rippled across her perfect stillness. "There's no such thing. People pick their path. Some heal bones, others break them. That boy was amusing. You don't see many wealthy kids coming around here for that learning."

"He's not a wealthy man."

"Wealthier than us, with a coin in his pocket to spare."

"And you sold him dangerous spells."

"I had a child to feed and there was little danger in it. They've taught you spells, I'm sure of it. Your father believed, same as the others before him."

She thought of her father, of when he spoke to the crops and of the superstitions that her mother disliked because they were the mark of uneducated country folk. Alba knew snatches of folk magic, spells for securing a sweetheart or attracting good luck. But she'd never thought that meant anything of importance.

"What happened then?" she asked.

"He turned fourteen and your father sent him away. Off he

went, and when he came back to visit, he was a young man. He must have honed himself in that time, because as soon as I saw him, I felt his power, and I was afraid because his heart was full of spite. I said, *You don't come back to bother us, you go away.* The trouble was, my Elena was not afraid. All she saw was the pretty mister, and even though I told her, *Don't you go crossing that man's path,* she didn't listen."

The wax from the candle had dripped down onto the table, tracing slow, pale rivulets. Alba touched the hardening wax with the edge of her fingernail.

"One night, when I was busy with other things, she left the house. She didn't come back. I looked, but I never found her. I know he killed her."

"How could you know?"

"Teyolloquani, they make their magic with blood. They drink the blood, they eat the heart. If someone is favored, the blood is potent, and my Elena had the gift, too. He ate her heart raw."

"I know Arturo—"

The woman smirked. "You know the pretty mister in his suits. You don't know the warlock that turns his enemies into animals. Or maybe you simply don't want to see him clear."

She slowly lifted one of the hands she'd kept in her lap, under the folds of her long shawl. Three fingers were missing from the hand, the stumps ending at the second knuckle. She remained serene; she was like a saint exhibiting the wounds of her martyrdom.

"After Elena went missing, I tried to kill him. I failed and nearly paid with my life for my failure."

"Your fingers . . . he couldn't have done that."

"Bitten off. By a wild animal. Just like a wild animal bit the throat of your friend."

"Arturo is not a monster."

"He can make monsters."

"But he isn't—"

The saint gave way to a woman who spoke in a hoarse voice, balling her hands tight. "He smells of carrion if you wash away the cologne. You have a gift; you know I speak the truth. Maybe you're as foolish as Elena, or worse than her."

Alba squeezed her eyes shut. Neither one said a word, not for a long time. When she opened her eyes, the woman had hidden her hands away again.

"Someone told me you tie a rope; you tie it, and you speak—"

"He's stronger than that. Words don't bind him."

"Then what can stop a sorcerer?"

"Nothing. Take your pistol and leave. I warned your brother back when it might have done some good. I told your brother to send him away, and maybe he might have gone. Now he has the scent of blood, now he's tasted prey."

"But there are stories of how to subdue a witch. Bullets! Bullets that are blessed!"

"You've seen what he did to me. No bullets will nick his skin. Certain tricks will work on lesser warlocks, but not him."

"Valentín, he told stories, and the knots worked! They did . . . the . . . I killed . . . so something else . . . something must be possible," she said, and then she couldn't speak because the memory of her dead brother, of the mess of feathers and flesh that dissolved between her fingers, was too powerful.

She pushed her chair back, grabbed her pistol, and stood up, yanking aside the thin curtain that led to the entrance. She looked back at the woman, who sat with the shawl pulled tight against her body.

"Tell me, if only for the sake of the child you lost," Alba said.

They stared at each other. The woman shifted in her chair.

"There is one story," Perpetua said, and her voice was a murmur. "It's about a young woman who finds herself under the spell of a sorcerer. He flies into her room each night and bites her on the neck. For six nights this happens, and her family is distraught, because each day she grows weaker and sicker, but on the seventh day her brothers consult a wisewoman.

"The wisewoman tells them to burn a painting of their mother, who loved the girl and has died. Mix the ashes with salt and the crushed wing of a moth and place them in a cup filled with wine. Whisper to the wine, telling it to protect the young woman. Then have the girl drink the wine and open the window to the chamber so that the sorcerer may fly in. The wisewoman tells them the sorcerer will drink from the girl, but the blood will be like a slow poison to him. His veins will be filled with the drugged wine and he will fall asleep. Then, when he is unconscious, the brothers must walk in and cut off his head.

"They do as they've been told and burst into the room. They find the sorcerer asleep and cut off his head. But when they turn to their sister, they realize her body is cold and dead." Slowly, Perpetua pressed her hands against the table, her eyes fixed on Alba's own. "That is the story I know."

"Thank you," Alba said.

Then the witch nodded and extinguished the candle.

WHEN ALBA RETURNED TO Piedras Quebradas her mother and her uncle had yet to come back. She told the maids that she did not feel well and would be napping and taking her supper in her room. Then she rushed up the stairs and threw herself on the bed, burying her face in the pillows.

She could not sit at the dinner table with Arturo and the others. Her blood rushed wild and discordant through her body. She feared she'd faint if she walked into the dining room. She closed the curtains and lay under the bedsheets with her back to the door. Later, her mother came.

"What is wrong?" she asked.

"A cold," Alba said.

Her mother pressed a hand against Alba's forehead. "I told you you'd make yourself sick."

"It's nothing. I'll be fine tomorrow."

Her mother was quiet. Alba felt her hand sliding against her hair, smoothing down a lock.

"Don't forget your prayers before you fall asleep."

"I won't."

There she lay until the house grew quiet and still. Midnight fast approached; they'd all gone to bed. She threw a robe over her nightgown and went down in search of the white pot in which the carnations bloomed. She cut a single crimson flower and walked up the stairs.

The hallway that led to Arturo's bedroom was vast and dark, so dark that with the dim light of a single candle to show the way it became cavernous, black and soft as velure. She moved quickly and when her hand fell upon her uncle's door, she hoped it would be locked and she would not be able to enter.

But the door gave way to her, it was unbarred, and she hesitated at the threshold before plunging inside. She knew the room; she knew the house. The furniture and the paintings and the mirror on the wall were all familiar and she charted her course toward the bed with ease. Yet his presence had turned the chamber alien. On a chair he'd draped a coat as thick as the pelt of a beast, and before the mirror there was a table with his shaving implements—the razor, the brush, the soap cake—and the bottle of cologne. The room had changed, had become his.

The hallway and the room had morphed, they were unrecognizable, but in the light of the candle his face was the same handsome face she knew. She let out a sigh of relief. Perhaps the witch was mistaken, or she had lied. Alba had felt her honesty, but it might have been a ruse. There was her uncle, his head peaceful against the pillow, his eyes closed, his breath gentle, and he was no monster with vicious teeth that could gnaw hearts and pierce the skin.

For a moment she thought to step out and let him be, but in her left hand she held the freshly cut carnation. She leaned over him and held the flower close to his lips.

The carnation wilted between her fingers, each petal curling and shrinking and blackening.

She sprang back in horror, and before she could even think to scream she was shoved against the armoire. She dropped the candle and it rolled upon the floor and was extinguished.

In the dimness of the room, she felt more than saw his eyes, now open wide, boring into her own. His hand pressed against her mouth. He pulled her away from the armoire and shoved her into an armchair at the other end of the room. At once she stood up and dashed to the door. The door slammed shut in her face, as if a gust of wind had rolled through the room.

"Come here," he said, and even though he was many paces from her, something dragged her back, pulled her as easily as a rag doll, and she was shoved back into the armchair with such force that she was left breathless.

He picked up the candle she'd dropped, lit it again, and set it atop a table.

"If you try to scream, I'll bind your tongue. It is not as if anyone would be able to hear you while you're in here anyway. I could shoot an elephant in this room and they wouldn't know. So let us be civilized."

She shrank back into the armchair, grasping it tight. His face, it seemed different. Not uglier or more handsome; the features were not altered, yet it was as if he'd removed a veil. There was the arrogance he'd always possessed, but now she saw something else. Power. Raw, heady. She could almost taste the magic upon her tongue.

She swallowed. "It's true. You're a sorcerer and you killed my brother and you killed Valentín."

"No, Tadeo killed Valentín and *you* in turn killed your brother," he said wryly.

"I didn't know it was him. You transformed him into a vicious animal. How could you learn dark magic and these evil things?"

He sat in an armchair directly across from her. His eyes were alert and fixed on her, unblinking. "You've been learning a few spells of your own. Tying knots and making talismans."

"To protect myself."

"Long before that."

She ignored his words and shook her head. "Why would you hurt us, frighten us?"

"Tadeo wouldn't sell the farm. With him out of the way, I thought it'd be easier to convince your mother. All those animals dying, all that bad luck . . . eventually, even the most stubborn of people will yield if everything goes wrong. Incidentally, I think very soon we'll be accepting an offer from the Molinas."

"You want my father's money. That's what this is all about?"

"It's one of the things I want," he said languidly.

She recalled the shadow that had sneaked into her room and bit her. She pressed her palm against her chest, upon the spot where she'd been wounded.

"Tadeo was right, you're a parasite."

"Careful, now, I said we'd be civil."

"You want to kill me. Like the girl. Elena. You leech."

For the first time he seemed surprised. His mouth curled with something that might have been distaste.

"You ate her heart; you drank her blood. You've drunk mine. And poor Valentín, you tore him to pieces."

"Poor Valentín, yes, meddling in affairs he shouldn't have meddled in. Was he the one who showed you how to kill your brother?"

"You destroyed my brother, not me. Same as you destroy everything around you. Carrion eater."

He stood from his chair. Lightning quick he was in front of her, his fingers upon her jaw, her neck, as if looking for a pulse point. She did not recoil at the anger on his face, she could not, too furious to fear him in that moment.

"Will you cut me open for your spells? That is what you do, isn't it?" she asked, and thought perhaps he might slice her from chin to navel in that instant, so bright and incensed were his eyes.

But he laughed, low and bitter. "Do you remember how you were so eager to know the name of my lover? I said I had none, even if there was a woman I wanted. Do you know her name this time around?" he asked.

He parted his lips and one of his hands was now in her hair. She stared into his sharp eyes, brimming with avarice, and she tried turning her head away, because she couldn't look at him any longer, couldn't speak to him. But the hand in her hair tugged hard, holding her in place.

"The one thing I've wanted the most is you, just as you want me. Wanted you quietly, for a long time now. You want me back. Didn't you wonder why your talisman didn't work? That sad dead bird. You must be careful with spells. You never barred *me* from your room. I've always been invited there."

"No."

"'Nothing you'd say would alter my feelings,'" he told her, repeating her own words.

"No," she protested, but it was a reflex and a lie. She remembered when she'd spoken that sentence to him, and she realized the power of such words. Magic wasn't about powders or birds, like that witch had explained. It was more than the mechanical repetition or a list of ingredients. She'd undone any magic, canceled any wards that might have kept him away, because she'd wanted Arturo close to her.

His fingers brushed against her mouth, traced the contours of her lips. "You summoned me. You called to me, and I came. Do you remember, when you knotted that cord around a piece of cloth, what you asked for? What you desired? Magic is desire, Alba."

"I didn't ask you to hurt anyone," she said.

"No man may escape the limits of his nature."

His eyes were impossible to behold, uncanny, and she feared his gaze would scorch her skin. He bit down on her mouth, drawing blood, and then he kissed her; so quick and fluid was the motion that at first Alba did not react. Rather than igniting, she became stone. But then her flesh softened, she opened her mouth, kissed him back, closed her eyes, forgetting all the terrible things he'd said, or rather remembering the strength of her desire.

For she had wanted him very much, quietly, for a long time. He'd spoken the truth.

She tasted shadows on his lips, the coppery trail of her own blood, relished it. Yet the memory of her brother's crumpled body was like a searing iron pressed into her brain and the outline of Valentín's coffin was painted a stark white against her eyelids.

Her fingers scrabbled at his shoulders and she shoved him back.

She ran to the door and attempted to pry it open. It would not yield. Then his hand fell upon the door handle, and she looked up at him. A drop of blood stained his lips. He licked it and turned the knob, holding the door open for her.

She hurried back to her room and found her brother's pistol then turned toward the doorway, thinking her uncle might have followed her. But she was alone. She stared into the dark hallway, the pistol heavy at her side, and remembered the witch's mangled hand. There was no use for bullets; she had been warned and knew it to be true. She'd felt his might. He'd shown her his true face. He'd done this because he knew himself invincible, immune to the petty weapons of men.

Alba closed the door and slid the pistol back into the drawer.

# 1934: 7

GINNY WAS QUIET THE day she went missing. Thérèse Audrain had offered me lodgings during the winter break, which I greatly appreciated. I did not have the financial resources to head off campus and vacation in a distant locale, like some of the girls would, nor could I avail myself of nearby relatives. I detested the idea of obtaining a special dispensation and remaining at Stoneridge, the lone inhabitant of the dorm. The previous winter, I had spent my break at Carolyn's house, but this year she was expecting visitors and I had not been invited.

Mrs. Audrain and her family would provide me with a home-cooked dinner and a measure of merriment. In exchange for their generosity, I had agreed to assist her during a dinner party she was throwing for other faculty members to celebrate the end of the term. This task would consume much of my day and I knew I was expected to stay during the party. I told Ginny as much.

She was sitting at her desk, a pile of books dominating the space, and scribbling in a notebook. Her basket with her knitting supplies, her needles and scissors and yarn, was atop her reading chair.

"You'll be fine, I trust? I'll be back before curfew."

"Don't worry."

"What time is Edgar picking you up on Friday?"

"Two o'clock," she said.

"Why don't you go to Carolyn's room and read there?"

"I'm fine."

"The girls are probably up to some fun, I bet—"

"I'm safe from any curses in this room."

I had been tying a scarf around my neck but I stopped when I heard that, and before I could think better of it, I spoke in exasperation. "Good God, Ginny, do you even listen to yourself anymore? You really do talk like you've gone insane!"

She raised her head and set her pencil down, resting her hands in her lap. Then she looked at me but didn't speak. I felt wretched. I knew how much my words pained her, how she feared people perceived her. She was going to spend the break with Edgar's family, but the thought of it made her terribly nervous. The idea of the sanatorium, of confinement, lingered in her mind, and she suspected the man she loved would one day label her a madwoman.

I knelt next to her side and clutched her hand. How soft it was, how thin and fragile.

"Ginny, forgive me."

"I'm not angry."

I didn't know how to help her, how to soothe her, but it was Ginny who soothed me, running a hand down my hair. I rested my head on her lap. The grandfather clock struck the hour downstairs and I stood up, weary.

"I'll leave you the number of Mrs. Audrain's house, in case you need me," I said, and scribbled it on a scrap of paper. "Promise you'll call if anything's wrong."

She tucked the piece of paper under her notebook. "I'll be fine."

"Well, then call if you're bored."

"I'll finish knitting that hat that I promised you. Don't you worry," she said, and she gave me the most dazzling of smiles.

I hurried out of the dorm and met Mrs. Audrain. Her house was in Temperance Landing. She was an awful hostess who would burn soup if left to her own devices, but she had a cook and each season she'd avail herself of a student or two who would walk around a room with a tray of canapés, place coats in the closet for guests, or set the table for her. I was used to paying for my room and board one way or another, and I ventured into the kitchen to assist with the preparations with a smile.

It was almost seven o'clock and the guests were streaming into the house when the phone rang. Mrs. Audrain turned to me.

"Won't you take a message for me, dear?" she asked.

I lifted the receiver and expected to hear a professor offering an excuse about why they wouldn't be able to make it that evening.

"Hello, Audrain residence," I said.

"Betty, it's me. I know who's bewitched me."

Ginny's voice sounded low and strained. I could hardly make out the words and adjusted the receiver.

"Ginny? What happened?"

"I know their names, but I can't speak them. They've tied my tongue. If something goes wrong, find bell, book, and candle."

"What?"

She hung up and when I dialed back the line was busy. A second felt like a week as I clutched the telephone receiver against my ear, and I feared I would not get through to her.

I was not supposed to leave Mrs. Audrain's house until much later, and she had promised to have me driven back to campus after the party concluded. But the cryptic call immediately had me putting on my coat and making a feeble excuse. Before Mrs. Audrain could protest, I ran out the front door and down the steps into the chilly December night.

Without a car I'd have to walk back, and in the snow; what might have been a leisurely stroll would surely become a much slower and more cumbersome task. But I could not think what else to do. There were no taxis in town. Forty minutes. It would take me forty minutes to walk back to our dorm.

Luckily, it had stopped snowing. I stuffed my hands in my pockets and hurried down the road. It was an easy path to Stoneridge from Mrs. Audrain's house—the street that took you to the college was the main artery of the town. It swept by the library and the park with its gazebo, rounded the central cemetery, and then curved by the ocean. I had walked this route many times.

However, the snow on the ground and the night altered the town and certain landmarks vanished. Predictably, I found myself suddenly walking down Neptune Street rather than following Pickman Road. I was walking in the wrong direction.

I turned around, changed course, but I was growing cold. My breath was a plume of smoke. Only once did a car traverse the street I was following, and it didn't stop when I waved at it, hoping I might hitch a ride.

I tried to walk faster, pushed myself until I was running, and by the time I reached the front of Joyce House beads of sweat rolled down my neck. I stormed inside and almost lost my footing on the staircase.

When I reached our room, the door was wide open.

Ginny wasn't there.

Her winter coat hung from a hook, her scarf and gloves were on the shelf where she normally left them, and her boots were tucked under it. Her knitting basket lay on the floor, overturned, but otherwise nothing looked amiss. She couldn't have stepped outside without her winter clothes. She had to be inside the dorm.

I rushed down the hallway, hoping I'd find her in Carolyn's room or with another of the girls. Carolyn's door was closed and she didn't seem to be in. I bumped into Bertha Trumbull and asked about Ginny. Bertha hadn't seen her.

I ran downstairs and found the house phone. The receiver was off the hook. I carefully put it back in place. Dread pooled in my stomach. I felt that time was running out.

I stepped outside, walked around the house, and found a trail of footprints leading away from the dorm, away from the college grounds. It had stopped snowing a scant hour before, which meant the prints were freshly made.

I followed their trail. The light of the moon reflected on the snow was so bright the land around me seemed to glow, and I had no trouble seeing where I was going.

Abruptly, the footprints became a confused jumble and the trail ended by the bend of a road, under a tree. On the snow there was a single smudge, like a red flower poking through the bone-chilling whiteness. It was a drop of blood.

The sight of it terrified me.

"Ginny!" I screamed at the night, but there came no answer.

My hands felt frozen stiff and the sweat that had trickled down my neck was growing cold. I stumbled down toward the road clumsily, not knowing where I was headed.

Then I stopped.

I had the sensation that there was something nearby, something dangerous and cunning and sharp. I saw nothing, heard nothing, yet my heart beat quickly and my dread was bubbling up, becoming panic.

"Ginny!" I cried out.

I stepped back, retreated toward the tree, my hand pressed hard against its trunk. The bark bit into my fingers.

It was starting to snow again, and as I squinted into the dark, I felt a deep alarm. It spread down my nape, my back, down to the very soles of my feet, making my eyes water and my teeth chatter violently.

Once, when Irene and I went camping in Arizona, we accidentally stumbled onto the nest of a rattlesnake. When I saw that reptile, my reaction was swift and immediate; I jumped back, driven not by reason but by blind fear. It was, perhaps, an instinctive reaction to encountering such an animal.

I can compare that moment in the snow to my encounter with the snake. It was as if the dark held a primeval terror, and upon encountering it my only possible reaction was the limbic response of flight. I ran away, stumbling madly through the snow, unseeing.

I did not stop running until I reached our dorm, and it was only after I flung the front door open, clutched a cup of hot tea, and spoke in anxious murmurs to our house mother that the feeling that something hungry and dangerous lurked outside began to fade away.

FROM THE OUTSET, THE investigation into Ginny's disappearance was botched; the twin forces of propriety and prejudice seemed determined to stifle any leads. The incompetent police officers who appeared at our doorstep were dismissive of the case. They said Ginny was probably out late, at a party, and would surface later. Edgar's desperate pleas for help finally moved them to ask a few questions and gather statements during the subsequent days.

Yet scant progress was made. Soon, the theory that Ginny had run off with Santiago had taken root and they seemed to lose interest in the case, if they'd ever had any. Ginny's family back West, made aware of the rumors of a secret love affair, seemed glad to let the issue drop.

I learned, after talking to Ginny's father, that she had eloped with a boy two years before—Terry, who'd stolen a car—that they had been brought back home after a couple of days and the whole matter hushed up. This seemed to seal the case in most people's minds. Edgar loudly declared that he didn't believe Ginny had run away on him.

People pitied him. They said that he was naïve.

There was some chatter about local legends, including stories concerning the Witch's Thicket. A teenage girl had gone missing near the college, more than fifty years before. For a few weeks all the women at Joyce House spoke in whispers, nervously, about these old ghost stories and a few more realistic fears. A madman might have taken Ginny. Who knew if he might take another girl? Or else perhaps it was the Devil, who was said to dwell in that patch of trees, Briar's Commons, the Witch's Thicket.

The students walked in pairs at night and keenly observed any outsider who might park his car and knock on the door of a dorm. But the winter continued quiet and ordinary, and soon enough the students breathed a sigh of relief.

By March, the house mother had boxed up Ginny's belongings and shipped them to her family and returned her books to the library. I had a new roommate. Joyce House buzzed with preparations for the spring cotillion and Ginny had been forgotten.

I GRADUATED FROM STONERIDGE with honors and headed west. I secured a job, traveled a little, fell in love, fell out of it, met

Irene, made a home in Arizona, returned to the East Coast, loved again, lived alone.

I wrote short stories in my spare time. Strange, ghoulish narratives that appeared in small magazines. Eventually, I penned a novella, a novel, kept writing. Tired of it. My hair turned gray and the seasons changed.

Periodically, I thought about her. She seeped into the lines of a manuscript, infected the keys of my typewriter, her mystery lingering and tantalizing me decade after decade. Where did she go? What happened to her? Who hurt her?

There were never any satisfactory answers, or there were, perhaps, too many to be able to glimpse the truth. A mystery is the most seductive of poisons; it intoxicates the soul.

Irene never comprehended this. Carolyn didn't, either. Benjamin empathized. Most people thought it was madness to dredge up the past as I did. Let it go.

Edgar alone understood. We were stricken with the same malady. When the leaves changed color and a chill descended upon Temperance Landing, I made my way to his house to share gloomy ghost tales and to paste the stories we'd carefully clipped out of newspapers into our black scrapbook.

But we never inched closer to the truth. Ginny's disappearance remained unsolved. Unlike other people who went missing, she never had her face decorating any posters, she was not listed in any database, her story did not show up on a cheap TV show. Ours was a private pain. Perhaps some people might think this was a kinder fate, but it isolated us. It made us the lone receptacles of her memory.

It made us morbid, that was what Carolyn said. She was correct. We swapped our newspaper clippings and told each other ghost tales to ease our pain.

Why return to that moment, why return to her?

It was not a choice we made. We were afflicted with a disease and it sprouted anew, like mushrooms that rise from the damp black earth, their long yellow filaments seeping into dead matter and decayed wood.

Once, while shopping for a new coat at Filene's Basement, I

saw a red scarf that reminded me of the exact shade of that drop of blood upon the snow. Red on white. So stark was the memory that my hands shook.

On another occasion, while riding the Green Line, I saw a girl standing by the doors who reminded me of her. From behind her hair was the same as Ginny's, long and dark. When she got off the subway, I followed her up into the Back Bay for a couple of blocks before I regained my senses and turned around, for the girl was sleek and young and Ginny would have grown old like me by then.

And there was an evening when, upon walking in front of a store displaying used clothes, I wept at the sight of a mannequin wrapped in an ancient green coat that looked like something she might have worn.

STORIES HAVE A RHYTHM to them. A beginning, a middle, an end. Mysteries beg for answers, narratives demand conclusions. Perhaps this is why Ginny made such a powerful impression on me: her story had no proper finale.

It was a never-ending loop, a perfect circle.

Open one door and Ginny has eloped, heedless, into the arms of a secret lover.

Open another door and Ginny has walked into the snow, mad, her mind finally cleaved by a secret malady.

Open another door and Ginny is the victim of a terrible crime. A stranger glides down the snowy road, drags her into a car, murders her.

Open another door and it is not a stranger. A stalker, concealed by shadows, walks into the dorm, forces her out of the house, kidnaps her.

Open another door and a monster, a devil, a supernatural fiend spirits her off into the depths of the earth.

But which door to pick?

None and all.

THERE ONCE WAS A large boulder in the vicinity of Dighton that caught the attention of early colonists with its petroglyphs, and though now it sits in a museum instead of a riverbed, no one can tell what its figures and lines mean. The Native American tribe that carved Dighton Rock—perhaps the Mashpee Wampanoag— left us a story, but we cannot interpret it properly, for we lack an understanding of its symbols, its metaphors. Nevertheless, such markings upon rocks indicate a place of importance, a place of power, and a place of memory.

It is like this with me and Ginny. Although she is long gone, and although I cannot comprehend the ending to her story, I return to it because it has power and must be remembered for that reason. Therefore, I have set it down as best I can, with the frail implements of paper and a typewriter, that it may preserve a fraction of Virginia Somerset's memory, as I knew her in 1934.

# 1998: 11

IT WAS RATHER COMICAL how, upon waking after a night when her dorm had been literally shaken to its very foundation by a supernatural force, Minerva's first concern was the coffee. She was running low but thankfully was able to get a pot brewing and poured it into her thermos.

She had a meeting at the Willows that day, and she didn't think she'd be able to function without caffeine coursing through her veins. Before she stepped out of the dorm, she checked her email and was delighted to see Christina Everett had finally returned from her vacation and was willing to meet with her. Minerva hadn't mentioned she was interested in talking about Thomas Murphy, figuring it would be too lengthy and odd an email to type, and instead had crafted a vague missive about needing a third person on her thesis committee. Which was true, but she hadn't really thought of Everett for that position. After a couple more emails, Minerva had secured an appointment for Monday.

Caffeinated, with the promise of the meeting in her inbox, Minerva walked toward the Willows with a heedless optimism she had not felt in a while, though as she approached the house her good spirits waned.

She had spectacularly managed to block out what had happened to her the previous night, but the wind rustling in the trees and the quiet streets she was following evoked a lonesomeness that made her pause. She wondered if Ginny and Betty had walked down the same street she was following, on their way to Carolyn's home. Then came a thought of her great-grandmother, dead now many years.

She walked with her hands in her pockets, feeling strange, like the child in a fairy tale who ventures into the dark forest. She kept going and soon the Willows was in sight, and she was turning onto the path that led to its front door.

Noah once again admitted her into the library and she grabbed the boxes with archival material and placed them on the table.

"Carolyn says she'll meet you at one o'clock. I'll come and fetch you."

She nodded and began taking out items from the backpack. The notebook, her pen, the camera. Noah watched her with interest. "You're very organized," he said.

"You can't get far without a certain sense of discipline."

"That's what Carolyn thinks."

"What do you think?"

"I try not to," he said breezily. "I called you last night. You didn't answer."

"The phone wasn't working."

She didn't specify that she'd disconnected it because it kept ringing, as if infected by whatever magic had been swirling outside the house. For there had been magic; this she didn't doubt.

She took off the lid from a box.

"You're not going to ask why I was calling?"

"I have a feeling you'll let me know." He snorted and she looked up at him. "Well?"

"Patricia's party, it's tonight. Did you want a ride?"

"Hideo will get me there," she said. She couldn't remember if he'd said he would. She was damn tired, hadn't slept well after the disturbance. But she refused to alter her planned schedule.

"I suppose you want to work now."

She didn't reply. Instead she put on her headphones, pressed her lips together, and began paging through Ginny's papers. He seemed surprised by her curt demeanor, maybe a little hurt, and he opened his mouth as if to ask her something, but she stubbornly looked down at the desk and pumped up the volume.

He left her alone, which was what she wanted. People made her nervous and right now she was jumpier than usual. She would have to find an excuse to leave the party early. There wouldn't be wards there—she'd be exposed. Although she'd have the talisman, which she carried in her backpack. Still, it seemed more dangerous to go out at night.

"Damn it," she said. She didn't want to start thinking like that. She didn't want to view the world as a vast collection of perils.

Something had to be done; a solution would have to be crafted. But she didn't know quite how to proceed. For now, there was research. Concentrate. Carefully write in the notebook. Drown out any noises with the sound of Neutral Milk Hotel in her headphones.

Eventually Noah came back for her and marched her into the living room. Carolyn Yates sat in her black armchair with the high back and her father's portrait behind it. There was no tea on this occasion. Noah did not join them.

"You've had a productive morning?" Carolyn asked. She wore her usual turban, this time black and gold, and around her neck there was a heavy necklace encrusted with gemstones. On her hands, multiple rings sparkled as she motioned for Minerva to sit down. She had the appearance of an idol sitting in a shrine.

"Yes, very."

"I wanted to get a better idea of how your research is proceeding. You've been here a number of times and I'm wondering how many more visits you might require to complete your work."

"Am I bothering you, Mrs. Yates?"

"No, not at all. I'm simply curious. I take an interest in the research of young scholars."

Her band of prodigies, as Noah had called them.

"Like Tom Murphy," Minerva said.

"Mr. Murphy, yes." Carolyn nodded. "A smart boy. I was sad to hear he transferred."

"He dropped out."

"Did he? Well. I can't remember all the details of the students we fund. Incidentally, my secretary will have to get in touch with you about filling out the paperwork from the foundation. For your next term. Well? What can you share with me?"

Minerva shifted uneasily in her seat, exhausted, trying to summon the proper words. "I've finished reading Beatrice's manuscript and her journal covering 1934. I'm afraid I haven't dug too much into other matters; it's been a complex read. I have a better understanding of what I'm looking at and what I need now that I've talked to Mr. Hoffman."

"You talked to Benjamin?"

"I went to see him and looked over the materials he's stored."

"Did you find anything useful?"

"Perhaps. It seems that Santiago was working at your father's factory in December. It seems he also went missing that month."

"Well, of course he would have gone missing. He ran away with Ginny," the woman said dismissively.

Carolyn's tone stirred something angry and raw inside her; Minerva's voice was sharper than it should have been.

"He went missing before Ginny disappeared. Betty or your husband must have discussed this detail with you."

Carolyn's red lips parted into a half smile. "Betty and I seldom discussed Virginia Somerset."

"What about your husband? He must have asked you to check the factory personnel records, back in the day."

Carolyn's smile receded. She rested her chin on the back of her hand. "My father saw no need for that. As I said, everyone knew they'd run off together. The person who came up with a different theory was Betty, because she had a writer's imagination. Dear Betty, always with her fanciful tales."

Minerva had caught the scent of something. This was important. She knew it. But she couldn't exactly figure out how it all fit together. She yanked at the thread, wondering where it might lead her.

"Benjamin didn't believe that Santiago ran off with Ginny, and

I doubt Edgar did. He loved her, he wanted her art preserved. I
don't think he'd do that if he really thought she abandoned him."

"As I said, my father ran that factory, and he never made mention of anything interesting in the personnel records. All there was,
anyway, was Santiago's address at that guesthouse. Not exactly a
great clue."

"So you did check and he was employed there? Because you
didn't say he worked for your family before. In fact, you told me
the factory records would be powder by now, but your father
pulled them out, or you wouldn't know about the guesthouse."

"You didn't have to pull personnel records to know Santiago
lived at the guesthouse."

"Why? Did you talk to him? Did he tell you where he lived?" she
asked, and she knew she was upsetting the woman. Soon the vague
amusement in her eyes would turn into exasperation.

Carolyn flicked her fingers as if chasing away a fly. The gemstones sparkled, catching a beam of light. "I have no idea why
you're talking about any of this."

Carolyn stared at her and Minerva knew better than to press
further. Yet the ending of Betty's manuscript lingered in her mind,
full of questions and dead ends. "When Betty went to the dorm the
day Ginny disappeared, she saw a drop of blood in the snow. It is
possible—"

"Virginia Somerset was a troubled young woman who thought
she could speak to the dead and who had been behaving errati-
cally before she went missing," Carolyn said, her voice hard and
unyielding. "And if she took up with a man like Santiago, and if he
hurt her, then she alone is to blame."

Carolyn glared at her, sitting back in the chair with the air of a
petulant empress, her chin held up high. Minerva looked into her
eyes, which dared her to keep talking, and tugged at the thread
once more.

"I don't believe Ginny ran away with anyone."

The thread snapped. When Carolyn spoke, she sounded indig-
nant. Her hands shook and she clasped them together.

"You're like them, whispering and trading idiotic theories.

Betty and Edgar could never stop their mad twittering. As if what happened sixty years ago should matter. She's gone." Carolyn's eyes fulminated, and she rose from her seat. "If you'll forgive me, I have more important matters to attend to."

"Mrs. Yates—"

"Good day."

That was that. She'd exhausted the woman's goodwill, and Noah's, too. He did not bid her goodbye, nor did he offer her a ride. Minerva was actually relieved; she hoisted her backpack onto her shoulder and stepped out of the house. She didn't really want to talk to either one of them, didn't really want to dig into the mystery of this missing girl. She was tired. Everything around her was infected with the stench of witchcraft and she walked quickly, her hands jammed in her pockets, Nine Inch Nails playing loud in her headphones, until she reached the dorm and tossed the Discman on the couch with a heavy sigh.

She lay down, draped her arm over her eyes. She thought once more about the last story her great-grandmother had ever told her. About the witch who'd haunted their farm.

She fell asleep. When she awoke, night had fallen. The house was a den of shadows. She turned on all the lights in the apartment and jumped into the shower. She put on a black dress with a print of silver flowers that reached her calves, black tights, and a pair of black boots, smeared eyeshadow on, and twisted her hair into a bun. She felt like neither dressing up nor going out, but if she tried to escape this party Hideo would ask what was wrong, and she didn't need him telling others that she was losing her mind.

She'd pinned the photos she'd taken of Ginny's painting and drawings on her corkboard. She stared at the patterns as she readied herself.

When Hideo arrived, Minerva quickly stuffed the bird talisman into a purse and stepped out. Fortunately, Hideo wanted to play her a Luna Sea CD he'd burned, and they spent the short drive listening to the music, which suited her.

The party, however, gave her a headache, as usual. Music, people, laughter, and she had to smile at Patricia and Hideo and everyone else. After a while, she realized that the headache was not from the noise, but that once again there was that pernicious sensation at the back of her skull. A portent.

She felt a pair of eyes boring into her back and turned around to find Conrad Carter staring at her. Of course he'd been invited. Patricia was friends with practically the entire student population of Massachusetts. He raised a bottle of beer to his mouth and smirked at her.

Minerva sank into a chair and rubbed her temples, making sure not to look in his direction. Still, she felt his eyes on her. She drifted into the cramped kitchen, which turned out to be a bad idea because people kept streaming in to grab beers. Conrad slid into the kitchen and she glanced at the linoleum floor. She didn't want to strike up a conversation with him, but he kept looking at her. Before he could open his mouth she went out of the kitchen and locked herself in the safety of the bathroom.

It seemed she always ended up there. She'd forgotten her aspirin and ransacked the medicine cabinet for a couple of pills, which she swallowed quickly. She leaned both hands against the bathroom sink and stared at her reflection. In the mirror she traced circles, remembering the witch marks.

When she stepped into the hallway and glanced into the living room Conrad Carter looked in her direction, then he laughed and turned away, busy talking to a young woman. Minerva felt someone's heavy gaze on her, although this time she could not say where it was coming from.

*It's here,* she thought.

She couldn't see anything strange, but the house seemed to have grown darker. Something stirred the shadows and made the CD that was playing skip. The light in the hallway behind her grew dim. Her eyes were watering and her throat felt constricted, as if she'd come in contact with a toxic substance. It was terribly warm inside.

She stuck her hand into her purse, clutching the talisman, and hurried out of the party. She bumped into Hideo, who smiled at her. Minerva mumbled something about getting a little air. Once outside, she walked quickly from the house.

A summer breeze stirred the trees. She took a deep breath. A handful of paces from the house she was able to breathe properly. The night air refreshed her strained lungs and the tension in her body relaxed. She wiped her sweaty brow with the back of her hand.

A few blocks from the house it returned, that sensation that she was being watched.

She turned around, peering at the hedges and the houses. A lamppost at the corner flickered like a firefly. She walked faster and scooped out the talisman from the purse, carrying it in her left hand.

The clopping of her shoes seemed to echo down the street, clearly indicating her path. Behind her something was slithering along in the bushes; she felt it staring at her, trailing her, and went faster. Another lamppost flickered ahead and she made a sharp turn to the right, jaywalking across the street. It followed, sleek and silent.

She ran, thinking of the safety of the dorm. Around her the streets were calm and quiet. the picturesque beauty of New England on display, and as she moved toward Neptune Street there was the scent of the ocean and the sound of the waves. This was the shortest route back to Ledge House.

Something slammed into Minerva hard enough to send her rolling onto the ground. She lay sprawled in the middle of the road, her ears ringing. The invisible something that had been chasing her through town had caught up with her.

She squeezed the talisman tight. A pin bit into the flesh of her hand, and the presence that was chasing her wavered, slipped aside like smoke rising toward the sky. It lifted away and was gone.

Minerva managed to get to her knees and open her hands. She sat like that for what might have been a minute, or ten.

She breathed in and stood up on shaky legs, stumbling down the road. A blinding light hit her face and she heard the screech of tires, the dim rumble of a motor.

"Shit! What are you doing there? Are you okay?"

She held a hand up and blinked. Noah Yates had jumped out of his Jeep and was helping her toward his car.

"What happened to you?" he asked.

"My purse," she said. "Where's my purse?"

She looked around. The purse had slipped from her grasp and was on the ground, along with her keys, her wallet. Everything had spilled out of it. Minerva desperately stuffed her belongings back in, looking for the talisman. Where had it gone?

"Fuck."

"Minerva?"

"I lost something."

"What?"

The talisman. But she couldn't say that. She turned around and stared at him. She'd skinned her knees, the palms of her hands were raw and ached from the fall, and her head was near to bursting. She'd bitten her lip. She could taste blood and swallowed it.

"Can you get me back to my dorm?"

"Jump in."

She climbed into his car. Noah side-eyed her as he drove.

"I was heading to Patricia's party. Were you coming back from there?"

"Yeah."

"What happened?"

"Nothing. I need to get back to campus," she said, lowering her head and touching her cheek.

"Are you high or something?"

"Do I look high?"

"You were stumbling around." She didn't reply. "Look, I'm not going to judge," he said. "We met because I was puking in the bushes."

*I'm bewitched,* she thought.

"I'm okay" was what she told him.

She closed her eyes. When she opened them, it was because they had reached Ledge House. It stood pale and lonely in the moonlight, cradled by darkness. Noah looked at her curiously. She brushed her hair back from her face and grabbed her purse. He extended a hand and caught her wrist.

"If you need to see a doctor—"

"I'm fine."

She stepped out of the car. He did too, rounding it and frowning. He wasn't convinced. She fished out her keys from the purse and glanced up at him.

"You're not going to tell me what happened to you," he said, crossing his arms and leaning his back against the hood of the Jeep.

"It wouldn't do any good."

"I thought we were friends now."

"We're somewhat friendly, somewhat not," she said.

"Okay. So you're my friend only when you need something from me, like a ride or information," he said bitterly.

"I didn't ask you to give me a ride. I didn't ask you to give me a tour of the factory. I didn't ask you to grab a bite to eat. Don't act like I'm the one demanding—"

"Well, fuck me for caring about what happened to you, huh?"

"I'm busy," she said.

What she really wanted to tell him was that she didn't trust him. She didn't trust anybody. The world had gone mad and she was attempting to make sense of it, to piece together answers. She went up the stairs to the dorm. His mirthless laugh made her pause at the door, and she considered asking him in for a cup of coffee, conveying an apology.

But she needed to be alone, and once she locked the door she slid down to the floor and rested her back against the wall, feeling the boards beneath her feet and the secret markings she'd hidden under there.

SHE MADE A SECOND talisman before leaving the house for her meeting with Christina Everett on Monday, stuffing pins into the body of a hummingbird. Her fingers stung with the pinprick of the needles, and with something else. A faint buzzing filled her ears.

She called a cab and it dropped her off in front of a Georgian red brick house with an old-fashioned iron knocker on the door. Christina guided her into her home office. She was fiftyish, her blond hair was up in a ponytail, and she wore a sweatshirt with the logo of the college printed on it.

"Sorry to drag you over to my house, but with all the remodeling around campus, my office there is a mess. They're redoing that wing of Elroy Center practically down to the studs."

"Yeah. They're tackling some of the dorms in the fall," Minerva said. She sat down in front of a large desk that was almost buried under a thick cover of papers, books, and magazines. "Joyce House is being restored, and Thistlewood, too."

"The library will be next, you know? Won't that be a mess," Christina said, throwing her hands in the air. "So Nell Quinn is your adviser?"

"Yes, and Brian Derleth has agreed to be on my thesis committee. But I figure I could use someone outside of the English department. I'm looking for someone who can help me with the witchcraft angle of the thesis. I think you were working with Thomas Murphy on something similar. You were his adviser, correct?"

"Ectoplasm," Christina said. "Tom was looking at Spiritualism and art, like in the work of Mondrian, but focusing on American artists. He was investigating the work of an artist who attended Stoneridge."

"Virginia Somerset," Minerva said. The name was almost like a spell by itself, conjuring secrets.

"Yes. Were you a friend of Tom's?"

"I was his resident director. But I thought he was looking at witchcraft in colonial America," she said quickly, trying to side-step questions about her relationship with Tom.

"I'm afraid we didn't discuss that. Although I wouldn't be surprised if he was changing the focus of his research. Tom was smart, but he tended to lose interest in things quickly. I was disappointed when he dropped out. Despite his eccentricities, I thought he had a knack for history."

"What eccentricities?"

"The Ouija board and the tarot cards. He loved to do readings. He thought it brought him closer to the ideas of the people he was studying."

The Ouija board. Suddenly she remembered that break-in at Joyce House right before Halloween and the hastily abandoned Ouija board and candles. She'd suspected the freshmen were responsible for that, but what if it had been Tom Murphy sneaking into the dorm to commune with the dead? Specifically, with Ginny.

"Now that I think about it, that book he left was on witchcraft," Christina said. "Where did I put it?"

"He left a book with you?"

Christina swung her chair back behind the desk, scanning her shelves. "He forgot it after our last meeting. I was going to return it to the library, but I thought it might be useful. You see, I teach a seminar on religion in Puritan New England and I wanted to give this a look for the section on superstition—"

"AMS 513."

"That's correct." Christina was moving aside books and papers. "Oh, here it is."

Christina held out a copy of *Bell, Book, and Candle: Witchcraft in the New World.* Minerva opened the book, her fingers careful upon the leather cover. On the title page someone had drawn a symbol she recognized: the witch mark with the overlapping circles, and underneath it the words "Look beneath the floorboards."

She flipped to the back of the book and found an ancient borrowing card with the dates on which the book had been checked out. Few people had asked for *Bell, Book, and Candle.* It had lain forgotten in the stacks for many years. Until, there it was, 1997, it had been checked out. By Tom. But decades before, in 1934, under the column ISSUED TO, there was another name: V. Somerset.

Ginny had written that message on the front, in a book she'd borrowed, which had likely been returned to the library upon her disappearance, and no one had read it, no one had realized its importance. But Minerva understood.

She clapped the book shut and looked at Christina, trying to seem calm and to steady the rapid beating of her heart.

"Could I borrow this?" she asked. "I've been looking for it and it was checked out."

"Be sure to return it to the library before the beginning of the term. They'll have my head if I keep forgetting the due date. So what exactly is your thesis about?"

Minerva mumbled about literature, horror, and legends of New England and managed to get through the meeting without a hitch. By the time she shook Christina's hand, she'd promised to send a full bibliography and a more coherent thesis proposal before mid-September, and Christina in turn had said she'd seriously consider being on Minerva's committee if she could furnish these items and fill out the proper paperwork. Then she let Minerva use her phone to call a cab, and she was heading back to campus with the book under her arm.

# 1908: 12

DREAD SEEMED TO BLOT out the sun. She must tell her family about Arturo's awful misdeeds, yet she feared his wrath. She hid in her room, unsure of what to say and how to say it. In despair, she buried her face in her pillow and pretended to sleep.

Her mother came by at midday to check on her.

"You still feel unwell?" she asked. "We'll have to call for the doctor if you continue like this."

Alba did not reply, pulling the covers tight around her and looking away.

"What is it?"

"Mother, he—" she began to say, but as soon as she opened her mouth she coughed. She tried to speak, tried to tell her about Arturo, but the coughing increased in intensity.

Her mother touched Alba's forehead. "My God, child, you have a fever. I'll boil you a cup of linden tea."

Alba shook her head but could not utter a word. She pressed a hand against her mouth to muffle her cough and fell back upon the pillows, exhausted. Her hair was plastered against her forehead with sweat.

Outside her room she heard her mother talking to her uncle.

"How is she?" he asked.

"She's caught a chill and has a fever. Our bad luck does not cease."

"This farm is too humid and musty. It would affect anyone's lungs. Once we've sold this place and moved away everything will be better."

"I don't know if I can sell the farm."

"It is cruel to keep her here. Not only is the environment foul, but she'll have few prospects with the way things are going. All those superstitious neighbors talk about curses. The surname Quiroga is becoming infamous."

"I know that! Arturo, even if I was ready to sell this place, I wouldn't know how to arrange it, how to go about it. The strain of these past few weeks is unbearable."

"Don't you worry. I'll help manage the transaction. I'll always help you."

The voices went quiet, but when she opened her eyes, Alba saw that Arturo was standing by the doorway and looking at her with an amused smile.

"It's very easy to cast a spell to prevent people from gossiping about you. You take the tongue of a small animal and drive a nail through it into the ground," he said. "Sprinkle a smidgen of grave-yard earth upon it and you're done."

Alba stared at him with wide eyes, and when she tried to scream, she was reduced to another coughing fit. He drifted away and her mother hurried into the room with a cup of tea upon a tray.

"Have this," she said, pressing the cup against her lips. Alba sipped the warm liquid.

She spent most of the day in bed, one moment shivering and the next burning like a hot ember. The room around her seemed deformed, the edges of it frayed. Her mother pressed cold compresses against her forehead and before nightfall her fever had gone down and she coughed no more. Her mother kissed her on the cheek and slipped away.

The next day, Alba went to the river, contemplated its waters for a long time, traced the contours of the riverbank where she'd played with Tadeo, found that old tree where she'd killed the thing that he'd become. It was late by the time she returned home. She was still unwell and had her supper in her room. Alone, she stood in front of her brother's watercolor portrait and tried to pray.

Once the house was still and quiet, Alba opened a window. The cool night air prickled her skin and she rubbed her arms as she stared at the moon. Tears streamed down her cheeks. Unable to remain standing, she knelt on the floor, muffling a sob.

Something brushed against her hand, and she opened her eyes.

A brown moth lay upon her fingertips. She looked at it in wonder as it drifted onto the palm of her hand. Alba closed her fingers, crushing the insect. This was a sign, she must proceed, and yet she sat still for a long time before dropping the dead moth into a bowl.

In the kitchen she found a bottle of wine and took it back to her room, along with a small container filled with salt. Once again, she stood in front of her brother's portrait and thought about the story the witch had told her.

In the watercolor, Tadeo's eyes were reduced to a smudge of brown, but they had been almost black, and the painted smile did not match the mischievous smirk that adorned his face when he was teasing Alba. This was Tadeo's likeness, yet so much of Tadeo had not been captured by the strokes of the brush even if it was the most accurate portrait of her brother. This only intensified the feeling of loss inside her chest. Tadeo was gone, destined to fade from memory and thought.

She pressed a candle against a corner of the portrait, letting the ashes fall into the same dish where the mangled body of the moth lay. She poured a cup of wine and added to it the ashes, the crushed wings of the moth, the salt.

"Keep me safe, brother," she said.

She drank the liquid, and when she stood up, she felt light-headed. Her forehead was uncomfortably hot. The fever had been ignited again, or perhaps it was the wine warming her skin.

She took off Valentín's medallion and instead fastened the golden chain with the pearl around her neck, feeling its cool smoothness against the hollow of her throat.

Alba held up the brass chamberstick and quietly walked out of the room and down the long, dark hallway. She wore her nightgown and did not bother putting on a robe over it. When she reached Arturo's room, she opened the door and let herself inside.

She drifted by the table with its mirror and shaving implements, setting the chamberstick upon it. Then she walked toward the bed and her fingertips brushed against the heavy coat that Arturo had draped over a chair, soft and luxurious.

"Uncle," she said.

He opened his eyes and looked at her. He was either a light sleeper or had not been sleeping at all. He stretched his arms above the headboard, lazily, like a cat, and sat up.

"Are you feeling better, my sweet?"

"No thanks to you," she said. "You've made me ill."

He smiled and shrugged. His nightshirt was of a dark color, navy or gray, and in the dim light of the candle it made him blend into the shadows. The room felt rather cold, cold enough she thought her breath might turn into fog. She wondered if it was his presence that made it so, chilling her every bone when she'd burned feverishly only moments before.

"Perhaps you'll learn to keep quiet about certain things."

"And if I don't, then what? Will I catch a dreadful chill and my death at the same time?" she asked, a hint of panic in her voice, but she smothered it, looking down at the floor as she sat on the chair by the bed, her left hand clutching his coat. "I want to know what you intend to do. You are pressuring my mother to sell the farm. What'll happen to us if we have no place to live?"

"You'll have a place to live. Perhaps in Pachuca. I will, of course, administer the finances for your mother, it'll be my obligation now that she is a widow and her sons are not of age. I shall make frequent visits to your home, don't worry."

"Yes, I suppose travel won't be an issue if you have the money for it."

"You're correct, it won't be any trouble. I'm considering a tour of Europe and its greatest cities. A young man is expected to see a bit of the world. Of course, it would have to be after my father's funeral. The dear old man has been sick for quite a while. I suspect he won't make it to the end of the year. My sister Julia is a dear but something of a hypochondriac. I wouldn't be surprised if one of these days she grows truly ill."

Alba shook her head, dismayed. "I suppose you know about sickness, and you intend to collect two inheritances, then."

"I'll soon be an independent man. As you can see, you needn't worry about your mother. She'll be cared for. As for my beloved niece, I would think it would do you good to see other countries. As long as a responsible member of the family can watch over you, I don't think anyone would object."

Even in the darkness his eyes burned bright, and when he smiled there was a flash of sharp white teeth. Everything about him was sharp and she had the burning need to take three steps back for fear of being snagged between his mandibles. She dug her hands into the softness of the coat on the chair, willing herself to remain there.

"It will be delightful. We've talked of Paris, haven't we? Dancing the waltz, attending soirées. Upon our return, you might remain in my house. A bachelor such as myself needs a reliable housekeeper, and it wouldn't be unusual for a family member to slip into the role."

"Especially a girl with few prospects, and I suspect I won't have many in the future." She watched his lips curl back into an even bigger smile, sharper now. It was a blade. She clenched her fists. "I don't want the farm sold." Her voice was strained, barely a faltering murmur, shy and scared as she was, caught under his intense gaze. "This was my father's land and his father's before that. I hope it'll be my siblings' land one day. If you are to inherit a fortune from your father anyway, then the farm can't make much of a difference. You'll have your independence."

"I'd much rather have two fortunes than one. And you come free in the bargain. Flesh and blood."

"Then I was correct and you'll drain me dry."

"I hardly think a nibble now and then would qualify as draining."

"Do you drink blood for pleasure or to kindle your magic?"

"For both. Besides, it need not be painful."

"When you came to my room you hurt me, here," she said, touching her chest. "It felt like a needle was driven through my heart."

"A small mishap, easily corrected. I was angry and jealous."

"Valentín," she whispered.

"I smelled him on your skin, your lips."

She let out a deep, shuddering breath. She thought of poor Valentín's disfigured corpse. He'd paid a high price for his affection. What might Arturo do to her if he should suspect treachery? The words she'd thought to speak were lodged in her throat.

"I can refuse you," she said at length.

"I'll have you, one way or another," he replied simply. He had a conqueror's boldness. Doubtless he imagined that the deed to the farm, once in his hands, entitled him to possession of every single item inside it, and every single person. Including her.

Alba stared at him and laughed, which seemed to bother him. His face soured; the smile was wiped off.

"No. You wouldn't like it that way. It wouldn't be as you imagined it. I believe you've pictured it quite a bit," she said, her voice low, but it didn't falter now. "After all, I've wondered about it myself."

She'd schooled herself into dismissing stray thoughts about kisses, about him, fearful of where such wild imaginings might lead her. But she'd had those thoughts, and he knew it, and in turn he must have thought many times about her, desire seeping in between the words he spoke, nestled in the silences.

He lowered his gaze, almost shyly, as if wishing to curtain off his thoughts.

"It would ruin it, if it had to be that other way," she continued. "I will fight you; I swear it. I'll scream and kick and scratch your face. It'll be terribly unpleasant. I propose something different."

"Oh?"

"The farm won't be sold and I will acquiesce."

Alba stood up, abandoning the safety of the chair. She was shivering. The room was made of ice and the nightgown provided no protection against the cold. She sat on the bed and reached out to him, pulling his face close to her own. He looked into her eyes, curious, measuring her boldness, and they sat like that for what seemed like a long time. He was mesmerized, she too.

Below, the clock in the sitting room chimed the hour.

"I don't need to bargain with you," he said, as if the sound had broken a spell, and caught her hand, his grip tight around her fingers.

"Then kill me now and eat my heart, and that is all you'll ever have of me. A rotting piece of meat. You've toyed long enough with me. Accept my terms, or kill me like you killed the others, and the only pleasure you'll ever find with me will be in the grave," she swore.

He snarled and pushed her hand back, bending it away from her body, making her wrist ache. She didn't yelp in distress, though it hurt, instead staring at him.

She went on looking at him, and he at her. His eyes were feverish and dark, mirroring her own.

"It need not be painful," she said.

He grunted in irritation and released her. Before he could either coax or curse her, she kissed him, and he might have pulled away, but she set her hand behind his neck and held him in place. Perhaps he thought she'd been bluffing, for he seemed rather shocked. Nevertheless, he kissed her back with a quick, boiling eagerness. She turned her head sharply and looked away, evading him.

"You know my terms," she said, and waited, her heart racing.

He idly ran a nail against the gold chain, flicking the pearl back and forth, like a cat that plays with its prey. Then his thumb brushed the hollow of her throat.

"Very well, then," he whispered against her ear. "I've never been able to refuse you anything."

She offered him her mouth.

# 1998: 12

IT WAS DUSK BY the time she arrived at Ledge House. None of
her witch marks had been disturbed. She knew it, and she knew
she must venture into Beatrice Tremblay's old dorm that night.
That pinching feeling in the back of her skull had returned but
now seemed to radiate farther down, and she kept thinking about
Ginny's note.

She grabbed the thermos she'd filled earlier in the day and
drank from it. For a while she stood in the middle of the library,
looking at the shattered shadow boxes with their insect specimens.
Butterflies and moths and a few bright beetles. On the walls, the
birds hovered in midflight. She took another sip.

Afterward, she pulled the toolbox from under the sink and rum-
maged through it, finding a hammer and a chisel. She tossed them
into her backpack along with her flashlight, a box cutter, and the
keys to Joyce House.

Walking through Briar's Commons did feel like walking through
a witch's woods that evening; the tree branches above her head
seemed to meet and clasp one another and the path she followed
was like a tendril of faded black ink, like in the illustration for a
fairy tale. But her great-grandmother's stories had been darker
than most fairy tales, drenched in blood.

She moved at a steady pace, one hand clutching the strap of her backpack, and listened intently for the sound of footsteps or a branch breaking. But if anyone was following her, it was a stealthy stalker.

A few minutes later she stood in front of Ginny and Betty's old dorm. She looked up at the second floor and felt the electric tug she often experienced when gazing at it, especially at that one window. Before, she had thought it was merely her appreciation of the old house, but now she recognized it as something else: the faint tracery of magic.

Minerva unlocked the front door and stepped inside, flicking on a light switch. The house was oak paneled, its walls stained a dark brown that was almost black, its ceilings soaring high. This grande dame was past her prime—the rug that had once covered each of the steps on the staircase had been rolled away, its paintings in gilded frames had been packed into storage units, and it was now filled with shadows and dust. But Minerva could still spot the glamour and glitz of Joyce House as it must have been when wealthy socialites chatted in the foyer.

Once she reached the top of the stairs, she found another light switch and the hallway before her was illuminated. She looked at the numbers on each of the doors until she reached the correct one.

Number 11. Ginny and Beatrice's old room.

She opened the door and stepped inside. The single bulb in the ceiling gave off an anemic light. No matter, she'd known it would be like this; with the house locked down for renovations, she was lucky that they had even left the lightbulbs in place.

She turned on her flashlight.

During her previous incursion into the room, on that night when she'd found the Ouija board and the candles, Minerva had been too busy talking to the security guard accompanying her to give the space a proper look. If she had been alone, perhaps she would have realized that this room was the same one she often stared at, her eye reflexively drawn to that particular window in Joyce House.

The house had been interested in Minerva long before she had become interested in it. Now it welcomed her: a crackling, almost electric shock spread down her spine as she stepped farther into the room. It was the sharp sting of a whip and her ears rang. She rubbed her head, remaining still until the sensation dissipated.

She aimed the beam of light above the doorway and noticed a carving there, on the wood of the doorframe. A witch mark, much like her own. She approached the window and ran her hand around its frame, brushing the dust away, until she felt the whorls of another witch mark beneath her fingertips. This time there was no electric shock, simply the texture of ancient wood.

Ginny had safeguarded the door and the window. Safeguarded herself and Beatrice. No evil entity could slip into that room. Although one must have breached the barrier, because Ginny had disappeared, had likely been taken from there. The witch marks had not been enough, or there had been a flaw in their design, even if they were still potent years after their making, so potent that Minerva had felt them even if they were not meant to harm her.

But like Nana Alba, Minerva had portents, and she was growing attuned to them. She no longer dismissed them as a simple migraine. Perhaps this was enough to trigger a response, however small, from the room.

She looked around and tried to picture the room as it might have been when students had lived in it, imagining the location of the beds, the desks, the chairs. She poked her head into the bathroom, which had an old-fashioned toilet with an overhead box and a pull chain and a claw-foot tub.

She peered into the mirror above the sink, found her tired face staring back at her.

Something brushed against her body, like the filaments of a spiderweb stretching against her skin. She turned around, the flashlight illuminating a bare wall. There was nothing there, but something was close to her. Something that could not be seen, but that she felt, inches out of reach.

Ginny's ghost. She knew it, could sense it. It was a talent. Nana Alba could predict the arrival of a guest at their apartment long before they rang the bell, could chatter with a dead parrot. Minerva had thought her a tired, half-asleep old woman, whispering old stories under her breath, but Nana Alba had power.

Now Minerva focused and tried to look beyond the tiles of the room, the peeling paint, and glimpse something. She was unsure of how to proceed, how to coax the dead out from the shadows.

"Virginia Somerset," she called out. "You were trying to speak to Tom. Won't you speak to me?"

The ghost did not reveal itself, there was no milky-white apparition, no ectoplasmic manifestation, but she felt it again. Something out of reach.

It was nearby.

She stepped out of the bathroom, pulled the thermos from her backpack, and took a sip. Her throat was dry as dust. She wiped her mouth with the back of her hand and unzipped one of the backpack's pockets, digging out an old black-and-white photograph. It showed Betty and Ginny together, smiling at the camera.

"I learned your story from Beatrice Tremblay, but not the ending," she said, holding the photograph up. "I'd like to figure it out."

There was no answer at first. The ghost was coy, did not know whether to trust her, or perhaps it was a frail, dim presence that could not manage much. The minutes slogged by.

She heard a faint scratching, which might have been simply a rodent rushing across the room. But she suspected not. She swung around and aimed the flashlight at a different spot in the room, and the noise seemed to move across the floor, so she moved her arm, the beam of light illuminating one ancient floorboard after another.

The noise ceased.

Minerva stuffed the photograph in her pocket, took a few steps, and bent down.

One of the floorboards had three circles scratched upon it. A small, crude design that people wouldn't have bothered to look at and recognize as a witch mark, safeguarding whatever lay beneath from sorcerous hands.

Time and the elements had shrunk the edges of the floorboard, leaving a gap, and she slid the wide-bladed chisel into this gap with ease. Then it was a matter of using the hammer together with the chisel to pry up the board.

And there it was, a yellowed piece of paper that had been slipped in between the edges of the floorboards many years before. Ginny must have tucked other pieces of paper under the floor, drawings with concentric circles, charms to keep evil away. But this one board and this one piece of paper were special.

The floorboards creaked and groaned, and there was a bump against the wall, then another. The ghost in the room was restless, perhaps afraid.

She unfolded the paper. There, in Ginny's beautiful handwriting, was the name of her murderers. The name that Beatrice Tremblay had longed to know and never suspected. It was a familiar name.

"Wingrave," Minerva said, reading the piece of paper.

The old lightbulb above her head grew dimmer and flickered. The silken, spidery threads brushed against her arm again, tugging at her with such force that Minerva stumbled back and bumped against the old-fashioned radiator. The ghost dragged her farther into the room, pulling her as far as it could from the entrance.

The house seemed to shiver, unnerved.

She heard footsteps and the creak and crack of old wood as someone moved down the hallway and stopped.

Carolyn stood outside the doorway. She was wearing one of her expensive turbans and a long, dark blue coat with a huge fox-fur collar that completely hid her neck. The woman parted her crimson lips and gave her a smile. Her teeth seemed blindingly white, and dangerously sharp. It was the grin of a predator, of a creature of abyssal depths.

"What did you find?" she asked.

Minerva clutched the slip of paper between her hands. It almost felt warm to the touch, this paper, or else it was her fingertips that seemed to have caught on fire. A combustion beneath the skin, smoldering powder caught in her grip.

"Your name. She couldn't speak it, but she could write it. You were the one bewitching her," she said, for it was useless to act coy now. There was only one reason why Carolyn would be standing beyond the threshold, staring at her.

"If you want to be technical about it, it was my father."

"Why?"

Carolyn's fingers brushed against the fur of her collar, smoothing it down. She motioned in the direction of the stairs. "If you would simply step out of the room, I'll tell you the truth."

"Why don't you step in?"

She couldn't. Ginny's witch marks still had power. Especially with her ghost in the room. Something about the spectral presence combined with the markings helped maintain the space safe from the influence of an evil sorcerer. That was why the piece of paper had remained beneath the floor. That, and Carolyn probably had no idea it was there. Ginny had left a message for her friend scribbled inside a book, but Betty had never read it. Thomas might have been close to discovering the note, but Minerva must have interrupted his séance.

Whether he'd had an inkling of the note's existence or not, the room was shielded and Minerva was safe within its confines. The room would not allow Carolyn in, nor one of her minions. Dark magic had no place within it.

Carolyn tapped her fingers against the wall. "You really should step out," she said softly. It was a vicious command wrapped in silk.

Minerva shook her head. Carolyn sighed. She tapped the wall again, once, twice, thrice. Her eyelids trembled and her eyes rolled back until the whites were showing. "Your friend owns a blue car, doesn't he? From his rearview mirror hang two air fresheners in the shape of palm trees."

Minerva did not respond. Her hands curled, balling up the piece of paper. She swallowed and her throat was now so dry it ached.

"Young people these days are careless. They drive too fast at night; they don't pay attention to the traffic signals. Your friend, he's reaching the bend of a road," Carolyn said, and she raised her hand, her fingers describing a sinuous curve.

"You can't do anything to him," Minerva said, but of course Carolyn could. It was a meaningless objection.

"Did my grandson ever mention how his parents died? It was a car accident. Anything can happen when you're driving at night. If you're a young man heading back to campus, you might be changing the radio station when suddenly you swerve and there's a tree—"

"Stop it! He doesn't have anything to do with this."

"That's up to you," Carolyn said.

Carolyn smiled at her with that predator's grin, with that smile that was all teeth. She'd smiled like that at Ginny many decades before and Minerva felt her power; it was a brutal, steely force that seemed to gnaw the walls around her.

Ginny's ghost brushed against her arm, as if clutching it for a brief second, warning her to remain where she was. But Minerva picked up her backpack and stepped out of the room.

Carolyn blinked, her eyes fixing on Minerva. In the hallway, the temperature had dropped; the warmth of summer had been vanquished and instead Minerva's breath came up in a plume, as though it were a chilly December morning. She was by the doorway and perhaps might have leaped back into the room, crouched in a corner, and waited for dawn to arrive. *But you can't outrun a witch. Not like this.*

"What now?" Minerva asked instead.

"Now we go for a drive."

# 1908: 13

ALBA DID NOT HUNT with her father and brother. It did not appeal to her, and her mother would have thought it unladylike for her to stumble through the mountains in search of deer. But she knew a good hunter was an excellent scout who was familiar with the terrain. They were also quiet, stealthy. A hunter must walk soft and slow, think before moving, and wait. Patience is the hunter's greatest weapon.

When you're hunting deer, it's relatively easy to remain concealed behind a tree, to hold the rifle with a firm grasp. But when there's a mountain lion a few paces from you, it's harder to steady the hands, to keep yourself from running away for fear that the shot might miss and the mountain lion will sink its fangs into your leg.

When she kissed Arturo, it was equally difficult to remain in place, to stop herself from bolting out of the room. For there'd be no turning back after this; she had chosen her path.

She stood up by the bed and he narrowed his eyes, perhaps thinking she meant to run off after all, but Alba took off her nightgown and let it fall to the floor. She stood naked now, her long hair covering her shoulders, half hiding her breasts. She shivered, at the cold of the room and the weight of his gaze. Then he lifted his nightshirt above his head and discarded it, stretching a hand toward her, and she breached the short space between them, sliding into his bed.

She'd grown up on a farm and thus understood the coupling of animals. Her father's books—the tomes on anatomy and the leather-bound encyclopedia—had provided her with precise knowledge of biological processes. She grasped what this would entail, even if she had only skimmed the edges of lust.

She'd thought of him during the past couple of years in a way that flirted with the inappropriate yet never became full desire. Now they embraced and it felt like a fever dream, her lips burning as he kissed her, the room growing dim and dark.

It would have been a lie to say she was indifferent to the press of his body against her own, to the way his hands moved down her breasts, making her skin tingle. But dread echoed each motion, and she could hardly respond to him, her body stiff and drenched in fear as she recalled Valentín's coffin and her brother dying in her arms, and in turn Arturo must have felt this fright and been repulsed. That was not the bargain they had made. He shifted his body as if to slip out of the bed.

She panicked, distressed at the thought of losing this chance, her one chance perhaps, and clutched his arms, pulling him atop her, kissing him. Then his mouth was upon her throat and her hands curled around his shoulders.

Dread was drowned by desire as his fingers caressed and probed her with caution, as if her skin were porcelain he must not damage. He kissed her hands, her wrists, her pulse quickening with every touch.

"We'll leave this place. You'll go with me, won't you?" he asked, and she gasped in response, a flick of his thumb making her hips buckle.

His tongue flashed between his teeth and she moaned, which seemed to please him very much. "I'd tear the world apart to have you. Say you love me."

"I love you," she said. He smiled, delighted.

His teeth carefully pierced the soft skin of her wrist and he licked the wound as she tipped her head back. There came a kiss between her breasts, and the sting of teeth once more, startling her, and she was caught between the twin waves of agony and lust.

"You'll be mine, always," he said, and lowered his head, sipping the blood from above her breast as he caressed the nipple.

She fought to breathe, to think, but her mind was growing hazy. When he slid into her, it was a smooth, easy motion, the twinge at her groin echoed by the pain above her heart. Time slowed down; she felt she'd been with him for an eternity. His movements were utterly unhurried, and her heart was hardly beating.

Her breath escaped in one low whimper as he surged into her. He embraced her tightly after his completion and she rested her forehead on his shoulder.

"You're too pretty for words and you taste exquisite," he told her. The honest contentment in his voice tugged at her soul.

He ran his hands through her hair, down her body. His knuckles traced the bumps of her spine, each caress gentle, attempting to erase whatever ache he'd caused her. He stroked her like one might pet a favorite cat. She was a lovely plaything he'd wanted for so long. Now he owned her.

Alba took a deep breath and turned her head to look at him.

He'd dozed off. In his sleep he was as beautiful as a statue, his whole body seeming carefully carved and devoid of imperfections. He slept peacefully. Alba lay at his side; the sweat covering her body had cooled and felt like a thin layer of frost. Her limbs were leaden and her eyes fluttered shut.

Alba curled her fingers and dug her nails into the softness of her palms, forcing herself to sit up. She remained perched at the edge of the bed for a few seconds. The bites on her wrist and breast stung, but he'd hardly drunk from her, a sip or two and nothing more. Yet the strength of him was a frightening thing.

She picked up her nightgown, slipping it over her head.

At last, she stood up and went toward the table with the mirror. She trembled. The surge of feelings overwhelmed her mind—he might wake in an instant, and even if he didn't, what was she doing?

Hunters can be injured in the pursuit of their quarry. One wrong step, one wrong movement, and the chase may end in death.

When Alba reached the table, she had to lean on it for support. She took a deep breath. Arturo's silver-plated grooming set glinted next to the light of the candle. Her fingers brushed the tops of the bottles, his comb, before settling on the razor.

She held it up and walked back to the head of the bed. Arturo slept on, eyes closed tight, and her hand shook as she bent down next to him, blade in hand. The anatomy books and encyclopedias mapped the veins and arteries in the human body. The carotids ran on each side of the neck.

She leaned down, closer, one hand grasping the razor, the other clutching the bedsheet.

He opened his eyes.

She gasped.

In an instant, before she could strike, he had sat up in bed and his fingers were around the hand that held the razor. Alba froze, mouth open, staring at his bright, amused eyes.

"I could sense your deceit the moment you stepped out of bed," he said. "Let go of this toy."

His hand tightened around her own, holding her with a bruising force, and she dropped the razor. He released her and she stepped away quickly, bumping into the table with the mirror in her haste, but just as quickly he was behind her, his chest pressed against her back and a hand at her waist.

"How should I punish you for this insurrection?" he asked.

She looked at their reflection in the mirror, peering into his large eyes, which shone in the dark like those of an owl or a cat. When he smiled, he showed her his teeth, ivory white and far too sharp.

She grabbed the candle upon the table and thrust it up against his face.

He let out a mighty howl of pain and unhanded her.

Alba ran. She rushed down the stairs and toward the door. Outside there were the fields of barley, turned gray and colorless under the light of the moon. The earth was moist and soft beneath her feet; the mist that descended from the mountains had dampened it. It made her movements trickier. But she knew the land, could trace its contours with her eyes closed.

She must head toward the river, near the spot where she'd shot the thing that had been Tadeo. The barley rustled behind her, stirred by a breeze, and she ran down a narrow dirt path, pushing forward.

The chill and the dampness of the night did not cool her skin. It was on fire, and her heart was a smoldering coal. Her lungs burned as she stumbled and pressed on.

She'd almost reached the large, ancient tree where she'd once hung her oil lamp when she was sent crashing against the ground. She attempted to rush away, she kicked and whimpered and shivered. All struggle was futile. Strong arms held her down and she stared into Arturo's face.

"Don't hurt me," she pleaded.

"But you may hurt me? It hardly seems fair."

"I thought you'd drink me dry."

"I should."

"It aches," she said. And it was true, it ached, not only the hurt of her body, but the hurt of her heart.

"Good," he said.

"Arturo—"

"Where did you think you were going, hmm? How quickly you seem to forget: you're mine now."

"I know!"

"You're such a pretty liar, professing love—"

"I do love you and you know it! I'll go to hell for this. I will." She sobbed. This was also true, it was real, every word.

A part of her still loved him, wanted him. He was the ideal of the man that she had imagined, everything from his voice to his looks to the way he played the piano seemed exquisite, and there was the bond of long-honed affection between them. They'd been so close, so well matched.

"You're a fool," he said. She wasn't sure whether he meant she was a fool for fearing the fires of hell or a fool for loving him. His fingers dug into her flesh.

Before he had shown a measure of restraint, but now he was angry. Their confrontation had stripped away the thin veneer of gentlemanly consideration he'd exhibited. He'd sipped at her blood before, nothing more. Now he pinned her down and gulped greedily. The pain he gifted her was razor sharp, stinging her skin, making her wince. She wrapped her arms around him and pulled him unbearably close, kissed him hard on the mouth.

He could sense her deceit, he'd said. But he slipped into her again with a thoughtless ease, primed perhaps by the chase through the fields. Or perhaps it was her vehemence that fired his desire.

His voraciousness was not only for the blood now, but also for her body. He'd been kind to her before, he'd played the sweet lover, moving gently. But that was not his nature. He was a glutton.

She'd thought to make her flesh into a snare, but he was terribly strong, and as he burrowed his head into her shoulder, muttering a word that was more a growl, she wondered whether he'd trapped her instead.

He enveloped her, pressed her hard into the earth, and the weight of his body was like being buried alive, like descending into the underworld.

Her pulse raged as he nipped and bit and licked her neck, her breasts. She fought to breathe, to think, while he scratched the soft skin of her throat and thrust into her. Her blood stained his lips. Maybe he would drink her dry after all. Maybe they'd find her body in the morning, floating down the river. She clutched him with heated desperation as she felt the fullness of pleasure and closed her eyes.

When she opened them again, he was rutting into her harder. She stared into his eyes, which were wild and hungry. He was panting. His breathing had grown labored, and he shook his head, his body faltering, growing still.

"What have you done?" he asked.

*I've hunted you,* she thought. But then again, the hunt is not over until the quarry lies unmoving and cold.

"Poison," she said. "Poison for witches."

"Foolish girl, what have you done?" he repeated, as if he could not believe it, could not fathom such audacity.

At the corner of his lips there was a trace of blood. He began to cough. His hands slid from her body. A swift, unmistakable change had taken hold of him. Her blood, which he'd lavishly enjoyed, had been laced with magic, yes, infused with poison. In the fury of their coupling he had not paused, even for one second, to consider the effect it was having on him, until it was too late and he was clutching at his chest. He'd been half mad for her, but then she'd been in the grip of madness to be able to weave such a scheme. Now he saw it, this madness, this ploy, and snarled, his fingers snagging in her hair.

She shoved him aside and managed to stand up, her knees weak, and for one terrible moment she thought she might collapse next to him. But she was able to reach the tree and ran her hands along its roots, searching for the feel of fabric.

She unwrapped the axe and turned around to see that he remained on the ground, his face pressed against the dirt, but he was attempting to stand up. His spine arched violently and he raised his head, those glowing, treacherous eyes of his narrowed and fixed on her.

# 1998: 13

"WHERE ARE WE HEADED?" she asked.

Although she was sitting in a car in close proximity to a witch and murderer, the question was made in a neutral tone. Minerva was more curious than afraid. At least for now.

"The factory."

"Is that where you normally kill people?" Minerva folded her hands on top of her backpack. When no answer came, she spoke again. "You said you'd tell me the truth."

"Yes, that's normally the place," Carolyn said. She didn't sound anxious or agitated, either. It was a bit amusing, how they both were able to converse amicably.

"There was blood on the snow the night Ginny disappeared, though. And her ghost lingers at Joyce House. For a moment I thought you might have killed her there."

"Most ghosts cling to the place where they died, that's true. But a few may return to a spot of significance to them."

She wondered if Ginny's ghost had drifted back to Joyce House to be near Betty. What a sad thought it was that Betty, desperate to find Ginny, might have been next to her all along.

"What happened that night in December?"

"She'd gone downstairs to the phone, and attacked me with a pair of scissors when she saw me. The idiot. I still carry the scar,"

Carolyn said, and Minerva looked at her fingers upon the wheel and the ugly line that ran down the back of her right hand. "Then she ran off into the snow. My father was waiting outside. We both chased her and caught up with her."

That meant the blood in the snow had been Carolyn's. She must have hidden her wounded hand under elegant gloves or warm mittens immediately after the incident. After winter break, the hand would have been healed, or an excuse would have been furnished.

"She didn't last long," Carolyn said, and she sighed. "It was a pity. We'd planned to keep her for a while. Pain and fear sweeten the blood."

"Is that the way your magic works? You must drink blood?"

"It makes it more potent."

"And the heart, it's also potent."

Carolyn smiled. It was a thin sliver of a smile, like a crescent moon.

"You seem to have learned a thing or two about witches."

Ginny had learned a thing or two about witches as well, but it hadn't done her any good. Her witch marks had been no match for the Wingraves; they'd caught her all the same. But that had been years ago. Carolyn had been younger, stronger.

"Not enough, it seems," Minerva said. "Why did you kill Ginny?"

"She had the ability, she spoke with ghosts. Oh, you can cast a spell with the blood of any old fool, but the blood of someone with the ability, that is precious. It's like wine. There are simply wonderful vintages and then you have your cheap table wine. Anyway, we needed her blood, needed the power. My father's business was failing."

"You killed her because of business problems?"

"Would it be better if I had killed her because I wanted Edgar for myself?"

"Did you?"

Carolyn looked ahead, her hands careful upon the wheel. The corners of her thin lips twitched into a smile.

"I met him before she did. We were part of the same social circles. We were much better suited to each other."

"Yet he never forgot Ginny. He kept all those drawings of hers like a shrine to his true love," Minerva said.

Carolyn's reaction was, as she'd expected, a mixture of irritation and pride.

"No, Miss Contreras. *I* kept her drawings and Betty's manuscript. I could have disposed of them after Edgar died, but I didn't. And you know why? They were never a shrine to Ginny. They were a trophy. A reminder of my success. I killed Virginia Somerset and no one ever suspected the truth."

She remembered what Benjamin had said, that Carolyn had adored Edgar. He'd been wrong. She'd *coveted* him. He'd been another kind of trophy that she'd won. Another marker of Carolyn's brilliance, her achievements.

The car slowly, gracefully, followed the bend of the road, slipping farther and farther from the college. Minerva clutched the backpack, felt its weight on her lap. She had the box cutter and her thermos inside it. Carolyn had not bothered going through it.

"What about Santiago? What happened to him?"

"We wanted two people. A man and a woman. The spell would work better that way. He also had the ability, though it was dimmer than in Ginny's case. I flirted with him a few times, convinced him I was interested in him, and then arranged a rendezvous."

"Then the woman they saw outside with Santiago was you. But no one knew, and when she went missing you must have fanned everyone's suspicions, told them she'd run off with him."

"Girls gossip in close quarters," Carolyn said with ease. For a second, Minerva could picture her at twenty, blithely going from a debutante ball to the scene of a murder with a shrug. It disgusted her. Minerva was quiet. She didn't want to ask any more. But she had to. She needed the answers. Besides, if she remained silent it would be worse. Fear would overwhelm her. Words kept terror at bay. This way she could pretend death didn't await her once they reached the factory.

"What happened with Thomas Murphy? I don't think you met him by chance."

"I like to look at the new crop of students we support through the foundation each year. Sometimes by looking at their records, or casting a simple divination spell using their photos, I can sense if they have the ability. Of course, the best, most accurate method is to simply touch a person and feel them like that. We had a function, and I shook his hand."

She remembered the first time she'd met Carolyn and how she'd helped her pour a cup of tea. Afterward, Carolyn had offered to show her Betty's papers. No wonder.

"I arranged for Thomas to tutor my grandson to get a better sense of him. Sometimes that first impression is incorrect and the ability is stunted, dim. Useless."

"But in Thomas's case it wasn't stunted. He had a Ouija board and read the tarot cards. He was the real deal."

"An amateur, but yes. Good enough."

"Did you tell him about Ginny and her artwork, or was he researching her by chance?"

"I made sure he learned about her. It fires the imagination, doesn't it? Young girl, gone missing many years ago. Leaves behind those abstract images and nothing more. And he, of course, tries to find out more about her, and Ginny's sad, poor ghost tells him half a story about witches and spells, and when something begins haunting poor Thomas, he is deathly afraid. The silly boy nearly wet his pants one night."

"Weren't you worried he'd find you out? That Ginny would tell him you were behind it all?"

"She couldn't. Ghosts are coarse things; communicating with them is difficult, and Thomas was not an experienced medium. At best, he learned enough to become terrified and paranoid."

"Which suited you."

"His blood did have a lovely tinge of dread. I kept him alive for a whole week. I might keep you longer."

That was why she was speaking to her, to induce a sense of

dread. Minerva wondered if she'd done the same with Ginny, explaining everything that would happen to her.

*I'm going to die,* she thought. She ought to have run off, although that's what Ginny had done; it hadn't helped her. She'd run through the snow, terrified, clutching the scissors, only to stumble directly into the arms of the Wingraves. Maybe they'd shoved her into a car much like the one Minerva was sitting in. Or else, through more esoteric means, they had transported their victim to a secure spot where they could devour her at their leisure.

"You have an exceptional spark, you know? You cut your hand a few weeks ago. My grandson must have lent you his handkerchief because it was in the laundry, smeared with blood. I sniffed it, tasted a drop of it." Carolyn grinned. "It's delicious."

Minerva pictured the woman rifling through Noah's clothes and pressing her tongue against the dirty square of fabric, licking the dried blood, and shuddered at the thought.

"Ah, here we are," Carolyn said as they reached the gates of the factory and she parked the car.

They stepped out of the vehicle. Minerva looked at the building warily. Carolyn opened her purse and took out a set of keys and unlocked the gate. She turned to Minerva.

"Go ahead," Carolyn said.

They walked into the workroom with the green walls and the pile of red fibers. The same room that had repulsed her when she had explored the factory with Noah. She had felt a foulness in the air. Now it hit her harder and almost made her gag. Minerva stood at the room's threshold and pressed a hand against her mouth while Carolyn turned on the lights. The fluorescent bulbs glowed bright above them.

"Come on, sit," Carolyn said. "If you don't cooperate it'll be very unpleasant for your friend, I can promise you that."

Minerva took two tentative steps and looked carefully around the large space. Two metal chairs had been dragged to the center of the room, and a worktable, which had been empty the last time she was there, was covered with a thick red cloth.

"Someone died here," Minerva said, recognizing what she had failed to see the first time around.

"Of course they did," Carolyn replied pleasantly. "Sit, please."

*I'm going to die,* she thought again, and almost had to bite her tongue not to laugh.

Minerva sat in one of the chairs. Carolyn tugged at the red cloth, tossing it aside. Upon the worktable there was a wide assortment of rusty old tools. A bucket full of nails. Wrenches. An axe. Carolyn opened a black box.

Minerva couldn't see what was inside. She craned her neck while slowly tugging at the backpack's zipper. Her fingers stilled as she felt more than saw a shadow hovering at the edge of her vision. She had the same sensation that she'd had at Joyce House, that something was there. Noah had said he'd seen a ghost at the factory, a man in overalls and a flat cap. Minerva had the same impression, lightning quick, of a man. Santiago, perhaps, tethered to this room decades after his death, like Ginny seemed tied to Joyce House.

"You won't get away with it, you know," Minerva said for the sake of covering the soft sound of the zipper with her voice. "They'll investigate if I go missing."

"Students stop attending classes, they drop out."

"Wait. How many students from Stoneridge have you killed?"

"Very few, actually. But when I did, nothing came of it. Thomas, Ginny, now you. Oh, a couple of others a few decades ago. My father and I focused on those who wouldn't be missed. The occasional hitchhiker, the illegal worker with few ties to this country, or poor young fools looking for handouts through our foundation. You are an only child, far from home, with no money and few people to wonder what happened to you. Besides, you're witchborn. You're worth the trouble."

"I have no idea what that means."

"It means you have an interesting family tree. And I need your spark. Frankly, I'm famished and you're a delicious dish. I've looked for a long, long time for someone like you."

Carolyn grabbed the black box and held it in front of Minerva for her to see. It was lined with red velvet and contained a thin, sharp knife with a golden handle. Carolyn set the box back on the table.

"For the grand finale. It's an athame. I thought you might appreciate the workmanship. And you do have a love for the dramatic, don't you? How you love Betty's cruel horror stories."

Carolyn unbuttoned her coat and carefully draped it over a corner of the table. She was wearing a white blouse, but the woman quickly grabbed a long red sleeveless tunic and slipped it over her head. Minerva almost laughed, thinking that it would cost a lot to get bloodstains out of the white fabric, and wondered if sorcerers had a special dry cleaner for that.

The ghostly presence drifted across the room; she could almost see it. It possessed a soft kind of shimmer, like an oil slick that faded in and out, yet it was also a shadow, a darkness that almost formed the outline of a man. Could Carolyn also see it? Maybe not. Or maybe she didn't care.

"You're rich. I doubt killing me would make you much richer," Minerva said as the shadow-shape slid next to the pile of red fibers, making some tumble to the ground as it brushed against them.

"I need to buy more time."

"I don't understand."

She finished unzipping the backpack's pocket. Carolyn's back was to her, but she looked over her shoulder at Minerva and Minerva stilled her hands.

"The ability runs in my family. But sometimes it skips a generation, or if it manifests, it's too weak. One of my sons had it, and he rejected it; he stunted his power with drink and drugs. And he wouldn't let me near Noah." Carolyn sighed. She picked up a golden pendant with a great red stone and placed it around her neck as she spoke. It occurred to Minerva that it was like watching a knight dressing for battle, or an actor putting on a costume. Perhaps it was necessary for whatever ritual she'd perform that night. Or maybe Carolyn also fancied the dramatic. "Such a disappointment."

"So you killed him and his wife."

"I thought if I had Noah to myself, I could rear him properly. Teach him, the way my father taught me. But I was too late, or there was a flaw in his constitution. Perhaps he simply takes after his father, seeking booze and cheap thrills. He's stunted, too. There was nothing I could show him. But I've arranged a good marriage for him. He'll have a child soon, and that child will have power. I know it. This time I'll get it right. I'll raise that baby. And for that, I need more time. We're rather long-lived, witches. My grandmother died at the age of one hundred and three. But I've had a few health snags."

Carolyn carefully removed the turban from her head, revealing sparse tufts of silvery hair. She was nearly bald and her hands trembled a little. Her painted face and carefully made-up eyebrows, her fanciful outfit, and the extravagant jewelry concealed the frailty of her age. And glamour, a hint of magic, had camouflaged the wounds of time. But now Minerva glimpsed her mortality.

"I need twenty more years and I can make a warlock out of my great-grandson," Carolyn said as she folded the cloth and set it aside on the table.

"Poor Noah. I suppose he'll have an accident after he studs a kid for you."

"Every family has their share of tragedies."

"The child might turn out useless, too," Minerva said. "Maybe your power has simply run out."

"It's in our blood, girl. Generation after generation." Carolyn bent over the worktable, her fingers brushing the handles of tools and sharp instruments.

"Except when it skips one or two. Could be you're the last of your kind. An atavistic remnant, a vestigial tail."

She whipped out the box cutter from the backpack.

*I'm going to die,* she thought. *I'm going to die, but I'm not going down easy.*

Without turning to look at her, the woman spoke. Her voice was magnificently serene. "My dear, it won't do any good to try and attack me," she said.

"I had other plans," Minerva said, and she slashed at her left wrist.

Carolyn let out a furious scream. Minerva was shoved back by a powerful force, her chair toppled over, and she hit her back against the floor. The box cutter went flying through the air and landed in a corner of the room.

"Silly girl," Carolyn said, slowly approaching her. "You can't get away from me."

Minerva could not sit up. The same force that had tossed her back now pinned her down. The ghostly presence in the room shifted from one side of it to the other, restless. Minerva grunted and tried to push herself up.

Carolyn knelt next to her. *They are gluttons,* that's what Nana Alba had told her. And Carolyn herself had said she was famished. Thomas had gone missing in December. Maybe Carolyn hadn't indulged her murderous tendencies since then. Who knew how often she killed, or whether the quality of her victims had been substandard. Minerva felt, at any rate, like she had waved a piece of meat in front of a great white shark.

Carolyn's nostrils flared and her eyes shone as she licked her lips. "You have a talent for being extremely dislikable. I'm going to thoroughly enjoy drinking your blood and eating your heart."

"I hope you choke on it."

Carolyn scoffed and roughly pulled Minerva's wrist against her mouth. The witch's lips felt like sandpaper as she licked her blood, and her hands were cold as ice, making Minerva shiver. She tried to flex her fingers and failed: she was frozen in place. She squeezed her eyes shut and then the woman wasn't merely licking the wound, she was biting her, and the pain of her arm was so great Minerva opened her eyes again and began to yell even though she felt out of breath.

Carolyn chuckled; the laughter was muffled against Minerva's skin. She tossed her head, tried to shove the woman off. Her body was a limp, useless mess, and the more she struggled the more tired she became.

Minerva had drunk almost the entire contents of her thermos

before venturing into Joyce House, the potion her great-grandmother had told her about. Poison for witches. It ought to work. Then again, it was simply a story she'd heard late at night. It might have been made up. It might not work on someone like Carolyn.

She lay staring at the ceiling. She'd stopped screaming. The fluorescent lights hummed—it was almost like a whine, a wheezing. Or maybe that was Minerva who was wheezing. The memory of Nana Alba's voice soothed her.

*Back then, when I was a young woman, there were still witches.*

Carolyn coughed. The noise was sharp; it echoed inside the cavernous factory space. Again there was the wheezing and pain. Then Carolyn coughed again. She coughed a third time.

Suddenly Carolyn stopped feeding from Minerva and touched her neck. She gasped, scuttering away from her. All the while she coughed.

"What . . ." the witch said.

Minerva's body seemed to jolt awake, the numbness receding in an instant, and she pushed herself up. She had all the coordination of a drunkard, but she was standing up. She managed to stumble toward the worktable and clutched it with both hands. Her fingers slid against the handle of the axe.

"You little bitch!" Carolyn roared.

Minerva couldn't even raise a hand to defend herself. Before she could react, Carolyn had jumped to her feet and was squeezing her hands around Minerva's neck, her nails digging into her skin. Again she felt the terrible iciness of Carolyn's touch and attempted to yank the hands away. Carolyn continued coughing; her bloody spittle flew through the air and stained Minerva's face.

Her hold on Minerva slackened and she stepped back. Minerva pressed a hand against her neck. She flung herself against the table, trying to get hold of anything that could be used as a weapon, but the nerves and muscles in her legs were twitching, a cramp ran down her lower body, and she clutched the table like a drowning woman holding on to a plank of wood.

The shadow-thing shimmered for a second. It stood at the other end of the table, close to where Carolyn was glaring at her.

"Help me."

Minerva's voice was hoarse, more a whimper than anything else.

*I'm going to die,* she thought once more. And although the idea had danced inside her brain, now it was a reality. Now death was there. There was nothing she could do except die the same way Santiago and Ginny had died. Bleeding to death, her heart carved out, her ghost left to haunt an abandoned, decayed building. She'd accomplished nothing, only delayed her grisly end.

But the shadow turned its head in Minerva's direction. It was looking at her. Then it looked back at Carolyn.

*Help me,* she said. She mouthed the words; no sound made it out of her throat.

Carolyn shook her head and extended an arm. The ceremonial knife jumped into her hand. The sharp, ugly blade glinted as she stepped forward, ready to plunge it into Minerva's chest.

"Help me!" Minerva said, and this time the words were clear; the command echoed around the room.

The shadow-thing seemed to acquire a solidness for a moment and sent the can full of nails flying. The rusty bits of metal hit Carolyn, embedding themselves in her face and neck. She shrieked, spinning around, her fingers madly trying to rip out the projectiles.

*You simply live through it.* Minerva remembered the words and her fingers tightened around the handle of the axe. Her vision was a throbbing burst of red and her body threatened to sink into unconsciousness, but she bit her tongue viciously. The stinging pain, the blood on her tongue, awoke every nerve in her body.

Minerva grabbed the weapon and rushed forward. She swung and stared into Carolyn's startled eyes as the blade sliced her head off.

"STOP," ARTURO SAID, ONE palm up in the air, the other against the ground.

Alba shook her head, her shoulders hunched with the weight of the axe. She could hardly stand. But he could hardly speak, lying there in the dirt, looking up at her, feebly attempting to sit up. His eyes were terribly intense, his voice so forceful that she lowered the axe for a moment, uncertain and afraid.

"We belong together, you know it," he said, his voice raspy. "No one will ever understand you like I can. And I can give you everything you want, everything you've always dreamed of."

His eyes vivisected her where she stood, even as his voice was a velvety whisper, and she knew he did not lie. His sincerity made her want to weep. She cared about him, even if he was monstrous.

More than once, Alba had comforted herself with the thought that they were the same, he and she. He had embodied gallantry and romance. Tarnished, lying in the muck, he still maintained a brightness to his expression, a terrible, damning beauty. And he was so young, boyish still, it made her hesitate. But Tadeo had been younger yet, as had Valentín.

"Do not forsake me, Alba," he pleaded.

Arturo extended a hand toward her, and she brushed her fingertips against it. Under his skin she felt the throbbing pull of magic, the power embedded in his bones, and, deeper yet, the awful extent of his appetite. He'd eat her whole. Maybe he wouldn't savor the taste of her bones, but he'd eat away at a part of her anyway, mangle her soul. Pull her deep into shadows that she might dwell in darkness until the end of her days. "My love," he said. His voice was appallingly soft, tinged with an unbearable affection that was ghastlier than his cruelty.

Alba pulled her hand back and pressed it against her lips. They stared at each other. Longing and fire and rage mingled in their eyes. Her tears scalded her cheeks and her whole body shook as she looked at him there, crouching low against the dirt, reaching for her once more so that she might help him up.

"I won't let you destroy me," she said. "I will live through this."

His eyes widened and he yelled for her to stop.

She cut off his head all the same.

MINERVA FELL TO HER knees, still clutching the axe tight. Black spots danced before her eyes. She blinked them away and looked down at Carolyn's body. It was melting, like hot wax. Rivulets of darkness spread across the floorboards and bones poked through the softening, peeling tissue. With each minute the body decayed more, becoming, at last, nothing but a fine layer of dust. Even her jewelry, her vestments, her shoes, grew rusted and brittle and disintegrated. Every item she'd brought into that room vanished as if it had never been, leaving behind only a sour scent.

The taste of her own blood in her mouth and the powerful stench made Minerva want to vomit, but she managed to resist the impulse. Instead, she bowed her head and let go of the axe. It landed with a thud on the ground. The edge of its blade was clean, though a faint tendril of smoke seemed to rise from the metal and vanish in a heartbeat. The noxious smell also dissipated, and then there was only the scent of decay and humidity that naturally permeated the factory.

Eventually, very slowly, Minerva raised her head and took a deep breath.

SIX WEEKS PASSED BEFORE Alba returned to the shadow of the tree, to the river. The spot where she'd killed Arturo, where his body had seeped into the grass, was blasted and barren. Nothing would ever grow there. It was as if his blood had poisoned the flowers and the plants that had once sprouted by the water.

But aside from that desolate piece of earth, the land was peaceful and the river gurgled merrily.

The people in Paraje de Abedules claimed that the Quirogas were cursed, that a foul monster must have taken Arturo as it had taken Tadeo, and made the sign of the cross when they approached their farm. Her family was becoming infamous, but the reticence of the village people meant they asked few questions about her uncle's disappearance, and they did not disturb Alba's peace.

Alba leaned her back against the tree and listened to the river's current and the way it spoke, sharing secrets with her. Above her, the tree spread its branches wide, shading her like a jade parasol.

She'd woken to a portent that morning, knowing she'd birth a child. It would be a girl. The townsfolk might declare she was

Valentín's bastard, or a demon's daughter. Who could tell, with the Quirogas? They were cursed, after all. And her mother might have questions, her eyes still damp with grief, but she'd welcome the baby.

Her fingers rested against Valentín's locket. She'd flung Arturo's necklace with the single pearl into the river, along with the axe. It would rest there, in the muck, in the dark. Let the water have this present and do what it will with it.

She'd name the child Tadea, after her brother. One day, when her daughter was older, Alba would tell her stories about witches and curses, for her own protection.

The world, after all, was rife with dangers and traps. To explore it was to venture down a path paved with knives. Yet, as the river demonstrated, there were also chances for beauty and quiet.

She brushed her hand up the tree's trunk, feeling the texture of the bark.

"Bless me, Tadeo," she said, for under the shadow of the tree her brother had perished. Two deaths there, side by side, but the spot where his body had fallen was dotted with yellow wildflowers and the land there had not withered.

"Bless me, Valentín," she said, kissing the locket, for if the dead ever paid any heed to the living, she hoped he would be kind.

Of Arturo, she did not ask a blessing. She'd survived him, and that was enough of a gift.

# Epilogue

MINERVA HAD FINISHED CARVING the pumpkin when the cat alerted her to an approaching car. The college held a trick-or-treat day for local children the evening before Halloween. They would go to designated dorms and knock on the door and the resident assistants would hand out candy. It was popular with the kids of the college's faculty and staff.

Briar Hall was already decorated, with the appropriate cobwebs and plastic spiders dangling by the doors. Joyce House remained shuttered; the renovation had been postponed until next summer. She'd walked through its hallways, curious to see if she might speak to Ginny. But whatever presence had lingered there had vanished. Perhaps Carolyn's death had liberated it. If that was the case, Santiago's ghost might also have vanished. But Minerva had not gone back to the factory to check.

Ledge House was almost ready to receive guests. She had bags of candy and Hideo had helped her hang cutouts of bats around the porch. But she thought the pumpkin would make for a nice touch, and the children wouldn't be stopping by until Friday. She had two whole days to spruce up the decorations.

Minerva washed her hands in the kitchen sink and dried them quickly. She pulled down the sleeves of her sweater, hiding the scar on her arm, and grabbed the pumpkin. Then she walked toward the entrance of the dorm and opened the front door at the same time that Noah Yates was stepping out of his Jeep.

"The dorm looks good," he said, pointing at the scarecrow that sat in a chair by the door. Hideo had also helped her make that. They'd spent an ungodly amount of time stuffing its body with hay.

Hideo knew something had happened to her but not exactly what. He probably thought she'd cut herself on purpose, the stress of her research getting to her, no matter that she'd made up a story about stumbling onto a jagged piece of metal while looking for something in the basement and having to get a tetanus shot. He'd been around often all through the end of the summer and into the fall but had relaxed recently, apparently convinced the incident had been a one-off occurrence. She couldn't explain what had really taken place and instead accepted his attention in silence.

"Maybe you can beat Hancock Hall for best decorations this year," Noah said.

The wind ruffled the trees, sending a cascade of brown and yellow leaves spilling across the ground. She set the pumpkin down by the scarecrow's feet.

"I haven't seen you around," she said. Then again, she hadn't looked for him. She'd phoned him for the sake of appearances when his grandmother went missing, but they'd talked for only a few minutes. She'd left it at that.

"I've dropped out."

"Really?"

"College is a waste of time for me. Plus, I'm moving to Boston. The Willows is too big and lonely with only me there."

"Have they found anything?" she asked.

Carolyn Yates's disappearance had been big news for a few weeks, but the furor had died down. There had not been a speck of bone left after she cut off Carolyn's head. She'd scattered the tools that had been in the room around the building, tossing them into dark and musty corners. She'd left the car exactly where Carolyn had parked it. They had fingerprinted it, which tied Minerva to the vehicle, but she'd been conducting research at the Willows and had ridden in the car before. Her fingerprints were not terribly unexpected, neither in the vehicle nor in the factory, which she'd toured with Noah.

Fingerprints or not, the police had not asked her any deep questions. A detective had phoned her, and another dropped by one day. Minerva told him about her research, explained that she had met Carolyn and Noah while gathering material for her thesis, and enumerated the times she had visited the Willows. He seemed interested in information about Noah rather than herself and she had answered his questions honestly. The detective took notes, thanked her, and never returned. It was not surprising. She didn't know Noah well and couldn't provide any interesting material. She hoped they would not contact her again.

"No, they don't have anything. She's gone. Eerie, isn't it? Like in Betty's horror stories," Noah said. His face was inscrutable. She couldn't draw any conclusions based on his expression.

"And not a clue, is there?"

"Not one. She was sick. I didn't know, she never told any of the family about it. Apparently it was more than arthritis, so there's the thought she might have killed herself. She'd given the staff the day off and I was in New York for some last-minute business she wanted me to take care of, so it makes sense that she drove herself and attempted something. But nobody can figure out why she would have parked at the factory and walked away, if she did walk away from there. The cops are baffled."

Minerva hid her relief by rearranging the scarecrow's cowboy hat and nodding. "No theories, then."

He knelt to look at the jack-o'-lantern, running his fingers around its jagged smile. "There are a few message boards where they say I chopped her body into pieces and threw them into the sea. Can you believe it?"

He glanced up at Minerva. His tone was casual; she couldn't determine how much he knew. She hadn't been able to figure it out. Her wards were intact. She'd sensed no magical dangers. Carolyn had said he didn't have any abilities. But did he retain a rudimentary appreciation of spells? Might he guess what Minerva had done? Did he even care one way or another?

"Why would I kill her?" Noah continued. "I have my trust fund, always did. My uncles can bicker over the rest of the money, I don't mind. Although I suppose some people might say she kept me on a leash. That I'm free now."

"I suppose you are," she told him.

He stood up and smiled wryly. The expression reminded her of Carolyn. Minerva lowered her eyes, looking at a leaf that was stuck to her shoe.

"How's your research going?" he asked.

"I have an outline and a few good pages."

She had more than a few good pages. She'd been feverishly at work, the piles of notes multiplying. Her meetings with her adviser had gone well and she was already looking at fellowship applications. With some luck, it wouldn't be only Betty who would be rescued from the jaws of oblivion; Ginny's art might also gain recognition. It was, at any rate, the beginning of something.

"Excellent. I can't say I understand the desire to spend your life sinking into the pit of academia, but then again, we're different. And yet alike, I suspect."

"In what way?" she asked, leaning against the house's wall, arms crossed.

"Our basic building blocks," he said as he took out a cigarette and lit it with nimble fingers. "Our foundations, if you want to put it that way. If you twist it a bit, you could be me and I could be you."

"I don't know about that."

A slight bemusement tinged his face, but he remained opaque. As she'd told the police, she didn't really know him, probably never would.

"Anyway, I'm hoping we can remain friendly even if I'm moving away."

"Are we friends?" she replied.

"I don't think we're enemies. Not yet," he said. That might have been a joke. Then again, it might have been something else. His tone was light, but his eyes, as he raised his cigarette to his mouth and took a drag, had a chill to them.

"That can change."

"Sure. We're not entirely in the clear." He laughed; it was like a fresh breeze ruffling a pile of leaves, toying with them and tossing them around.

His face now was warm, charming, as he tilted his head. Yet the gesture seemed practiced.

She nodded at him and looked over her shoulder. "I should get back inside. I have a staff meeting in an hour."

"You're not inviting me in for a cup of coffee?"

She dragged a hand against the wall of the house, feeling the web of wards wrapped around it, and shook her head. Never. You didn't invite a witch into your home. And maybe he wasn't a sorcerer, maybe he was a bored rich kid who had a little time to kill, but she didn't wish to find out.

"I've sworn off coffee," she said.

"That's a pity," he said, his voice smooth and his smile wide. "See you around sometime."

He walked back to his car and drove off. Minerva remained by the door, staring in the direction in which he'd gone. Would he be trouble, one day? Would she walk into her house and find all her wards defaced? He'd been in her kitchen one time before, and might that render her safeguards useless? She couldn't tell.

For now, she'd simply check on the witch marks. It was logical, with All Hallows' Eve creeping around the corner. And then there would come the Day of the Dead and her altar to Nana Alba, even if she didn't have that sepia photo of her anymore because she'd burned it to make the potion that had ultimately saved her life. But she could still bake bread, light candles for her departed. Add extra ones for Ginny, Betty, and Santiago, so that they might be remembered.

She snapped her fingers, summoning the ghost of the cat. She didn't understand all the properties and peculiarities of ghost animals, but after finding it roaming by the house, she'd been able to press her hand against its invisible body for a brief moment, and now it tended to follow her around. Maybe that was how it had happened with Nana Alba's parrot; its ghost simply flew into the room one day and perched on her shoulder.

She supposed in Puritan New England they might have called this creature a witch's familiar. Mummified cats or skeletal horses perhaps roamed the houses where they'd been interred in previous ages and could be pressed into service as guardians of those abodes. Perhaps, and maybe. She hardly had all the answers, but then that went the same for researchers and academics marching through their own esoteric labyrinths of learning.

Minerva brushed her fingers against the cat's head and looked at the trees dripping with withered leaves.

"Keep watch, will you?" she told the cat as it rubbed itself against her legs.

Curses and spells persisted, even in the era of fiber optics and telephones. Atavistic, yes, but not extinct. Maybe Noah wasn't a warlock, but there might be others. Caution, thus, was the answer.

Though, at the same time, one couldn't live in fear. There was a thesis to finish and a second pumpkin to carve. There were the paths carpeted with leaves that crunched under her boots, the chill of the October evening, and the setting sun painting steeples and roofs golden.

"When I was a young woman, there were still witches," she said, bidding Karnstein goodbye.

She opened the front door, walked past the threshold with its witch marks, pressing her palm against one of them, feeling its power. A secret and a spell etched in wood. *May it keep me safe on the nights when witches carouse across the sky.*

# Afterword

MY GREAT-GRANDMOTHER USED TO tell me stories about growing up in the Mexican countryside, and about witches.

The witches of my great-grandmother's youth were very different from the witches of our modern pop culture. They were malicious entities who blighted the crops or called forth storms; they sucked the blood of their victims and turned into giant balls of fire. There was even a town inhabited by witches in the mountains where she lived.

Such folklore was typical of many central Mexican towns and seemed to mix both European and pre-Hispanic elements. For example, in pre-Hispanic lore witches were "born," and the day of their birth determined their fate. However, some of the methods for catching or repelling witches included saying the Lord's Prayer or hanging crosses around a room.

My great-grandmother, poor and illiterate, wouldn't have understood words such as "syncretic," but that was the nature of the world she inhabited. Snatches of this syncretism survive to this day.

WHEN I WENT TO college abroad on a scholarship—two, if we must be precise—I worked on campus in a variety of jobs, including as a resident assistant, to make ends meet since I was a struggling student with very little cash and big dreams. The school I attended—Endicott, once a women's college—is located in Beverly, Massachusetts, and I learned a whole different set of stories about witches there.

This college and the nearby town served as the inspiration for Stoneridge and Temperance Landing. Paul Tremblay, the horror author, grew up in Beverly, though he went to school in Providence, Rhode Island. Providence is, of course, the home of H. P. Lovecraft, whom I first read at the age of twelve when my mother gave me one of his short stories. Shirley Jackson, another early favorite of mine, lived for many years in Bennington, Vermont. Stephen King is from Maine, and the fictional towns of Derry, Castle Rock, and Jerusalem's Lot are all inspired by his home state. New England naturally seems to breed horror writers and left an impression on me.

Eventually I finished college, headed back to Mexico City, and was filled with wanderlust again. I drifted to British Columbia. Here I've remained, putting down roots, juggling jobs, and growing silver hairs at my temples. I wear my bracelet against the evil eye on my left hand.

## About the Author

SILVIA MORENO-GARCIA is the author of the novels *The Seventh Veil of Salome, Silver Nitrate, The Daughter of Doctor Moreau, Mexican Gothic, Gods of Jade and Shadow,* and a bunch of other books. She has also edited several anthologies, including the World Fantasy Award–winning *She Walks in Shadows* (aka *Cthulhu's Daughters*). She has been nominated for the Locus Award for her work as an editor and has won the British Fantasy Award and the Locus Award for her work as a novelist.

silviamoreno-garcia.com
Instagram: @silviamg.author

## *About the Type*

THIS BOOK was set in Old Style 7. Old Style faces are based on sixteenth- and seventeenth-century faces of the Dutch, English, and French designers. They are characterized by definite strokes and bracketed serifs. The original Old Style is based on an English old face. Old Style 7 appears smaller than the original and has much less contrast between thick and thin. Old Style was cut in 1905 for the Mergenthaler Linotype Company, which also had variations of the face for distribution.